Off the Hook

JULIE OLIVIA

Author's Note

Off the Hook is the first book in *Never Harbor*, a series of interconnected stand-alone contemporary romance novels inspired by *Peter Pan*. They are not a retelling of the original story.

Please be advised that this book is a **slow burn, open-door romance**, meaning there is **on-page** sexual content. Some of these characters are inspired by fictional pirates, so expect profanity as well. Mature readers only.

Finally, while this book is full of light-hearted humor, Off the Hook also explores grief and loss surrounding the death of a friend (accident, off-page, prior to the story). Be kind to your heart as you read, friends.

Now, go! Fly off to Never Harbor!

xo Julie O.

To those of us who experienced childhood through books and stories.

I'm glad we never grew up.

Playlist

"Father And Son" - Yusuf / Cat Stevens
"In Dreams" - Ben Howard
"I Sat by the Ocean (live)" - Queens of the Stone Age
"Sea Legs" - The Shins
"Cyclone" - Maude Latour
"Wicked Game" - Chris Isaak
"Runaway" - AURORA
"All I Want" - Kodaline
"Lighthouse" - Dirty Heads
"Darling I Do" - Ezra Williams

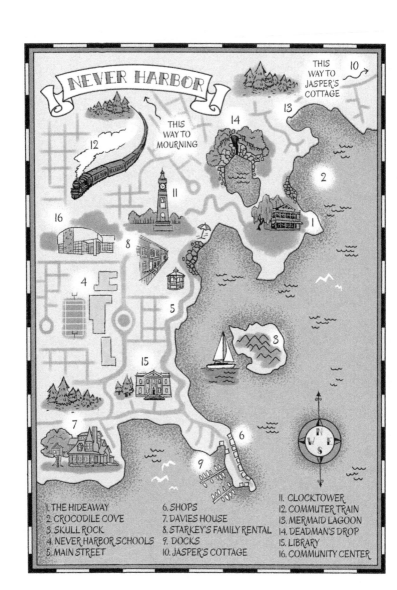

Chapter 1

An Awfully Big Adventure

Jasper

I STOPPED BELIEVING IN A NORMAL, uneventful life around four years ago. Parenting a six-year-old boy who always plays pretend will do that for you.

"Avast, ye!"

A thankfully *very* pretend cutlass smacks my thigh. And thank God for child-safe plastic because my boy swings it with the full force of a kid mid-play.

I accidentally fumble my coffee cup—my favorite one, too, with the #1 *Captain* scrawled on the side in Sam's wobbly handwriting—and it shatters in the sink.

Sam's face falls.

Entangled in the fun as well, is Roger—my one-hundred-thirty-pound dog—skidding around the corner with his tongue lolling out, chasing after a now-frozen Sam. I twist at the last minute to shield Sam from Roger barreling into us, but I bang my hip against the cabinets in the process while Sam topples over anyway.

"God—" I grit my teeth together, catching the curse word before it leaves my mouth.

I wish I could say that was the end of my unfortunate morning. But life doesn't play silly little games with me. It waits until my agenda is perfect, until I've got this parenting thing down to a science, then delights in slamming the hammer down. We play chess, not checkers, around here. Simplicity is never enough.

"I got a job this summer."

My eyes widen at my little sister, sitting across the kitchen island with her thumbs twiddling together in mock innocence. She was mid-sentence before all this mess, and I wish she hadn't finished.

"Are you *fucking* kidding me—" I bite my lower lip even though the curse word has already floated down to my boy's ears. He blinks up at me through blurry eyes.

You can't win them all. Or even most.

But my sister's news can wait.

Instead, I crouch down to the more important issue—the jumble of little boy legs and long dog limbs on the tiled floor below. I remove Sam's red beanie and run a hand over his featherlight blond hair, smoothing it to the side, peering around for anything I don't want to see.

"Your mug—"

"No scratches on your head," I observe out loud.

"But your favorite—"

"It's fine," I insist, cupping Sam's cheeks and tilting his head up. "Wanna know why?"

"Why?"

"Because I see no bumps or bruises on you."

"None?"

"Not a one."

Once I find that this is actually true, my heart rate

lowers by a fraction. At least until I spot his bottom lip wobbling, which means we're ten seconds away from total meltdown. Whether it's from the sadness of breaking the mug he gave me this past Father's Day or thinking he might get in trouble for running in the house like some wild animal, I don't know.

I take that unsteady lip and tug it to the side, peering at his gums.

"Hmm ... no scurvy either. And let me check for gangrene too. Pirates *always* have gangrene."

A small giggle slowly bubbles out. Adjusting his thick coke-bottle glasses, he says, "I don't have gang green."

"You're sure?" I ask with faux skepticism.

I reach for his arm, continuing to pretend like I'm some sort of doctor, but Sam brandishes his plastic sword in the air between us.

"I'm fine!" The words are stated more confidently than I expected—and far from tear-filled.

Crisis averted.

Roger, our massive Irish wolfhound, howls in agreement.

"I'll have words with you later," I assert to Roger with a pointed finger, but Sam gives a little, "Woo-woo," in boyish solidarity.

I roll my eyes and shove Sam's beanie back on. I give it an extra rustle because it makes him laugh and I'm convinced not many sounds top this delightful kid's laughter.

"How about we take this pirate raid outside, okay?" I suggest.

"I found treasure!" Sam says.

"All right then." It will always amaze me how little kids survive off non sequiturs. "Show me real quick."

Dutifully, Sam digs into his fanny pack—a peeling faux leather relic from Never Harbor's 2002 Pirate Festival—and presents a clear box of screws in his tiny hand.

"Are these from my workshop?" I ask.

"No."

I lift a single eyebrow. "No?"

His lips curl in, and he nods through a giggle. "Yes."

I hold out my palm, gesturing toward me. "Hand them over."

He sheepishly drops them into my hand.

"Don't take any more screws from the workshop, okay? Saws and nails are not for little pirates."

"I'm sorry about your mug," he whispers.

"Hey, I can fix it, all right? Just maybe use your inside feet for steering next time. Now, I bet you'll find better treasure out on the deck or garden."

"Yarr!"

Bonnie lets out a small laugh, and I pass my sister a glare that says, *I'm not even remotely done with you.* She cups her hand over her mouth to stifle any additional laughter, but I can still hear the muffled taunts through her palm.

"Can I get a yes instead?" I prompt Sam.

"Yes, Captain!"

"Attaboy."

I stand, patting Sam's back as he scrambles toward the back door in a heartbeat. The fanny pack he wears smacks against an old, cracked leather belt of mine slung around his waist. It clangs from his spoils—spoons, bottle caps, and action figures—creating a symphony in our otherwise quiet home. He rips open the sliding back door and rushes out. Roger regains his footing as well, skidding across the hardwood after his playmate.

"And close the back door!" I call.

Sam's hand reaches in like a theater hook to crane the door closed. The squeaky hinge is masked by his laughter. After it snicks shut, the faint soundscape of nearby waves disappears to the house's dull hum.

"Christ," is the only exhaling word I can get out before I'm interrupted by my sister's cackling.

Right. The enemy.

I swivel to face her. "Now, what did you say to me again?"

"What?" she asks innocently. "When?"

I shoot my sister a look that would intimidate even the meanest of my tattooed employees at the docks. But leave it to my seventeen-year-old sister with her tipped-up chin to appear unbothered. I guess that's the type of resilience you gain after growing up with four rowdy older brothers and two younger ones.

"When I was getting pummeled in the leg by a sword," I indicate.

Bonnie snaps her fingers and tips her head to the side. "Oh! The whole *I quit* thing?"

I run a palm over my beard—anything to slow my heart from sinking into my stomach.

"That isn't a funny joke, Bon."

"I'm not joking."

Down, down, down ...

I steady my palms on the countertop, leveling her with a stare. "Okay then. Do you want higher pay?"

"I don't want money."

"Lies."

Bonnie grins. She has the same grin as our mother, which shouldn't be possible, considering we don't share actual blood ties. You can spot it everywhere else, like how my pitch-black hair and easily tanned skin directly opposes

5

Bonnie's red waves and fair complexion. But somehow, the Davies family mischief always peeks through. Nurture overpowers nature's genetics every time.

"Well, I don't want *your* money anymore." She leans back in her barstool, crossing her arms, coated in summer freckles. "I landed a real job this summer."

"Where?"

"I'm not telling."

"Why?"

"I don't need you getting all testy."

I grunt in response.

I don't get testy.

"It's at Jukes's Jambalaya, isn't it?" My tone is, admittedly, harsher than it should be.

Her face breaks into a smile again, clear braces peering back at me.

"*Testy*," she singsongs. "And no. Ew." Her face scrunches up in that disgusted way only she can achieve. "That place smells like fish. But, well, I guess ... so do you."

I don't counter that claim. Working as a port captain has its drawbacks. Depending on the day, it's a toss-up on whether I'll come home smelling like the combination of stale walls and coffee from my small port-side office or fish bait from catches of the day.

"Then, where are you working?" I press on.

"I'm not telling." Bonnie shakes her head. "You have that red in your eye. Stop. It freaks me out."

"My eyes aren't red."

I don't know which of my brothers started the rumor that my eyes get red when I'm angry, but it's somehow clung like glue in our small town. Maybe I do see red. I would believe it more if I felt anything aside from tired these days. I don't have much time for anger.

She barks out a laugh. "Oh-kay then. Sure."

Teenage sarcasm will be the death of me. Whenever Sam grows up, I know I'm in for a world of hurt.

"Are you working at Mermaid Lagoon?" I ask.

"No. I can't swim. You know that."

My jaw clenches. "Then, come on. Where?"

"Okay, okay. I'll tell you. You'll find out anyway. Promise not to freak out though?"

I lift an eyebrow in response.

She blows out air. "I got a hostess job at The Hideaway."

Damn.

The Hideaway gets all the good summer workers eventually. Leave it to my brother to steal my employee away from me.

"Christ ..." I grumble.

Part of me can't blame her though. Working there is practically a rite of passage for youth in Never Harbor. Plus, it's supposedly the most fun a teen can have at a summer job, which doesn't surprise me, given who owns it.

"Jas, I'm seeing red in those periwinkles again."

"That role involves talking to people," I barrel on, ignoring her accusation. "You'll have to be nice. You hate that."

I'm of the belief that living in a nosy small town naturally leads to some level of disdain for the general population. Even though my parents and happy-go-lucky brothers are practically the welcome committee for Never Harbor—participating in every event from Art in the Park to Halloweenfest—Bonnie and I have instead always agreed that most people suck.

"Well, Lu got a job there—"

7

I slowly nod in understanding. "Ah. There it is. Best friend jumps off a bridge, so you do too?"

"Okay, *Ma*," Bonnie shoots back. "Maybe I want to work a real job."

I tap my finger on the kitchen island in conflicting irritation. I'm not accustomed to having a responsible sibling. At seventeen, my younger brothers were still pulling pranks and avoiding detentions. Bonnie at seventeen is far more rational. She's the only girl in our family, and I'm starting to think teenage girls are just made of a different, harder steel than us boys.

"Okay, what if I paid you fifty dollars a day instead?" I counter.

"Nope. You can't buy me out."

"Not even for a hundred a day?"

"You would never."

"No, I wouldn't," I agree. I reach for my cell phone, running my thumb over the cracked screen. "Fine. I'll call Nana then."

"Nope, she's gone."

I place my phone back down on the counter. "How long is Nana on vacation?"

"Oh, she's gone forever," Bonnie says.

"She's *dead*?"

"God, no! She moved to Aruba."

I blow out an exhale. "Christ. You can't just say an eighty-year-old woman is gone forever."

"Whoops," she says with a playful grin. "But, hey, you'd know that if you came into town more."

Not the first time I've heard that. But there's a reason I bought this fixer-upper cottage, sitting a lengthy fifteen-minute drive out from Never Harbor. Sure, I craved a slice of land bordering the peaceful seaside—you really can't beat the view from our back porch—but it's also secluded.

Never Harbor is one of the most walkable small towns in North Shore, but I personally prefer not to be within strolling distance of everyone I've known since birth. I might miss some important things, like my long-term emergency babysitter retiring to paradise, but at least town gossip stays in town. At least I'm left alone.

Plus, I can work on the house, and nobody complains about the loud hammering. It's just us and the seagulls. As long as they keep their nests away from my current renovation project, I'm fine with them. They don't squawk nearly as much as the locals.

I clean up the broken cup in the sink with a rag, empty it to the side to repair later, and rip open the fridge door. "You're telling me you want another job—"

"*Have* another job," Bonnie corrects.

"And Sam's summer break starts next week."

She cringes. "Okay, I do feel a little bad about that."

"You couldn't have told me this a couple of weeks ago?"

"I just found out I got it this morning," Bonnie pleads. "I promise. Izzy literally *just* texted me the job offer."

"Izzy *texted* you a job offer?"

My brother's bar manager is more on top of things than I am.

"Yeah," Bonnie says. "Everyone texts everything nowadays, except you."

"I text."

"You text like a serial killer."

"I do not."

"You wished me a happy birthday, and it felt like a threat."

"I get to the point."

She scoffs out a laugh. "You are *so* old."

"Thirty-three isn't old."

"Denial," she accuses.

"I'm not in denial. You're just young, so everyone not at your high school feels old."

Bonnie reaches her hand out and places it over mine, the one with the discolored scar slashed over the back, and coos, "You know ... this sounds like an awfully big adventure for you."

"Hilarious," I deadpan, tugging my hand away.

An awfully big adventure is what our mom preached to us as kids. No matter what the universe throws our way, everything is just one more exciting event to tackle. As long as we stay true to who we are—continuing to always act kindly, even in the face of unkindness—we'll be okay. Once my siblings grew older, the phrase turned into more of a joke for when we felt like being asses to each other. But Ma wasn't wrong. She rarely is.

I plop a Tupperware full of watermelon on the kitchen island. Red juice sluices over the edge and onto the counter. I hang my head with a sigh.

Definitely an adventure.

Bonnie's eyebrows tilt in. "Want me to get you a rag?"

"I got it," I murmur.

I grab a clean one from a nearby drawer and wipe up the sticky watermelon juice.

Bonnie joins with a paper towel as I sigh out a small, "Thanks, Bon."

I fetch cleaner from under the sink and spray it down. It will be one of many stains removed due to the hectic life of my boy and every adventure that comes with him. And now, I've got nobody to watch him for the summer.

"Hey," Bonnie starts slowly.

"Hmm?"

"You gonna be okay?"

"We'll be all right."

"You're just scrubbing extra hard, is all."

I pause. The watermelon juice has transformed to pink suds. I toss the finished rag into the sink.

"Y'know," she continues, "maybe Dad is—"

"I don't want Dad's help," I cut in, my eyes flashing up to meet hers.

Her head juts back at the motion.

"Or anyone else's, okay?"

She shakes her head, lips parting. "But why?"

"Because we'll be *fine*."

They say it takes a village to raise a child. When I moved back to Never Harbor four years ago with Sam in tow, my small village-sized family halted their lives to be present for me and my boy. I got lucky that Bonnie needed a summer job the last couple of years, but the rest of them are adults. I might joke that they are still children at heart, but they have lives. Responsibilities. And now, so does my little sister.

My ex was right. I took too much from my family those first few years with Sam. I won't do it again.

I gather two forks and carry the watermelon out through the sliding glass door and to the back porch.

"Breakfast, bud!" I call out.

Sam is down by the rocky shore, running on the very small area of the beach that isn't littered with craggy seaweed-ridden rocks and pebbles. Roger is at his heels, bounding from rock to rock on lanky limbs, his wiry fur likely littered with sand by now.

"Hey, don't go down there without me. We've talked about that."

Julie Olivia

"Aye, aye, Captain!"

The mix of laughter and dog barking has the side of my mouth tilting up in a smile. This will be a treasured moment that, hopefully, Sam will remember forever—summer memories with just a boy and his dog. I can only hope it will overshadow the bad.

I only have three days to figure out how to handle this summer. Today is the last day of school. I don't have time to consider day care for next week. Our local center is likely all full by now anyway. I can't ask Betty to house one more child.

It's fine. I am perfectly capable of balancing work and a loose-cannon six-year-old pirate all summer. Sam deserves a godfather who can care for him. I might not be even a sliver of the man Sam's father was, and our adventures likely aren't as fun as his parents would have managed, but I'm trying. I can only hope I'm doing right by them.

My chest aches, and for a moment, I feel that familiar weight. The one that settles in the pit of my stomach, pointing like a magnet toward the floor, rooting me to the spot. The one that comes when the memory of Ed and Stacy hits me. I shift from one boot to the other, ensuring I can still move. I finally breathe when I realize I can.

Bonnie's eyes flick over to me, and for once, it doesn't look like a sarcastic comment is locked and loaded.

"What?" I ask.

"I just ... I don't like you two being out here alone all summer, Jas."

"We'll be fine," I repeat for what feels like the tenth time—or maybe I just say it in my head a lot nowadays. *We'll be fine. We'll be fine. We will be fine.* "Just don't tell the others."

Bonnie lets out a combination of a laugh and an exhale. "You know they'll find out eventually."

I give her a pointed glare, and she raises her hands into the air with a grin.

"Okay then. Won't leave my lips. But, I mean, you're still coming to dinner tonight, right?"

"No."

Her grin grows more sinister.

I exhale. "You already told Ma I was coming, didn't you?"

"I already told Ma," she confirms, and her smile says, *Checkmate, old man.* "Seriously though, take a shower before dinner tonight," she adds. "I'll barf if you smell like fish."

"That sounds like an awfully big adventure for you."

Chapter 2

The Unserious Place

Wendy

I'M in a cocoon of affection and despair.

"Don't leave, Miss Wendy!" my kids chorus through tears as their tiny arms wrap around my waist and thighs.

This is customary for the last day of school. Crying children, tight hugs, and chaos. I continue to pat their heads like the cute little ducklings that they are.

"I'll see you next year," I soothe. "I'll be right down the hall."

"That's so far away!" one of my kids whines.

Their parents watch our scene from the car-rider line with stars in their eyes. Some are less enthused—I swear I see Lewis's mom tap her watch—but the majority of them just like seeing their kids happy. That's the best part about being a first-grade teacher in Never Harbor. Parents actually care.

"But what happens to Cinderella?" one of my more tenderhearted children whines, and then it's like they all realize they need to know as well.

14

"What happens?!" they chime together, voices overlapping others.

I could tip them off to one of the many adaptations recounting that particular fairy tale, but they're probably too fragile for that right now. Instead, I go with, "Well, she lives happily ever after, of course."

"Knew it," one whispers conspiratorially.

"Give us a new story!" they demand.

Children love demanding things. *Insatiable, I swear.*

"With Jill!"

"Yeah!" they say, along with, "Love Jill!" and, "Jill rocks!" and, "Jill's a badass!"

"Hey now," I warn.

The child guilty of too-harsh language for a seven-year-old curls his lips in with a sheepish smile.

"We'll see. Maybe I'll write her story over the summer."

"Promise?"

"Oh. Um ..."

Crap.

If you ever need someone to say no, don't choose me. I'd say yes to that sly snake offering an apple in the Garden of Eden if he asked politely enough. Heck, I'd agree if he asked rudely, just so he wouldn't slither away in anger.

I'm a people pleaser through and through. And saying *yes* is my not-so-hidden love language.

"Okay. I promise," I finally commit. "Now, shoo, you wild children. Go get sunburned and sick on taffy and fudge and whatever else kids find in the trash."

"YAY!"

Their collective cheers concern me that they'll take the advice seriously.

I wave from the sidewalk as they all pile into cars or walk down the street, hand in hand with their parents. The tears from a sorrowful last day of school are already wiped from their eyes, fading away, alongside the worries of homework and catching the bus before dawn. No need for them to remember this place for another three months.

It's magical to be young in Never Harbor. Summer break is when time disappears. When you bike around town from sunup to sundown. When you eat gelato on the pier. When you leap into the quarry water at the hottest part of the day. Well, only if your parents are particularly irresponsible. Or if you have no parental supervision at all.

Tomato, tomahto.

The thought of a Never Harbor summer as an adult sounds far less exciting. Instead of having the freedom to eat so much fudge that you puke, I'm saddled with not having any additional pay for three whole months.

Some school districts split a teacher's salary to include the summer season. And while Never Harbor's district has a lot going for it—good pay, non-fussy parents, nutritious lunches—their salary is only split evenly through the working months.

When I moved back one year ago, I was fully aware of the cycles, but I was also desperate to get back home. I snagged the only house available to lease—Charles Starkey's family rental by the sea—even though it was far outside my budget. At the time, I didn't care about an unbalanced budget. I just needed to get back to Never Harbor—to the only place that'd felt like home.

I don't recommend my hurried move across the country. I also don't recommend the ex-boyfriend who drove me to it, but oh well.

I was shortsighted in my desperation to move back. Now, I'm stuck with the looming threat of rent being due and only a couple of weeks of stockpiled salary to pay it.

Instead of buying new bathing suits for the beach, I'll need to find secondhand slacks for a part-time job.

"Wendy!" a parent calls from her car, pulled over to the sidewalk near me. "Are you volunteering at Taste of Never Harbor again?"

"Yes! Well, maybe." *If my future part-time schedule permits it.*

"Let me know!"

I sigh. "Will do."

I continue waving to the cars, pausing only to see my principal, Donna, poking her head through car windows, smiling from ear to ear as she talks to parents. She loves her job, and I love her for it. But the truck she's currently poking into was likely a wrong choice.

Jasper Davies sits in the driver's seat of his black pickup truck. A zip of nerves strikes through me at the sight of him. At his jaw, shrouded by the thick black beard. At the rolled-up sleeves of his navy button-up, highlighting tense forearms that flex with each grind of his fists over the wheel. At his light-blue eyes bordering on silver, the stare that razes Donna down until she gradually gets uncomfortable enough to inch away from the window, cautious smile still plastered.

This is the first I'm seeing Jasper in almost one month, and the eldest Davies brother is just as he's always been—silent, irritated, handsome in that weird, menacing way that feels both dangerous and exciting. It's funny how I can be so close to his family and this man is still a stranger. When their house became a regular hangout in middle school, Jasper was already in college. Summers kept him at sea, and he was a strange presence on fall weekends, like a frigid breeze whipping through the autumn leaves. He moved back permanently four years

17

ago, but that only means his shadow is around more—not him. Not really.

I wonder if he's coming to dinner tonight.

In the back seat, his child, Sam, looks out the rolled-down window. Spotting me, he gives a big, frenetic wave. I return the gesture. He's a cute kid. Far less menacing than his guardian.

Jasper's truck inches forward, and Donna follows it. After two more times of him letting off on the brakes, she finally takes the hint and waves goodbye. Driving off, Jasper takes a left turn at the end of the street instead of the right that leads to his parents' house.

I guess he won't be coming to dinner tonight.

I wait until the last few cars empty out of the elementary school lot—more questions about volunteering at events I can't guarantee—before I grab my tote bag from the patch of grass I laid it in, then walk down the sidewalk. Sure, I'll need to come back next week to clean out my classroom for summer break, but right now, I'm enjoying the last day of school like the kids do—with no worries.

Except for that whole lingering rent thing.

Hands in my sundress pockets, I walk down a block and turn the corner toward Main. The ocean breeze drifts between the alleys of each building—a little salty, a little seaweedy, and cool enough to break the heat of incoming summer.

Never Harbor's Main Street is right along the coast. It's a collection of artists' galleries, souvenir shops, ice cream parlors—you would think four is too many, and you'd be wrong—local restaurants with signature lobster rolls, and tiny parks scattered throughout. A bench here, a gazebo there, a stretch of rocky beach with just enough sand for some chairs and umbrellas and joyfully screaming kids to chase waves.

It's perfect. It's home.

May is bumping up to tourist season, where locals from Boston hop on the commuter train to vacation on weekends. Shops stay open later, and the smell of sweet vanilla ice cream tempts you toward their thresholds well into the evening. If you're lucky, you might catch the pirate performers roaming the streets at night with bottles of fake rum in their hands and a swing in their step. Though that signature sway is probably due to some real alcoholic influence.

My ex-boyfriend hated this place. George only cared about fancy galas, his expensive watch collection, and whether people knew his name. And even with the layer of wealth Never Harbor has in the houses along the shore, the locals never met his classist standards. Locals here don't peacock enough. The richest man on the coast is more likely to be dressed in ripped jeans and flip-flops than a tailored suit. When I pointed out that Mayor Barrie still gardened his own yard, George looked at me like I had no brain at all.

He always looked at me like that though.

I was almost relieved to find George in bed with someone else. That woman looked like she found kids to be a nuisance, understood how to balance a checkbook, and didn't own a single pair of sneakers in her closet. She looked very ... serious. George liked serious.

So, after he hired movers for me—how *gentlemanly*—I ran back to my very *un*serious place. I escaped back to a very unserious person and his silly family. Because there's only been one boyfriend who came close to truly understanding me, and it wasn't George.

It was my ex-fiancé, the second-oldest Davies boy.

Our engagement was a disaster. I was naive to think I could force him into commitment. Recognizing that is probably why we stayed so close after our breakup, why we still chatted through my relationship with George, and why we continue being friends now. When you're small-town sweethearts—when his mother takes you in after your own parents couldn't care less—it's hard to let someone like that go.

It's hard to let the Davies family go.

While my parents were busy working, it was the Davies boys who became my best friends. My dad traveled for work, leaving me with just some cash for pizza, and David Davies offered a home-cooked meal instead. My mom needed to be in Boston during most of my soccer games, and it was Maggie Davies who took me to her clinic and stitched up my injuries afterward.

Some people learn they never want children only after they have them; my parents fall into that category. Other people, like David and Maggie Davies, find they want more children until they cannot stretch their love any further. But for them, that's an impossible task, which is probably why they always keep the front door open.

Unlike their eldest son, Jasper, who almost runs over a principal on the last day of school, I attend every Friday night family dinner at the Davies house. I can't say no to any of them. And in this case, I don't want to.

I open my phone, fingers poised over the screen, scrolling down to Maggie's number, asking if we're still on for dinner. It's every single Friday without fail, but there will always be a small part of me that wonders when my invitation will expire. They have their hands full enough with seven children.

Less than ten seconds later, I receive a text back.

Mags: What a silly question. Remember to come over early. I set aside dresses for you.

Wendy: Bonnie didn't want them?

Mags: I saved her the combat boots. Dresses are for you.

I smile, pocketing my phone back and taking out my notepad.

Maybe my class was right. Maybe it is the summer for good memories and big dreams. For writing the book about my imaginary pirate captain, Jill, that I've been wanting to write forever. Maybe it's time for my swashbuckling stories to come to life.

I journey down the sidewalks away from Main, scribbling dreams onto paper as I cut off the main road and stroll down the pedestrian footpaths. These are my favorite shortcuts in Never Harbor. Tall grass on either side and the sea as my silent companion. The ocean waves aren't wild and insistent, like beaches elsewhere. They're peaceful. Calm.

When the footpaths empty back onto the main streets, I finally spot my favorite place in the world.

The Davies House.

Even one block away, the tippy-top of the turret pokes out from the crowd of trees. I spent my high school years up in the crow's nest, peering down at the town below, cheek resting on the glass as I made up stories about adults as they walked past. If only that Wendy knew what growing up would actually be like.

Bills to be paid. Disappointment in love. Not at all like the fairy tales I used to love writing. The only fairy tale remaining in my life is this house and the family within.

The Davieses' home looks like a crayon drawing of what a child thinks a house should be. A conglomeration of wood

21

and brick. Added onto and removed and then pasted back on again.

There's a wraparound porch that stops short of a tree house in the backyard. A staircase winds up the opposite side, leading to an apartment above the open garage. The front door is a different color than the railing and the mailbox and the shutters. Smoke billows from the kitchen window, which could either be Mr. Davies's cooking or one of Bonnie's candles left unattended.

It's not neat. It's not uniform. But it's perfect.

A figure crawls out from the crow's nest window. Long limbs recline on the roof, forearms relaxed on knees and hard jawline angled to the sky. His hair is haloed in a thicket of messy golden locks, glowing as if born from the sun itself. His eyes flicker down to the sidewalk, and I spot that familiar mischievous grin—the grin I reluctantly decided to leave behind so many years ago when it was directed toward someone that wasn't me.

"Wendy!" he calls down.

I slowly tuck my notepad back in my pocket, back to where dreams stay in fictional worlds.

The Davies House is the closest thing to a dream I will ever know.

Except this beautiful haven belongs to my ex-fiancé, Peter Davies.

Not me—the woman who simply wishes she were part of the magic.

Chapter 3

Part of the Magic

Jasper

You'd think hosting weekly dinners would accomplish some sort of organization on my parents' part.

You'd be wrong.

My parents *encourage* the chaos.

The moment my truck rambles onto the gravel driveway, Sam unbuckles out of the back seat and leaps out before the engine is off, hauling ass up the porch steps and through the front door, which is swinging wide open.

Because, of course, it is.

We're late to dinner because we stopped by the house after I picked up Sam from school. I needed to wash the fish bait scent off me. It had been a busy day that involved a lot of hands-on work outside my office. Not exactly *with* bait, but close enough, and I wasn't risking my siblings' whines all night.

I park my car beside the other familiar cars spilling onto the grass. Dad's rock playlist of R.E.M. billows through the open windows, along with his usual smoking stovetop. I shut my car door and take the uneven stone walkway toward the porch. I already hear my mom's voice filtering out the open door.

"Boys! Go outside if you're gonna play with the water guns."

"Liam started it!" I hear Levi accuse.

"I do not care who started it. Let's end it."

I scuff my shoes on the entry rug and walk through, stopping short of the living room, where Levi and Liam zoom past, arms loaded with plastic artillery, nearly knocking into me with a collective, "Sorry!" before they're down the hall and out to the backyard.

My littlest brothers, Levi and Liam—or, as they're affectionately called, The Twins—are eleven-year-old shots of chaos that were delightful "uh-oh" babies for my parents. *Very* uh-oh.

My mom bustles around the corner, frazzled with frizzy black hair, streaked with gray, and dresses folded over her arm.

Her eyes widen. "Jas!"

She runs to me like I'm a soldier home from the war, gathering me in her arms and holding me against her chest. My mom normally gives the best hugs, but this is borderline threatening. I haven't been to a family dinner in a month, but to her, that's basically a year.

It's not that I don't want to be here. It's that, whenever I do come home, there's an insistence on taking Sam for days or even a couple of weekends each month. I love my family and how much they give, but I've taken too much from them, especially when it comes to Sam. I don't want to say no, but I'll do it.

Pulling apart, she smacks my arm. "Where *have* you been?! And no Sam around either?" She holds up a finger, lifting a single eyebrow. "And don't you *dare* say you were busy."

I open my mouth, and she slaps my shoulder again.

Maggie Davies is short but fierce. Slightly plump because she loves Dad's cooking too much not to be, but with the secret, hidden strength of an ox. She prioritizes weight training, even at fifty-three, just in case she needs to deadlift her children to safety.

"Been busy," I tease, pulling her in for another—gentler —hug as she lets out a, "Oh, *you*," burying her nose into my chest.

"How's the clinic?" I ask.

"Fine," she says with a breathy sigh. "With today being the last day of school, I worry."

"I know."

My mom has been Never Harbor's local physician for almost twenty years. The summer is always the busiest. Then again, Never Harbor kids on the loose are always the wildest.

"Oh, can you give this to your dad? He was looking for it."

I look down at the bottle of spice she's shoving into my chest.

"How did he lose this?"

I don't receive an answer before she pats me on the shoulder and a childlike, "Stop it!" rings out from the backyard.

Mom slaps her hands on her thighs before power-walking off and yelling, "Twins! Is there a problem we somehow cannot solve on our own?!"

I exhale, journeying down the opposite hall toward the kitchen. Floral wallpaper is barely visible behind framed family memories. Polaroids are tucked into the corners, and crayon doodles are shoved between those. My parents believe photo albums are a waste of money when walls will do.

Even with missing spices, the kitchen still smells of too many. I find my dad wiping his hands on his apron. He takes the spice from my extended hand and sets it down before pulling me in for a hug. One, two, three claps on each other's back, and we exchange the most awkward hug in human history. David Davies isn't nearly as affectionate as my mom, so the family leaned into it over time, making his awkward hug style extra obvious.

"Jas! Can you pull the pork out of the oven? Thanks, son. How's the house?" he asks, flustered-sounding thoughts oddly always organized.

I place on mitts as he goes back to cutting vegetables.

"Still coming along," I answer.

"Any day now, huh?"

I huff out a breathy laugh, pulling out the sheet of pork chops and depositing it onto the stovetop, next to a pot of mac and cheese.

"Any day now," I echo.

It's another inside joke because I'll never not be working on my house in some capacity. When I bought it, it was a shell of the cottage it is now. But that's how you get property on the seaside—find a fixer-upper and learn carpentry. Not only is it practical, but it also helps to keep my nightmares at bay. Which is exactly why I might never stop working on it.

I turn toward the creaking staircase, where Bonnie descends, lowering her noise-canceling headphones to her neck. I gifted them to her last year. The house might be down to only four siblings—her, Cassidy, and The Twins—but that's loud enough to need assistance.

"How're you holding up?" she asks, punching me in the shoulder.

"Holding up?" Dad asks. "Is something wrong?"

My eyes dart to her in a secret *you promised* gesture.

"Oh, no," she covers quickly. "Jas just wanted advice on a rash on his butt."

My dad's face falls, taking his thick mustache with it. "Oh. Well, y'know, I've got something upstairs I can grab—"

"No, Dad—"

"No, really, it's no issue. Easy application too—"

"No thank you," I rush out. "I'm fine. Nothing is wrong. Bonnie's just being mean."

Dad shrugs. "Happens."

"Ooh, are those homemade pickles?" Bonnie asks, changing the subject as she reaches for the unlabeled mason jar.

Dad gives a smile. "Only take one. They're not for you."

"No, you take none. You'll ruin dinner." My mom's voice precedes her frenzied rush into the kitchen. "Outside," she demands. "Too many cooks."

My mom's no-nonsense parenting complements my dad's permissive one well.

"One pickle?" Bonnie whines.

"No. Out."

Her lips twist to the side before she walks through the open back door.

I follow behind, almost shutting it before I hear Mom's call of, "Keep it open! It's too hot!"

"Seriously, you should consider Dad for the *you know what* job," Bonnie whispers as we exit the kitchen. "He'd love it."

"No," I answer.

Our father has held his dream job as a stay-at-home

father for nearly thirty years. He thought he would retire after Bonnie, but The Twins held other plans. Sam could definitely join his uncles for the summer, but Dad is getting older, and he only has two hands. I won't place that burden on him—not on any of my siblings. Not when every time we text, they're volunteering or running a restaurant or simply having a social life, unlike me. It's not fair to ask that of them.

We empty into the yard, and it's a cacophony of sound. The Twins are climbing the tree house stairs, fumbling over their feet to reach the top deck, where my three other brothers—Milo, Cassidy, and Peter—stand, poised with battered plastic swords from our childhood at the ready. Near their feet stands Sam, his tiny chest puffed out, prepared for a fight against the solo battalion on the opposite side.

Standing across the hanging bridge, swinging a sword at the four of them as their group takes comical steps backward, is Wendy Darling.

Wendy is the ever-present ex of my brother. Always here with her tendrils of long, dark brown hair tucked back into a powder-blue ribbon. Her sundress, with its cinched-in waist, billows behind her, exposing slender legs and delicate ankles. Her plump pink lips form a type of knowing smile that's indescribable. Exciting yet secret, as if the true smile underneath is being saved for something special—or someone.

My jaw tenses, and I look away.

But a cocky, loud voice brings me back. "Come and join us, you old codfish."

I look back to find my brother Peter standing with his sword pointing in my direction. His wild dirty-blond hair and crooked grin accompany the domineering stance. He

28

might be thirty, but his heart always seems to remain young.

Not like me.

The *codfish*.

I'm the eldest of our seven-sibling crew, and apparently, just because I don't want to join in on their childish activities, it means I'm an old *codfish*.

Also, sure, I smell like fish from time to time. That doesn't help.

I level a look at Peter. He laughs, undeterred by my nonresponse.

"Are you adults or children?" Mom asks.

"We're fighting Pirate Jill!" Sam calls down.

Mom nudges me with her shoulder. "You sure you don't want to get up there too?"

I grunt. I don't need to play when my brothers have the entertainment covered all on their own. They've always fared fine without me.

Peter is three years younger and my only brother by blood, aside from The Twins. Until I was eight years old, it was just the two of us, fighting and punching and doing what boys did. I always thought that Peter and I fought like normal brothers, but my mom said it was more than that. She said we never truly saw eye to eye—me too quiet and him reacting too loud, as if making up for my silence.

It took *the* fishing accident for my parents to decide they'd had enough and needed more playmates to round out the natural hostility. But while they tried to have more children, the universe cruelly frowned upon their attempts, so they adopted instead.

First to join us was Milo. He was the same age as Peter but far quieter. The childlike giggles we'd expected were hidden behind books and shy smiles. When I first took Sam in, it was Milo who dropped by with no less than fifteen parenting books despite not being a parent himself.

Next was Cassidy. He was a mess of curly, dark hair and dimpled laughter. With Peter and Milo being four years older than him, they became Cassidy's idols. He and I weren't close until we were both adults, but he always found my and Peter's fights entertaining. Then again, he's always found most of the world to be one big joke.

Once all four of us were old enough to drive around and cause teenage-boy shenanigans, my parents hated the empty nest, so Bonnie arrived next. They wanted a little girl to pamper with pretty bows and pink onesies. But the first time I held Bonnie in my arms, I received a swift balled-up baby punch to the jaw. She must have known she'd have to be tough among all her brothers.

My parents intended to stop at five, but sometimes, surprises happen, and The Twins were no less than a miracle. Rambunctious, but miracles all the same.

Then came Wendy Darling.

Since my college years, she's always just *been here*. Cassidy came home from middle school, begging my parents to invite her to dinner, claiming that she basically had no mother or father. So, they gathered her in their arms, like they do with everyone in town. She became another staple in the Davies family.

My parents were ecstatic when she started dating Peter a few years back. Like most lost souls, she was drawn to my younger brother's charisma. And Peter, being who he is, was drawn to anyone who would show him the attention he craved. Wendy and Peter were engaged for a short bit, but my brother's hubris was always going to be his downfall.

The ass never stopped flirting with other women.

I don't know how far his escapades went, and I don't

care to know. I'm afraid too much information might make me think differently of my brother, and I don't want that. The only facts I have are that Wendy forgave him, and after all that, she still adorns our tree house instead of another woman.

She's Peter's Wendy through and through.

I watch her now—for probably too long. Longer than I should because her eyes find mine.

Her eyes.

Blue, like the color of Never Harbor's ocean. Vast and unpredictable. Calm but somehow deeper than they seem.

Pretty.

Yes, Wendy Darling is undeniably pretty.

"What about Wendy?" Bonnie asks from beside me.

I shake my head, almost choking on nothing. "What?"

She nudges my shoulder and says far too loudly, "Wendy could be your babysitter for the summer."

"You need a babysitter?" Dad asks, poking his head out the kitchen window.

Oh Christ, here we go.

My mom whips her head to Bonnie. "You're quitting?"

Bonnie juts her chin up proudly. "I got a job at The Hideaway."

"You're welcome," Peter adds, giving a low bow.

"Oh, about time!" Cassidy calls over, averting his attention enough to get barreled into by The Twins with an *oomph.*

"Wait, so Sam needs someone to watch him?" Milo asks, eyebrows cinched in.

"No, I—"

"Yes, he does," Bonnie says.

"Well, Bonnie's right then," Mom adds. "Nobody knows kids like Wendy."

I shake my head. "That's not what—"

My family gets like this. Nosy and pushy and wanting to be involved. I know they're just trying to help, but I'm perfectly fine on my own.

"You want Wendy?" Peter asks.

His question silences the rest of us.

Peter can always quiet a room. Or a yard.

Everyone shifts their attention solely onto me.

Wendy is frozen in her piratey stance, cheeks flushed that beautiful rosy pink. Those ocean-blue eyes blinking in anticipation. I swallow under their stare.

"No," I find myself answering. "No, I'm fine."

I don't know why I say it. Maybe because I don't want my family's help again. Though, no, Wendy isn't family anyway. She's far from it. Maybe it's her age—a twenty-six to my thirty-three—but who cares how old she is? Maybe it's because she's my brother's ex. But that shouldn't mean anything either.

Right?

I can't cycle through my thoughts fast enough before my family descends like vultures.

"And why not?" Mom demands.

"Son," my dad chastises.

"You won't find someone more qualified than Wendy," Bonnie adds in.

"Yeah! Wendy's fun," Sam says, swinging his sword in her direction.

"Sam—" I'm in the middle of trying to find a reason my six-year-old will understand when Peter speaks up.

"No, I get why he doesn't want to hire her. I mean, Jas doesn't want a nanny that's *too* serious, right?" he says with a boyish laugh.

I see the moment Wendy's face drops.

A chill seeps through the backyard—a type of cold that shouldn't belong in Never Harbor during the summer.

I love my brother, but, God, even as an adult, he can't find the right thing to say. I've always respected Wendy for ending things with Peter. My brother runs solely on the pleasure part of his brain. He doesn't think before he speaks, and he *definitely* doesn't consider how his ex-fiancée might feel if he says she's too *serious*. Or, really, too *anything*.

I can see the rest of the world disappearing around Wendy as she wilts on the spot. I know because I feel it too —the hole in my chest widening as she fades like a bird shot from the sky, flitting down to the ground.

The longer the silence, the more my blood boils.

My eyes flash to Peter, who takes a tentative step toward Wendy, his eyebrows cinched in. He has the courtesy to look genuinely sorry.

"Hey, Pete," I call. "I saw smoke when I pulled up. You're not burning the chicken again, are you?"

The abrupt subject change isn't the most effective, but Peter's face still splits into a smile. And the attention isn't on Wendy anymore either, which was the whole point.

"Dad's fault for letting me help," he crows.

The yard bursts into loud yet friendly accusations and fighting that will mean nothing in another five minutes.

I look around, finding Wendy walking back into the house alone. But before she crosses the threshold, her eyes flick up and find mine. And an odd *something* in my chest lights on fire.

Chapter 4

Grumpy Brother One & Cocky Brother Two

Wendy

PETER'S never met a window he didn't like—especially mine.

Thirty minutes after I arrive home from dinner, his bright face jumps through my open window frame, a stark contrast against the black night behind him.

My hand shoots to my chest. "Peter!"

I should have listened for the familiar leaves rustling beneath his boots, but I've been too lost in my head. Too distracted by dinner and the disaster before it.

"I'm sorry," Peter says, but it's not in response to scaring me. It's as if we were continuing a conversation we weren't having. He crawls through the window, bringing a leaf or two with him. He sweeps them back outside. "I'm sorry, Wendy."

I sit in the love seat across from him, my cross-stitching project in my lap a distraction from everything else. Peter's comment before dinner. The awkward silence. And Jasper diverting the conversation.

Leave it to boy wonder himself to drop by and remind me of it.

I sigh. "What do you want, Pete?"

"You know I think you're fun, right?"

"Then, why'd you say I was too serious?"

Peter runs a palm through his hair, messing up the ends. But even messy, it's still devastatingly beautiful.

"Jasper didn't seem into the idea of you working for him, so I was giving him an out," he explains. "It wasn't meant to hurt you. I'm really sorry."

His eyebrows are tugged in the middle. His mouth in a sorrowful frown. He *does* look sorry—I'll give him that.

"It's okay," I say, shaking my head. "It is."

I curse the words in my head the moment I say them. But staying mad at Peter means interrupting the wonderful companionship we've built since breaking up, and I can't sacrifice that.

His shoulders slouch as he sighs. "You know I'd be lost without you."

"I know."

A soft smile spreads over his face, and I return the gesture.

And that's that.

Problem solved.

I like to make people's lives easier. I know I'm not Peter's top priority, and I won't ask him to choose between me or his brother. Peter melts for his family, and he looks up to his older brother more than Jasper will ever know and more than Peter himself will ever admit.

Jasper is the only brother who truly eludes him. Heck, the one who eludes me as well. He's too busy to hang out with his brothers, too many years older to have much in common, and with the addition of Sam four years ago, too preoccupied to think of anything but his boy.

When I first met the Davies family in middle school, I remember seeing Jasper looming in the corner of the living room, an unsmiling college boy. No, a college *man*—he was always a man. He stood with bulky, crossed arms and piercing eyes that stared me down like a hawk. Those steady eyes—pinprick irises with lake-water blue bordering on silver around them—could be seen as menacing, but the threat of it all was exactly what drew me in.

That day is the only time Jasper has given me a second glance. I don't think he finds time for anyone, aside from his family, and no matter how long I've hung around, I've never been granted entry to that list.

Not tonight though. Tonight felt like the first time we'd met all over again. Those eyes found mine in a flash. And he stared with a knowing look that said maybe *he* understood how I felt.

Yeah, right.

Jasper's knee-jerk reaction to hiring me was a very clear, resounding *no*. To think Jasper Davies would want to spend a whole summer with me—or anyone other than his son for that matter—is absolutely laughable. Would I even want to spend a whole summer with his grumpy self anyway? Not a chance. I'd break out in hives from the anxiety of it all.

Peter falls into the twin armchair across from me, tossing his phone up and down in the air before pocketing it and staring out the window. He gets like this after people get mad at him—quiet and distant. At his core, he loves everyone, and he loves deeply. The funny part is, when Peter is contemplative, he looks calm for once. Possibly even thoughtful.

He almost looks like Jasper.

36

I stare, entranced, as he stands, ambling across my small reading room. Whereas Jasper entranced me from afar, Peter was always barely in reach. Not fully there, but close enough to think you could grasp him. Cassidy's charismatic older brother. Flirtatious. Beloved. Even prom king. Somehow, I captured his attention at one point. And even when I lost his focus, it felt weird to have had it at all.

He heads to the wall of bookshelves, stacked with a range of genres. Some read, some not. I'm of the firm belief that collecting books and reading books are separate hobbies anyway.

Peter then walks over to the side table and picks up my notepad.

"Wait, Pete—" I protest.

He spreads it out like a pinup centerfold. "You're writing again?"

"Sort of. But don't read it."

"Why? I always loved your stories," he declares, as if I just accused him of not loving them.

"They're just silly stories," I utter.

"The world needs more silly stories." He places a finger on a random page and peers up at me through teasing eyebrows. "I bet this one's good."

I laugh. "You assume all of them are good."

"I do," he answers with a flash of a smile.

It's only an assumption though. Peter's never read my stories. Maybe in the beginning of our relationship, right when I was out of college with my education degree and creative writing minor and I was the center of his world. But like everything in Peter's life, it was only important for a short time. His attention is fleeting.

George was similar. Interested, doting, and exciting

from the start, but something about me deterred him, and I don't know what.

That's the most irritating thing about both of my previous long-term relationships. The question that snags at me like a loose thread, begging to be pulled, an end never in sight.

What did I do to deter them? What about me was wrong?

Though, while George sent me packing, Peter has remained a friend. He's much better at that anyway. I think he understands the significance of his family to me without me explaining it. I've spent over ten years of my life on Davies summer vacations, with a parking spot reserved in their driveway, at their house for Christmas, having my own stocking. They make me feel like I *belong* even if I never actually have. Peter shares his family with me, even after we split, and for that, I think I'll always forgive how he acted.

Peter lays the notepad on the lip of the bookshelf he's leaning on and crosses his arms. "Have you thought about Jasper's nannying job some more?"

"Should I?"

"You should text him."

"I don't have his number."

"Huh." He blinks like this is news to him, then shrugs. "Well, y'know, I think you should work for him."

I burst out laughing. "You're kidding."

Peter raises his eyebrows.

"Oh. You're not."

Peter scratches behind his head, ruffling the locks of sunny hair.

"Why?" I ask.

"You know Jas."

I snort. "I don't."

"Well, he won't ask for help," Peter continues. "And you *would* be really good at the job."

"I don't know ..."

"I just want to make sure he's okay." He sighs, then adds quickly, "And you. Of course I want to make sure you're okay too."

"I'm fine."

He scans the room—from the open floor plan with the armchair and love seat to the wall of books with the rolling ladder and through the wide threshold into the kitchen and hall leading to my single bedroom.

"What else are you doing this summer?" he finally asks.

"What do you mean?"

"You should at least get out of the house."

"Why? Are you hiring?"

He barks out a laugh. I laugh with him.

Peter's bar and grill, The Hideaway, is my least favorite place in town, and we both know it. It's not that it's a bad place exactly. It's actually quite lovely with its string lights and outdoor patios. But I'm not a partier. Never have been, never will be. It's part of the reason why we ultimately didn't work.

I haven't told Peter about my money problems. I've been too ashamed to. But I won't need to come clean if I can stumble into working at his bar.

I've reached a new low.

"Izzy could always use the help," he says, calling my bluff with a teasing smile. "If you want to."

"Then, maybe I will."

"Fine."

"Good."

He smirks, maybe impressed I called his bluff in return. "Well, you'll just be here, in this house, all summer. You seem like you need ..." He waves his hand at my notebook full of stories with a smile. "I don't know. Something."

"Something," I echo in a whisper.

I can tell what's going unsaid. *Writing* is apparently not a fun enough summer activity. I open my mouth to say otherwise, but before I can, Cassidy's voice appears from behind me.

"I thought you were gonna apologize, Pete."

I let out a wail at his sudden appearance, and both men laugh.

"When did you get here?" I ask him, out of breath with a racing heart. "And how?"

Cassidy throws a thumb over his shoulder. "Your front door was unlocked."

His broad shoulders barely fit through the threshold. When I first met him, Cassidy was just a short, chunky kid with curly hair. But that middle school baby fat transformed into a linebacker build once he discovered weight lifting.

"Hey, at least it wasn't the window," Cassidy adds.

"I'm always invited through Wendy's window," Peter says with confidence.

I gape, find a pencil on my side table, and toss it at him.

"Not like that!" he counters, batting it away as his grin widens.

"Still not hearing an apology," Cassidy says, throwing me a quick thumbs-up. "Got your back, Wendy."

"Thanks, Cass."

He lowers into the armchair Peter occupied minutes before. All the Davies brothers fit differently in that armchair. Cassidy, too snugly; Milo, too stiffly; and Peter with a recline of confidence.

For a split second, I wonder how the last brother might fit, sitting across from me like we were friends instead of bodies just orbiting near each other every few weeks at the Davies dinner. I bet Jasper's muscles, built from hours of—I don't know ... working on his house? Hoisting barrels at the docks? I have no idea what Jasper does to maintain his bulk, but there's no denying his strong biceps and thick thighs would overflow that chair.

Would his stare freeze me like it did earlier tonight? Would I float away under his silvery-blue gaze?

"Wendy?" Cassidy asks.

"Sorry, what?"

"Man, they really shook you tonight, huh?"

"Who?"

"Grumpy brother one and cocky brother two."

"I'm not grumpy," Peter counters.

"Never said *you* were the grumpy one," Cassidy shoots back with a grin. "Have you ever seen Jasper's texts? It's like reading an alien's attempt to exist among humans."

Peter's aforementioned cocky smile grows until his green eyes center back on me. They're light, but they're nowhere near close to silver, like his brother's. Filled with mischief, but not mystery.

"So, did you?" Cassidy asks.

"Yes, I've apologized," Peter says, waving his hand like he's dismissing the thought of it. "I'm trying to get Wendy to work for Jasper now." He lowers his chin down. "Come on, Wen."

"Come on what?" I ask on a laugh.

"Jasper needs you. Work for him. You don't want to hang out at my restaurant. You'd hate it."

Raising my chin, I defiantly respond, "Don't tell me what I would like or wouldn't like, Peter Davies."

"You'd really rather play hostess with Bonnie?"

41

I narrow my eyes and give a playful smile. "You're trying so hard to give me to your brother."

"*So* hard," he teases.

It's tempting. It would be far more enjoyable than The Hideaway. But it's also Jasper. Jasper would never hire me.

Which is why I call his bluff and say, "Fine. If he agrees, why not?"

But the moment the words leave me and the more Peter's smile grows, I know I've made a very grave mistake. Just like I can't say no, Peter doesn't accept no. He never turns down a challenge.

Chapter 5

The Captain

Jasper

Peter: We need to convince Jasper to hire Wendy.

Bonnie: Wow. Thanks for taking credit for my original idea.

Peter: I thought it was mine?

Bonnie: No, I'm clever like that.

Peter: Oh, wee baby sister, don't you know I'm the clever one in this family?

Bonnie: Hilarious.

Milo: You're the adventurous one, Pete.

Cassidy: Yeah, I think Milo gets the clever points. Or me.

Bonnie: Cass, didn't you just claim at dinner last night WITH YOUR FULL CHEST that Pluto was still a planet?

Cassidy: And how am I supposed to keep up with Pluto's changing planet status???

Milo: I think that's fair.

Bonnie: Enabler.

Peter: ANYWAY, so how are we gonna get the old man to hire Wendy?

Jasper: Please stop referring to me as if I'm not in the group chat

Peter: There you are! Why didn't you come over for First Day of Summer breakfast? The Twins requested snickerdoodle muffins. Dad really outdid himself.

Cassidy: They tasted like heaven.

Jasper: I was at work

Milo: Where's Sam?

Jasper: With me

Peter: That's no fun for a growing boy.

Bonnie: Bring Your Kid to Work Day is so '90s too.

Cassidy: Uh-oh. Your age is showing again, Jas.

Jasper: I'm literally only three years older than Milo and Pete

Jasper: I'm not old

Bonnie: Prove it. Use one emoji.

Peter: We dare you.

Cassidy: Double dog.

Bonnie: Triple.

Jasper: Children please

"Captain, we've got a problem."

I swivel my eyes to my office doorway. Charles Starkey's square head peers past the threshold, five-o'clock shadow growing its way down his collared work shirt.

"That's not a sentence I want to hear," I respond.

Starkey tilts his head side to side. "Well," he says, dragging out the word on a raspy breath, "that's the only sentence I got. Wanna come see?"

Reluctantly, I nod and lock my computer, catching eyes with Sam. That's when Starkey finds him, too, sitting in the corner of my office.

"Oh, hey, kid."

Sam, holding his gaming console way too close to his eyes, gives a short, "Hi," but nothing more.

I hate it when Sam spends too much time looking at screens. He gets dismissive and careless. But what else is a boy to do here? He tried reading a book, but that only lasted an hour at best. He's not at the level of chapter books just yet.

Peter was right. The docks are no place for a growing boy. Instead of running in the sun, he's curled in the corner chair of my dingy office, looking like half the kid he was just three days ago, excitedly playing pretend pirates with his uncles. His trusty plastic sword is tucked away in his belt loop while his fingers knock around buttons and joysticks.

I sigh, standing from my desk. "Be right back, okay, bud?"

He gives a noncommittal hum. I use my finger to tilt his screen farther away from his eyes—because I definitely think they're about to melt out of his head—until he finally looks up at me.

"How about when I get back, we take a break?" I suggest. "Maybe go for a quick walk or something."

His back straightens slightly, and I see a spark of hope. I ruffle his red beanie in my palm. He swats me away with a small laugh. *There's that smile,* but it fades away when his eyes drift back to his gaming console.

I walk outside, the smell of the docks hitting my nose in

a wave of fish and seaweed and bait. Distantly, the clock tower on Main tolls. The gentle lapping of waves on the hulls echoes through the outdoor walkway.

I catch Starkey staring at the office door as I close it behind me.

My gut clenches. I know how it looks. I come off like a terrible guardian, taking my kid to spend his first day of summer here—and likely most of his future weekdays as well. I wouldn't want it this way either, but what options do I have?

My family wants me to hire Wendy for the summer, but I don't want my family's assistance anymore. When Sam became my whole world four years ago, I did everything I could to be the best guardian for him. I moved back to Never Harbor with their excellent schools. I got a job on the water—it wasn't marine biology, like I went to school for, but I took what I could get. And I asked for help from my family, just like Ma always said we could do.

But I took too much. My ex, Jessica, didn't like that they babysat as often as they did. I know she was right. My dad already had The Twins to look after. Ma had a whole clinic to run. Peter was taking time away from his restaurant. Milo was volunteering around town less. Hell, even Cassidy backed off from the gym, which, for him, is like cutting off his arm.

After realizing the effect I had on my family, I took fewer shifts at the docks so I could be more present on my own, living on the strictest budget in our cheap cottage so that I could pay for Sam's day care. Once he graduated to preschool, I hoarded dock hours like a man desperate for water. I climbed the workplace ladder tooth and nail, leaping at the role of port captain once my old boss retired. I tripled my salary in less than two years and spent my weekends renovating our little fixer-upper with my bare hands into something resembling a home.

And I'm proud, damn it.

Maybe I should have been more driven from the start, read more parenting books—doing it all and then some. I shouldn't have depended on my family as much. Jessica was ultimately right.

So, potentially hiring Wendy? It feels too close to home —too much like defeat.

Plus, it's Wendy Darling.

Blue eyes. Pink cheeks. A delicate smile.

Nerves run across my chest. I shake the image from my head before the heat can roll up my neck.

No, Sam and I can handle ourselves just fine.

Starkey's face shifts to an apprehensive smile when he catches me looking at the door. I try to adjust; I wonder if I was accidentally sneering. That tends to happen. They call it my resting captain face.

"Y'know, Marina would have killed to play video games all summer as a kid," he comments with a chortle, rough as rocks and wet from his lungs.

I scratch through my beard, running my palm up the sides.

"Yeah," I respond noncommittally, the word fading off.

Starkey's trying to be nice, which is funny, given he looks like the type of guy you wouldn't want to meet in an alley at night. Some people have trouble seeing past the sheet of tattoos on his skin—mermaids and seagulls and lobsters spanning from his ankles up to his neck. He's a sailor at heart, and he swears like one too. But he was also a single parent himself. His daughter, Marina, now in her twenties, is his pride and joy.

"So, what's the problem?" I ask.

Starkey and I walk side by side down the dock, the wood creaking beneath our dirty boots as he explains, "Check-in for bay eight got mixed up in the schedule. Noodler's here at the same time as Turk."

"Christ."

Hooks and chains clank as we walk past, clunking up the wooden steps to the upper deck. I peer out, and sure enough, those two idiots have their boats at an impasse, squared off like a game of Battleship.

"Give it to Noodler," I decide.

Starkey guffaws. "Why? Because Noodler's Noodler?"

"Exactly."

"You cut him too many breaks."

Noodler is one of three managers reporting to me, alongside Starkey, but he might as well operate with his hands on backward. He's a good man, but he's not the sharpest hook in the tackle box.

"He needs all the breaks he can get," I grumble.

Starkey smiles, then crosses his arms. "Hey, Cap?"

"Hmm?"

"Can I be honest?"

I lift a single eyebrow and lean against the railing. His confidence falters a little under my gaze. I know because I have the same eyebrow lift as my mother, and I'd rather run into oncoming traffic than encounter my mother's questioning stare.

"You've never not been," I observe.

"True. Well, I know what you're thinking."

"Do you now?"

"You're thinkin' that dirty office is no place for a kid in the summer." I sigh in response, and that must be answer enough because he asks, "What happened to Bonnie?"

"She decided to get a life with her friends," I answer, which is true.

I saw her and Lulu cackling in Live, Laugh, Taffy when I walked past the window to grab lunch for the harbor crew. I gave a small wave, but her widened eyes told me she didn't need her old-ass brother making her look like a loser in front of her best friend, so I just threw her the middle finger instead. Her subsequent grin told me I'd made the right move.

Blaming my loss on teenage friendships is better than saying my brother stole her for his own restaurant.

"Hey," Starkey offers, clapping a hand on my shoulder. "Sam'll be fine here if that's what you need to do."

I tongue my cheek, but the thought that's been at the edge of my mind all day is already burrowing further.

"I thought you were honest, Charles."

His face falls, but he doesn't hesitate. "All right then. Kid needs a summer."

There we are.

I agree. I can't keep my boy cooped up in an office on a sunny summer day every week. Which has me asking myself the true question: What would Ed and Stacy have done?

I hate when I ask this question because I have *no clue* what they would have done because they're not here anymore.

But I can guess.

Stacy would have taken him snorkeling. Ed would have had Sam already swimming with the dolphins somewhere in the Caribbean.

The kind bastard.

I will never be the gentle animal whisperer that Sam's father—my best friend—was. Nor will I ever capture the

49

adventurous and open-minded spirit of Sam's mother—my other best friend.

At two years old, Sam was much too young to lose both his parents. But I suppose growing up starts at two, when you learn language and view the world around you for what it truly is—full of infinite disappointment.

Sam will never see the look on Ed's awed face after catching his first fish of the day. He'll never hear Stacy's triumphant laugh when she makes a breakthrough in the lab.

He'll only know me. His godfather. Just a guardian.

Sam refers to me as Captain because it's the first thing he ever wanted to call me. He watched some cartoon about pirates far too young in life—another failing from my parenting, I'm sure. But I accepted the title, mostly because the thought of him calling me anything else felt wrong. The name Dad sends shivers down my spine, icy cold and sharp like nails. I will never be Ed.

It feels like yesterday when I stood at the front of that chapel, cradling baby Sam in my arms. None of us could have known my godfather duties would come to fruition. Nobody could have known I would be his only lifeline after Ed and Stacy's research boat capsized at sea.

The familiar weight is back again. The harrowing tunnel vision that always comes at the thought of my two best friends. I grab a railing and steady myself.

Sam once asked why this happens—why I need to take moments to myself. I explained that I get dizzy, which isn't untrue. But I can't talk to him about why. I don't know how I'd react if I let the memories flood in. And if I'm not strong for Sam, then what type of godfather am I?

Swallowing, I let the feeling creep over my shoulders and slink away.

"Cap?" Starkey asks.

I nod. "I'm all right."

I walk back to my office with Starkey trailing behind. When I open the creaking door, the first thing I notice is Sam's empty chair.

Empty?

"Sam?" My eyes scan the small office. His gaming console is on the floor, and his pillow sits lifeless on the hard chair. "Starkey!"

Starkey pauses in the doorway. "What's up, Cap?"

"Where the hell is Sam?"

His eyes widen. "Oh sh—"

Starkey and I rush out the door. I power-walk down the dock until I'm suddenly full-out running, calling out Sam's name like my life depends on it.

My heart is racing, pounding, practically exploding out of my chest.

My boy is gone.

The harbor isn't meant for kids. Sure, I know my men are trustworthy, but the tourists that dock here sometimes? I don't know them. Sam is smart, but he's also six years old, walking around on his own. Not to mention all the hooks, chains, and various other dangers lying around.

He can't swim. Bonnie was his babysitter for the past two summers, and that girl has never learned how to stay afloat herself.

What the hell was I thinking, bringing him here? What if he fell in? What if—

I hear it in my head. The gargling. The choking on water. The sounds that haunt my nightmares.

No, no, no.

"SAM!" My voice is loud and harsh and cracking.

"Captain! He's in here!"

51

My chest is tight as I follow Starkey's voice, rushing down the moaning wooden planks and turning the corner to the grungy break room. Sam stands between the cluster of chairs and crowded tables, his wooden sword drawn out and directed at Noodler.

I barrel over to him, chairs clattering out of my way, before pulling him against my chest, skewing his glasses off his nose. I don't care. If they break, I'll buy him new ones.

"Sam, what in the world are you doing?"

Sam's muffled voice says, "Noodler said he would duel."

Over his shoulder, Noodler adjusts his cap. "I did say that, boss."

"Utter one more word, and you're fired," I bark, biting back the curse words I wish I could send flying instead. I refocus again on Sam, my palms cupping his shoulders. "Why did you leave without me?"

"I wanted a drink," Sam says.

"I said I'd be back in a minute."

"I just wanted a drink," he murmurs quieter.

Then, I realize he's leaning back. Maybe scared. Maybe intimidated. Maybe wondering why the man who should be the steady image of calm is freaking out at him being gone for less than five minutes.

I clear my throat. "You can't run off next time," I command, running my hands over his arms. "You got me?"

"Yes, sir."

Not even a playful Captain in sight.

Sam needs a fun, safe summer, and I can't give it to him here. I can't be the father he deserves if I'm too busy with work to properly watch him. And I absolutely cannot react like a helicopter parent with my rotors spinning out of control if he's out of my sight for more than one second. I can't see him scared like that again.

My ex's voice floats through my head. *"You're not enough for him."*

Jessica was always right.

I pull out my phone from my pocket and let my fingers hover over the screen before shooting out a text.

Chapter 6

What Freaking Shack?

Wendy

Unknown Number: Hello Wendy
Wendy: Hi! Who is this?
Unknown Number: Jasper. Would you like to work for me for the summer?
Wendy: How'd you get my number?
Jasper: Peter
Wendy: Wait, did you just text me a job offer?
Jasper: People text job offers
Wendy: I didn't know that.
Jasper: Let me know by tonight if you're free
Jasper: I need you to start tomorrow
Jasper: I pay competitively
Jasper: Thank you
Wendy: Wow. So formal.
Jasper: It's a job offer
Wendy: Sure it's not a ransom note?

Jasper: Yes or no

Wendy: Yes. I'm actually free as a bird. What time should I be there? Sundown? In the cellar?

Jasper: Seven in the morning will do fine

I'd be lying if I said I wasn't terrified. Because, ransom note or no, Jasper Davies doesn't seem like the type of man to appreciate my jokes. Or to want me around at all.

A job is a job though, and I'm not an *A average on my graded paper* kind of girl. I go for the A-plus.

I set my alarm at five thirty in the morning to get in a morning walk, winding down the empty sidewalks with the hushed influx of the tide on one side and the paintbrush strokes of pink and orange above me.

I stroll into my favorite coffee shop the moment it opens.

"Mullins!" I call, the bell over Peg Leg Press's door dinging as the lanky owner wanders out of the back room, grinning in my direction. "Any idea how Jasper Davies takes his coffee?"

Bobbi Mullins, brewer of the best coffee in the world, narrows her eyes, wrinkling the lines beside them on her brown skin.

"And what does a sweet girl like you need to know Jas's order for?"

"Ah. So, he takes it black," I assume.

She laughs. "That he does."

Bobbi is a staple in the Never Harbor community. Her wiry gray hairs sticking every which way are normally tucked back with a braid, spoon or pencil, and her gap-toothed smile is one of the first most people see on their way to work. Because why would you make your own coffee when her heavenly roast exists?

"I'm his nanny for the summer," I clarify.

Her eyes widen. "No kidding. So, no volunteering this summer, huh?"

My stomach drops. "I'm so sorry. It's just ..."

"No, it's good. Those boys need a ray of light like you out in that shack."

I blink. "Shack?"

"You know Jas," she says, as if that clears up anything.

I lift my eyebrows. Why does everybody keep saying that when I absolutely do not? Does anyone *know* Jasper? Bobbi laughs at my blank expression.

"They live out in the middle of nowhere," she explains. "That man does the best he can, but, yeah, it's just them all the way out there."

So, if I'm hearing correctly, I agreed to nanny for a man who texts like Hannibal Lecter in a place where nobody can hear me scream.

A shack? *A shack?*

"I'm sure it's ... quaint," I say, reassuring myself more than Bobbi.

She holds her hands up in the air. "All I'm saying is, good luck. So, one black coffee and ..."

"One regular. But double the sugar. And something for Sam too."

"You got it."

When she walks off, I let my shoulders fall.

Jasper's house can't be that bad, can it?

Five minutes later, I carry the to-go drink holder to my car, enter Jasper's address into my GPS, and drive. And Bobbi's right; it's definitely a *drive*. It's still close to Never

Harbor, but while most people live within fifteen minutes of walking to town, at max, Jasper is close to fifteen by car. Truly absurd by small-town standards.

I'm still driving long after the town fades away, when the colorful buildings on Main are only a memory and the only roads remaining are barren two-lane highways with seagulls scouting the coastline by the cliff's edge.

After a few treacherous, winding turns, my navigation empties me onto a single gravel lane. My car kicks up dirt while tall seagrass breezes by on either side. And at the end of the road, a little red cottage grows larger.

Shack?

What freaking shack?

This property is nice. *Really* nice.

I pull into the open space that could easily fit two more vehicles, right next to Jasper's parked black truck.

Hopping out of my car, I cross the gravel and peer over the edge of the cliff, down the flight of wooden planks leading to the beach. The paint looks new. Everything about this place does.

I turn back to the seaside home before me, guarded only by a white picket fence and rose bushes.

A white picket fence?

Is this seriously Jasper, the angry hermit's, house?

Maybe this place was once a shack, but that's not the case anymore. I wonder how few visitors swing by that nobody in town has noticed the transformation.

Crunching back across the gravel, I ascend the front porch steps. A bench swing hangs from the roof, creaking on its chain in the salty breeze. Beside it is a kid's bike, tipped onto its side. The front basket is decorated with barely visible superhero logos, too layered behind various other stickers. I bet Spider-Man would feel awful, getting one-upped by the Red Sox and a peeling Transformers logo.

I knock, and within moments, the door swings open.

Jasper leans on the threshold, palm pushed against the other side. The sleeves of his navy-blue work shirt are rolled up to his forearms, revealing a single tattoo of a fishing hook along the inside—right next to the veins that trail down to his defined wrists and fingers. His damp black hair, likely fresh from a shower, hangs loose with a single strand shadowing over his blue eyes, which look more translucent and silver this morning. His full beard appears freshly groomed, the fade that journeyed down his neck from last Friday now shaved away.

"Wendy." It might be a greeting if I thought he wanted me to be here.

Just like his devastatingly handsome looks, his voice is debilitating as well. Low. Decisive. Jasper's never *not* been intimidating, but being here on his property now feels more intimate and unnerving.

He lifts a single eyebrow, and I realize I haven't responded.

"Jasper," I finally counter, as if we could possibly be on even footing in this scenario.

I'm in linen overalls with straps that tie like ribbons on my bare shoulders, and he's straight out of a handyman porno. Except Jasper looks more likely to kill me than kiss me.

Jasper's wicked eyes flick over to my to-go carrying case, full of coffee cups.

"Oh, right!" I blink back and focus because I am totally professional and he is, technically, my boss now. "This is for *you*." I exaggerate the word as I take out the cup with the black slash on the lid. "Mullins said it was your go-to coffee."

He stares at it for a moment, like he's never heard of the word *coffee* in his life, but then he brings it to his mouth, his lips caressing the lid as he sips down the first few drops. The whole thing feels methodic.

Jasper eyes the two remaining cups. "Sam can't have coffee."

I laugh, and it's too high-pitched. "Oh God, of course not. No, that last one is lemonade. Figured he'd want it for lunch or something. I didn't wanna show up with nothing for him, y'know?"

I think I see something in his eyes—curiosity or maybe just plain old judgment—before he nods.

"He'll like that."

Point for me. I'll take it.

Jasper clutches his coffee loosely by the lid and walks across the hardwood with his work boots clunking into the echoing silence. I stand awkwardly in his doorway, popping my lips before taking one tentative step in and shutting the door behind me.

The interior is just as surprising as the outside. It shouldn't belong to a man. Not to say men can't be clean, but Peter lives his life in happy chaos, and George always depended on me to be his maid. But Jasper's house is immaculate. I bet I could eat off the dark hardwood floor. The only colorful decor are the crayon drawings and school projects layered on the fridge.

Jasper stands on the opposite side of the kitchen island now, sheets of paper scattered out in front of him. He brings the cup back up to his lips, and I shamelessly watch him. The way his throat bobs with each swallow. The way his piercing eyes dart over the documents. I can't seem to look away.

I take a seat at the barstool across from him and twiddle my thumbs. "Wow, so when company comes over, you mean business, huh?"

His eyes swivel up to me, acknowledging my attempt at small talk.

"What do you mean?"

"It just looks like you spent all morning cleaning," I observe, taking the opportunity to look around more.

Beyond the kitchen is a parlor with a green couch, matching armchairs, and a small musical keyboard in the corner. Floor-to-ceiling windows display the back porch outside, overlooking where the open sea meets the horizon line.

You've got to be kidding me.

"I didn't," Jasper says. I look back to him, confused, so he clarifies, "I didn't spend all morning cleaning."

My eyes widen before I can steel my expression. "You're telling me it *always* looks like this?"

He blinks rapidly, opening his mouth, shutting it, then nodding.

He says nothing, as if he can't find appropriate words to reply to a pseudo-compliment, which is why I add, "It looks nice."

He pauses his pen over the paper for a moment before murmuring, "Thanks."

I glance at his hand. A raised scar is slashed and discolored across the back. A watch sits just above it, resting over his bony, defined wrist. The face of it is cracked. Unlike the house and surrounding property, both the scar and the watch do not look new. Far from it.

Everything in this house seems perfect, all except those details. What other imperfections are lurking in his mind?

There's an array of schedules and numbered instructions and Post-it Notes before him. Even the *J* in his signature swoops into a beautifully thin, curved hook.

"I've got a makeshift agenda set out," he says, and my back straightens. "Sam likes breakfast at nine and quiet time at one."

"Quiet time?"

"He goes to his room and plays on his own. Helps with independence."

I want to ask why the heck he still has quiet time. Anyone six years old and up, especially with no siblings, doesn't exactly need that time. But to each their own.

"Okay," I say. "Well, I was thinking I'd take him to Mermaid Lagoon and—"

"No," he interrupts. "He can't swim."

I bust out laughing before I can stop myself, but when Jasper's eyes meet mine again, heat rises to my cheeks, and my smile disappears.

"You mean to tell me that sweet boy lives in Never Harbor and he can't swim?" I ask.

Jasper lets out a heavy breath. "I never got around to teaching him, and Bonnie never learned either so ..."

"Well then, he'll have to take swim lessons. Laura, over at the community center, normally hosts a cute little camp in the summer. I can get him in. He'll love it."

Jasper instantly shakes his head. "I ..." His words fade off.

I wait for him to finish, but he doesn't.

I know everything about this man's family. I went to middle school with Cassidy, I have reading dates with Milo,

Bonnie and I go thrifting with Maggie, and Peter and I are, well, whatever we are.

But Jasper himself? He's a missing piece in the Davies family quilt of knowledge. I might be a bonus guest at their house on a normal day, but here, I'm a downright stranger.

I furrow my brow. "Swimming should be a normal life skill. It'll be in a supervised environment. He'll be fine."

Jasper's jaw grinds. "Let's just move on."

And he does. Jasper continues with Sam's full schedule, what meals he likes, what his favorite television show is, and exactly how many blueberries will settle in his stomach before he starts to feel sick. He's in the middle of explaining Sam's tendency to leave doors open—and how that is absolutely *not* allowed—when he lets out a little tsk.

"I forgot the house key for you. Be back."

Then, he walks off, leaving me to sit awkwardly by myself. It's the second time he's just kind of ... left. I wonder if he does that often. Or I wonder if it's just easy to do around me.

I lean back to steal another peek at the ocean I get to admire all summer, but instead, I spot Sam out on the back porch. A massive Irish wolfhound sits next to him, nearly twice his height and still as a statue. The sliding glass door is left open, and the salty breeze floats through the house. I smile to myself.

Unclosed doors indeed.

I stand from my barstool and cross the parlor, walking through the open back door. I plop down on the opposite side of the dog.

"Hey, Sam," I say, peering around the wiry fur to see Sam doing the same.

His smile is growing by each second.

"Hi, Wendy."

"Who's this?" I ask, nodding to the wolfhound.

Sam places a tiny hand on the dog's spine. "Roger."

"Roger," I echo, reaching out to pet him as well, but stopping midair. "Do you mind if I pet him?"

Sam nods enthusiastically, so I pat and stroke the coarse coat. Roger leans into it, but keeps his paws firm on the porch planks beside Sam.

"Does his job well, doesn't he?" I observe. "Likes to protect you?"

"Yeah. He doesn't bite."

"I feel like every time I hear that, a dog does bite." I playfully narrow my eyes. "Are you tricking me?"

Sam giggles and insists, "No! He doesn't."

"You sure?"

"Yes," he replies, the answer mixed with bubbled-up laughter.

"Okay then. I *guess* I'll believe you. So, what do you like to do around here with Roger?"

"We play pirates."

I grin. "You know I'm a pirate sometimes."

"Jill?"

"That's right."

His eyes brighten. "I love your Jill stories."

"Think she can join your crew?"

"If Roger says it's okay."

"Well, *of course*," I say, stroking a hand behind Roger's ears.

His tongue lolls out between his whiskered beard, and a moment later, he barks. I raise my eyebrows at Sam in anticipation.

Sam's head bobs up and down, his thick glasses jumbling around with the motion. "He says yes."

"Whew," I say, wiping fake sweat from my brow. "Close one."

"Now, you need the captain's permission."

"And is that you?"

A low voice behind me, so gravelly that a shiver tickles my spine, says, "No, that's me."

Jasper stands in the threshold, leaning against the door-frame with crossed arms and an impassive stare. He looks down at me. I suddenly feel so childish, sitting cross-legged on the ground like this.

"Can Wendy join the pirate crew?" Sam asks.

With a small twitch at the corner of his lips, Jasper throws a nod at Sam. "Consider her part of the crew, bud."

"Nice," I whisper to Sam, holding my fist up and letting it bump against his.

Jasper clears his throat as he bends to hand me a key. I tuck it into the front of my overalls.

He tosses his head back toward the kitchen. "A word?"

"I'll be back, Sam. Prep the ship while I'm gone."

"Aye, aye!"

I stand, dusting my pants off, as Jasper continues like our previous conversation never stopped, "He gets one hour of screen time total. Split it however you'd like. He also likes vegetables, but he doesn't like squash or zucchini. But he will *try it if Miss Wendy makes it, won't he?*" The words are pointed toward Sam, who gives a cheeky smile and nods.

Jasper guides me back over the threshold, and for a moment, I feel the warmth of his palm hovering behind the small of my back. He slides the door shut.

Once it snicks closed, he adds in a murmur, "He'll also want chocolate pudding after lunch. Don't give it to him."

I laugh. "He can't have chocolate? Is he a puppy?"

"Specifically pudding. He won't survive quiet time if he gets it."

"Heck, I wouldn't wanna endure quiet time either," I tease with another laugh. "Pudding or not."

That comment causes Jasper to pause in place. He runs a hand through his hair, tousling the black strands, somehow making it more heartbreaking than it was before.

"Wendy, listen, I trust you. But I have rules. And I want to ensure they'll be followed. Can you please assure me that will happen?"

I see the concern etched in the little indents between his eyebrows and the lines beside his eyes. This is more than just simple dad responsibility. There is something more rooted beneath the surface, if only I could grasp it. But I don't think he'd ever let me.

So, I just tell him, "Yes, I promise."

"Good."

Yet before he can walk off, my childcare-loving brain puts my foot in my mouth anyway.

"But he should take swim lessons. Seriously. If he's gonna live near the water, it's less of an issue of missing out on fun and more of a safety concern." Jasper stares at me in the silence, and teeming with discomfort, I quickly add in, "You just said you trust me."

Jasper blinks at me, shifting his gaze between my eyes before assessing my lips and back up. I hold my ground, but my body wants nothing more than to melt through the floor like lava.

After another few seconds of quiet, he finally says, "Okay, sign him up."

He walks back to the kitchen counter without another word.

I can't pin the oldest Davies sibling down. He's cold. Distant. Guarded.

But why?

And why do I even care? It will only bring me stress. He clearly has no interest in being friendly. Which is okay. I'm here to get summer funds. That's all. I need to pay rent so I can stay in Never Harbor—in the place I call home.

It's not my job to worry about the closed-off state of Jasper Davies even if my curiosity demands another say. But I learned my lesson about curiosity with a Davies man once before. I know better than to do it again.

Chapter 7

The Wendy Bird

Jasper

THE DREAMS ARE BACK.

I shoot up, my soaked shirt sticking to the damp pillow-case as I gasp for air. I expect to see waves before me. A storm. The edge of the ship. But instead, it's just the darkness of my bedroom. I bury my head in my palms, exhaling a heavy breath that feels like an imitation of the one in my dream.

After a couple of weeks, the nightmare has returned. I was wondering when it would pull me back.

The dream is uncomplicated with no variation.

I'm looking over the edge of a ship. Rain is plunking on the railing while my hands clutch tightly until my knuckles are white. My skin is pruned, as if I'd been stagnant for too long. And every time, I still do nothing as I watch Ed and Stacy drown.

They're fighting, choking on water, gargling it as it consumes them. I watch them go under right before I wake up, and I never wake up in time to look away. It's as if my mind insists on confirmation that, yes, they're gone.

Ed and Stacy are not coming back.

Waking up, drenched in sweat, seems almost cruel, as if the storm followed me back home.

I wasn't on the boat the day Ed and Stacy went missing. It would be impossible to know what actually happened, but the dreams have been convincing enough.

I remember the call like it was yesterday.

The officer asked if I was sitting.

I sneered a sarcastic, "Sure," before collapsing to the floor, hand clutching the corner of my kitchen counter. The hollowness shot through me like a bullet.

Within two days, I was on my way to pick up Sam. Both Ed's and Stacy's parents were pieces of shit, and my role as godfather became too real when I was listed in their will as Sam's legal guardian. I'll never forget Sam blinking up at me with those big eyes, a confused boy at two. I was equally unsure with my fumbling hands shaking to figure out the new car seat before leaving the police station.

I climb out of bed, stripping my bed and pillowcase and tossing them in the washer. I walk out to the quiet kitchen, pouring a glass of water from the fridge. There's a clicking of nails on the hardwood as Roger sleepily pads over to me, nudging his nose against my leg. Patting his head, I walk down to the hall to open Sam's door.

I find Sam fast asleep, unburdened by memories—real or not. His mouth hangs open as little child snores leave like tiny puffs of air.

Back then, I know he had a sense something was wrong. But he was so little that all he did was cry, as if confused why two familiar faces no longer greeted him every morning. Now, all Sam has are stories, and I hate that I'm so bad at telling them, if I can even tell them at all. It's been four years, but still not long enough for me.

I allow the door to silently shut behind me as I cross to the back porch. I pause when I see an unfamiliar notepad resting on the side table. The front is a very plain yellow, and Sam normally prefers superhero stickers plastered over his. It can't be his.

Picking it up, I flip through the loopy scrawl, a delightful cursive inked in purple. There are notes, little observations, little half thoughts.

Stories.

It must be Wendy's. It's weird to see a little piece of something different in this house—yellow contrasted with our blank walls. A spot of color.

My chest tugs into a knot, so I place the notepad back down, tilting it to the side to look like I never touched it. I slide open the back door to the porch. I nod my chin toward Roger, and he lopes out after me.

The moon hangs high, its circle reflecting onto the water. It must be the middle of the night because there's no sign of a sunrise anywhere on the horizon. I sit on the stairs. Roger rests his head in my lap.

Jessica always hated when I woke up in the middle of the night, especially if it was in a cold sweat. She'd say it was like Groundhog Day and then walk herself to the couch without another word. If this is Groundhog Day, it's the shittiest time loop I can imagine.

It's always weird to me how everything seems normal, but then the knowledge hits again and again and again, like an alarm blasting me to the present. My best friends are gone, and they aren't coming back.

I close my eyes. I enjoy the calmness of the waters out here. The waves are more audible at night, but they're nothing like my dreams. There's no rush. No storms. No coughing.

Sam is taking swim lessons now, and I know I should have taught him years ago. But I couldn't handle hearing the noises from my dreams. Not with him.

But he's learning now. Wendy is making sure of that.

She's protecting my boy.

Even now, I can't do what needs to be done for him. I can't be the parent he deserves.

I sigh.

It's going to be a very long day.

WENDY DARLING LIKES to stay out of sight. At least out of *my* sight.

It likely has something to do with how little I talk. But the moment I walk through the door after work, whatever game she and Sam are in the middle of instantly turns into an exchange of awkward smiles and small waves, and within five minutes, max—timed on my watch—her car leaves with a plume of gravel dust kicking up behind her.

I suppose it doesn't matter whether Wendy wants to spend extra time here. What business does she have with me anyway? It only matters that Sam is happy and fulfilled, and that boy would already defend Wendy with his little life.

I asked him one night before bed what they had done that day, and he proceeded to speak—at length with barely any breaths in between words—about her stories. Nothing about their actual day, just fictional adventures.

Wendy had tried to talk to me after her first day, but she hasn't tried since. I must have had on my resting captain face. I can't blame her, but I miss knowing what's going on.

"So, you're doing all right?" I confirmed. "Swim practice was fun?"

His little brow furrowed before saying, "Wendy is the best, Cap."

He could have added a *duh*, and it would have carried the same inflection.

So, that was that.

In the first week alone, I came home to Sam's childlike giggles in the garden, the back porch, hiding in the beach-grass, and under my bed, waiting to grab my ankle.

I screamed. He laughed. And then Wendy left in silence. Again.

Always leaving without even one conversation.

I could feign innocence about why Wendy dislikes me so much, but why lie? It's not anything I did. It's just who I am. Quiet. Icy. Emotionally unavailable. Jessica always told me the latter was my worst feature. My lack of openness was why I didn't have friends outside of my family or Starkey.

Just two days ago, I pulled into the driveway to find Wendy and Sam down by the rocky shore, tiptoeing over the pebbles in old sneakers, picking up shells and laughing. Sam's arm floaties squeaked with each turn, and Wendy ...

Wendy.

It had been a while since I'd seen a woman in a bathing suit. Granted, it wasn't even that revealing, just a simple one-piece. She was wearing bright yellow swim shorts, which I was sure were better suited to running around with a six-year-old than bikini bottoms. Very practical.

But the back of her bathing suit sank low, kissing the top of her shorts and exposing the slender length of her spine with that delicate dip along the center. And right around there was where I noticed something I'd never seen before.

A bird.

It was a simple tattoo, but the appearance of thin black lines on such soft skin felt like I was looking at something I shouldn't. A piece of Wendy she kept for herself. I hadn't even known she had secrets. Like Peter, she'd always appeared to be an open book.

Peter.

I walked back inside before I could look again.

It's best for me to stay distant. Not only is she my nanny —my damn employee—but she's also my younger brother's ex-fiancée. I can recognize when a line needs to be drawn.

So, I take her cue and stay quiet as well.

Day after day.

A wave. A weak smile. A car departing.

She can pretend to be nice to me in front of Sam, but it's simply pretend. And pretend is only for children, isn't it?

On Thursday, I walk into a house devoid of the usual laughter I've gotten accustomed to lately. No pitter-patter of child feet. No smacking of Wendy's flip-flops on the floor. Even Roger's paws padding over the hardwood is absent.

I tense at the pit forming deep in my stomach, and I can't find my voice enough to call for them. But that's when I hear her. Out in the garden through the kitchen window.

"So, there I was, sword in hand."

"On the plank?" *Sam.*

"That's right," Wendy continues. "I stood at the end of the plank, looking just over the edge. Me and the ocean. And then ... *a crocodile!*"

"No!" Sam's voice echoes through the yard, fear laced in the outburst.

I cross the kitchen, avoiding the squeaky planks near the cabinets to silence my approach.

"Yes!" Wendy spouts with fervor. "A crocodile! With an open jaw and gnarly teeth, just waiting for me to hop right in. I knew if I were to jump, I would be gone forever."

Journeying out the front door, I walk quietly down the porch steps and around the corner toward the rose bushes.

"So, what did you do?" Sam asks.

"I demanded to speak to the captain."

A silence falls over the breezy yard as Sam asks in a hushed whisper, "Who was it?"

"*Blackbeard,*" Wendy says, and the word is spoken so low, so haunting, that it practically hums. Hell, it sends a shiver down my spine.

I reach the garden gate, then stop. Quickly, I rotate so my back is flat against the bushes.

It's not eavesdropping if it's on my own property, is it? It's not being nosy if it's simply a *story*, right?

Sam gasps. "What did you do then?"

"Why, I dueled him."

"*You did?*"

The cushion on our patio chair squeaks. I wonder if he's scooting closer to the edge of his seat.

"I sure did. What could Blackbeard possibly do to me? I'm Jill! The mightiest female pirate on the seven seas!

" 'Girlie,' Blackbeard said. 'You shall surrender your weapon to me this instant. Or I'll swash you down like the ... the *jerk* that you are!' "

"He called you a jerk?"

"Okay, well, he said something far less savory," she says with a laugh. "But yes."

My mind swims with that laugh. Light. Airy. Genuine and pure. Almost regal.

The way she continues to weave the adventure is so confident. So captivating. If I didn't know better, if I suspended disbelief for even a moment, I'd think she had lived the adventures herself.

I have to stifle the smile that wants to break through. The little glimmer in my chest. The slight shift that feels ... *uncomfortable*. New.

"And then ... Sam joined me!"

"Avast ye, Jill!" he bellows, and that's when I finally turn the corner. As if my body subconsciously wants to join in on the fun.

She screams. Sam screams. Roger rises from his sprawled position on the grass and runs forward. There's even a hint of a growl until he realizes it's me.

"Writing a story?" I ask.

"Oh," Wendy says, her face flushed pink, hand close to her chest.

I like the way she looks surprised.

"Yes. But it's just an idea."

"She's been on *loads* of adventures!" Sam says excitedly, bouncing on the cushion. One of his eyes is covered with a patch, and his sword is withdrawn.

"What happened to your eye?" I ask.

"Blackbeard took it a week ago," he groans in another *duh* tone.

We'll need to discuss this newfound attitude later.

"Uh-huh," I muse, nodding slowly before looking to Wendy. "And is that one of your stories as well?"

"What?" Wendy asks. She looks almost taken aback, like she's shocked that I asked at all.

"One of your stories or something," I clarify.

Her face falls, and the mood shifts. But I can't place my

finger on why. I don't know what I said. What I do know is her frown has my nerves tangled in knots.

"Yeah. Something," she quietly agrees.

I don't like her lack of smile.

I dislike even more how swiftly she pulls Sam into a big hug, murmuring, "See you tomorrow, kiddo," before turning to leave.

She's checking out so fast, just like she always does. But I don't like it this time. I want that beautiful laughter again.

Quickly, she's walking through the gate, bypassing me altogether. My feet walk forward before I can stop them, pushing me toward her car, chasing the new feeling that's leaving just as fast as she is. I'm crunching through the grass until her key is in the lock.

Then, I blurt out, "Hey."

Like an idiot.

Like a grade-A moron.

She turns on her heel, eyes wide.

"I, uh ..." I can't find the words because, quite frankly, I didn't have any. I hold out my palm, squeeze it closed, then let it fall by my side. "Thank you?"

I have no idea what I'm thanking her for, but Wendy's eyebrows tilt in, and almost imperceptibly, her lips twitch into what could be a smile.

"You're welcome?" she answers, playfully mirroring my tone.

Then, she gets in her car and leaves once more.

But that glimmer in my chest only grows brighter.

Chapter 8

A Pocket-Sized Pixie

Wendy

"Okay, so if we sneak around the other side—"

"No. We'll get caught in two seconds."

I lean on the counter with my cheek in my palm, watching Cassidy and Peter scour over the new quarry map that he somehow acquired from city hall.

Deadman's Drop is our required summer activity—at least according to Peter—but this year, entrances have been blocked off because some of the pools are now being used as the town's water supply. Not all of them, but enough to have Officer John surveying regularly. But you try telling Peter Davies he can't do something, especially something concerning tradition.

"This feels illegal," I muse.

"It's not illegal," Cassidy states with far too much confidence for a man who doesn't actually know.

I squint right as Peter throws an arm around me and tugs me close. He smells good today, like citrus and tea tree.

"Wendy," he chides, "my little rule follower. Let's live a little."

"I live," I argue, rolling my shoulder to remove his hand.

He peers down at the map again and runs a hand through his hair.

Once he's not looking, I let out a small breath.

Peter is handsy with everyone, and it has nothing to do with me. But the shame I feel every time he touches me ... the wrongness ... I wonder if he feels it too. As if our already-precarious situation suddenly feels very untenable.

Knowing Peter, he probably doesn't notice at all. Because what worries an average person simply doesn't make sense to him. It's both his best and worst feature.

SLAM!

My head shoots up. So do Peter's and Cassidy's.

"Are we running a business today or not, Pete?"

In front of us, with one palm slapped on the high-top, is the face of a woman absolutely *done* with Peter.

"Ooh," Cassidy taunts, wiggling his fingers in Peter's direction. "You're in trouble."

Peter rolls his eyes with a crooked grin, hopping off the counter. He runs a large hand through his hair again—never allowing it to look neat for one second—and grins down at his bar manager, Izzy. And *down* is the correct direction because his six-foot-something frame towers over her five-foot-nothing one.

"Sorry, Bells," he says to her with a shrug. "But we've got two hours until opening. That's more than enough time."

She gives him a sarcastic smirk. "I'm not afraid to kick them out."

But as Izzy says it, her eyes flash specifically to me.

My eyebrows cinch in, and I tilt my head to the side, as

if to say, *I thought we were on the same team.* The team of being Peter's best female friends. The ones who whip him into shape.

What a silly thought.

I should know by now that Izzy only exists on her own team. And at this moment, her bar needs to be opened soon, and the owner is spending time with me instead of doing administrative tasks, like an owner should.

But I needed the small escape—to hang out with familiar faces when I'd spent the last couple of weeks avoiding the new grumpy one in my life. Cassidy and Peter are breaths of fresh air, open books, as opposed to their oldest brother, who isn't even written in the same language.

So, I went to The Hideaway.

"All right then," Peter says, clapping his hands together. "Let's run a restaurant."

"Good," Izzy says, shooing him off.

He turns back around to flash a grin.

She rolls her eyes. "Keep walking, Pete."

He tosses her a cheeky wink, which only has her crossing her arms and lifting an eyebrow.

Cassidy stretches next to me. "I'm gonna get a drink."

I look to the clock on the wall. "It's barely after three."

"It's five o'clock—"

"Somewhere," I finish with a smile. "I know."

He grins. "Pink drink, Wendy?"

I laugh. "Are you trying to kill me?"

He flashes me a finger gun. "One pink drink then."

"Only one!" I insist, holding up a finger and letting it fall when he ascends the stairs to the bar.

The Hideaway's three-tiered wooden tree house–like structure has everything for everyone. Families mostly stick to the first-floor restaurant. The second floor is always full of local bar flies, playing ping-pong and secluding themselves to their drinks and hearty laughter. The third landing is an open balcony, overlooking Crocodile Cove—an exclusive space for private parties or anyone Peter deems worthy.

This place is Peter's prized possession. It's nestled in the far corner of town and found at the end of a long, winding road, curtained by drooping willow trees, making it a literal hidden hangout.

Overall, the customers are always kind. But there's also the no-nonsense bar manager, Isabel.

I knew Izzy briefly back in high school, a senior with Peter when I was a freshman. She was quick-witted and sharp, making comments that had his head flying back with laughter. I admired his laugh back then, the kind that bobbed his throat and displayed his beautiful white teeth. He has the type of laugh that invites you in like a siren's song.

For a small moment after college, after I moved back to Never Harbor, Izzy, Peter, and I were a trio, grabbing coffee, taking beach days, and cliff-diving into the quarry. But when Peter and I started sneaking around, she showed up less. Looking back, I wonder if she felt left out. Not that we were shy about how attached we were because when you're twenty-two and the man with all the charisma in the world turns his focus to you, it's hard not to drown in the attention.

I guess they got close again after our breakup when I left town. Now, Izzy works as his bar manager, and I swear this woman is made of different stuff. Harder stuff. A pocket-sized pixie with an attitude.

"Hey," I whisper to her once Peter's out of earshot. "Sorry for distracting him."

Izzy barely shifts her body to face me. Her blue eyes

scan from the top of my ribbon-tied ponytail down to my colorful sneakers.

"It's fine," she says, glancing back down at a clipboard in her palms. "You know he doesn't focus well."

I laugh. "True. How's business lately?"

"Fine," she repeats. "Aren't you working with Jasper this summer?"

"Yeah. I'm Sam's nanny, but I don't go on weekends. Kind of savoring this day off."

"Must be nice."

I blink at her.

Well, someone *needs nap time.*

"Oh," I say, trying to keep my voice reasonable and happy. "Well, yeah, I'm enjoying it."

But Izzy seems distracted.

I hate that we're not the trio that we once were. And maybe we'll never be, but Izzy and I had good memories.

She was the friend who barked at insistent men in the bar. She's the one who dropped by my house with chocolate when I was on my period, making light jokes about how *Eve really dropped the ball for us* as she popped in my comfort rom-com. She's the type of friend you want in your corner, and I miss her.

"We should get coffee sometime," I say.

Her eyes swivel to me. I can see the unease slice between her blonde eyebrows. She shifts from one foot to the other. "Oh. Sure."

"Still prefer lots of sugar?"

"I've actually switched to black coffee."

"Oh."

She nods slowly, and it's awkward. Part of me wishes I hadn't brought up the subject. She's not being mean; I simply don't know her anymore.

She points a finger over to where Peter is standing, looking at signs on the walls with his hands on his hips. "I should ..."

"Oh! Sure. Yeah. Definitely," I say, waving my hand. "Go! Open the restaurant."

Izzy nods, flitting off to Peter, leaving me to stand alone. Embarrassment rolls over me.

My phone buzzes in my pocket, and I fumble to pull it out, swallowing back the anxiety still catching in my throat. But just when I thought I couldn't get any more uneasy, my breath hitches even more. I start to cough, choking on my own air.

"You okay over there?" Peter calls across the room.

I give a weak thumbs-up and swipe open my texts to see the full message.

Jasper: You left your notepad

That's the whole text.

I don't know what to make of Jasper or his serial killer–level messages with zero punctuation.

Part of me thinks he likes being alone. But sometimes, he has this look that makes me wonder if there's something he isn't saying. His eyebrows cinch in, his mouth opens, then closes, and he comes up with something so unnatural that it cannot possibly be what he intended to say in the first place.

Whenever I get peeks of it, my body has a knee-jerk reaction to it—a stutter. Like it's saying, *Go, go, go. Tell me what you really want to say.*

Wendy: Oh no! Call the police.

I send the joke and am unsurprised to only receive back—

Jasper: It's on the side table

A smile twitches onto my face. I kind of like his directness. Even if it does set my nerves on fire.

A titter of laughter echoes through the empty restaurant. Peter flips through paperwork on a clipboard, giving Izzy that devious grin of his and saying something that has her rolling her eyes with a smile.

He slaps the clipboard on his palm and hands it back to her. She snatches it with whiplike precision.

"We need to talk to Wallace about the lights issue on floor two."

"Done," she responds.

"Also, I got a call from Bobbi. Her health inspector came early, so we should keep an eye out."

"She called me too," Izzy says, striking her pen across the clipboard. "Not a problem."

"Have we started a checklist?"

"Don't insult me. I've crossed half the items off."

"God, I love you."

She smirks. "I know you do."

A quiet stare passes between them after.

I have mixed feelings about seeing Peter in the restaurant scene. He's confident. Passionate. Knowledgeable. It's where he always took care of me—yes, making me three too many specialty drinks but always tucking me into bed afterward.

But bars are also where I found him flirting with women constantly. And this bar is where he stood with one hand on the lower back of whoever that girl was. When he's in charge, Peter isn't the same man who whisks you from your window in the middle of the night for an adventure. He isn't the man who invites you to family dinners because you don't have your own. He's the literal boss. And while he's great at what he does, he relishes in the power.

He's the king, and he knows it.

Peter leans down, palms wrapping around Izzy's waist, and my stomach drops.

"Pete, no. Don't. Don't you dare." Izzy's protests turn to reluctant laughs. "Peter Davies, I swear to—"

Peter picks up Izzy in his arms, tossing her over his shoulder and pushing into the kitchen. The sound of their combined joy fades until I'm left standing in the center of the empty lobby, surrounded by crowded tables with over-turned chairs.

And suddenly, I feel very alone.

Chapter 9

A Boy Raised by Wolves

Wendy

"The captain will be home in three hours!"

Sam says this every single day immediately before the sacred quiet time, which, by the way, is not my idea of a good way to spend an hour in the afternoon.

But, hey, not my monkey, not my circus.

Or not my pirate, not my ship, I suppose.

Sam likes being loud. He loves anything outdoors on the grass or the sand or even in the ocean. We've gone to a couple of weeks of swim camp, and he's taken to it like ... well, like a fish to water. He graduates next week, and I'm seriously considering getting him a little cap with a tassel and all. Though I think he'd much prefer a pirate hat.

He's a funny kid, the kind who likes learning new facts about the world and asks so many questions that I always have my phone near me just so I can confirm the answers. He's also obsessed with chocolate pudding, which we make sure to only have *after* quiet time, per his dad's instructions.

But more than anything else, he loves Jasper.

Captain—not Dad, not Father, not Papa—gets home every single day at four o'clock, right on the dot like clockwork. And I am reminded every single day.

After I put Sam in his room for quiet time, I sit on the couch, trying to savor the hour to myself. And somewhere in the silence of threading my sewing needle through the cross-stitch hoop and Roger resting his head on my feet, I look out at the porch.

As of two days ago, the railing has been stripped off, and a fresh pile of wood now sits at its base. Another one of Jasper's construction projects.

I see them each week. Paint cans. Stacks of lumber. Shovels. This house is a constant work in progress, and I wonder what his end goal is. When will this house ever be considered finished in his eyes?

I can't say I hate it. I arrived yesterday morning to discover him in the garden, spade in hand, black T-shirt straining over his biceps, sweat rolling down his neck.

I didn't say a word. I couldn't find a single one in me, so I quietly bypassed him into the house.

When he came back to get ready for work, I was already prepping breakfast for Sam and exclaiming, "Oh, I thought you'd left!" which was ridiculous because his truck was obviously still parked here, and I know he wouldn't leave Sam home alone.

In that moment, Jasper probably thought I was just as dumb as George did because his jaw clenched and he walked to his bathroom without a word. But even that, the intensity of him, had my body reeling with energy.

Maybe this is my problem. I'm attracted to mean guys.

I mean, I'm not *attracted* to Jasper.

Not when he does that *single eyebrow lift* thing, the one

that says, *Can I help you?* in what I only imagine is an arrogant tone that demands to be talked back to.

Well, okay, so maybe I am attracted to Jasper.

I loved playing with George's irritation. It made me feel wanted—sexy even—when he said he couldn't wait to get me home and put me in my place. At least until it became less playful and more like he just genuinely hated when I questioned him.

With Peter, I wasn't allowed to be the playful one. Not that he ever told me not to be, but when two people who both love to tease get together, well, not much gets done in the bedroom. So, I bent to be whatever he needed me to be. I tend to always fall into that role. It's easier that way.

Distracted, I set my cross-stitch aside to instead whip out my notepad. I found it on the side table, just where Jasper had promised it would be. When I think about the fact that maybe he read it, I start to reel. *Feeling mortified* is a better phrase.

I wonder if Jasper thinks my stories are ridiculous, just like George or Peter.

I've been trying to jot down the adventures Jill and Sam have every day. I want to keep track of plot ideas, but the words themselves never flow quite the way they have in the past. It's just a jumble of words or scenes. But it's better than nothing.

Today's words are slow, like usual, but then my mind wanders. Escapes. Daydreams. My pen scribbles across the lined notebook in a stream of words that shift from bullet points to sentences and suddenly prose. A vision slides into focus, like a haze parting over morning waters.

A pirate captain. Quiet. Reserved. But nonjudgmental.

Maybe he'll have longer hair, a big captain's hat with a

beautiful little feather. Maybe he's badass so he has an eye patch or a peg leg.

Or a beard.

Or piercing blue eyes.

Maybe. Just maybe. But then again—

A loud crash sounds from down the hall near Sam's bedroom. I toss my notebook into my tote bag and run, but I stop short of Sam's door because *boundaries*. Even kids deserve those.

I rap my knuckles on the door.

"Hey, buddy? You all right?"

What I hear in return is the screech of a banshee. The wail of a siren across the sea.

I creak open the door, and staring back at me is less like Sam and instead a wild boy. Crazed. Wide eyes. Feet tapping the floor.

And the worst part?

Covered in chocolate pudding.

"Oh my God, Sam, where did you get those?" I breathe, blinking at not one, but two pudding cups on the ground. Not a trace of chocolate in them. Licked completely clean.

Sam zooms past me, crawling like some possessed spider along the hardwood and laughing the whole way.

Oh my *God*. This is a horror movie.

Jasper Davies is going to murder me.

I try to steady my panicked breathing, watching Sam as he bounces on the couch cushions, where, two seconds ago, I was lost in a fantasy, picturing some hunky pirate.

A fantasy that suddenly feels incredibly inappropriate.

It's fine.

This is fine.

I can fix this.

But quiet time? We're way past that.

When kids get like this, there's only one good solution.

Run him ragged.

I sprint into the living room after him with a loud, "YARR!" as his giggles turn to screeches.

We run through the kitchen. I let him climb on the counters, picking him up and throwing him over my shoulder when he gets too high.

He loves it.

He demands we go outside, so, buddy, we go outside and run up and down the deck stairs, skipping steps and ascending again, only to tumble back down toward the shore with Roger barking behind us.

Minutes pass. Maybe hours.

Good *Lord*, does this child's energy ever cease? Like, what the heck do they put in those pudding packs? Why are they even in the house?

Eventually, I'm exhausted. I'm sweating under my boobs, and a drop slides down the center of my stomach. My ribbon has fallen from my hair and is tucked into my pocket. Sam has now ripped off his shirt. I'm trying to toss it into the laundry hamper when the front door opens.

I pull out my phone from my front pocket to check the time.

Four o'clock.

Oh God.

Before I can stop him—or even maybe give a pep talk of *hey, let's tell him the truth gently*—Sam barrels through the living room and into the kitchen and bombards Jasper with one massive hug, nearly knocking him over by the thighs.

I can't help the cringe overpowering my face.

Perfect. Just perfect.

Jasper ruffles his son's red beanie—somehow the one thing above his waist that didn't get removed—and swivels his eyes to me. With his head still tilted down toward Sam, the stare is absolutely menacing. Yet, somehow, that twists my stomach in a different way. A *not entirely upset about it* way. My thighs press together as I try to stifle the anxiety filtering down from my stomach to my pelvis like little drops of rain.

And it hits me.

This is the pirate captain I was writing earlier.

It was Jasper freaking Davies in all his intimidating glory.

"He had pudding," he snaps.

And there's my bucket of cold water. Splashing over my head and bringing me back to reality.

I blow out a breath of air and shake my head, trying to smile.

"Wow, you clocked that fast," I joke.

His eyes entertain zero humor. For a second, I might even see red, but that's probably all in my head. Just a rumor Cassidy spread in middle school.

But Jasper is mad. Very mad.

Sam is now hugging Jasper's legs even tighter. Jasper scoops him up into his arms. Then, he twists away from me, nuzzling his nose closer to Sam's chubby cheek, sending Sam roaring into a fit of laughter. The moment is soft and secretive, almost as if Jasper wanted that moment for himself.

A tiny arrow snags at my heart. If I felt bad before, now, I feel terrible.

Jasper sets Sam down, gesturing to the back porch, where Sam runs to without any verbal command. Maybe their connection is just intuitive. Or maybe Sam is simply off the rails right now, and any old gesture will do.

He flies out the door with Roger, the door still slid open.

I swivel my body around slowly, knowing I'll find Jasper staring right at me. And he is. His arms are crossed, stretching the fabric of his collared work shirt under his biceps. His legs are shoulder-width apart, his chin tipped up, eyes raking over me. I'm not the shortest woman, but Jasper is over six feet tall, and at my five-six, I'm feeling the rays of disappointment like a bright sun—no, like an eerie moonlight—shining down on me.

I want to recoil, but I also want to lean in, a moth drawn to a flame.

"He won't sleep tonight." His words are spoken low, expectant and commanding even though the sentence appears rhetorical.

"I don't know where he got them," I counter.

"The pantry."

"Well, obviously, the pantry."

"Did you leave him alone?"

There are times when I think I could connect with Jasper like I do with the rest of his brothers. Little moments where he stumbles over his words or picks up Sam after a long day at work, burying his nose into his neck, like he's been waiting all day to inhale his son.

And then there are these moments like this.

"Did I leave him alone?" I echo. "At what point?" I give a half-hearted laugh because my body is sizzling with nerves. "My eyeballs can't find him all the time. Maybe when I was getting water or using the bathroom—"

"I cannot believe—"

"Women use the bathroom, Jasper," I say with a scoff and smile.

He steadies a look at me, which causes my heart to sink.

Okay, not in a joking mood then.

Though when is he ever?

But the insinuation that I'm not doing my job well enough, it settles in me uncomfortably and irritatingly, like a little pebble in my shoe.

"Listen," I start, trying to get calming words in before this can escalate further, pulling on all my teacher training. I've dealt with far more irrational parents, but that doesn't mean it makes me any less uncomfortable. "If you have impossible expectations, don't expect me to meet them. Mistakes happen. He's six," I say, accidentally hissing the last word, the sound like a sword coming to a duel. I dial it back with a sigh.

He means well. I know he does.

My own insecurities are poking through. That's all.

Jasper's eyes dart between mine.

"Not every day is going to be perfect," I continue. "Not every decision is the right one. And, by the way, parenting books say a lot of things, but you've gotta take them with a grain of salt."

"I'm doing my best."

"Maybe quiet time works, maybe not, but—"

"I said, I'm *doing my best*, Wendy."

My head rears back. His eyebrows tilt in, and his face falls, but Jasper doesn't look upset. Something different is in there. Fear. Or maybe concern.

No, worse than that.

It's a look that screams, *Please*.

It's the look of a single dad. The desperate eyes. The tiredness. The real face underneath his surly mask. I see it occasionally at parent-teacher meetings. There are a couple of single parents in town, but somehow, none look as tired as Jasper.

I blink, trying to process the unspoken words. The silence between us is louder than it has any right to be.

I swallow and answer with, "Okay."

He nods. "Okay?"

"Okay."

Then, he does that thing again, opening his mouth, finding words that won't come, then closing it once more.

Tell me. Tell me what you need to.

But Jasper shakes his head and tongues his cheek.

I won't push him to speak. I silently grab my tote bag from the living room. Jasper is still staring, following each step.

I feel weirdly ashamed, like I got reprimanded. I desperately want to leave. I want to cry maybe, but it's only because I'm so overwhelmed and confused.

But he's the one hurting, isn't he?

I was always taught by Jasper's own mother to never make someone who is hurting feel any worse. So, I pause and reassure him the best way I can by saying, "I'll see you on Monday. And hopefully at the family dinner tonight."

Then, I walk past, the warmth from his body radiating toward me like a storm cloud, and for the smallest second, I think I hear a low hum, like the words are finally there on the tip of his tongue, begging to be said.

But nothing comes out.

Chapter 10

A Davies Girl

Wendy

JASPER ISN'T at the family dinner that night, and I don't know if I'm upset or relieved.

Cassidy tosses me a furrowed brow, and even though he mouths, *You okay?* I just nod with a smile.

I'm not sure if I'm okay. I'm not doing unwell exactly. But the grasp I've held on my knowledge of Jasper feels weaker now. Unsure.

I want to know why he isn't here tonight.

If I were to ask anyone where Jasper is, it would be Peter. Peter knows him best, which isn't saying much, but he might have some insight. But Peter didn't show up for dinner either. I consider whether he's spending time with Izzy instead, but just as quick as the thought found me, I let it go.

Peter is gonna be Peter.

I honestly only care about why Jasper didn't turn up.

I attempt to distract myself, helping Maggie set up the picnic table in the backyard, arranging the casserole and salad on the kitchen counter for David. At one point, he slips a jar of homemade pickles into my tote bag with a wink.

It's the little things that re-center my focus, reminding me that I'm here to spend time with *them*—David and Maggie, the family that brought me in even though they had more than enough of their own kin. Who do things like make jars of pickles just for me.

On nice summer days, the Davies family feasts outside with a portable speaker blasting classic rock from the picnic table and food served buffet-style. We always bump Cassidy to the end of the line because he eats like a starved man and won't leave any green beans for the rest of us. The Twins insist he go first for this very reason, but they're shuffled to the front instead, a heaping spoonful of sloppy greens loaded onto each of their plates, much to their chagrin.

"I don't see why we can't make two dishes for everything," Cassidy says, his hulking body taking up half the bench seat.

I squeeze in next to him, playfully nudging his elbow away from mine.

"Feel free to join me in the kitchen next time, Cass," David says with a knowing grin.

"Please no," Bonnie laments.

"He'll burn it all," I add.

"Oh, come on, everyone. Cooking isn't that hard." David laughs.

"Cass can't follow instructions to save his life," Bonnie throws in with a snort. "Ask Milo about the time they tried to build a bookshelf."

"Let's not relive that disaster," Milo bemoans, giving a half smile.

"Disaster?" Cassidy's incredulous voice booms through

the yard. He's taken aback by our accusations. "We finished it, didn't we?"

Milo squints. "Was that when I went to the hospital for a broken thumb?"

"No, that was the sofa," Bonnie corrects.

"Still finished putting together that one too," Cassidy mumbles. "And, hey"—he points his fork, rotating it around the entire table—"none of you will be laughing when I get my new place all fixed up. Furniture and all."

"Finally," Bonnie says, dramatically throwing her head onto the picnic table with an exhale.

"Finally," Maggie echoes with a wink, but I see the hidden pain in his mother's eyes. She doesn't want her son moving out.

"Well," Cassidy says, "I can't exactly bring dates back here so ..."

"Son," David warns.

"I mean, *friends*," Cassidy corrects, eyeing The Twins. "I can't bring *friends* back here."

"Oh, *please*," Bonnie counters. "You're not getting any women anyway."

I tilt my head side to side, as if to say, *Well* ... and when Bonnie catches it, I burst out laughing.

Then, one of The Twins says, "Ma, can we bring friends home?" and we all join in on the laughter.

Cassidy definitely gets women. I've seen the looks he gets at The Hideaway. He's always been more like a brother to me, but you'd be blind to not see the appeal. Or, I suppose, you could also be his seventeen-year-old little sister.

After dinner, we disperse to our usual spots. Cassidy and Milo tackle the dishes; their dad watches some game on the television, kicking his feet up after an evening of cooking for eight; and The Twins play with water guns in the yard, savoring the perfect summer evening. Maggie, Bonnie, and I journey to the front porch, grabbing three rocking chairs and settling into our respective hobbies.

Maggie crochets. I switch between my cross-stitch hoop and notepad. Bonnie has her drawing tablet with noise-canceling headphones pulled over her ears.

If I let my thoughts wander, if I get my hopes up, I start to think this is *my* home. My mother sitting next to me. My teenage sister zoning us out. My little brothers squealing in the backyard.

I've created many fantasies through my stories, ones with mermaids and pirates and fairies. Adventures and make-believe. But this is the most captivating pretend game of all—the one I get lost in more than the others. The life of a Davies girl.

My parents weren't around much. They'd thought they wanted a child, but even by the time I was seven, I could tell that wasn't the case. I remember asking if I was adopted, as if that could be an explanation for why I felt so different. My seven-year-old brain didn't understand how insensitive that thought was because family never means only blood relation. The Davies family taught me that. Maggie and David have always been good to me.

I tap my pen on my notepad, waiting for the writing inspiration to come soaring in, like it did this afternoon. But after the weird moment with Jasper, I'm finding it hard to write about a pirate captain when said captain inspiration might still be mad at me.

"Are you writing?" Maggie asks, nodding to my still hand.

I shake my head from my thoughts and nod. "Trying.

Sam likes to be told stories, which is giving me a lot of ideas."

"I'd love to see you finish a book."

I give a half laugh. "You and me both, Mags."

"You can do it, you know."

"I know," I agree, but that's not entirely the truth.

I'm not sure what I'm capable of anymore. George never thought I could finish a book. And he wasn't wrong. I never have. I've barely had inspiration since George.

Well, until the thought of the pirate captain earlier today. Until words were pouring from my fingers, desperate to escape the prison I'd kept them in, eager to describe this new character in detail. His beard. His stare. His eyes.

I clear my throat, snapping the book closed.

Maggie eyes my jerky motions. "How's it going with Sam?"

"Good," I say, thankful for a subject change. I'm happy to think about anything that isn't the captain. "Sam's a good kid."

"And Jas?"

My heart catches in my throat.

"Fine," I answer stiffly, opening the notepad again even though I have nothing to write. But I still poise my pen over the paper because it's better than doing nothing and appearing bothered by this conversation, which I'm absolutely, definitely *not*. "He's quiet. And intense sometimes."

"Sounds like Jasper," Maggie says.

"Y'know, he got mad today because Sam ate pudding."

"Oh, I'm glad Sam still likes those. I wasn't sure if I should stop picking them up."

"Wait, do *you* buy him the pudding cups?"

Maggie waves me off. "Oh, you sound just like Jas. Let me feed my grandson."

"He's nuts when he eats them though!" I say with a laugh. "You have no idea. It's like he turns into a boy raised by wolves."

"He needs a little fun. I worry about them all alone in that house."

That has me slowing down, quieting my laughter, and readjusting in my chair. It's not the first time I've heard that.

"They seem to like it," I respond.

"Do they?"

The words are sudden and sharp enough that my eyes dart to Maggie. I see the same look in them that I've seen in Jasper's. Something beneath the surface. Except where Jasper won't use his words to express the hidden emotions, Maggie has no issues putting everything on the table.

"I don't believe so. Jasper has been building walls for years." She goes back to her crochet, albeit with a little more jabbing involved. "I miss my boy a lot."

"Being a single dad isn't easy."

"There's more to it than that."

"What do you mean?"

She heaves a sigh. "He's been dealt a rough hand in life. Too much for any good man to handle, if you ask me. First his best friends, then Jessica coming in and ..."

She huffs out an irritated breath, snorting through her nose, and I half expect flames to shoot out with it.

My stomach coils.

I remember when Jasper got custody of Sam. Mostly, I recall how Maggie pulled the family aside and introduced us to her meal-plan system. Every sibling was assigned a shift, and we weren't allowed to bring it up to Jasper—ever. I recall Peter's hand giving mine a very tight squeeze. It was one of the first times I saw Peter look sad.

As for Jessica, I barely remember her. She attended a

dinner or two, but mostly stayed out of the Davieses' house. I picture Jasper kissing her neck, and the weird sensation travels over me again. A wrongness in it.

Maggie tilts her head to the side, pausing mid-crochet. "Do me a favor?"

I blink. "Anything."

"Just ... get him out of that house, okay? For me."

I can hear the worry. The sound of a mother desperate to reconnect. I already know I'll say yes.

"Mags, I'm only babysitting Sam, you know," I tease with a smile.

Her eyes twinkle as she returns the gesture. "But you've never been one to do the bare minimum though, have you?"

"No, I haven't," I agree. "Of course I'll try." I let out a lighthearted laugh. "But just know that you're asking for the impossible."

Her soft hand covers mine. I look down to see her golden wedding band and emerald engagement ring, dulled from years of wear. From years of love.

"You know what, my Wendy Bird? This sounds like an awfully big adventure."

I smile. "It does, doesn't it?"

"But I believe in you."

Then, as if that statement doesn't completely rock my world, Maggie Davies goes back to crocheting. That's that. Like believing in me comes as natural as breathing, and I suppose it does for her.

I'd do anything for Maggie Davies. And if I'm being honest with myself, I'm more curious about her pirate captain son than I'd care to admit.

Chapter 11

Keep Talking

Jasper

I'M A CREATURE OF HABIT. I arrive at the docks at the same time every morning; I have repeating tasks blocked out in my calendar; I eat the same chicken and broccoli leftovers for lunch; and meetings never run past their allotted time on my watch. But the most important part of my schedule every single day, without fail, is when I get in my car and drive away at three forty-five to finally see my boy.

So, tell me why it's getting close to that time, and I haven't completed a single damn task I've started today.

I have a sneaking suspicion. Something has sprouted in my brain like a weed, growing through the cracks and grooves. No, not something. Some*one*.

Wendy Darling.

I'm still unsure what happened last Friday. Every version of the situation I run through feels more uncomfortable than the last.

It felt like I was suspended in time. My only thoughts were that Sam was suddenly wild, and Wendy had let him be, and I'd granted her the wiggle room to allow that, and how could I have been so irresponsible, and it could have—

My mind spiraled until my brain felt like it was drowning, my nose barely cresting the waves to gain air.

Normally, I'd bring that situation to a hard stop, just like my meetings, just like my employees once they get rowdy. I'd narrow my eyes, and that'd be that.

But Wendy didn't care how I looked at her. She stared me right in the eye and explained the situation. She was honest, forthright, and confident.

So damn confident.

Wendy was right to question my rules. Even after the fourth year as Sam's guardian, I still don't know what the hell I'm doing. Parenting books are all I have.

After, I was scrambling to say something—anything— that would let her know I was backtracking my thoughts, stumbling into an uncomfortable territory of wrongness. And just when I thought I might have ruined our whole arrangement, she said she'd be back Monday.

That was what got me the most. That was what shook me to my core.

All weekend.

All of today.

That, despite my anger, she said she'd be back.

I couldn't possibly face her at my parents' dinner on Friday. I couldn't endure my own embarrassment about how I'd acted. And now, I'm stuck at work, falling behind on paperwork as my thoughts continue to circle the drain.

I text Wendy around three thirty, telling her I'll be back later than expected. She says it's no problem.

Of course she does.

By the time I'm pulling down our long gravel road, the

sun is setting over our cliff, illuminating the white staircase leading down to the beach in shades of orange and pink.

The door creaks open when I key in. The floorboards sound squeakier than usual. The kitchen lights are off. The dishwasher is running at a low hum, and it smells faintly like lemon cleaner.

I kick my boots off and walk to the living room, where Sam is at one end of the couch, conked out and curled in a little ball as the television plays the same dragon cartoon he's been watching for months now.

My eyes trail to the other side of the couch, where Wendy sits with a cross-stitch hoop in one hand, half-finished flowers adorning the fabric interior. Her hair is tied up with the familiar blue ribbon, strands lightly curled at the ends. Her knees are pulled close to her chest, and I think I spot goose bumps.

"He wanted to wait up for you," she says.

"It's not that late, is it?" I glance down at my watch and feel my cheeks burn. "Shit," I hiss, pushing a hand through my hair.

Wendy's eyes follow the motion before she turns back to her hoop.

"I'm sorry."

"It's all right." Her shoulders shift, and I see more of a chill run over her skin.

"Are you cold?" I ask.

"A little, but it's fine."

"Oh. Um ..." I look around, but there're no coats hanging on the coat rack. So, I remove my own jacket instead.

She stares at me, even as I tug down my undershirt when it rides up too high. I hold the denim jacket out to her. Wendy looks at it like she's seen a ghost.

102

"Oh," she says, blinking. "Thank you."

I cringe. "It might smell like fish bait but ..."

She gingerly takes it from me before I can finish, sliding her arms through the sleeves. It swallows her whole, pooling by her wrists, not matching her outfit one bit but still cute all the same.

Cute.

I wait for the inevitable—for her usual routine of packing up quickly and drifting past me like she was never even here. After Friday, I wouldn't blame her. I wait and wait, but she doesn't move.

Finally, she asks, "How was your day, Jasper?"

It's like my gut has been hit by bricks.

How was my ... day?

My lips part, but I'm not sure what to say. Because I genuinely don't know the last time someone asked me that question.

"It was ... fine." The words are slow on the exit, but what do people answer when they're asked that question? Do I tell her what I had for lunch? Do I talk about the small fight I had with Starkey because he claimed I was distracted, which I was, and that I couldn't focus, which I couldn't? Do I include that I was running late because of her? Because I was still parsing through apologies for how much of an ass I had been last week?

Wendy blinks at me, so I repeat it again. "Yeah." I clear my throat. "It was good."

"That's good," Wendy answers.

She's quiet for another moment, as if allowing me room to speak if I have more to say, which I don't. I wonder if my jacket *does* smell like fish. It probably does.

I swallow. "And yours? How was your day?"

Her face slowly lights up.

103

"Good," she says. "Real good."

Her smile grows, first with the twitch of her full pink lips, then gradually into a grin, accented by two dips in the corner of her mouth. I didn't know she could smile like that in front of me, but she's pulling her feet onto the cushion, tucking them underneath her before firing off like a cannon.

"Sam did great at his swim lesson. He had a little trouble with floating on his back, but once he got it, he was a total natural. Laura says he should be ready by graduation on Wednesday. Sam absolutely cannot wait. We had a snack afterward with no pudding, I swear. But I did kind of give him one after quiet time. He was wild, but I think it tuckered him out."

The smile after those words is so playful that it has me lowering into the armchair across from her, balancing my chin on my fist. She watches the movement and bites her lower lip.

"Should I keep going?"

"Please."

She smiles again, then continues, and I sink into the gold mine of information.

The memories from the day are precious nuggets from Sam's life that I would have missed otherwise. Things I wish I'd been there to experience alongside him, but am still happy he lived regardless.

Is this what I've been missing by crossing paths with Wendy like ships in the night? By refusing to be cordial?

"Thank you," I finally whisper when she's finished.

She blinks. "For telling you about our day?"

I nod, and I must stare at her for too long because the smile she once had fades away. Her cheeks flush, and I find I like the color more than ever before.

She hesitates for a moment before saying, "Come with us to his last swim lesson on Wednesday."

I let out a huff of a laugh, ignoring the twinge in my chest, before running a palm over my beard. "I don't know ..."

"Oh, it's a whole graduation ceremony and everything. It's really quite cute."

"I can't."

"Why? Take the day off." She blows out air, as if it were the simplest thing in the world. As if I'd be silly not to. "You're the boss, aren't you?"

I tilt my head to the side. "It's very last minute."

She waves her hand. "It's twenty-four hours' notice. More, if you email everyone now."

I open my mouth, and a small noise leaves me, the start of a word at the tip of my tongue. A sentence begging to be released. I want my answer to be *yes*, but my brain is pushing a *no*.

Then, Wendy says, "Sam's been practicing, and he's really proud of himself. I think it'd mean a lot if his captain was there."

I glance down at the sleeping boy, his thick glasses askew, the red beanie halfway off the couch. Running a palm through his soft blond hair, I ask the same question I fall asleep to every night.

What would Ed and Stacy do?

They'd cancel everything. They'd shut down research for the day. Hell, they'd abandon the entire ocean if it meant seeing their six-year-old son swim for the first time. Or seeing their son at all.

I nod, moving past the croak in my throat to say, "Okay. Sure."

Wendy's beautiful smile greets me once more. Those

precious little dips in the corner of her mouth. The sparkle in her blue eyes, like stars staring back at me. And, God, part of me wonders if this is what Peter came home to once upon a time.

I know Wendy wouldn't be looking at me like this if we weren't talking about Sam. But sometimes, adults can play pretend too. And I pretend that smile is just for me.

Chapter 12

The Hook

Wendy

Jasper is intense.

I sit next to him on the bleachers, both of us watching Sam down at the pool in his cute Spider-Man swim shorts and red goggles. But next to me, Jasper's hands are wringing together, that cracked watch glinting in the sunlight with each turn.

I swear tension radiates off him in waves as he rubs his palms and tries to steady them on his thighs.

"Hey. Relax," I find myself saying after a minute.

His head jerks to me.

My words nearly catch in my throat under that gaze, but I somehow get out, "You're making me nervous."

I'm not sure in what context I mean it either.

While he's been sitting there with a tapping foot, I've noticed just how muscular his thighs are, how tightly they stretch the fabric of his denim. His henley exposes the definition of his collarbone, granting a slight peek of wiry chest hair peering out the top. There're lines beside his eyes and a small crease between his brows, which make me wonder how regularly concerned he is for a man in his early thirties. His lips are pink, peering out from his stark black beard that is scruffier near his ear, like maybe it's the day before he needs a cleanup. But even the scruff is attractive with little flecks of gray in the longer strands.

Then, there are his hands, winding around each other, wrists bony with spidery veins trailing over the backs. I never considered myself a wrist-loving girl before, but maybe it's because I've never witnessed Jasper's wrists. And on his right hand, cut deep along the back, is that scar. Whitened and raised.

"It's just a swim class," he says.

"Right," I answer with a laugh. "Just a swim class."

"All right, let's go, buddy!" Jasper claps his hands, sitting up straighter, looking like he's at a Red Sox game rather than a child's summer camp.

I look out to see Sam stepping into the water. He gives us a big thumbs-up. I clap alongside Jasper, but my eyes won't leave Jasper's clenched jaw. His steady stare.

"Sam's a natural," I assure him.

"Makes sense."

"Why?"

"His parents were too."

I pause. Is this territory we don't cross?

But Jasper's jaw twitches, and I can't help but ask, "Are you okay, Jas?"

His keen eyes land on me, darting between my own. What is that? Disbelief? Concern? Anger? I wonder if his employees get intimidated by that stare. I sure do, but in a way that makes my stomach drop, going down, down, down to somewhere I shouldn't be imagining Jasper at all.

"Yes," he says.

"Uh-huh." I nod in understanding, looking over as Sam's entire torso dips into the water and seeing the subsequent tightening of Jasper's hands. "Because it seems like you're freaking out."

"I'm not."

"Oh, okay, sure. The tapping foot means nothing."

His penetrative eyes slide to mine once more. My mouth goes dry.

I like that menacing look too much.

And I'm not sure why, but my hand extends out to touch his forearm because that always works to calm my first graders. But this is a grown man, and I underestimate him. I didn't realize the touch would feel like fire.

"He'll be fine," I say, the words as gentle as I can make them to counter all the blood in my body rushing to my head.

Jasper looks at my hand. Slowly, he nods, and his tapping feet quiet down.

I can't handle the heat anymore, the way my neck starts to sweat and my cheeks grow hot.

I've been burned.

Engulfed in his flames.

My first thought is, *Maggie would be proud I've gotten him out of the house.*

But the next more sinister and lingering one is, *God, what would everyone think if they knew I'd touched him?*

I jerk my hand away.

$\int$

SAM PASSES his swim camp graduation with flying colors. Not like they'd flunk a kid during the summer anyway. But I make it a cause for celebration, instantly shuffling the boys to Sam's favorite sandwich shop and setting up a picnic in the middle of the park on Main.

On a Wednesday afternoon during summer, it's a little crowded, but not too stuffy. Slightly loud, but in a field large enough that the noise turns into more of a pleasant hum. And breezy enough from the nearby beach that the colorful bunting hung between lampposts sway in the wind. It would be easy to close my eyes and let it lull me into sleep.

I love moments like this in Never Harbor. The quiet times without expectation. As a kid, it felt like summertime lasted forever out on that rocky beach, playing mermaids and layering sunscreen every few hours. We'd inevitably forget once or twice, forced to lie on the cool tiled floor in the Davieses' kitchen to soothe the burn.

"It's already one o'clock?" Jasper asks, causing me to pry open my eyes and glance down at my phone.

"My clock says it's twelve thirty," I respond.

I follow his line of sight to the clock tower. His eyebrows scrunch in confusion.

"Wendy says the clock tower is never right," Sam chimes in, crunching on his turkey sub, dribbles of red tomato running down his lips.

I reach for a napkin in the bag at the same time Jasper does. Our fingers bump, sending sparks zipping up my arm and straight to my sternum. I instantly pull back, glancing away as Jasper hands the napkin to Sam.

Jasper clears his throat. "Well, that seems problematic. To not have the right time."

"You didn't know?" Sam asks.

Jasper shakes his head. "Never spent much time here."

My lips part. "You've lived here your whole life, and you've never hung out in the square?"

He shrugs. "Why would I when the time is always wrong?"

It feels like a joke. I think it might be one. I'm not sure I've ever heard Jasper tell a joke. I give the tiniest of smiles, but he's already looking in the opposite direction.

"Why haven't they fixed it?" Sam asks. His feet kick up behind him as he takes another chomp from his sandwich, which is ninety percent ciabatta bread.

"They tried," I answer. "But it demands to be wrong."

Too many town hall meetings ended with promises to adjust it, but three cherry pickers and a week's worth of hammering later, the darn thing continues to be a minute ahead or three behind or sometimes a full hour in either direction.

As teenagers, the Davies boys and I would run back to Maggie, just barely missing their curfew of midnight, always with the excuse of, "But the clock tower said eleven!"

Maggie was never mad; she always joked that the clock tower insisted upon more fun. Sometimes, I wonder if it has a mind of its own too.

I push onto my side, resting my cheek in my palm and squinting at the sun. "Why do you need to know the time, Jas? Have somewhere to be?"

"Yeah, have somewhere to be?" Sam teasingly echoes, rolling over the floral blanket spread on the ground, rustling the grass beneath.

I hold out my arm to stop him from accidentally crushing his bag of chips.

Jasper gives Sam the slightest of smiles—a simple twitch at the edge of his mouth that sends my heart racing in my chest. It must feel special to be on the receiving end of such a rare smile.

Sam stretches out on the blanket like a starfish. His hand almost touches my arm. His foot is already on Jasper's shin.

"This feels like camping," Sam says. "Wendy, let's go camping!"

"I've never been, but I guess it's an adventure we can have together."

"You've never been camping?" Jasper asks.

"I was told it wasn't for girls."

"By who?"

I snort. "Your brothers. I mean, they were young. They don't think that now. I don't know. Maybe Cass does."

I give a playful smile. Jasper shakes his head right as Sam picks up the pickle spear from his plate and drops it onto mine.

"Oh, thanks, bud."

Sam then reaches across the blanket to snatch Jasper's, who quickly lets out a scoffing laugh, covering his plate with his palm.

"And what do you think you're doing?"

"Give her your pickle," Sam demands.

Jasper's eyes widen right as I sputter out part of my water, droplets spewing onto the blanket.

"Pardon?" Jasper asks in his low tone.

Sam giggles. "*Please* give her your pickle."

"And why should I?"

"They're her favorite."

Jasper looks to me, then his plate, and without additional hesitation, he picks up his pickle spear.

"Oh, no, you don't have—" I start, but it's swiftly placed next to Sam's offering on my plate. I can feel my body heat with embarrassment. "Thanks," I murmur.

"It was soaking my plate anyway," Jasper says, wiping his fingers on a napkin.

Jasper continues to surprise me, but I don't know why. Sure, he's not the brother who reads with me or takes me to the gym or ... well, dates me. Proposes to me.

I shake my head, blinking from my thoughts. When I look back at Jasper, a singular eyebrow is raised. His blue eyes, nearly clear in the sun, raze me to the ground.

"What?" he asks.

I see bits of Peter in Jasper sometimes. It's hidden in their smiles, in the little line darting down the side of their lips. Though while Peter's is cocky, Jasper's is reluctant.

"Nothing," I respond. "Just thinking."

"About stories?" Sam whispers conspiratorially.

"That's right," I singsong. "Always brewing up new things for ya. Just wait."

"What new things?" Jasper asks.

Bouncing on his knees, Sam takes another bite, mouth stuffed with bread as he exclaims, "Wendy's writing a book!"

"Chew and swallow, then talk, bud," Jasper says.

The subtle smile is back. I wish a bead of sweat didn't roll down my back at the sight. I also wish I could blame the sweat on the sun, but I know better. Jasper's care for his son is attractive in a way nothing else is—not even his handsome pitch-black hair or gorgeous eyes or beautiful hands. Nothing compares to his love for Sam.

Sam barely finishes swallowing before saying, "A book about pirates!"

"Oh, yeah?"

"It's just something," I say, taking a piece of my bread and ripping it from the sandwich.

"About Jill?" he asks.

My heart stumbles in place, freezing me to the ground.

"Yeah. How'd you know?"

Jasper shrugs. "I listen."

My mouth dries out, and I laugh before I can do anything else, averting my gaze.

"Well, if I could actually get some words down ..." I say, nervously ripping another piece of bread from my sandwich. "Maybe Jill will have better adventures by the end of the summer. Who knows?"

"I like her adventures," Sam counters with crossed arms, as if disappointed I'm not giving Jill enough credit.

This kid's my biggest fan, I swear, which has me grinning from ear to ear. But he's not the only one noticing my smile.

"Why haven't you finished it yet?" Jasper asks.

I raise a shoulder and let it fall. "I don't know. I guess there's a lot of research I still need to do. Like, I don't know the first thing about pirate ships."

"Do you need to?"

"Sure. I like the authenticity."

"Of pirates?"

And I see the twitch at the edge of his lips.

Is he teasing me?

"Well, not if you're gonna be a jerk about it," I joke.

But he's still giving me that half smile.

"Oh!" Sam exclaims. "Can we go to work with you? Can we?"

"I thought you hated my office," Jasper says, resting his forearm on his raised knee.

"Yeah, but you can teach Wendy stuff about boats!"

I laugh at that, but nobody else does. And I realize how weird that is, so I stop, especially when Jasper's already looking at me again with a decided look on his face.

"Sure," he answers. "Come to work with me."

"You're kidding," I breathe. "For book research?"

"Why not?"

The silence that follows is deafening—at least until the clock tower suddenly chimes. It echoes through the park, giving its little *bong* not once, but twice, a third time, and up to twelve, beating to the off-kilter strum of my heart.

Jasper nudges Sam. "Well? What do you think?"

"Yes!"

"Maybe we'll play ..." I bite my lip. "Pirates on the docks?"

Jasper's face instantly falls. "Okay, that's where I draw the line."

"We should! Cap is *so* funny as a pirate," Sam adds, already trying to stifle his own laughter, as if the thought is just *too* funny.

"Is that right?" I playfully raise an eyebrow at Jasper. "You play pirates too?"

"I dabble," he answers, and it's so nonchalant that it almost feels friendly.

Are we ... friends?

"Well, go on," I insist. "Show me your best pirate impression."

He looks to an invisible something in the corner of the park, tonguing the inside of his cheek. "No, let's not."

Sam shakes the crook of Jasper's arm. "Yes! Come on, Captain! Please?"

Sam's face is giddy with excitement, and I can practically see the gears turning in Jasper's mind. The twitch of his jaw.

All of a sudden, Jasper hooks his finger—the one attached to the scarred hand.

And Sam squeals, scrambling to his feet and yelling, "Not the hook!"

"Ye get the *hook*, Sam!"

Jasper's ridiculous accent takes me by surprise, and I burst out laughing as Jasper chases after Sam.

I twist at the waist, watching as they race through the park, Jasper's boots catching on the grass and Sam's giggles growing more panicky and heightened, but only in the way kids do when they're on the verge of both fear and sheer joy.

The thrill that spikes through me at the sight, at the menace of Jasper, is enough to have me shifting on the blanket. My cheeks flush hot. And just to shut my own mind up, I shove the other pickle spear in my mouth and wince at the sour taste.

Chapter 13

Just the Three of Us

Jasper

WHEN WENDY TAKES NOTES, she bites the corner of her mouth. It's a detail I wish I didn't notice, but once it happened the first time, I can't unsee it.

After deciding to visit me at work, Wendy and Sam came to the docks the very next day. They've been following me around all morning as I check on the incoming ships and cycle through my usual rounds of paperwork.

"What does this tie to?" Sam asks, picking up a thick coil of rope.

"Boats," I deadpan.

Sam scrunches up his nose, a gesture I mockingly return, before dropping it and asking about the next thing. He wasn't nearly this curious on the first day of summer, but toss in Wendy Darling, and he's got enough questions to fill our employee handbook. Wendy, on the other hand, is quiet, dutifully jotting down everything she sees.

And biting that damn lip.

"Getting anything good?" I ask.

She peers up from her notepad for the first time in five minutes and shakes out her hand, the pencil limp in her grip. "Getting tired is more like it."

"What's the plot?"

She nonchalantly shrugs, and she lets out a laughing, "I don't know. Pirates?"

"Got any names picked out?"

"Jill," she answers with a playful smile.

"Uh-huh," I coax. "And?"

She blows out a breath before lifting her shoulders again. "So many questions. They're just ideas, Jas."

Wendy does this a lot. She talks about her writing the same way I talk about my work. It could be interesting, sure, but at the end of the day, who cares? It's boats and seagulls and the pungent smell of fish.

But Wendy is writing a *book*. That's far more interesting. Yet she brushes it off like it's nothing. It's like talking to a blank wall.

Hell, is this how it feels to talk to me?

That's harrowing.

Before I can ask a follow-up question, Sam is running toward us with something glossy and wriggling in his palm.

Wendy gasps. "What in the—"

"Sam, did you just catch that fish with your bare hands?"

My boy nods feverishly, his toothy grin so wide that his gums peek through. It's the look of satisfaction.

Hell, I'd be proud too.

Trying to hide the chuckle that wants to bubble up, I shake my head.

"Toss it back, bud. Yep. No arguments. Toss it in."

His face melts into a frown before he absentmindedly flings—literally *flings*—the creature back off the dock. But in the process, he slides on the slippery wood and lands on his knee. I catch his face screwing up before the wails erupt like an engine backfires.

"That's enough fishing for today, I think," I say, scooping him into my arms and carrying him down to my office.

There, I take a wet wipe and dab around the scrape. I pluck out a Band-Aid from my drawer—Spider-Man-themed, which is his favorite—and spread it over the wound.

"Better?" I ask.

Sniffing, he nods, barreling his face into my chest. I hold him, patting his back, while Wendy looks on from the doorway, a gentle smile crossing over her lips.

"Lunch?" I offer.

"Sounds delicious," Wendy quickly agrees.

"All right. Think you can go wash your hands, bud?" I ask, patting his back. "Or do you want me to go with you?"

"I can go," he murmurs, swiping the back of his palm over his nose.

"Maybe blow your nose too?"

He nods. I gesture him toward the restrooms, which he sprints toward. He's gonna risk a scrape on the other knee if he's not careful. But I smile because that boy only has one speed and it's *go*. I wonder if I ever had that same enthusiasm.

Growing up with my brothers felt so chaotic that the years blend into a mess of accidents and fights and subsequent solidarity, as if we'd gone through the same war together. But I was happy, I think. I love my brothers even if they were a crew outside of me.

I was only three years older, but that distance felt like a lifetime when they were still in middle school as I got to high school or high school when I was close to graduation. I was always the odd man out, trying to find my place between being too young to fit in with the adults but too old to play with my siblings.

I found my place in college.

When I met Ed and Stacy in my hall our freshman year, it was like perfectly sliding into a puzzle. All three of us were coincidentally marine biology majors—Stacy carrying us through the labs, me creating the study guides, and Ed being the comedian that kept us awake as we worked overnight at the student center.

Even when Ed and Stacy started dating, I never felt like the third wheel. When Stacy would leave on the weekends to visit her parents, and Ed and I would watch sports we didn't care about. And when Ed would work, and Stacy and I would disappear into the familiarity of bar crowds, getting an odd comfort from loud conversations that could only come from being a part of big families.

At the end of each week, the three of us would find time to fish at the docks during sunset, imagining a life post-graduation, when we would be researching out at sea.

Just the three of us.

But that dream passed with them.

I turn the corner into the break room. It's a dingy place that isn't much different from other break rooms near water. But I noticed the mold more after losing Ed and Stacy. All of life's grime and mildew came to the surface after their deaths, and it's like I don't have a sponge rough enough to clean it off.

"Sam seems like he's having fun."

I blink from my thoughts, greeted by Wendy's small smile.

"Oh," I answer. "Yes, he does."

Her eyebrows tilt in. I wonder how long I was quiet.

"I think he might want to be you when he grows up," she adds.

I run my palm over my beard. I wish he didn't. I wish he wanted to be like his parents, not me.

"Maybe," is all I respond.

"Definitely."

Wendy's so confident in her response. She's confident in the way she carries herself with pretty bows and those curled ends of brown hair. In the clothes, shifting from sundresses one day to bike shorts and a loose tee or overalls, like the one she's wearing today. In how she whips out her notebook from the chest pocket, turning away from me to quickly scribble down words.

Okay, so a little *less* confident in that.

I squint, taking a tentative step forward, granting myself a little nosiness, a question I want answered. I see the words curving from her pen.

He questions everything with a furrowed brow, like he can't trust other's feelings. Or maybe he can't trust himself. The pirate captain is always considering.

"Is that about me?"

Wendy jumps with a peep as she takes one, two, three steps away from me. As she moves, I catch a passing scent of fresh laundry. Clean. New.

Not at all like the grime around us.

"You," she says, poking her pencil in my direction with a sly smile, "are not supposed to read an author's first draft. It's always trash."

"Didn't seem like trash to me."

"Like I said, just silly ideas."

I squint. "Why do you do that?"

She blinks at me. "What?"

121

"Dismiss yourself."

A laugh bubbles out. "I mean, they're just stories."

"No, they're not. I don't think Sam wants to be like me," I say. "I think he'd prefer to write stories, like you."

She blinks at me with her lips parted, and suddenly, it feels like there's a rope tied tight between us, just like the one Sam found outside. If he asked me again what it was for, I don't know if I'd have an answer. I don't know if I could form any words. Because the threads tangled around my stomach now tug in a direction I wish they wouldn't.

They pull directly toward Wendy.

The *something* is there again, crossing from her world to mine.

"So, packed lunches?"

"Yes," I answer, clearing my throat, walking with purpose to the fridge and ripping it open.

I can't be thinking of tight ropes and connections or *somethings* with Wendy. When did that even start? And why is it still happening?

I pull out Sam's lunch box and the two brown bags I packed this morning for me and Wendy—hers scrawled with a *W*. I place her lunch down.

"Thanks again," she says, grabbing a seat. "And, hey, don't tell your dad, but I'd take packed sandwiches over casserole any day."

"You're gonna break his heart," I comment, which has her granting me that light and airy laugh, the one I like so much. Though it normally comes out due to Sam's ridiculousness.

Me making her laugh? That's a different, wonderful kind of high.

I dig out my own sandwich, along with the ziplock bag containing a pickle and a pudding pack.

"Ooh," Wendy says in a mocking tattletale tone. "Sam's gonna be mad."

"Nah, I packed him one too."

Wendy gives an over-the-top gasp. "Look at you," she teases. "Pudding before quiet time? Breaking the rules."

"It's just pudding."

"It's not *just* pudding," she says, mocking my tone back to me from earlier.

I like this banter we're forming. Each moment spent with her feels more relaxed, like I'm settling into a new rhythm of conversation I haven't had in so long.

She unpacks her own bag, pulling out the sandwich first, then rummaging at the bottom of the paper until she emerges with her own clear ziplock bag. But then she pauses, staring at the one extra pickle inside.

Wendy's eyes slide over to me. "You packed two for me?"

My body heats across my chest and up my neck, and suddenly, it feels too weird that I remembered that detail about her. Not only remembered, but acted on it.

"You said you liked them," I answer.

"I do."

"Then, why wouldn't I do something simple if you like it?"

She blinks at me, but doesn't answer.

And when the silence wears on, I clear my throat. "I'm gonna go find Sam."

Chapter 14

How Crass of You

Wendy

I LOVE READING during the summer. It's the only time I can fully disappear into a story without the subconscious stresses of coming up with lesson plans or answering emails or dealing with *people*.

But I haven't picked up a single book in the past week.

I've been writing instead.

The ideas started with my notepad, getting more ragged as each day passed, and then my hand started to throb, so I switched to my bulky, laptop from college. I've barely used it past graduation, and at this point, it can only run one application at a time. Forget trying to play a single song. The whirring fan sounds like it's taking off to space.

But for daydreaming?

The old clunker is perfect.

Every evening, I sit on my cushioned windowsill, the window open, feet tucked underneath my pajamas as words leave my fingertips in sparks. Sometimes, I'm accompanied by Milo sitting in the armchair, reading his book in silence. Then, maybe Cassidy barges in to steal food from my fridge or Bonnie interrupts to give me the latest teenage gossip, complete with boy crushes and best-friend disagreements with Lulu. But even the usual distractions can't keep me from getting lost in this new world. Jill and duels and excitement, but also ... there's him.

The pirate captain.

Exciting, but in the way of beards and hidden smiles and tight pants. Very tight leather pants.

I take my laptop to work, trying to get in extra words during Sam's quiet time. It's not a lot of words at the end of the day, but it's something. It's only alarming when I hear the telltale thumping of work boots crossing the kitchen at four o'clock and look up to see familiar shadowed eyes.

Sure, the real question of *is this fictional captain actually Jasper* has crossed my mind, and I've told myself a firm, assured *no* several times. The captain in my story is new, unique, and doesn't even have tattoos. But when Jasper rolls up the sleeves of his work shirt and toes off his boots in the foyer in one smooth motion I wasn't sure could be hot until now, I realize I might be crossing a very fine line between employer and fantasy.

A very, *very* vivid fantasy.

"Would you like to stay for dinner?"

I freeze. "What?"

Sam clings on to Jasper's ankle, and Jasper walks Sam like deadweight across the floor. I slam my laptop closed right as he lifts an eyebrow.

Credits roll down the television as the movie Sam and I were watching finishes. I hadn't realized it ended.

I shake my head to reorient my thoughts.

"Stay? For dinner?" I ask.

Jasper nods silently.

"Oh, I don't know ..."

"Please, Wendy!" Sam yells from the floor, pressing his cheek into Jasper's leg.

I swear he uses his cuteness as a weapon.

"No pressure," Jasper adds.

This seems like a bad idea. A terrible, irresponsible, misguided—

"Sure! Why not?"

And that's how I end up on the back porch with Sam and Jasper, our three sets of feet swinging off the side of the deck, watching the waves roll in and out.

"I bet I could swim all the way out," Sam says proudly, forking out a bite of spaghetti from his bowl.

"Out where?" Jasper asks.

I was about to ask, too, but I'm too busy savoring Jasper's meal. He whipped this up in thirty minutes like it was second nature. Absentmindedly seasoning while listening to Sam talk about our day and occasionally peering at me for confirmation.

It felt so domestic. So real. And even now, as I sit with my palm cradling the bowl of precious Parmesan pureness, my heart settles into the warmth.

Once we finish and our bowls are set aside to bask in the sun, Jasper gathers them up.

"Oh, please, let me do that," I offer, scrambling to my feet and crossing through the sliding glass door after him.

He shakes his head and exhales a huff of near laughter. "Please, Wendy. I'm not making you wash dishes."

"But you cooked."

"And you're my guest."

It might be small, but something about *my* guest versus *our* guest seems ... different. And I can't shake it.

My guest.

"Wendy, let's go down to the beach!" Sam calls from the open door, already slipping on his sandals.

Jasper tips his chin. "Go," he commands.

"I feel bad, leaving you here to do everything alone."

But he lifts his eyebrows, as if to say, *Didn't you hear me?* and I can't help but give a little laugh.

I hold up my hands in a gesture of surrender, walking backward toward the door. "Fine. Have it your way."

"Next time," he says, and I almost stumble my way out the door at the thought.

My guest.

Next time.

No, I'm just imagining things. It's the pirate captain I'm fantasizing about.

Not Jasper.

Except, I think, maybe even for a second, before I close the sliding glass door, there might be a sea shanty humming from his throat as the sink water turns on and bubbles start to expand.

Sam insists on walking down by the shore, so we do, thumping down the wooden steps and hopping over rocks until we reach the sand.

Sam barrels into the water, so I call out, "Hey, stay close, please," and he does.

After a few minutes of giving Sam the occasional thumbs-up when he displays seashells for my viewing, I'm hit with the same scent I'm starting to recognize as Jasper's cologne. Sea salt and cinnamon and maybe a slight hint of bait, too, but it's not bad. Not really. It reminds me of spending time in The Davies House, when David would come back from fishing and start cooking his catches of the day.

It feels a little like home.

Jasper takes a seat on the rocks beside me. Both of our knees are pulled up, his legs far longer than mine. From the corner of my eye, I catch him looking at me, roaming from my shoulder down to my spine and back up before swiveling back to Sam out in the water.

"I don't know if I ever thanked you," he suddenly says.

"For ..."

"The swim lessons. That was ... well, Sam needed them."

"I know he did," I tease with a scoff.

Jasper lifts a single eyebrow, the corner of his mouth twitching up into a small grin. My chest sinks into the rocks below, falling into the grooves like cooling lava. I realize something else—it's the first time he's resembled Peter. Almost cocky. It's a little too similar.

Jasper's face falls. "What?"

"Nothing," I answer, rolling my lips together.

"Nothing?"

"I can just see the resemblance, is all." Then, I try to play it off with, "All you Davies brothers look the same."

"You know half of us don't share genetic material, right?"

"I stand by it," I continue through a smile, tilting my chin up to further the joke. But I've already outed myself.

His mouth opens, and he sighs out a weird kind of laugh. A knowing one.

"Can I ask you something?" he asks.

"You just did."

Another half chuckle leaves him. "What a teacherly joke."

I grin. "Yes, you can ask me something."

Jasper sucks in a breath and lets it out. "What happened with Pete? If you don't mind me prying."

The iron cage surrounding my hearts rattles in my chest. It's not that I love Peter anymore. It's that, even after two years, the situation still feels raw. Even though the relief of forgiveness goes away, betrayal likes to linger.

I must be silent for too long because he interjects, "If you don't—"

"No, it's fine. I just don't know the last time I was asked this. If ever, honestly. It's such a small town, y'know? People know. Truth is, I guess Peter just loves everyone," I admit, and my shoulder rises to my ear, then drops. "That's it, really."

Jasper doesn't reply, just keeps his focus on the ocean and Sam, splashing in the shallow water. But it doesn't feel like he's ignoring my answer; it's like he's giving me room to think through it. To breathe.

I run my thumb over the hem of my skirt. "I caught him flirting with someone else at The Hideaway. He didn't know I was gonna show up that night. But I figured I'd surprise him, y'know? Pete loves adventure. And surprises."

"He would plan his own surprise parties as a kid."

I laugh. "That is not at all shocking."

Jasper gives a little smile and a nod. "Sorry. Go on."

"It's okay. But, well"—I let out a weak laugh—"there he was. I found him standing so close to this woman. Cornering her at the bar, like he would to me. Smiling bigger than I'd seen in a while. I didn't know her. I didn't even know how long *he* had known her. She could have worked at the bar or ... I don't know. And it's odd; it's not like they were kissing. But ... it was a weird moment. Peter flirted with everyone. This wasn't new. It was just the final straw. I think I just knew ... Peter would always want more. More fun. More excitement. More ... than someone like me."

The waves are quieter somehow. My breath exhales in a low hum.

I trace my finger over the sand as Jasper says, "I'm sorry."

"It happens," I sigh. "My boyfriend after him was worse."

Jasper's eyes dart to me. "Worse?"

My heart ratchets into my throat, and I cough out a laugh.

"Not anything *bad*. Just, unlike Pete, he *actually* got his dick wet, which sucks."

Jasper's eyebrows rise, and a small chuckle leaves his mouth. "How crass of you."

"What? Saying dick?"

"You're an adult. You can say what you like." He clears his throat. "You're just not normally so ... blunt."

"Is that bad?"

"No," he adds quickly. "Absolutely not. Blunt Wendy is entertaining."

I laugh. "Oh, Jas, you don't even know the half of it."

"That right?"

His eyes meet mine, darting between them before tracing down over my cheeks and to my lips, where he lingers. Maybe it's for a minuscule second, but it feels like forever. Shivers roll down my back. Maybe the breeze stops. Maybe it gets quicker. Or maybe it's all in my head.

"So," he continues, his eyes flicking back up to mine, "tell me about this wet-dicked asshole."

I bark out a laugh. "George."

"George," he sneers. "What a fuckin' name."

"So crass," I mock back.

He gives a smirk, and it's the first time he's looked rakish. I like it.

"Yeah. Found him in our bed with someone. They were going at it like bunnies."

"Christ. Your own bed?"

"It was funny, kind of. He looked *off* from that angle." I squint at the memory. "Honestly, I was more embarrassed for myself. I slept with someone who had sex like *that* for an entire year. But so it goes. So, those were my two big relationships. Big heaps of disappointment. Sometimes, I wonder if good relationships are just a fantasy."

Jasper nods. "Seems that way."

"Oh, ho-ho. Does Jasper Davies have a story for me now?"

"Ah ... I don't know," he says, shifting uncomfortably on his rock.

"Oh, please. I shared. Plus, I *love* stories."

"I know you do."

"Oh, come on, Jas."

"All right." He clears his throat. "Well, I dated someone—"

I gasp. "Scandalous." He snorts, and I ask, "Jessica?"

He nods. "Yeah. And it was ... I don't know ... a couple of years ago now. Well, she ... so, this one time, I was trying to find her a birthday present, right? Her birthday was a few weeks before the holidays, and she liked whales a lot. A collector kind of girl. Some on the mantel. A bookshelf full of them. One that winked at me while we slept."

"Creepy."

"Not the best." He inhales. "So"—he exhales it out—"I found this Christmas tree ornament with a whale. Simple. Just a flat circle with a whale drawn on. She always talked about how she wanted more decorations for the holidays, and it seemed up her alley. Not too fancy. I thought she'd love it."

"Did she?"

Clicking his tongue, he shakes his head. "She said she didn't want to get a Christmas tree that year. She said I would be better off returning it."

"She said *what*?"

"Yeah. And I think I was so upset, so taken aback, that my mouth just spouted ... stuff."

"Oh God. What'd you say?"

"I just said, 'Well, y'know, I bet you could put a magnet on the back and put it on the fridge.'"

I stifle a laugh behind my hand. "You didn't."

"I did. God, she was so angry."

He starts laughing, and then so do I until I'm clutching my stomach and he's chuckling in his palms, hiding his smiling face from the world. Almost like he can't stand the idea of people seeing he's happy. It's so tragically beautiful, like a marble statue captured in a museum.

I nudge him with my shoulder. "It's okay to laugh about it, Jas."

His eyes peer out from his hands, and he shakes his head. "Nah. It was rude. And childish. And I don't know ... I guess I regret it."

"You shouldn't."

"Maybe," he muses. He straightens up, letting his head fall back to look at the sky, brushed with the strokes of an orange-and-purple setting sun. "It's weird. She could be harsh, but it came from a good place. She always said I needed to be the tough one. Cassidy's the fun one. Milo's the smart one. Pete's the one with charisma and confidence and ... I don't know. All traits I didn't need to have. I just needed to be a good dad. And she was right."

My heart sinks, and something else sparks inside me as my veins pump with fire and my ears feel hot.

Anger.

Peter *is* the more outgoing one. He makes it clear that he's *there* and present. But Jasper is ubiquitous. He's the guy that will get you the whale ornament. Or that extra pickle in your packed lunch. Or run around the park after his son, finger hooked and snarling in a strange accent, without abandon.

"She was incredibly wrong, Jas. And I'm sorry she was so mean."

"No, it's fine. I don't really like to talk about it."

I smile at his honesty, the warmth spreading over me in steady waves, like butter sliding on a pan. I feel like I'm in a secret club, huddled around a fireplace in Jasper's mind, and I don't squander chances like that.

"Sam's lucky to have you, you know," I say.

"Nice subject change," Jasper grunts.

"I'm serious. He's lucky."

"Yeah, 'cause I'm all he's got."

"No. Because you're all he needs. You're a good dad, among other things. I bet he loves all the ornaments you get him."

"He's a child. He can't return them."

I lean my head back and laugh. "Okay, but he wouldn't anyway. Because *you* got them for him. You're thoughtful. And caring. And charismatic, I must say." He snorts in dissent, but I ignore him. "By the way, thanks for the extra pickle the other day."

"Don't mention it."

The worst part is, I think he's insisting. Jasper doesn't like anyone knowing how much he cares.

"Fine," I agree. "Then, I won't."

He smiles at me. He says nothing, but he doesn't have to.

That's okay. I'll keep his secret for him. I quite like having secrets with Jasper Davies.

Chapter 15

Something

Jasper

I TOLD Wendy about Jessica tonight.

I don't talk about Jessica to anyone. My ex-girlfriend is a slice of life that feels both like it occurred a lifetime ago and yet also like we split yesterday.

One month before Ed and Stacy's accident, we went on a date—just friends of friends of friends. The date was one of those where you keep tacking on new locations and ideas, just to have the night live on forever. I smiled more back then—laughed more—and Jessica had a way of pulling that out, even when I was only half a whiskey deep.

Things got muddled after the accident. Not just with her, but with me too. Despite that, Jessica offered to help me move back to Never Harbor. I'm not sure how I would have functioned during that first year without her.

She wanted so much more for Sam than I could provide. I can only imagine how frustrating it was to watch me struggle with basic parenting tasks, like bedtime stories or bath time, to be burdening my family on weekends for childcare, to wake up next to a grown man heaving into a sweaty pillowcase because he still had nightmares.

She saw me for who I was, and my shame was what broke us apart.

So, why did I open up to Wendy?

It was just the time, the place, the fact that Sam was out in the water—safe because *she'd* had the courage to let him learn.

Sam kept saying, "Cap! Cap! Look!" and showing me how he could dive under and come back up, float on his back, and paddle back to shore.

All thanks to Wendy.

After the sun goes down, Wendy tosses her tote bag over her shoulder, and we stand across from each other at the threshold of the house.

I lean in the doorway before pocketing a hand and grunting out a corny, "See you tomorrow."

"See you tomorrow," she echoes in that airy, light way she does.

"See you tomorrow!" Sam practically screams from the kitchen, smacking Lego pieces together.

I watch Wendy walk backward to her car, give another wave, then drive off. And my chest—a tight, looped lasso—groans and whines the farther away she gets. Like she's taking my secrets with her.

I put Sam down for bed after another hour. Instead of me reading to him, he tells me some grand adventure he and Wendy had today.

I kiss him on the forehead, tugging his blankets up so comically high that it has him pushing them down through laughter.

And right before my fingers click off the light, he whispers, "Cap?"

"Hmm?"

"I really like when Wendy stays for dinner."

The rope tightens around my chest and slides into a knot.

"Oh, yeah?"

He snuggles into his sheets. "Yep."

I click off his light with a chuckle. "Yeah. Me too, bud."

I shut his door and start my nighttime routine through the house, darkening each room as I go. Light after light, the snaps and clicks of turned-off lamps. Only the distant ocean waves and the smack of my bare feet on the hardwood left to echo.

I finally reach my bedroom on the opposite side of the kitchen, shutting the door behind me and letting the complete silence wash over me. But sitting in it for too long prompts that same rope, jerking my chest forward and back, securing its hold.

Securing my thoughts to Wendy.

I rip off my T-shirt, flexing out my hands as I walk into the bathroom, trying to shake this rigidity mummifying every tendon, zipping up my veins and stuttering into my heart.

I strip the rest of my clothes off, tossing my fishy shirt into the washer with a detergent pack.

God, I smell like *bait*, and Wendy didn't even say a word. Her nose didn't get that disgusted scrunch; the tilt of her pink lips didn't twist into a scowl. Then again, maybe she was just being nice.

Wendy Darling has always been polite.

But how well do I know her, really?

The polite Wendy I knew wouldn't have said her ex *got his dick wet.*

The echoing words have me chuckling all over again.

God, the Wendy I thought I knew wouldn't have been so forward. But I don't think I truly know this woman.

Who is Wendy when she's alone?

I twist the shower handle and step onto the cool tiles, letting the waterfall showerhead cascade rain over me. The water is cool, sprouting goose bumps over my shoulders.

Wendy looked interested in what I had to say tonight, blinking and nodding along with each word. I don't have a lot to say, and when I do, I'm sure it's about something dumb, like work. Who cares about work?

But Wendy laughed with me, and I felt *something.*

For so long, I've felt like I was floating—my body simply drifting from day to day, like a ghoul passing through walls. I've been so cold. But now, the bottoms of my feet are warm, the tiles suddenly feel like lava, and I'm burning. Toasting from the inside out, like being cooked by sparks bursting out of my chest, into my neck, and down to my stomach.

I twist the shower handle to a colder temperature, but even as it cools down, my body is still engulfed in flames. Steam feels like it's rising over my shoulders, a dragon breathing at my neck. My arms stiffen and release. My breaths come in stammered starts and reluctant ends.

Wendy laughed tonight, and there was that little indent in the corner of her lips that is becoming all too familiar as each day passes. It's like a hidden place for her cheeks to kiss her lips. A kiss visible to only a lucky few.

How does that kiss taste?

I pant out a breath, twisting the handle down again to as cold as it can go. The water is so frigid that it hurts, but as it streaks through my hair, drips down my beard, dribbles over my shoulders, and tickles down between my legs, I can still only imagine the heat of her stare. Her pouty lips and teasing mouth.

I look down. My cock hangs heavy, full and demanding. I have felt nothing for so long, but now, my body is brimming with *something*.

I take myself in my palm, running down the hardened length for just one stroke. That one touch has my body lurching forward, my hand slapping against the tiled wall, palm pushing into it as I steady myself. My thighs shudder so much; they might damn well take me down.

I stroke my cock again, flicking my thumb over the swelled head. I distantly hear my own huff of an exhale echo against the glass shower door.

Flexing my grip, I pump again.

God.

Everything is difficult—the tightening of my muscles, the rip of anxiety through my veins, the clenching of my jaw … the damn *work* it takes to remain standing as I stroke faster and faster, gripping and pumping and twisting and suddenly imagining.

Her ocean-blue eyes, her plump and parted lips, her long, pretty lashes blinking.

Her laughter.

What would her hair feel like, tangled in my hands? How would her breath feel against my cheek? Would her lips fit with mine? And how much would that kiss break me?

I choke out another guttural moan, water splashing over my fist as I pump up and down, the pain in my chest growing, growing, growing.

What noises does she make? What positions does she like? How would she *taste*?

The pleasure at my base reaches a new height until, suddenly, it plummets.

It's like a plug is ripped from a drain, sending my

thoughts, tension, *everything* spiraling. My orgasm releases onto the tiles for the first time in weeks.

My feet stumble in place, my thighs shaking beneath me, all while those blue eyes still linger in my head. My mind is spinning, and I'm dizzy, barely keeping myself upright.

I've gotten so accustomed to nothing. This *something* is scary. New. Exciting.

I release a shocked laugh.

Then, I feel the sting. The icy chill. I shiver as I rotate the shower handle back up. Until I'm standing, cold again, under the showerhead, blinking through the rising heat and steadily fogging glass.

Something.

Something, instantly followed by guilt.

Chapter 16

A Selfish, Rude Friend

Jasper

"You're late."

I've been at my parents' house for two seconds, and I'm already frozen at her words.

Because, somehow, Wendy found me before everyone else, then says in a low, accusatory tone, "You're late, Jasper Davies."

I shake my head as she bites back a laugh.

"I figured I'd wait for the party to start first," I say as we both wind through the hallways.

"Well, you know the party doesn't start till you walk in, right?"

"News to me," I grunt, which has her laughing, the sound stamping on my soul, even after it fades away.

The Twins barrel past us in the hall, forcing Wendy and me against the picture frames. My hand shoots out for her waist, steadying her on her lower back so she doesn't hit the wall. The fabric of her dress is soft, and the warmth of her body radiating through it has my face heating.

I thought about her again last night. Dirty and quick as I imagined us pushing into my bedsheets with her legs wrapped around my waist.

I close my eyes, mentally scrubbing the memories clean. I wonder how disgusted she'd be if she knew that a man seven years older than her—her *boss*, her ex's *older brother*—was fantasizing about his thumb rubbing between her thighs.

Another flash of her breathy moans, soft, just like her.

A spark of my palms gripping her thighs.

I jerk my hand away from her back, but I can still feel the sting in my palm, like guilt stabbing through me.

Wendy grins at me, none the wiser as she walks away to Cassidy and my mom. She fist-bumps my brother, just as she's always done since their middle school days, and she cocoons my mom in a hug. Sam runs over, nudging his way between their legs to join the party.

I cross back into the hallway, but that's when the conversation shifts.

"How's it going?" my mom asks her.

There's a silence before I hear Wendy murmur, "Um ... good actually."

Good.

"He's not giving you too much grief?"

"No," Wendy answers with a laugh.

And I don't know much about Wendy—I'm still learning every day—but the word sounds like a fading breath. A relief and maybe a smile even though I can't see it on the other side of the wall.

"No, not at all. Jas's been nice."

I smile.

"I actually really like it over there."

My body zings with energy, but before it can overtake

me, before I rudely eavesdrop anymore, I walk away. I continue out into the open backyard, my hands tucked in my pockets, the excitement ping-ponging through me.

Sam runs out after me, climbing into the tree house. I watch, alone, from the picnic table, leaning my elbows on my knees, my hands clasped in front, as The Twins push past each other up the tree limbs. Milo quietly walks behind them, like a sentry for his little brothers.

The sun is bright, but the air has a tepid feel to it. Storms must be rolling in.

I smile to myself, remembering days like this out on the docks with Ed and Stacy. Sam was only a baby, swaddled against Ed's chest as he flung the fishing line in the water with that winning smile of his. And my mood starts to drift out with the memory of that water, sinking down.

I tense, clutching my hands together as I pull in a shaky breath.

But then I'm pulled out by a melodic voice, humming, "Nice day, huh?"

Wendy sits down next to me, and like a tide rushing back in, there's that *something*.

She extends her legs out from her dress. There are freckles on her knees I've never noticed before. After a stretch, they disappear back underneath. Part of me—the selfish, rude part that wants and wants—wonders how soon I'll see them again.

"It is," I observe, but my eyes don't leave her shins until I rip them away. I squint up at the setting sun. "So-so."

I don't know why she's sitting here with me when she could be off with my brothers somewhere, playing their game of pirates and wild boys.

Wendy nudges my arm. "Want to place a bet?" she asks. "Sure."

143

"Sound a bit more excited," she says. I let out a small chuckle, causing Wendy to gasp and cover her mouth, whispering through the muffled hand, "Wait, was that a laugh? Oh, quick, hide it. Someone might see!"

I roll my eyes, but the smile is ever-growing on my face. "Okay, what's your bet?"

She places her hands on her knees—knees that I now know hide precious freckles—and leans forward, glancing in the kitchen.

"How long until Cass sneaks a biscuit?"

I grunt, "Oh, he already has."

"Yeah?"

"Definitely."

And like magic, Cassidy appears around the corner, half-eaten biscuit in his hand. We both burst into laughter.

"Darn," she says. "Thought I'd get you there. Fine. You win that one."

"I'll place another bet."

"Oh, please do."

"How long until Ma starts talking about holiday plans?"

"She does like to secure dates," Wendy says. "Hmm ... next month?"

"Better yet, when will she start getting those special-edition Hallmark ornaments?"

"Y'know, I hear you can make a magnet out of those."

My breath catches as I watch Wendy lean back on the picnic table, satisfied with her joke. The tree house casts her chin and lips in shadow, but a tiny sunbeam illuminates her eyes, highlighting the streaks of chestnut in her hair, confirming the errant flyaways beside her cheeks.

"You win," I exhale.

"Wendy!"

I jolt back as Peter pounces toward us, bouncing on the balls of his feet.

"I was just looking for you!"

She blinks up at him, hand rising to shield her eyes from the sun. "Were you?"

Then, Peter snatches her hand, pulling her to her feet. The look of her small hand engulfed in his suddenly makes me very aware of my heartbeat and how fast it's pumping in my eardrums.

"Sam told me you're working on your book," he says.

Wendy laughs. "I am."

"Well then, we should go to Deadman's Drop! To celebrate."

"Celebrate what?"

"Creativity."

"By jumping off a cliff? Did you ever figure out how to sneak in?"

"Of course."

"Well, I don't know," she muses, twisting her lips with a smile. "There's still a lot of other things I need to do for the book before I celebrate. Like, I need to learn sailing first."

That's when Peter points to me. "Oh, Jas can take you to do that. Jas, you still have that boat, right?"

My heart stammers as I run a hand through my hair. "I do."

"Then, take her out."

Peter is grinning, but I don't know how. He's practically shoving me into some romantic boating date with Wendy. Or maybe that's just me *wanting* again.

Wendy's eyes dart between us.

"Oh," I finally concede. "Sure. Yeah. I could."

The moment I seem on board, she's instantly grinning ear to ear.

145

"Oh, and Sam can swim now!" she says, clapping her hands. "That would be so fun. And I can drive the boat, right?"

I snort. "You'll send us straight into Skull Rock."

She tsks, waving a dismissive hand. "Oh, details."

"Important ones," I counter, but she smiles at me, triggering my own small twitching smile that breaks through the surface.

"So, are you two friends now?" Peter asks with a grin, pointing between us.

I blink back. I almost forgot my brother was there.

Wendy looks to me and shakes her head, as if to say, *Absolutely not.* Then, she scrunches her nose, smiles, and nods.

"I like to think so," she answers.

She would?

"I like that," Peter says. "You can make him a little less grumpy."

"I'm grumpy?" I ask.

"If you weren't, you'd have more friends," Peter teases.

"True," I concur with a joking eye roll. "But don't remind me I don't have friends."

"Well, *I'm* your friend," Wendy chimes in. "Come on. Don't tell me this is one-sided?"

She blinks at me, and I find myself saying without a thought, "No. I guess I'm yours too."

Yours.

It's a slip of the tongue I wish I could take back, but it doesn't matter because Peter's beaming again, and it bothers me just how happy he is for this new development. It's not because I don't like seeing my brother happy. It's because he isn't the least bit concerned. Of course he wants his best friend and brother to get along. Why would it matter if

Wendy and I are friends? At the end of the day, she's always *his* Wendy, and he knows that.

A wail echoes through the house, pulling me from the spiral.

"Ca-a-a-ap!"

I'd recognize that cry anywhere.

I jump to my feet, running toward the sound of the nickname that only comes from my boy. I dart through the kitchen, past the parlor, down the hall, where Milo is leaning with a book in hand, and into my mom's office to find Sam at The Twin's feet, holding out his red beanie, ripped and unfurled at the stitches.

"What happened?" I bark.

The Twins each point a single finger at each other. I sigh.

"Twins," I scold, "scatter."

As a unit, they scramble from the room. That's a talk for later.

"Cap," Sam cries from the ground. "It ripped."

I crouch down, gently taking his favorite little beanie from his grasp. I twist it between my hands. "I'll fix it, okay?"

He's sniffling over and over and nodding.

I hold out my arms for a hug, which he instantly stumbles into.

"Everything okay?"

I twist to see Wendy in the threshold, hands tucked into her dress pockets, biting that bottom lip in concern.

I nod. "Just an accident. Still figuring things out."

Peter appears behind her, balancing one long arm on the opposite side of the threshold. "You all right, little man?"

Sam, still sniffling, nods.

"We just need a moment," I say quietly.

Peter nods in understanding before wrapping an arm around Wendy's waist and dragging her off.

Blood shoots up to my head, and I feel lightheaded. But this is the reality, isn't it? Wendy is the type of woman Peter could win over with his charisma. Not me.

But before they're fully out of the room, she turns around, and I see that familiar smile with the secret crease in the corner.

Except it isn't directed at Peter. It's beaming right at me.

Chapter 17

Mermaids

Wendy

I'm excited when Jasper decides to take off work again to sail with Sam and me.

The boat, a Catalina model that looks old yet scrubbed back to new, rocks side to side as Jasper's muscles do the fabulous things muscles do when they're curling rope and tugging rigging.

Rigging? Is that what it's called?

I should be paying closer attention, taking notes for my slow-growing book, but when Jasper's head tilts around toward me, eyebrow lifted, my notebook remains blank. He knows I'm barely paying attention.

It must be obvious in how glazed over my eyes are, but I play it off with a laugh and a, "Are we swimming yet?"

Jasper rolls his eyes with a chuckle—a low, familiar, inviting sound I'm not sure I'll ever truly get accustomed to, but I've established we're friends now, and I guess laughing is what friends do together.

I like his laughter. He doesn't give it often, but I'm happy to earn it.

We dock near Skull Rock, a small island right off the coast of Never Harbor, which is usually crowded with paddleboats or camping teens—something I was never invited to by the boys because it was *a guys' trip*. But I've spent enough time here to know that right now, on a Monday at nine o'clock in the morning, it was bound to be just the three of us.

Jasper tosses his keys on the seat next to him, and I discreetly lean over to observe his fob. One key chain in particular stands out—a long royal-blue diamond shape that looks like it's from an inn. My curiosity is pulled away at the sound of Sam running across the creaking wood, life jacket secured, and hopping off the side and into the water.

I don't miss Jasper's subtle jaw twitch.

"Okay, if we're playing mermaids, you're gonna have to be more present," I joke.

The corner of his lips curls up. "Mermaids?" he asks.

"Oh, don't tell me you've never played *mermaids*."

I turn around, crouching down to dig out two pairs of goggles from my clear beach bag. I toss a pair toward Jasper over my shoulder. He catches them midair. But his eyes are focused on something different. They look to be steadied on the center of my back.

He swallows. "Can I ask you something?"

I grin. "You know you can just ask me things, right? No preamble?"

"What's with the bird?"

My stomach dips. My tattoo is in the middle of my back, so I forget about it a lot. I stand, absentmindedly tightening the goggle straps.

"I got it a couple of months ago," I say. "It's just a thing."

"A thing," he muses, nodding slowly. "Didn't peg you for a tattoo person."

I peer up at him through my downcast eyes. "What type of person do you think I am?"

His lips tip up, and mine do, too, a shift in my chest rolling around, like our boat on water. It's been doing that more. At the beach the other night. At his family dinner. It's a shiver that taps my shoulder, coaxing me to float in Jasper's orbit. But what happens if I get lost in space?

I glance down to the fishing hook tattoo on Jasper's forearm—the one that always seems to be hidden under a partially rolled sleeve.

"What's your hook mean?" I ask.

"I asked about your tattoo first," he prompts.

I grin. "Fine. Your mom calls me Wendy Bird."

"I'm surprised she didn't lose her mind at you having it."

"Is Jasper Davies scared of his mother?"

"No," he scoffs. But it does make him laugh again, and I really like that low laugh. "But I definitely didn't like the look I got when she saw mine."

"Maybe she just liked the significance of mine more," I jest.

"Oh, I wouldn't doubt that. Keep talking, Wendy Bird. What's it mean?"

Wendy Bird.

I bite my bottom lip because if I don't, my heart might beat right out of my chest.

"It's a reminder to keep flying," I confess. "That life will move on. That the Earth keeps spinning and the birds keep migrating regardless of what happened the day before. That I should keep flying too. It's dumb, I know, but—"

"I like it."

"It's cheesy," I continue, shaking my head.

"No, it's important to you. If we can't love the things significant to us without guilt, then what can we love? Your tattoo is important because you think it is. And that's all that matters."

I don't know why I bother writing a pirate captain when the real one in front of me feels too fantastical to re-create.

"Without guilt, huh?" I muse. "So, you're telling me you don't have guilty pleasures?"

"I don't."

"Tell me a secret then, Mr. I Don't Feel Guilty."

The air stills as his eyes roam down to my lips and back up, freezing me on the spot.

"I collect coins," he answers simply.

I choke out a laugh. "I do not at all believe you're a coin collector."

"I am. And you? Your so-called guilty pleasure?"

"Stamps," I answer.

"Well, now, you're just mocking me," he says, grinning.

I nod at his forearm. "Okay, so what about your hook? What's it mean?"

"Ah, story for another day."

I gasp. "You tease!"

"I thought we were playing mermaids?" he asks, narrowing his eyes with a smile as he points a thumb over his shoulder.

"Jasper Davies, oh my God."

I walk forward to playfully push his shoulder, except he grabs my wrist before I can, sending me off-balance. I laugh, and his smile bursts through the scruff of his thick beard. A hearty laugh, straight from his chest, erupts, too, and my body halts with tension. I reach my other hand to attempt again, but he clutches that, too, and suddenly, both my wrists are captured by Jasper.

The moment, once filled with laughter, now fades away. His piercing eyes dance over mine. My chest rises and falls. So does his. I don't know when we stopped smiling, but we did. When I stumble in place, he releases one wrist, instead placing a warm palm on the dip in my waist to steady me.

And he's looking at me in a weird way. Like maybe he's trying to parse through something in his mind.

"Wendy ..." The word is murmured softly, brushing across my cheek.

Then, the boat's ladder creaks against the waves, and Jasper and I rip apart before Sam can finish climbing up it.

"Can I take off my life jacket?" he asks, starting to tug at the belts.

We're close to the shore, but I glance at Jasper for confirmation, who slowly nods, "Sure, bud. Let me help you."

I look away, trying to shake the moment from my mind.

But what moment? There wasn't a moment, was there?

Jasper finishes snapping off Sam's straps, and he sets the vest down.

"Captain said he'll play mermaids with us!" I announce.

"You will?" Sam asks, eyes brightening.

I grin, expecting to see Jasper's—no doubt—miserable expression, but then it happens so quickly. Too quick for my heated brain to process it.

Jasper reaches across his chest, his fist clutching the corner of his shirt, and rips it over his head.

My mouth gapes, and I can't stop it. Jasper, shirtless, is just ...

He's tan, maybe a little bit uneven in parts—likely from working at the docks. But those same docks are why his forearms trail with veins and why his collarbone arcs over his shoulders, connecting down to the swelling biceps beneath. His chest is the kind only active men have. Dark

153

brown curls peppering over the broad surface, a thin path disappearing over the bumps of abs and reappearing on his lower stomach with a trail leading down to ...

Well ...

Then, Jasper smiles. "Whatever you want."

I don't know if he's talking to me or Sam.

But I know who I hope he's addressing.

"Whatever you want."

Jasper gathers Sam in his arms—against that hard chest —then cannonballs into the water, leaving me with nothing but the sizzling droplets cooling my flushed cheeks.

Chapter 18

The Ladder Accident

Wendy

MY WORDS ARE FLOWING like water now. Adventures about Jill and her trusty first mate, Sam, and the captain from the wrong side of the docks. It's fantastic, exciting, and ... well, a little hot now. My epic fantasy story has transformed into a romance simply because I know how to describe a shirtless pirate captain.

Jasper: Did the sailing research help

I toss my phone across the couch like it's a snake that just struck because he's *texting me*. But once I'm past the shock, I immediately scramble to pick it back up.

Wendy: Yes! Thank you! :)
Jasper: Anytime

Anytime.

"Whatever you want."

What does it all mean? And why does it matter what it means?

Jasper's probably just texting like the technologically unsavvy man that he is, as seen in gems like *home soon* and *weather isn't good.* Like, buddy, get some punctuation marks in there. That could mean rain or tornadoes as far as I'm concerned.

But because of this trend, that also means *anytime* could translate to *hey, anytime, friend!* Or *anytime, but please don't text me.* Or even *anything for you, Wendy Bird.*

I don't know anymore. Not after our arms got tangled together and the heat from his stare warmed me from my core down to my toes.

I got home that day, shut and locked both my front door and bedroom door, and lay in bed, staring at the ceiling in just a bra and panties.

I was ready to imagine it all over again. But my hand paused at my lacy hem, and my brain blocked it all.

It's wrong. Thinking of Jasper is the biggest form of betrayal I can imagine.

Jasper is my ex-fiancé's brother.

Peter's brother.

It was good I didn't follow through because hurried knocking came at my door and Bonnie bounded in with magazines and nail polish. I listened to her discuss the latest Hideaway drama among the hostesses, but my guilt still overflowed in waves.

It's been days, but I still groan, slamming my laptop closed.

My body is thrumming, my heart pounding, and I'm itching to relieve this pressure building, but I've got to find someone who isn't Jasper to occupy my fantasies. I walk to my trusty bookshelf wall. I trace a finger over the rows of books and find a perfectly good high fantasy with elves and wizards from the top shelf—the furthest thing from a *pirate*, that's for sure—but when I climb onto my ladder, there's a sudden crack under my feet.

I trip, slamming my face against the middle rung.

"What the—"

I stumble off the ladder, clutching my cheek. I wince at the touch.

Wonderful. Definitely a bruise.

That's when I notice the bottom rung of my beautiful dream ladder is now broken and deceased.

RIP.

This is what romance does. It ruins good things.

So, I do the only thing that makes sense in situations like this. I hunt for coffee. Just like our ancestors before us.

By the time I make it to Peg Leg Press, I make a beeline to the front counter.

Bobbi stares with wide eyes. "Good Lord. What happened to the other guy?"

"Iced coffee, please," I say, almost out of breath. "All the sugar and cream. Literally all of it."

Then, another familiar voice calls through my laser-focused haze, "Wendy!"

I turn, spotting Maggie sitting at a booth-table combo near the window. Bonnie is across from her, a split muffin in the center of the table.

Must be a mother-daughter date, which is enough to give my heart a little tug. I love that Maggie and Bonnie have that type of relationship. But before I can say hi, Maggie is rising from her chair, bustling over, practically tripping over her long skirt—a cute number with a slit up the side because Maggie is just that side of feisty.

157

"Oh my goodness, what happened to your cheek?" Her eyes are wide as they search my face. Her hands examine me as she goes into full physician mode.

"Uh, rolling-ladder incident," I respond with a weak laugh and smile.

Maggie lets out a small tsk and tilts her head to the side. "Books will be the death of you, huh?"

We both laugh together, and I wince in pain. But a piece of my heart—the one coffee was supposed to fill—heals a little.

I wave to Bonnie. "Midday coffee? Tired from work?"

She tucks her red hair behind her ear. "Not really. *Ma*" —she sends a pointed glare to Maggie—"doesn't like me working too late, so I don't get any of the good tips."

Maggie shoots her a look. "I don't want you partying there."

Bonnie rolls her eyes. "Lulu does."

"Lulu is twenty."

"Peter won't even let me serve drinks."

But another voice says, "No, *I* won't because it's illegal."

Izzy comes out of the restroom hallway, and my heart slices right down the middle.

Wait, why is Izzy here too?

I hate that my first thought is wondering why I wasn't invited to this intimate coffee date. I don't have to be invited, do I? I'm not part of this family.

But neither is Izzy.

I bury, bury, bury the hurt because it doesn't matter.

It doesn't matter one bit.

"God, you look like you got punched in the face," Izzy says from their table, head tilted to the side.

"That would be far cooler, I guess," I respond with a fun

—yep, totally fun and chill—laugh. "Can we go with that instead?"

But Izzy twists her lips to the side without commenting.

All right then, zero for fifty on attempts to gain Izzy's friendship again.

"So, just a coffee date then?" I ask, pointing to the table with a smile.

"Couldn't resist. It's a beautiful day, and I had time for a break between appointments," Maggie says, looking out the window to Main with dogs on leashes and colorful shop doors propped open.

Steve, our town's paper boy—well, paper *man*, I suppose —pumps his bicycle uphill with sweat drenching the neckline of his shirt. We all wave, and he tiredly returns it.

"Poor guy." Maggie tsks.

Bonnie lets out an exaggerated groan, leaning her elbows over the back of her chair. "I just wanted coffee by myself, but Ma tagged along."

"Am I not allowed to want coffee?" Maggie asks with feigned innocence before mumbling to me not too quietly, "Teenagers. Don't recommend." She swipes a thumb across my cheek before patting it.

Bonnie moans, rolling her eyes playfully, but there's no sign of actual disdain in them.

"We happily ran into Izzy too," Maggie continues.

"And I'm obligated to spend time with Mags whenever I run into her. It's a rule," Izzy says with a genuine grin that feels so foreign because I never get one anymore.

Although I feel slightly better that Izzy wasn't invited, my stomach still twists at my otherness in this moment and the sour fact that I'm satisfied Izzy wasn't invited. That's gotta put some points in the *bad person* column, right?

"That's great," I say, the words catching in my throat.

159

Maggie notices my cracked voice. She lifts an eyebrow, and even though I know that expression well—the one laced with concern because she can read me like a book—the worry somehow fades from my mind. Because I like that lifted eyebrow. I've seen it on her son so many times now.

She narrows her eyes, nods, as if satisfied nothing is actually wrong with me, then asks, "How's your book coming along, dear?"

"Oh, you're writing a book?" Bonnie asks from the table. "That's so cool."

I smile. "Yeah, it's been really fun."

Bonnie's face brightens. "Are you gonna publish it?"

"I haven't even considered it," I admit. And it's true. It's not like I want to write as a job. I love teaching and my kids. So far, it's just been fun, and I like fun.

"So, you're just gonna write a full book and do nothing with it?" Izzy asks.

Pop goes the balloon.

"Izzy, quit being snarky," Maggie quickly chastises, complete with a motherly finger point.

"I didn't mean it in a rude way," Izzy says, and her tone agrees. "Just ... why would you go through all that trouble for nothing?"

I want to argue that not everything should be monetized. Why can't my dream of finishing a book be enough? But Izzy wouldn't understand. She's the type of woman that likes purpose.

"That's a good question," I say. "Maybe I'll look into publishing or something."

I could. And maybe I should.

George would have expected it. Even Peter probably would.

But publishing feels so ... unnecessary. I'm doing what I

love already. Why should I want more? Is that weird? Abnormal?

The thoughts swim through my mind in waves of uncertainty, and suddenly, I'm lacking.

Not enough. Yet again.

Thankfully, this is about the time Bobbi appears at the counter. I grab my coffee, filled to the brim with enough sugar and cream to amp up a small child for days, and wave to the group. "Well, I should get going."

"No, sit with us," Bonnie asserts, scooting over on the booth, accidentally knocking into Izzy as she does.

"No, it's fine," I say. "I don't want to intrude or anything."

"But we love intruders," Bonnie says.

"And you're not an intruder, dear," Maggie argues, her eyebrows tilting in again.

"No, really," I respond with a forced laugh. "I should go work on the book or something."

Because that's all it is, I guess. A *something*.

I look at my phone, as if checking the time, but I'm not sure why or what I'm expecting. It's Sunday; I'm not on a schedule. But somehow, my finger swings to my texts of its own accord, and I reread the text from Jasper.

Anytime.

Maybe it means, *Anytime, I'd love to help with your book. Anytime, because your book matters.*

I pocket it again. "I should really get going," I insist.

Maggie pulls me into a bear hug, smashing me against her. I wince at the bruise on my cheek even though this is the best kind of hug. The kind where I inhale the smell of cookies and vanilla and a home I've never had.

"Let's plan our own girls' date soon," she whispers, and I nod against her.

"I'd love that."

She pulls away, patting my cheek again. "Good."

But somehow, I feel like all the cookie smell in the world can't overshadow my sudden sense of aimlessness and *lacking*.

Chapter 19

You

Jasper

I'm packing my lunch when Wendy walks in with a bruised face.

"What the hell?"

My blood pressure spikes, and I'm crossing around the kitchen island in less than two seconds.

Wendy, on the other hand, looks completely unbothered. In fact, the woman is smiling, holding her palm over her reddened face, as if embarrassed.

"It's all right," she says, shaking her head. "Really."

My hands fly to her face before I can stop them, my thumbs tracing over the inky purple splotch on her cheekbone.

"What the hell happened?" I demand.

"Nothing," Wendy answers, now laughing. "It was just a ladder accident."

"A ladder accident? What does that mean?"

My thumb gently analyzes the raised bruise. Not that I think Wendy would lie about getting sucker-punched in the face by a ladder, but my heart won't stop pounding, and the only thing helping me calm down is the feel of her smooth skin under my fingers.

"My ladder broke and ..."

For the first time, I notice subtle freckles dotting along her nose. Long, heavy lashes. Those ocean eyes have tiny flecks of green circling the irises, yet they look like deeper waters than I've ever seen.

"And?" I prompt.

Her eyes dart between mine. She lets out a soft exhale that tickles my beard.

"Wow," she whispers, popping her lips. "The Davies family has sure loved touching my face lately."

Oh God.

I rip my hands away.

I run a palm over my beard from the same hand that still lingers with the warmth of her flushed cheek—cheeks that are as red as apples, like mine probably are too.

I clear my throat. "That was—"

Inappropriate. Overstepping.

Wendy shakes her head. "No, really, I'm okay." But her face is falling, and she looks sad. "It's fine."

Not fine.

"It's—"

Like a taut slingshot being released, Sam barrels into the kitchen, belt clanging, a musical recorder held up to his lips. "Hey, watch this!"

And then he just starts playing random notes, his fingers pressing over the instrument's holes. We stand there, blinking at him—smacked into the reality that, number one, kids are weird and random, and, two, Wendy and I are here for Sam, *not* each other—until he pauses mid-play, eyes practically popping out of his head.

"Holy heck, Wendy."

Wendy grins, and even with the bruise, the energy in her smile is still palpable. "I got in a swashbuckling duel."

"That's so cool," Sam breathes, tossing the recorder onto the counter, next to his red beanie, still unstitched, waiting for me to sew it back.

It's been a long weekend, and I haven't gotten to it yet.

"Want to go reenact it with me?" Wendy asks.

Sam bounces on his toes. "Yes!" He snatches her hand and pulls her toward the back deck.

"Right. Well, bye, Sam!" I call sarcastically, but he and Wendy are already halfway through the parlor, his mind already lost to their pirate wonderland.

Wendy twists and throws a sheepish wave, face back into a small frown. "Have a great day at work!"

"I ..." I hold up a hand in response, then lower it, murmuring, "Yeah. You too," after they disappear out the sliding glass door.

I feel like I've just been assaulted by fifty things.

The bruise.

Her smooth skin under my fingertips.

My boy's ridiculous recorder performance.

But mostly how sad Wendy looked beneath it all.

The longer I stand here, the weirder I feel, so I grab my lunch off the counter and drive my truck to work, my fists winding over the steering wheel the entire way.

I'm distracted all morning. Each conversation blends together, and every time I look up, I expect to see a bruised Wendy again. I can only provide little *mmhmm*s in response.

I feel weird. I try to reason with myself that maybe it's the weather. Dark clouds have been gathering over the horizon, and the wind is picking up near the shore. It smells distinctly like seaweed, which is never a good sign.

"Hey, I'm gonna wrap up at home."

"You're ... what?" Starkey asks, blinking at me over his afternoon coffee.

"Yeah," I say, clearing my throat. "Gonna work from home. I've only got paperwork left anyway. And the storm, you know. I should make it home before things get worse. Everyone is back, right? You guys can call it early too."

Starkey narrows his eyes. "Call it ... early? You never work from home. Is Sam all right?"

"Yeah. Sam's fine." I push a hand through my hair. "I think I'm just tired. You guys try to beat the storm."

He's not convinced that everything is okay, but that makes two of us.

On my way out of town, I drop by the pharmacy and pick up various creams for bruises and cuts while sidestepping through aisles, so Ted, the owner, doesn't catch me in a conversation. I make a second stop at Jake's Hardware, where, unlike Ted, Jake understands the value of non-conversation.

By the time I'm driving down my gravel road, the sky is awash with black, so dark that even the clouds are barely discernible. Small droplets start to plunk on my windshield, and when I park, the rain is falling in sheets. I rush to the front porch with the bags in hand, ducking through the rain and wind and keying in as veins of lightning touch the horizon down by the beach.

Wendy is on the couch, sitting cross-legged and staring up at me with blinking eyes.

That damn bruise doesn't look any better. It might have just been an accident, but I don't like it. Not one bit.

In her lap is Sam's beanie, sewing needle paused.

Roger is in the dog bed in the corner, loud snores echoing through the silent room.

Sam isn't around. I check the clock over the television. It's a little after one o'clock. Still in his quiet time.

"You're home early," she observes.

"I ..." Then, I realize I have no idea how to explain why I'm here. Why I left early or that it was because I needed to see how she was doing. "You're fixing his beanie?"

"Yeah," she says, holding it up. "He doesn't seem like the same kid without it."

"I was gonna do that this weekend."

"You know how to sew?"

"I have a kid. I have to know."

Her smile has my lips twitching up into one, too, before her gaze locks on my wet hair. "Do you need a towel?"

"Oh, no. Thanks."

"No, let me get you one."

She gets up, crossing to the hall closet before I can protest more. She pulls out one of Sam's beach towels, unfolding it and walking closer. She gingerly places it on my head, running her hands over the top. Her palms massage into my scalp, and my gut clenches. Maybe she feels the same awkwardness because her palms pause and she takes a step back.

"Thank you," I say, touching where her hand was before, drying off my own hair as she lowers back down to the couch.

"You looked like a sad puppy," she says with a weak laugh.

But just as quickly as Wendy's smile came, it falls. Her eyebrows pull in as she switches her concentration back to the beanie. It's not just concentration though; it's melancholy beneath that bruise. Something is wrong, and

167

I don't know what to do about it. Maybe it's the ladder situation bringing her down. Or maybe it's something I did.

What if it's something I did?

I cross over to the couch, sitting down opposite her. I open my mouth to talk, but the words aren't coming out how they should. Hell, they're not appearing at all.

In the awkward silence, she pauses sewing again. Her eyes peer up at me through those beautiful lashes.

"What?" she asks.

"What?" I echo.

"You just seem like you want to say something."

"Yeah. Is everything all right?" I ask.

"Why?"

"You just don't seem okay."

"I'm okay."

"Wendy." I steady a look at her, and she lifts her eyebrows in return, trying to give a smile, but it's not one that displays the little dip beside her lips, so I tilt my chin down. "Talk."

She sighs. "I've just got a lot going on in my head. Back to school stuff in a couple of months. The ladder."

"Damn ladder."

She gives a breathy laugh. "Yeah. And I don't know ..."

"Yes?"

Her eyes swivel up to mine at the same time thunder rumbles through the house.

"I'm just ... I'm wondering why I'm even writing this book, y'know?"

"Because you want to."

"Okay." She drags out the word, then adds, "So, I write and then what?"

"I don't know." I hold my palm out and gesture to the

porch behind her with a small stack of wood soaked in rain. "I work on this house and then what?"

"You have a prettier house."

"And you'll have a pretty book to put on your shelf."

Her face falls again, and, God, I hate it. I hate that I don't know what to do. I can handle an upset Sam, but this? This is new. Wendy is bright sunshine with wonder and adventure. I'm not sure what to do with a sad Wendy, but I wish I did.

My eyes flash to the stitching in Sam's beanie. The thread is a darker maroon than the original fabric, but I like the added layer of quirkiness. My eyes catch on a thimble on Wendy's thumb. It's familiar, and I instantly smile in recognition.

"Is that my mom's?" I ask.

Wendy nods. "Yeah. When she taught me how to sew, she also gave me her thimble. Said that I should always think of her when I use it. Like it's some warm hug or something. You know how your mom is. So sentimental."

"She is," I agree, feeling my lips tipping into a knowing smile. "Always knows the right things to say."

"You get that from her."

I freeze, then clear my throat. "Can I see?"

She holds out her thumb with the thimble, and I reach out for it, my fingers sliding over that curved dip between her thumb and forefinger. Her skin is so soft compared to mine. Smooth, as opposed to my calluses and tanned work hands. Wendy is practically an angel. It feels like a sin to touch her.

I lift the thimble off her thumb, absentmindedly rolling it between my fingers as I try to look more interested in that than her. But I'm too distracted by how loud my breathing is. My blood is practically pumping through my ears.

When I hand it back, my hand bumps hers. I didn't realize how close we were sitting. Just like this morning, I see the freckles on her nose, the flush of her cheeks still bright under the bruise, and the thick lashes she bats up at me beneath hooded eyes. Now, I can hear her breaths, too, glimpsing her collarbone rising and falling over her chest.

"You keep looking at me like that," she whispers.

My eyes flick up to meet hers. "Like what?"

"I don't know. Like you've got a lot on your mind."

"I do."

"Sam?"

"Yes. Sam. Work. You."

"Me?"

"I ... yes. You."

Her breath hitches. The room shifts. That unconscious rope between us tightens, and we're both lassoed forward at once.

Suddenly, without thinking, without considering anything, I curl my palm behind her neck and lean toward her, Wendy following, and our mouths meet in the middle.

I'm kissing her.

I suck in a sharp inhale, like a sting of electricity finally touching ground. There's a rumble of thunder, and, God, I feel the clap. I feel it in my chest at the way she presses her lips against mine, opening and closing, hand curling into my shirt, chasing when I pull back, pulling me closer when I push.

My hand dips deeper in her hair, caressing the back of her neck, the ribbon in her hair tickling my hand. My heart is pounding so loud, banging like a reckless drum, sending my breath stammering out in heavy exhales.

I'm kissing her.

At first, it feels like another fantasy, but it's real. Too

real. I could never in my wildest dreams imagine her being this soft. The skin along the column of her neck. The silk of her dress captured in my other fist. The inhalations of her delicate perfume, fresh like cotton or laundry.

Wendy moves forward, her knees knocking against mine. I fall back on the couch with a low, involuntary grunt, grasping her dress, steadying her hips, and trying to find purchase—something to ground me in this moment as she crawls over me. Her slender legs straddle my thighs. My palms mess up her hair. My heart won't stop.

When Wendy kisses, she smiles.

Like kissing me could actually make somebody—*her* —happy.

I'm kissing Wendy.

I'm lightheaded, finding that I'm smiling back. She laughs against my lips. I kiss it away. She chases it with another.

The *something* that sparks through me is wonderful. Exciting.

It's so much.

Too much.

I sit up, holding her hips in place, kissing her over and over, cherishing this entire moment for as many eternities as I can until I set her back onto her side of the couch. Our lips fade with smaller pecks, like echoes of the fervor we once had. And when we finally pull apart, when the storm settles and the rain outside lightens to a small patter on the window, I realize what I've done.

I kissed my brother's ex-fiancée.

I swallow, my palm caressing her cheek and then down to her neck. I expect her to speak first, but she doesn't. She's simply breathing, the remnants of a smile still lingering on her lips. But I can't find the strength in me to return it.

My voice leaves in a low croak. "I should ..." I find my other hand stroking over her dress. I yank my palms back, clearing my throat. "I just ... I'm gonna go check on ..."

"Jas?"

"I should go check on the bed. The headboard, I mean. The ... I'm building a new one."

I'm already standing, running a hand through my already-haphazard hair—ruffled this way and that by her hands.

"Jas, I'm sorry—"

"No," I say, my tone sterner than it should be. "No, that was on me." I swallow. "You can head out when Sam is up."

Her lips, now bee-stung and tinted with pink from the scratches of my beard, tilt down on her once-giddy face.

"Oh, sure," she murmurs, sliding down on the cushion. "Okay."

I walk out of the living room without looking back. Because, if I do, if I see those beautiful eyes staring back, I might kiss her again. And if she looks half as guilty as I feel, then that will mean it's real.

That I really did kiss Peter's Wendy. And that makes me a terrible brother.

Chapter 20

Who Needs to Talk Anyway?

Wendy

I KISSED JASPER.

No, he kissed me.

Actually, I climbed that man like a tree.

If there was a word beyond *mortified*, I'd be right next to the definition in the dictionary.

Jasper's been avoiding me all week, offering a stiff wave when he comes home and immediately escaping to a different room to build something or, I guess, do anything that doesn't include me.

I want to talk about it. I like Jasper. I miss his subtle humor and rare smiles. I almost stopped him mid-stride on Friday evening just so I could shake him by the shoulders and say, *Hey, grumpy dude! It's fine! We can forget it!*

Except I didn't.

And now that it's the weekend, I'm sitting on my kitchen counter, crunching on a sunny-afternoon snack and wondering just how long we can go without discussing it.

Food helps me think, and I've needed a lot of brain power to process this.

I know our kiss was wrong. Twisted.

But when his lips touched mine, I wasn't thinking about him being my ex's older brother. I was thinking about it being *Jasper*. His coarse hands gripping my dress. His beard warm against my cheeks. That little rasping groan that left his throat when I crawled over him.

It's not just how hot he is though—which he totally is, holy *God*; it's how he makes me feel. How my blood boils over when he looks at me with a pointed, assured stare through almost-haunted eyes. How he's always asking about my writing, like maybe it actually matters regardless of my goals and ambitions. Just that writing the book is enough. Like maybe I'm enough too.

His clamshell exterior cracks open bit by bit as each week passes, and I like the pearl underneath. I don't want to lose the ability to admire its beauty. Because, if I'm being honest with myself, I really, truly like the eldest Davies brother.

No, he's my boss. Though we're way past that, aren't we? I'm at every family dinner.

Maybe our kiss will fade with time in a weird, impulsive, stormy-weather mistake. I'll forget an earth-shattering kiss if it means I won't lose him as a friend.

BZZT!

I still, pausing with my pickle halfway to my mouth. I have no idea what that—

Wait, is that a doorbell? I have a doorbell?

The usual visitors waltz on in. Even Starkey gives a single knock before automatically resorting to using his key —it is his property after all. So, why would any of the

Davies brothers use a doorbell when they can just waltz on in?

I snort at the thought, hopping off the counter, shoving the rest of the pickle into my mouth, and walk over to the door. I peer through the peephole and *HOLY*—

My pickle goes down the wrong pipe. I shove my fist against my chest. Coughing. Gagging. Finally, it squeaks its way down, but the strained lump in my heart and pounding through my veins doesn't lighten up.

Maybe it's because I almost died.

Or maybe it's because Jasper freaking Davies is standing on my front porch.

The doorbell buzzes again at the same time I rip open the door.

There he is, decked out in a plain white T-shirt that hugs his biceps far too well, and his hands—the same hands gripping my dress earlier this week—hold a plastic grocery bag, slacking with the weight of its items inside.

"Hi," I breathe.

"Hey," he says back, less out of breath than I am. Then again, he didn't just choke.

"Hi, Wendy!" Sam calls.

I barely noticed him waiting behind Jasper's legs, Roger by his side on a leash. Sam swats a bee buzzing near his face. The bee follows him, so he runs past me and into my house, Roger trailing behind.

Jasper sighs, then gives the smallest twitch of his lips. It could be a smile, or it could just be adoration for his son. I don't know which is more devastatingly attractive.

"Can we come in?"

"Oh, sure," I say, stepping aside. "Of course."

I shut the door behind him, the snick echoing through the house, along with Roger's clicking nails on hardwood and the sound of my playlist still thrumming from my laptop on the kitchen counter.

Jasper twists, the bag rustling with the movement. He pokes a thumb into blank air. "Cat Stevens?"

I nod. "Yeah."

"Good choice."

I smile, winding my hands together, feeling like a teenager with a schoolgirl crush all over again. I like that the cool, older boy likes my music.

I'm not normally this awkward, but I can feel Jasper's lurking energy from here, radiating in waves of sea salt and cinnamon.

Sam climbs onto one of my barstools and gasps. "Ooh, pickles!"

"Ask Wendy if you can have one first, bud."

"Wendy, can I have a pickle?"

I wave my hand. "All yours."

There's a wet splashing as Sam digs into the jar, then just the crunching of the pickle between his teeth. Roger waits attentively nearby, likely hoping for a dropping of any kind.

Meanwhile, Jasper's intense stare is locked on me, searching my eyes. His unspoken words as loud as they've ever been.

I glance down to the keys rattling on his belt loop and the diamond key chain still dangling beside them.

I pop my lips. "Sorry, why are—"

"Sorry, yes." Jasper lifts his plastic bag. I finally recognize the logo of Jake's Hardware on the side with the hammer and wrench. "I'm here to fix your ladder."

I blink. "You're ... what?"

"You said your ladder was broken. I wanted to take a look."

"You did?"

At that, his lips pull up into a lopsided smile, and heat rises up my neck. I'm starting to believe Jasper saves his smiles for when they'll be the most effective at melting my heart.

"Can I?" he asks.

I nod in agreement, unable to form words. Instead, I power-walk past him, ignoring the warmth of his body when we're too close. The linen curtains surrounding my open window blow in the summer breeze. My pillow cushions are askew because I spent all last night bingeing the final book in a fantasy series—definitely *not* featuring hot pirates. There's a speck of popcorn on the carpet I must have overlooked that now seems so messy and obvious.

Behind me, I hear a, "Stay in here, bud, and use a paper towel, okay? We'll be back."

I snatch the popcorn kernel and tuck it into my dress pocket.

"Aye, aye, Captain!" Sam calls.

Jasper rounds the corner with a raise of his eyebrows. I point at the ladder and toward the bottom rung, pathetically dangling down.

He nods, getting down to one knee as he digs into the plastic bag. Even when he's in that position, it's hard not to turn my head and admire him. His legs, clad in jeans that are rolled up over thick work boots. His forearm with that fishing hook tattoo. The deft hands with veins trailing under his skin. The slash of the scar I still know nothing about.

Jasper pulls out something that looks like maybe wood glue or normal glue—heck if I know—then grabs my ladder. It's somehow rough yet gentle. Confident but caring.

I blink and turn away.

I've gotta calm down.

"I like your wall of books," Jasper compliments, breaking the silence. "I should build something like this in my home."

This isn't helping. The knowledge that Jasper can just *build* something simply because he desires it is a whole new level of attractiveness.

"It's why I fell in love with the house," I say. "Well, and the fact that it was the first house I looked at. And the only one I could afford." *Sort of.* "But I think I would have gotten it anyway."

"I don't see a TV," he says. "Do you only read?"

"Well, I have my tablet for shows if I want one. But normally, yeah. Just reading."

His lips twitch up. "I like that. Seems peaceful."

I smile with him. "It is. Though, sometimes, Milo comes over and has reading dates with me. Then, there's a lot of discussion and—"

Jasper lifts a single eyebrow at me.

I grin. "Not an actual date."

He nods, then goes back to work, but his shoulders still look tense. It sends a thrill through me even if it might be short-lived.

I reach out and tap the toe of his boot with my sneaker. "Hey."

He keeps his hands on the ladder rung but turns his head to watch my foot against his. His eyes swivel up to me.

"Hey," he responds.

"Are we gonna talk about earlier this week or ..."

He huffs out a breath before saying, "I'm sorry."

I laugh, waving a hand at him. "You do *not* have to apologize."

"I do. It was unprofessional."

"I'm friends with your family." I squint. "I think we're a little past strictly boss and employee."

He nods in agreement. "Fine. Then, it was crossing a line."

"I didn't mind."

"My brother is—"

My heart twists and catches in my throat as I quickly interrupt, "Let's not talk about Peter, okay?"

Jasper's eyes are planted on me, rooting me to the spot, sending my mind whirling and spinning until I'm light-headed. Until I want to melt to the ground.

"But he is a factor," Jasper whispers.

Peter was once my entire world. He was the star in the sky I flew toward, which kept me feeling alive and young and adventurous. But that all disappeared when he flirted with other women—when he decided I wasn't enough. It seems unfair that—even though I called off the wedding, even though I made the decision that was right for the both of us—he's still a ghost that haunts my life.

I shouldn't have kissed Peter's brother, but I did. Jasper shouldn't be here in my living room, performing such a domestic task, but he is. I shouldn't want him so bad that my fingers are twitching to reach out to him, but they are. And I do.

"I think it's a little too late to worry about that," I whisper back.

Jasper's unmoving, except for his throat bobbing, and I wonder for a second if I crossed a line. Maybe even the insinuation of interrupting the careful dynamic the Davies family holds is enough to write me off.

"Can we please talk?" I ask, my voice almost a whining desperation. "I don't want things to be awkward and weird.

I like to think we're friends now at least. I like spending time with you, Jasper."

He blinks slowly, as if confused. "I like spending time with you too."

A slow smile rises on my face, and I try to remain calm under the heartbeat stumbling in my chest at that admission.

"Really?" I ask.

Jasper steadily rises to both feet, towering over me. His boots knock the ground as he walks forward. He's never been this close, this domineering, this intense, so much so that I walk backward. My back hits the bookshelves. His forearm lands beside my head, caging me in.

The room is electric. My heart is sparking, sending flames tunneling down my spine.

My back arches into him as he pulls in a sharp inhale, and when he lets it out, his head dips beside mine. His breath is warm against my neck. His black hair falls in strands against my cheek. Goose bumps roll over him, starting mine like a domino effect.

"Yes," he answers quietly, his eyebrows pulled in, as if he's in pain.

"And the other thing?"

"What other thing?"

I trace my index finger over his shoulder. "Well, I think I like kissing you too, Jas."

He lets out a heavy exhale. "Don't say that."

"I'm sorry—"

"Don't say that because I'll do it again." His nose trails over my cheek. "I want to do that and more."

I swallow. "What kind of more?"

"Terrible kinds of more."

His beard brushes down my neck, sending nerves skittering down to my elbow and hand, which I use to reach out and coast over his tightened stomach to clutch a fistful of his shirt. Our bodies knock into each other. My breasts shift against the fabric of my dress, catching on his shirt and hard chest.

"Sometimes, I can't breathe around you," he murmurs.

Jasper's lips purse against my neck, and I exhale a breath in tandem.

Every ounce of his kiss—the softness, the intensity, the care—seeps into me.

"This isn't exactly *talking*," I jokingly whisper.

His gravelly voice returns. "I've never been great at that."

"Who needs to talk anyway?"

I close my eyes as he places a second kiss against my collarbone.

But then I hear crunching in the leaves outside my window.

I push Jasper away from me in an instant, and his eyebrows tilt inward as he scans my face for what feels like forever. But I know it's only a moment in an eternity I wish we had because after that one stellar second, my head jerks to the window.

And as I expected, a familiar, grinning face pokes through.

"Oh. Hey, Jasper."

Peter.

Chapter 21

In·tox·i·cated

Jasper

Shit.

Peter climbs through Wendy's window like it's second nature, like this is his own house. And he's looking at us without a care in the world.

How often is he here?

"What are you doing here?" he asks me, plopping into an armchair, thighs spread like a king on a throne, green eyes dancing between me and Wendy.

He doesn't appear even remotely threatened by me even though my lips were just against his ex-fiancée's neck. Even though, seconds ago, I was breathing in her linen smell, indulging in her soft skin once more.

But she pushed me away just in time.

"I'm fixing Wendy's ladder," I explain, kicking my boot against the fixed rung.

Wendy tucks a strand of her hair behind her ear, looking at the ground, at the ladder, then back to Peter. Her bruise has nearly faded to a muddle of green and yellow, but she still has that natural blush that makes her appear so endearing. But I know Wendy Darling a bit more now. I haven't forgotten how quickly she crawled on top of me. There's so much more to this innocent teacher than meets the eye.

My stomach drops at the memory, and my eyes flick over to Peter, none the wiser.

I'm betraying my brother with these thoughts even if it's not crossing his mind. If it were, he'd be able to look at Wendy's flushed cheeks and draw conclusions. But it's so far out of his realm of possibility that even the obvious signs don't register.

Because why would his older brother chase his ex?

Because why would his Wendy fall for lonely Jasper?

"I couldn't reach my top shelf anymore," Wendy says.

"Oh no, you'd have to read the thousands of books on your other shelves," Peter teases.

Wendy tilts her head with a smile and rolls her eyes. "Hilarious."

Peter continues to grin back, eyebrows rising in a playful challenge. And Wendy smiles even wider.

I didn't think my stomach could twist tighter, but it's now in a death grip. I don't like that he jokes about her books, as if they're frivolous to him. But more than that, I don't like how she allows it to happen.

I've never considered whether Wendy still has feelings for Peter. Why wouldn't she? She might have broken off their engagement, but just because she did it out of necessity—out of her own self-preservation, which I respect—that doesn't mean the feelings wouldn't linger.

I wonder if I stepped into a situation rigged from the start.

"Jasper came over to play handyman," Wendy explains.

183

Peter points between the two of us, squinting. "Why does this feel like the plot to a porn—oh, hey, Sam!"

Peter holds his arms out while Sam sprints across the room and barrels into his uncle's chest.

He takes Sam's hands and sniffs them. "Your fingers smell like pickles, little man."

"I ate the whole jar!"

"The *whole jar*?" Wendy and I say in unison. Our eyes dart to each other, then break.

I run my palm over my beard. "We're gonna have a rough night."

"Well, that'll be Mom's problem," Peter says as Roger runs into the room, snuggling his big head into the armchair's cushion, next to Peter.

"Mom's problem?" I ask.

Sam's eyes widen. "I'm going to Grandma's?"

"It's summer solstice!" Peter says, hands flying in the air. The motion has Roger barking.

"Summer soul-sis!" Sam joins in.

I shake my head with closed eyes, trying to process. "Okay, and what does that mean?"

"I don't know," Peter says with a shrug, picking at a piece of lint on Sam's beanie. "It's just something Lulu is excited about, so I figured, why not make it a party?"

Peter doesn't need any excuse to throw a celebration. I could have said I stapled together a bunch of papers, and he'd toss some confetti at the office supplies for doing such a great job.

"It's Saturday," he continues when neither Wendy nor I respond to his supposedly brilliant idea. "It's the middle of summer. Who doesn't want a party?"

"I'm not the partying type," I say.

"Well, I know that," he responds with a scoff. "But I'm

still gonna try and get you out. I only came over to invite Wendy, but your house was next."

"Probably not for me, Pete."

"Oh, come on," Peter says, his eyebrows furrowing inward. "You're always cooped up in that cottage. Come and party with the cool kids. Wendy, tell him we need him there."

Wendy and I exchange another stolen glance. Just moments ago, she was pressed against me, and now, it's like we're simply family friends again instead of something more.

She swallows, her lips parting as she softly mutters, "We need you there. Come on, Jasper."

But if we were still only family friends, that plea would have done me in.

I clear my throat. "Fine. Sure. I'll go."

Peter bites his bottom lip and pumps a silent fist into the air.

"Perfect! You can keep us from making dumb decisions while we're—" His palms cover Sam's ears as he mouths the syllables to the word *in-tox-i-cated.*

Wendy giggles. "What, like we're gonna dive off Deadman's Drop?"

Peter snaps his fingers. "Now, there's an idea."

"No," I say at the same time Wendy laughs.

Peter slaps his knee, like we're ending court and his word is law. "See? Tonight'll be fun." His playful smile turns to Sam. "Grandma time?"

Sam bounces on his feet. "Yay!"

I sigh. "Does she know you've saddled her with babysitting duties?"

"Oh, please, she won't care."

Something tells me I'm gonna hate how right he is.

Something also tells me I shouldn't have accepted this invitation. But one look at Wendy's nervous smile confirms that I can't seem to say no to her anymore, and I'm not sure what to do about that.

⌡

I RELUCTANTLY DRIVE AWAY from my mom's house four hours later, Sam waving from the front bay window.

Peter was right, as usual. My mom instantly clutched Sam against her without a second thought, swinging him back and forth. Matching pajamas were set aside by the time we got there, and Dad had cookies in the oven.

Which means I'm headed to The Hideaway.

Part restaurant, part tiki bar, The Hideaway is a local escape. It's such a staple in Never Harbor that it's one of the few restaurants that doesn't strictly rely on tourist money even though the savvy tourists always scope it out. But the locals support it mostly on their own—enough so that Peter has enough capital to close it for his own personal parties, which range from Fourth of July celebrations to Thanksgiving for those without families to *I got all the red lights this week, and now, I'm sad; let's party.*

My truck rumbles between the aisle of willow trees, wilting over the road like curtains. Further down, music already thrums from the crooked wooden building, towering three stories tall. Edison lights are strung on trees. The interior glows with soft light.

I park farther down the road. I'm late, and cars are already lined up and down the drive.

You'd think everyone in town regularly celebrates summer solstice because the entirety of Never Harbor is inside. Jake sits at the bar with his wife, Steve's bike is propped against a table as he's on who knows which number lobster roll, and even Laura is poised at the bar. I'm pretty sure she only leaves the community center to have bottomless mimosas.

Unsurprisingly, I also spot Bobbi Mullins, Charles Starkey, and Will Jukes, owner of Jukes's Jambalaya, sitting at their usual corner table, drinking some specialty drink with umbrellas in it. I don't know the last time I stopped by The Hideaway, but even I know they're regulars. Inseparable, the three perform as pirates on Main a couple of nights a week. I joined them one time at the request of Starkey, but I won't do so again, preferring not to stumble home at four in the morning ever again.

I hold up my hand in a wave, and Starkey's eyes widen as he waves back.

"Wow, Captain, look at you! Out and about."

As I journey farther in, similar expressions follow me for the next five minutes.

"Jasper freaking Davies! No way! Sam all right?"

"Jas! What a sight. You doing good? Little man okay?"

I say the same lines over and over. "Good," and, "Doing fine."

I survive small talk with a forced smile, giving a polite nod and averting my gaze when someone else's eyes catch mine before they can flag me down.

Izzy sneaks me a double whiskey, neat, and gestures toward the creaking wooden stairs leading to the third floor. The second step from the top creaks louder than the rest, so I give it an extra press with my boot to double-check it, and then I make a mental note to fix that for Peter later.

It's quieter at the rooftop bar. Cassidy is chatting with Peter, leaning his forearms on the counter as Peter zips behind the bar, slinging drinks and likely being too generous with the alcohol content. Izzy ascends the steps behind me with some tattooed guy I vaguely recognize. Bonnie and Lulu are chatting with Milo at a high-top in the corner.

My brow furrows as I walk over.

"Jas!" Bonnie's hands are raised in the air, a yellow drink swirling in the tumbler lightly held by her fingertips. Pinkie up.

"Mom seriously let you come here?" I ask.

"Okay, narc," she sneers.

"Are you drunk?"

"No, Pete gave me stupid lemonade." She rolls her eyes. "You guys are too protective."

"Happy solstice!" Lulu woos, raising her drink.

I raise my whiskey in response, and Bonnie joins her best friend in some *woo*-fest.

The two of them are opposite sides of the same coin. Sarcastic yet giggly, gossiping and having one too many nail polish parties at my house while I'm at work. But while Bonnie consistently wears black, Lulu buys colors—pinks or greens or whites. Bonnie blasts rock in her headphones while Lulu prefers pop music in her convertible.

Opposites attract, I suppose.

"Having fun?" Lulu asks, bouncing on the balls of her feet and tossing her long black hair over her shoulder.

"Sure," I answer.

She continues to look at Milo expectantly, who gives her a half smile in return.

"Of course, Lu," he finally answers.

Her eyes scan him from the top of his head down to his sweater with the rolled-up sleeves. Lulu must not be satisfied with his response because her bright purple-painted lips twist to the side.

"What book are you reading today, Milo?"

He digs in his back pocket before displaying a decrepit copy of some novel I've never heard of.

"I've read that one," she says.

"And did you like it?"

"Loved it," she says with a grin.

Her confidence makes me wonder if she actually did. And if she didn't, why would she say she did?

"So, are you gonna dance?"

My brother chuffs out a laugh with a smile, pocketing his book back. "I don't think so."

She rests her forearms on the high-top, leaning forward and closer to him. "But what if I insist?"

He chuckles. "Lu, you know I'm not going to."

Her giddy face melts into a scowl.

"Fine. Hey, Bonnie, let's go dance."

"Hmm? Oh. Okay," Bonnie says, breaking her eyes from Izzy and her tattooed friend, who Bonnie was shamelessly staring at.

Lulu grabs Bonnie's hand and drags her downstairs to the dance floor.

I pull in a breath and let it out.

I glance around in the silence, eyeing Cassidy laughing with his head tipped back. Peter grinning ear to ear as he shakes a drink. Izzy talking to the tattooed guy, who is now lighting a cigarette. Everyone is in their own world, having fun, and I'm tapping my thumb on the top of the pub table.

I know who I'm ultimately searching for.

I want to know if Wendy is already here.

Milo nudges my elbow with his. "You look so uncomfortable," he observes.

"I'm ... managing," I say, struggling with the word and taking a large swig of my whiskey.

He laughs.

I suck in air through my teeth and place my glass down, winding it in the cool condensation, surrounded by the ghostly rings of previous drinkers.

"What are you doing here?" I ask. "Aren't you normally … I don't know … reading?" I gesture to his pocket.

He smiles. "If you're looking for quiet-brother solidarity, you're on your own. I bring backup options," he says, gesturing to his book. "But I still know how to have fun."

"Sounds awful," I deadpan, which has him laughing again.

"Nah," he says, leaning his forearms on the table. "I like the people-watching aspect. Where else can you see Starkey with an umbrella in his drink?"

"That Charles."

"Love the guy." We take another simultaneous sip, scanning the crowd. "You should get out more, Jas. We miss you."

"I'm busy," I say, shuffling my feet. "I've got Sam and stuff."

"So, what got you out tonight?"

Wendy.

If it wasn't for her, I wouldn't be here. I like the quiet of my cottage. I like the peaceful waves rather than drinks and loud music. But I also can't stay away from the woman with the ribbons in her hair. It isn't the alcohol that will end me; it's her intoxicating presence, poisoning my soul from the inside out.

"Uh, just figured, why not, y'know?" I answer.

"Right. Well"—Milo claps my back—"come on. Let's give Peter an excuse to get you drunk."

I sigh. "Fantastic."

Chapter 22

Pink Drink

Wendy

I'M FORCED to park at the end of the lane by the time I arrive at The Hideaway. I hate arriving at these things on time. Maybe years ago, I would have been first through the doors, but now, I don't trust myself to not have one too many pink drinks. It always ends with me cuddling the closest person near me or nodding along to the story of a blurry woman in the restroom and agreeing, "Yes, if you want to foster a fifth cat, you do it."

When I walk through the propped-open double-door threshold, marked in knotted wood and faded stain, I get a lot of comments on my bruise and how well it's clearing up. And definitely a lot of *you should see the other guys*, which is par for the course, especially for my landlord, Starkey.

"I'll stop by to fix the ladder," he decides, holding up his umbrella drink.

"I'm great with wood too," Bobbi offers.

Jukes puts his meaty palm to the side of his mouth, swaying as he murmurs, "You should see her with—"

"William Jukes, don't you dare finish that thought," Bobbi interjects, slapping him on his thick, hairy arm.

The three of them chortle with laughter.

"I've got it covered actually," I say, leaning back on my heels with a nod. "Jas stopped by to help."

I don't miss the halted look that passes between the three of them—like the heckling Muppets, stunned before breaking into a bit—so I quickly shuffle off before they can draw more conclusions.

Small towns talk, but the Pirate Trio talks more.

I grab a soda water with lime just to start the night off on a more optimistic foot, throwing a wave at Bonnie and Lulu on an active dance floor they probably started and climbing the stairwell to the top floor.

Like a zip of lightning in my soul, I instantly know Jasper is already here. Maybe it's the shift in temperature through my veins or the smell of sea salt in the air—likely just Crocodile Cove below—but I feel it, and I find him just as quickly.

Jasper is perched on a barstool, leaning forward with his arms on the bar top, hand wrapped around a glass and locked in conversation with Milo, Cassidy, and Peter. His boots are hooked onto the rung beneath him, his thighs stretching the fabric of his jeans, his tanned cheeks tinged with red from alcohol.

It always amazes me how well all the brothers work together, moving like a school of fish through rapid waves.

Peter is leading the charge, as usual, hands waving in the air as he likely recounts some over-the-top tale. Cassidy laughs at the punch line. Milo chuckles into his drink, getting a push from Cassidy, who still has his head leaned back. But then there's Jasper, listening attentively, face neutral, the small twitch of his lips still indicating that he is having fun. It's a subtlety I didn't notice before, but after half the summer has gone by, I can finally recognize his tells. And when Cassidy cracks a joke and the other two laugh, Jasper's twitch progresses into a full-on grin.

Maybe I'm staring at his gorgeous smile too long—teeth white and lines defined beside his eyes—but Jasper's head turns to find me. His mouth tilts up into a gentler smile, eyes crinkling at the corners. He gives the smallest of waves, and I return it.

Jasper's cute when he's a little tipsy.

The room feels like it narrows around us—all the ancillary string lights, high-tops, and booths blurring until it's just him on one side and me on the other. And the longer we stare, the more his face slowly starts to fall. It settles until his eyes are no longer lined with laughter. Until his eyebrows furrow in the center. Until he goes from cute to downright feral.

My stomach flips, and I lick my lips, my mouth suddenly dry.

"Wendy, come over here!" Peter calls. "Get yourself a pink drink!"

I snap back, puff out my chest to get some courage, and join them.

"Pink drink, pink drink," Cassidy repeats, his fist hitting the counter.

"Nah-ah-ah," I say playfully. "I'm taking it slow tonight. At least with your bad influence around."

I slide onto the only available stool—coincidentally the one next to Jasper and his gorgeous thighs. And once I settle in, his legs widen just a bit to rub one against the outside of my bare one. My body heats.

"Suit yourself," Peter says, knocking back a pink concoction of his own.

I wonder which number he's on.

"What's a pink drink?" Jasper murmurs beside me.

His breath has a bite of whiskey, and I wish I could lick it off his lips.

"Look at Jas," Cassidy says with a chortle. "Wondering what a pink drink is."

Jasper snorts and takes another swig of his drink, but doesn't reply.

"You'd know if you came out more, buddy," Peter says, leaning his torso over the bar to clap Jasper on the back. "It's Wendy's favorite drink."

"With consequences," Cassidy says with a barking laugh.

I squint and point a finger at him in warning.

"See?" Milo says. "Don't you miss this fun?"

"Yeah," Peter agrees. "I'll even let you drink on the house."

Cassidy's eyebrows furrow inward. "Hey, you don't let me do that."

"Yeah, 'cause you'd drink my bar dry," Peter replies, knocking back another shot—this time a green liquid. But then his eyes catch on something across the patio.

"Oh, Christ, hang on a sec," he murmurs.

Quickly, he winds around the bar. All our eyes follow him as he strides over to a couple in the corner. A woman is sliding away from the guy next to her as his arm sneaks closer to her shoulder.

Peter stands tall, towering over them as his jaw tics back and forth. I can't hear the words exchanged, but when the man tries to stand, Peter's palm rests on the man's chest, pausing him in place. He tries to puff it out, but it looks ridiculous. Peter's too tall. Too confident. Too domineering.

After a few more moments, the man is escorted out by

one of the bartenders, and Peter holds out his palm toward the woman, checking if she's okay. She bites her lower lip and nods graciously. I know that look. It's another person captured by Peter.

Peter's a protector. Anyone who steps through his restaurant doors is automatically his responsibility. Sometimes, I wish he could have been more responsible when it came to me. Sometimes, I wish the look on that woman's face didn't have him automatically grinning back.

But for once, his flirtatious behavior doesn't hurt me as much as it normally does. Not when Jasper's thigh presses against mine.

I turn back to the bar top, where Peter eventually rounds back with a sigh.

"Got it handled?" Milo asks.

Peter nods, shaking his head and blinking back. "Yeah. What were we talking about?"

"Jasper," Cassidy says.

"Oh. Right." He's distracted now but still trying to keep up the mood. Very typical Peter. He tips his chin toward Jasper again. "So, what's holding you back from coming here?"

"Well, men like that might be one reason," I joke.

"I don't put up with that shit," Peter says, and I can feel the irritation coming off him in waves. "Jas, seriously."

Cassidy rolls his eyes with a smile, but I watch Jasper clutch his drink tighter, jaw shifting as his eyes bore through Peter's.

My urge to learn Jasper's secrets is not nearly as important as my urge to protect them.

"We don't have to—" I start, but Peter interrupts.

"It's Jessica, isn't it?"

My body freezes. Jasper shifts uncomfortably in his seat.

"After Jessica, you stopped coming out," Peter continues. He scratches his head, ruffling the dirty-blond locks before leaning forward. "You stopped doing much of anything with us."

I suddenly feel like this is a conversation I shouldn't be a part of. Even Milo and Cassidy are looking anywhere that isn't here.

"I mean, I'm not imagining that, am I?" Peter asks, glancing at our awkward party before leveling a look at Jasper again. "We were close once, weren't we?"

Jasper clears his throat and nods. "We were, Pete. We are."

"No, we're not. I miss you, man. I miss your kid. I miss pretending I like whiskey when I don't, just so you'll drink here."

Jasper chuffs out a small chuckle before shaking his head. "Jessica was perfectly—"

"Perfectly not great," Peter finishes with a playful grin. "She made you feel awful, and you don't deserve that. You deserve someone good. Kind. Someone like …" Then he points to me, and my heart leaps into my throat. "Someone like our Wendy here. But obviously, *not* Wendy," he adds with a laugh.

My stomach churns. The side of Jasper's hand bumps against mine under the bar. His pinkie brushes along the outside, sinking into the dip between my fingers. Our hands hook for a brief moment before breaking away.

Jasper's tipsy smile has disappeared. He's nodding to himself, licking along his teeth, taking another drink of whiskey.

"Loving the sentimentality, guys." Jasper sniffs. "Now, can we move on?"

There's an uncomfortable silence between the five of us. A moment where my body feels twitchy and uneasy.

Peter reaches out his hand, covering the back of Jasper's scarred one with his palm as he grins. "Y'know, that sounds like an awfully big adventure, Jas."

There's a burst of laughter, breaking the tension. Guffaws and swigs of drinks and slapping each other on the back ensue. Cassidy demands another round for all of them. Peter obliges with a grin.

I love when the boys get together. I love how much they love each other. And I love how much family means to each of them.

But when I glance at Jasper, he's simply sitting there, swirling his drink in silence.

I STAND near the railing on the third floor, looking out at the darkened depths of Crocodile Cove, listening to the waves splash against the rocky shore. The sun has gone down, and The Hideaway's orange illumination makes it hard to see past the cliff's edge. It makes the water seem endless. I sip on a pink drink even though I know I shouldn't, but there're a lot of things I know I shouldn't do, and if I can't have one vice, I at least deserve another.

I feel him before I see him.

"Hey," Jasper murmurs.

A tickle slides over my neck and across my shoulders.

"Hi."

"So, pink drink, huh?"

I grin and hold it up to him. "Cheers."

He leans his forearms on the railing, clinking his glass against mine, the straw in my drink swiveling toward his.

"You're not gonna dance?" I ask.

"Should I?"

"You probably have some moves."

"No, absolutely none. I'm not good in front of crowds."

"That checks out."

"Though, one time, Peter put on a talent show for our family when we were kids. I was a magician."

"You know magic?"

He shrugs, and it almost seems embarrassed. "Secret talent."

"Let me guess ... pulling a rabbit out of a hat?"

"Coin tricks."

"Oh, please. Not this with the coins again."

He reaches behind my ear, and I gasp until he pulls his hand back to reveal a quarter.

I can't help the laugh that busts out of me. "A man of many secrets."

"Too many," he says with a half smile.

It's quiet, just the music from two stories down thrumming through the floor and the low hum of conversation behind us. But here, it's just us. And my slightly tipsy words are bubbling to the surface.

"I'm sorry they brought up Jessica."

"Eh," Jasper says, tilting his head to the side. "Pete's gonna do whatever he wants. He's always been that way."

"I know."

An errant wind whips through Jasper's hair, rustling the strands. Even though his face is in shadow, directed away from the light, I can still spot the embarrassed pink tips of his ears.

"So ..." he murmurs. "About him ..."

My stomach drops because I knew this conversation was coming. It's impossible to watch the Davies family interact and want anything less than perfect for them. Even though Jasper isolates himself, it's obvious they're all close, like some bond that can never be broken once you inherit the name. And as much as I crave it, I don't belong in that group, and I definitely refuse to disturb it. I should have prepared for this, but prepared or not, it doesn't change the outcome.

"I know," I interrupt.

Jasper's eyebrows furrow together. "You ... know? Know what?"

"That we can't do whatever this is. Pete's your brother. I know that you love him and you don't want to hurt him."

His lips part before he takes another sip of his drink, then lowers it back down, nodding to himself. I get the feeling he wants to say something, but he won't, so I say it for him.

"It's okay," I say. "Really. I get it. Family is important."

He clears his throat, shifting the drink from hand to hand.

"I ... well, if this is what you want," he says. "We can just be friends."

"Isn't it what you want?" I ask.

He exhales. "What I want," he muses, letting out a small, sardonic laugh. "You are ..."

But he can't find the words, and I don't mind because the fading sentence says more than either of us ever could.

He shakes his head. "God, you're like my star in the sky, Wendy."

"Your star?"

"My North Star. Always showing me the direction I should travel. I've never met someone like you before."

"Is that ... good?"

"Yes," he replies. "It's very, very good." He chuckles. "But it's also terrifically unfair."

I laugh with him, but I understand what he means.

I know Jasper and I can't be together. The amount of strife that would cause the Davies family would be unimaginable. I can picture it now—a family dinner with perfectly happy people, and then Peter throws a spoon at Jasper's head, and we're scrambling to hold them both back.

Or maybe I'm just being dramatic.

I can't hurt Jasper like that regardless. Or Peter.

But see ... that's where the cogs in my mind start to rotate in different directions, prompting my thoughts to break down.

Peter made his choice, didn't he?

Peter, of his own accord, decided to flirt with another woman while I wore his ring on my finger.

Peter Davies, in all his cleverness, didn't think past the here and now and his own charm.

So, it feels so unfair that the first person I've wanted since Peter, the first person who has made me feel like I matter, is his brother—a person who would do anything for Pete.

Jasper is off-limits, and he's also correct; it is terrifically unfair. But life never agreed to bend to my will.

I lean in, our shoulders brushing as I do, his T-shirt rough against my bare skin. Jasper doesn't move an inch as his eyes swivel to me, and he tilts his head to the side. The tips of his fingers find mine, ghosting over my knuckles before pulling away.

"Just friends?" I ask.

With a final pull of breath, Jasper trails his eyes from my chin down to my lips and back up. For a moment, I think he leans in, and my eyes flutter closed, only to open and see he's pulled away, making me feel more exposed than I ever have.

"Sure," he echoes. "Just friends."

He shakes his head and walks away, and I stand there, frozen, wishing for more.

Chapter 23

This Woman, I Swear

Jasper

THE ONE WOMAN I WANT, Peter got to first.

I hammer another nail into the wood, and splinters explode from the impact. I hurl the board to the side and bury my head in my hands.

What's happening to me?

What's happened?

My brothers were right.

Jessica wasn't perfect. She drew attention to who I actually was. Who my best friends needed me to be for their son. Where I was lacking. I thought she was only trying to make me a better guardian. A better father figure for Sam.

Wasn't she?

But then came Wendy, and she proved what a real partner could be. Kind. Caring. And too generous with her heart—so generous that she knew us being together would crack my family in two. She sacrificed herself for us because she's just that kind of woman.

"I surrender," a tentative, low voice says from around the corner.

I look up to see Cassidy with his hands held high, glancing from me to the destroyed plank.

"Hey," I say, running a palm over my beard, stretching out my mouth, feeling my jaw unclench. "What are you doing all the way out here?"

"Thought I'd ask the house expert about houses," he says, crossing over the deposited tools and array of spare wood.

I've been expanding my porch, trying to make it a wrap-around with a back door gate into the garden. With all the recent rain, I haven't had time to dive in as much as I'd like, so I'm taking advantage of the sunshine.

If I could focus on anything but Wendy for more than two seconds.

"But maybe I went to the wrong person," Cassidy continues. "You seem more keen on demolition."

"It's just a porch reno. It'll figure itself out." I squint at the sun before running a hand through my hair. "So, why do you wanna know about houses?"

"Moving out."

"Oh, yeah?"

"Figured it was time." He throws a thumb over his shoulder. "Where are Wendy and Sam?"

I try to overcome the pounding in my chest at her name. It's been a couple of days since The Hideaway's solstice party or whatever the hell that was. We've been circling each other, saying nothing yet everything as we pass. It feels like the early days of her nannying. The avoidance. The reluctant pull.

I got home earlier than expected today and ran into Wendy and Sam right as they were heading out for groceries. I said I'd hold down the fort. I had no intention of interrupting their schedule.

But when I sidestepped past Wendy, my arms feeling so tight that I could barely breathe, she leaned over to Sam and said, "Captain probably just wants alone time. Let's head out."

Then, she gave me the smallest of smiles and left.

"They're grocery shopping," I answer.

Cassidy nods. "And you're frustrated because ..."

I look around at the stacks of wood. "Building stuff is hard."

He laughs. "No kidding."

"So"—I wipe my hands on my jeans and stand, taking his proffered hand for assistance—"you're looking for a house?"

"Yeah. Figured you could help me see past all the cruddy listings online that claim it's a fixer-upper when it's actually a lost cause with rats for roommates."

We turn the corner toward the front of the house to see Wendy's car rumbling down the lane. Sam's head is sticking out the window, a tiny hand holding the Frankensteined beanie in place. Roger is already barreling toward them.

I whistle so he's out of their way when Wendy parks in her usual spot.

"Well, hi, Cass," she says, Roger barking for Sam to open the door. "What are you doing here?"

Cassidy shrugs. "Manly things. Building tree houses. Watching football. Making *no girls allowed* signs."

Wendy's laugh bursts out of her, making my heart stutter in my chest.

"Hilarious," she jests. "Like you could ever build a tree house on your own."

Cassidy turns back to me, jokingly murmuring, "This

woman, I swear."

This woman *is right*.

I didn't say what I wanted to say at The Hideaway. What I should have said was that I would make a lot of sacrifices to be with her—to the woman who makes me feel alive. But we can't. We both know that.

The moment she pops open the trunk, Cassidy and I descend on the groceries, hooking the bags over our arms and fingers. Sam clutches a half gallon of milk in both his arms, and Cassidy bets he can't carry it all the way to the kitchen. With a squeal, Sam runs up the porch steps as Cassidy chases after him.

Wendy closes the trunk, the sound an echo between us. I finally meet her eyes, sucking in a breath as I take the chance to wander over her. Today, she's in a yellow sundress and white sneakers. There's a slit up the side, exposing part of her thigh, secretly sharing the freckles on her knees. She gives a breathy, nervous laugh, and I awkwardly nod, as if agreeing to a thing she didn't say.

We're careful with each other now. Avoiding conversation, ignoring how magnetized we are. How that rope tightens around my stomach every single day. How it loops me closer and closer to her and how I'm desperate to saw at it with a knife. But every strand I break only stitches back together.

I carry my armful into the house. Sam is already running buck wild, bumping into a side table in the process.

"Inside steps, please," I call out.

I hear his shuffling steps follow suit, along with an, "Aye, aye, Captain!"

Cassidy barks out a hearty laugh as he places cans into the pantry.

"Damn, can I call you Captain too?" he jokes.

"Me three," Wendy chimes in, and her eyebrows rise in a beautifully taunting look.

I try to joke in return by pointing a finger at her. "Watch it."

It comes out more gravelly than I expected. Wendy's back straightens, and I see the dip in the corner of her mouth grow. Her cheeks flush red.

Does she *like* that tone?

I can still picture Jessica's little eye roll when I'd try to flirt. That pitying laugh she'd make when she said I was so terrible at it. She said I needed to focus on Sam and we could attempt flirting later if she was still in the mood, which she never was because why would she be when I was so hopeless at it?

But Wendy didn't look off-put by my comment. Not one bit.

Cassidy's mouth drops, and for a moment, I worry he's seeing the obvious energy between us. The lasso looping me to her tightening its hold once more. But, of course, he doesn't because there's nothing to see. She ended things before it could start, and I don't blame her one bit.

Cassidy's laugh booms from his broad chest as he holds up a hand for Wendy to high five.

"Is this what you two do all day?" he asks. "Play the *piss off Jasper* game?"

She smacks his hand and shrugs. "You're missing out, Cass."

Exactly. That's all we do. Joke around. Like friends.

But, God, I want to touch her more than I've ever wanted to touch another person in my life. I don't think friends want that.

A rumbling storm cloud hovers outside, and I wonder if it can sense the uneasiness in my soul.

Chapter 24

Just Friends

Wendy

NEVER HARBOR IS SHROUDED in rain for days, making the usual summer outdoor adventures impossible.

I'm pretty sure the rain is taunting me. That or it's a personification of my moods, which have felt significantly less happy since the party at The Hideaway.

I try not to think about my situation with Jasper, but it's difficult when he still looks at me like he's in pain, scouring my body, as if it's punishment for the thoughts he's had. Staring, but not touching.

My brain knows we made the right decision. I owe so much to the Davies family. Harming that dynamic would be irresponsible and selfish.

But my heart argues otherwise. It beats for Jasper when he does simple things, like carrying in groceries, or chasing Sam, or when I find a new jar of pickles sitting in the fridge. It beats at the sight of his tortured eyes as I mentally plead that it's not him that's the problem; it's the situation.

The week passes with blurry clouds and dreary rainfall.

Puddles form along the sidewalks on Main, making them difficult to maneuver, even with decent rain boots. The beaches are uncharacteristically empty, the symphony of waves now accompanied by plunks on the rocky shore. Shops, though open for business, feel shuttered as their cute hanging signs drown in droplets.

Sam and I walk down the street in our raincoats, Roger on his leash and covered in a clear plastic jacket of his own, ears flopping through the tiny holes in the hood. I promised Sam we'd go to the library, and after four days inside, I'm seeing to it that we get out even if we get drenched along the way. One more unnecessary breakdown about stepping on a toy, and both of us were going to start a violent pillow fight.

I open one of the library double doors for Sam, taking his coat off, then mine, and then Roger's. I loop his leash around the inside vestibule's bike stand and pat his head.

"Be back in five."

Sam runs to the children's section—*good Lord, please get that energy out*—as I mosey up to the front desk.

I rise to my toes and look at the volunteer on the other side. "Hey, dork."

Milo sits behind the desk with a book folded open. He peers up at me with his head playfully tilted to the side before dog-earing the page and closing it.

"Don't you know dog-earing is generally frowned upon?" I tease.

He lets out a rush of air through his nose, already smiling. Milo's smiles feel genuine. They always reach his eyes.

"I live life on the edge," he counters.

"Hardly."

"Oh, I'm sorry, is walking through the rain edgy now?"

"Well, it could be if I also said we listened to '90s rock on the way."

"And did you?"

"Sure."

"Then, sure. You win."

"Too easy."

He laughs, removing his horn-rimmed glasses and setting them to the side before leaning back in his seat and rubbing his eyes.

"How's Jas and his little pirate?"

I turn around, spotting Sam waddling through the bookshelves, his arms already overflowing with Golden Books and likely a couple of Pete the Cat novels.

"A handful," I answer.

"Jas or Sam?"

"Funny."

"He seemed to be comfortable on Saturday."

A little stutter echoes through my chest, and I twist my head to stare at him. His dark blond eyebrows rise.

Milo is deliberate and practical in every action he takes. He wears reading glasses because it prevents migraines. He volunteers at the library because he believes giving back to the community is what makes our small-town ecosystem work. He reads all genres from nonfiction boat construction to women's fiction because he says that's the only way we learn and grow.

He's very attentive. Too attentive.

"He had a whiskey," I comment. "Of course he was comfortable."

Milo nods with his bottom lip poked out. "Oh, okay."

"What?"

"I didn't say anything."

I shift on the spot, feeling the unease of the unsaid.

"Don't be shy," I coax.

He lets out an exhale, leaning back in his chair and

209

crossing an ankle over his opposite knee. "It just seems like you two are really getting along. It's good for him."

I smile, playing it off with a shrug even though my heart is hammering. It wasn't that obvious, was it?

"This summer has been good so far. Sam learned how to swim. Jasper took us sailing. We've had picnics." *We kissed.* "I can't really complain."

I keep replaying that kiss more than I should. His hand diving into my hair. The feel of his large thighs under me as I straddled his hips. The small groan that left his lips. And then him pressing against me at my house, kissing along my collarbone like it was a relic to be worshipped.

How would Milo react if I told him what happened? Would he be disappointed? Or would he simply be surprised that we even did such a thing?

Milo's eyes search mine before he shrugs.

"That's good," he says, stretching his legs back out. "I like seeing him happy. He should have a friend that isn't us."

Friend.

"Yeah," I agree, letting out a heavy exhale. "I like seeing him happy too."

"We're gonna do Deadman's Drop on Saturday," Milo says, flipping his book back open. "You should come. And bring your new friend Jasper with you."

I snort. "We'll see."

But with the low rumble of thunder shaking the library and the memory of that heated kiss on the couch, I wonder if jumping off a cliff would be the logical solution to my problem.

ʓ

THE RAIN DRENCHES my hair as I run behind Sam. His hand steadies his soaked beanie while he giggles. Waves rush onto the shore. Our feet pound against the hardened sand, and eventually, both his beanie and my hat get soaked enough that we deposit them on the deck stairs. The storms are heavier than they've been all week, but at this point, I don't care anymore. If we get wet, we get wet.

"Wendy, I want to go inside," Sam calls through the rain.

"Ah, why?"

Sam squints up at the sky, and I follow his line of sight. It does look like it's about to get worse. The clouds are so dark that it almost looks like nighttime, but I didn't notice with the back porch floodlights illuminating the beach.

"Good call, bud."

We run up the steps, me keeping behind him just in case he trips on the slippery wood. By the time we're inside and toweled off, Sam wants to change into pajamas for an afternoon movie. I stop in the kitchen to prep popcorn and trail mix, but Sam runs out in the hall in only his underwear.

I gasp. "Sam, clothes."

"But my beanie!"

"What about it?"

"It's still at the beach!"

"Okay, I'll go get it," I say, waving him away as I side-step him. "And finish putting on your PJs, kid!"

"Aye, aye!"

He runs back to his room, and I burst out into the rain again, barreling down the stairs and over the rocky shore, where his red beanie is sopping wet next to my baseball cap. I snatch it and turn around, ascending the slick stairs once more.

Julie Olivia

But when I reach the top, I'm greeted by someone different. Standing behind the large floor-to-ceiling window, right next to the sliding glass door, is Jasper.

I slowly walk across the porch, padding on bare feet as the rain plunks off the wood. Jasper's eyes drift down, and that's when I notice how my dress clings to me. My nipples are puckered against the fabric, visible, even through my bra.

I could say it's the rain, but it's Jasper causing this. Jasper's hardened stare. His clenched jaw. His clear, piercing eyes, tracing over my figure, assessing me from my chest down to where the dress gathers near my middle and back up.

He looks in pain again, tilting his head to the side, as if admiring a devastating painting.

I take a few more tentative steps forward until I'm under the awning, the remaining droplets from my hair trailing down over my nose and chin.

"Come outside," I say.

"In the rain?"

"It's fun."

"It's wet."

I bite my bottom lip and slowly nod back.

Jasper croaks out a small, "No. Come inside, Wendy Bird."

My back straightens at the nickname. It sets my soul on fire.

"Do you plan to drive home in this?" he asks.

He's changing the subject, which is clever, but I'm not letting him have it.

"If you come outside, I promise not to drive home."

Realistically, I shouldn't stay. But I'm feeling bold.

212

Testy. No, angry. Irritated with our situation. How much I wish it didn't exist.

The thought of being here overnight feels like we'd be stepping over the line, but I can't help it. Wasn't it his suggestion first?

Just friends, my ass.

"Wendy ..." he warns.

"Come outside for five seconds," I counter.

He bites his cheek, suppressing a chuckle. "This isn't a debate."

"But it could be."

He exhales so heavy that it fogs the glass.

"Come on," I beg. "Live a little."

The sliding glass door suddenly whines open, and I take a stumbling step back as he walks out. I didn't think he'd actually do it, but he's outside and already so close. His chest takes the place of the glass, pressing hard against my breasts. I can smell everything on him. The work from the day. The hints of the sea.

His hair is already getting soaked, droplets falling from the strands that drip onto his forehead. They roll over his cheeks and into his beard.

I smile. "See? Not so bad."

His eyes glide down my front and back up. "I like your dress."

My body heats, and words catch in my throat. They finally exhale in a jumble of, "I'm probably gonna have to change."

"You can wear my clothes."

I laugh. "I'll look ridiculous."

"You could never."

I tilt my head to the side, savoring the compliment. "How was work?"

"It was ..." He sighs, rain sliding down his nose. "Good. Starkey tried to get me to go pirating with Mullins and Jukes."

"You should. Bet you could outdrink them."

"But at what cost?" he asks with a chuckle.

"Well, are you a captain, or are you not?"

His mouth opens, then closes. His jaw tenses as he blinks through the rain.

It's quiet between us. I wonder what I said that was wrong.

"It's been more than five seconds," I observe.

"True. And are you happy?" he asks.

"Yes. You?"

Jasper's breath catches in his throat as he peers down at me. I wonder if he's angry with me. If he's annoyed by how much I'm pushing his buttons.

"No," he answers, placing one hand on the small of my back and leading me back through the sliding glass door.

How long until we break? Until this situation feels untenable? Until the opinions of others, the risk of how they'll react, no longer matter to how much we want each other?

Or am I the only one still wanting? Am I the only one desperate for this?

That thought alone has my stomach falling and my mind reeling.

It's always me who wants more.

Chapter 25

It's Just a Dream, Jasper

Jasper

I WAKE UP, covered in sweat.

At first, it feels like the rain from this afternoon. But I know better than to assume it's something as delightful as that.

I bury my head in my hands, my body rippling with anxiety.

The boat I never saw.

The devastating waves I only heard about.

My friends taking breaths I will never hear again.

There's a knock on my bedroom door.

"Sam?" My voice is a croak, still heavy and limp from the nightmare.

"No. It's me," a whisper replies.

I swallow. *Wendy.*

"Are you okay? I heard, uh ... something."

Shit.

"It's fine. I'm fine," I say, running a hand over my face

and across my beard, adjusting the sheets around my waist. "I'm sorry. I forgot you were here."

Wendy stayed after the storm when I challenged her promise to spend the night. I washed some linens and made up the pullout couch while the sheets were still warm. Sam even offered her his security blanket for the storm. She laughingly declined. Before I closed my door for the night, I observed her curling up with her laptop, settling in, silhouetted by the windows capturing the storm outside.

I'm glad I asked her to stay. Driving home in this thunder and lightning along the cliffside might have been perfectly safe, but I didn't want to risk it. Or maybe I was simply being selfish.

Part of me wonders why she didn't put up more of a fight—it's only a fifteen-minute drive after all—but I think she craved to stay just as bad as I wanted her to. Any additional hour together feels like a secret souvenir from a vacation we can't have, a memento from a different Never Harbor.

And now, she's here, in my doorway, and I'm coated in a layer of slick sweat.

Very romantic.

"Can I come in?" she asks.

My stomach drops.

Jessica was always here for my nightmares, except she was the unfortunate woman sleeping beside me.

"It's just a dream, Jasper. It's been so long."

She always claimed I moaned for a few moments until it progressed to a yell, waking myself up from the roars.

I wonder if Wendy heard that.

"I don't have to," she says. "I just figured—"

"Sure," I answer. "Come in."

The bedroom door squeaks open, the moonlight

216

through the kitchen windows flooding in, illuminating her figure. She's wearing an old T-shirt of mine—a homemade promo shirt from my, Stacy, and Ed's band, The Jolly Rogers. The hem is a little ripped, but it lands right at Wendy's thighs. Her body is stolen from me when she shuts the door closed once more, leaving us in darkness.

Rain pounds outside. Low hums from the wind knock against the wood. Wendy takes a seat at the end of my bed, depressing the cushions, the light squeak of my mattress echoing in the empty air.

"What did you hear?" I ask curiously.

She clicks her tongue. "Uh ... yelling."

"Fantastic," I drawl, running a palm over my face.

"Do you want to talk about it?" she asks, not lingering on my embarrassment. "If you want to, I'm happy to listen."

"I, uh ..." The words fade because I'm not sure how to react. Blood is rushing to my head, trapping me in a state of unease.

Jessica never wanted to talk about my dreams. Most of the time, she found her way into the living room, trying to escape from my shaking body and panting breaths. But with Wendy across from me, I'm breathing steadier. Calmer.

I swallow. "It's just ... a nightmare I have."

"A nightmare?"

"It's been around for a while. And, uh, I just keep picturing it." I hold a finger up to my head, tapping on my temple and looking down at the sheets.

She stays quiet, waiting for me to continue, but my words won't come. I adjust in the bed, sitting up more, running a hand through my damp hair.

"I had nightmares as a kid," she finally interjects into the silence. "Of some really mean mermaids."

I huff out a laugh. "That right?"

217

"Brutal. Pulled my hair. Called me names. I'm assuming those dreams aren't like yours."

"Not exactly." I let out a quivering breath, closing my eyes, and decide to let the words land where they fall. "I have this recurring dream about Sam's parents. The, uh, night they died, I guess. Or what I feel must have happened."

The room is deathly quiet before she lets out a very small, "Oh."

"Yeah. Not a very normal thing to dream about, huh?"

"What is normal anyway?"

I give a smile she likely can't see.

"So, what happens?" she asks.

"Ocean waves take them under. And I'm standing there, doing absolutely nothing." I shake my head. "It's just a dream."

"Doesn't mean it hurts less." My eyes haven't adjusted to the dark yet, but I think I hear her smile.

"What's weird is that I think I cherish the nightmares a little. Is that messed up? Because then, if I dream about them, they still exist even if in the worst of circumstances. Sometimes, I dream of our band instead. And that's nicer. But mostly it's the ship. At least it's something."

"You were in a band?" she asks with a stifled laugh.

"You're wearing the shirt."

"Get out. Do you have the album?"

I huff out a small chuckle. "Somewhere around here." *In the cabinet below the bathroom sink.* "It was just a little college thing. I was on keyboard."

She giggles. "You play piano?"

"Terribly."

"I'd love to hear it sometime. Has Sam heard it?"

"No."

"Do you ever talk to Sam about them?"

"I can't. It feels like I'd only be sharing bad things. *Here's why you lost them* kind of things."

"Well then, let's only talk about the good stuff."

I glance up. "About Ed and Stacy?"

"Yeah. Tell me what you love about them."

Not *loved*. Love.

I open my mouth, then close it. It's hard to remember them now. Jessica was right. It *has* been so long. I remember what my dreams tell me, but the little things, like Ed's crooning singing voice and Stacy's skills on the drums ... it feels so long ago, like a different lifetime, and the guilt of it trickles through me. I don't like the knowledge that, each day, they fade away a little more, even the pieces I so desperately want to hold on to.

My chest tightens. "I love ... everything about them," I admit. "Every single thing. Their outlook on life was spectacular. Like nothing would truly ever go wrong. I see it every day in Sam. And not just their personality, but also little things, like how his hair is just like Stacy's. That blond that's almost *too* blond, y'know? He even has Ed's teeth."

Wendy laughs. "His teeth?"

"The man never grew into his mouth, I swear."

Wendy laughs some more, and it's sweet, like candy. Soft like a breath of air.

"Maybe it's just the memories tainting my perception of them, but I remember them being so happy," I continue. "Indescribably happy. Sam is too. I think the joy must be genetic. I mean, couldn't have learned that from me. Sam's not the one with nightmares."

"Did he ever have them?"

"No. He was only two. He dealt with it well."

"Seems like you are now."

"I had to be okay. Everything was confusing in the beginning. I remember, one time, Bobbi found me in the grocery store, and I just ... couldn't remember why I'd gone there. Like I couldn't make sense of the world without them." I swallow. "I'd get jealous of friendships. Of my brothers and how close they were. I didn't think I could get that close to anyone again."

I feel the mattress inflate as she stands.

Maybe that was too much. Too real. Too depressing. Here is this woman, who, only last week, I was desperate for, who was desperate for me, and now, she's in my room, seeing me at my most vulnerable. At my most unattractive. My weakest.

But then I feel the warmth of her standing near me. She runs a hand over my hair, and without thinking, I lean into her.

I wrap my arms around her waist, resting my face against her. Her fingers comb through my hair, running through the damp strands, letting them fall down piece by piece. I close my eyes.

"I said I'd be your friend, Jas, and I meant it."

"I know you did," I murmur.

We stay like that for a moment, me holding her ... or maybe her holding me—I'm not sure. But it feels different. Right. Exactly where I need to be. Exactly how I wish I'd woken up so many times with Jessica.

Wendy lets me exist. She lets me feel. She lets me inhale this nightmare and exhale it out into new moments that are different and happy.

Good memories of Ed and Stacy.

Not the boat or the waves or the nothingness.

Something.

Wendy always makes me feel *something.*

I slide my palms down her waist, lingering as they caress the outside of her thighs before removing them completely. Her palm slides over my beard, and it feels better than any time I've ever done it myself. It's a relief.

"Thank you for coming in here," I whisper.

"Anytime," she says back.

I want her to stay. I want her in my bed. I don't even need to kiss her. I just need her here. But Wendy is smarter than me and starts to walk away, back to the closed door of my bedroom.

She creaks it open, her body glowing in the sliver of moonlight once more. She pauses mid-step and turns around to look at me.

"Milo invited us to Deadman's Drop tomorrow," she whispers. "If you want to go."

"Are you going?" I ask.

"Yes."

"Then, I'll be there."

I can feel myself already at the edge of a cliff, at the precipice of my cracked soul. Because, against my better judgment, I know what I want.

I want her.

Chapter 26

Come and Get Me

Wendy

THE TOP of Deadman's Drop is not the place to be if you're afraid of heights. Thankfully for me, I love flying off the edge. Unfortunately for Jasper, he doesn't share the sentiment.

My tall, bulky, bearded man is standing near the rocky edge with his hands on his hips, as if observing the exact measured height of the fall. He runs a palm over his beard, stepping back. He's never looked like more of a dad in this moment, and that only makes me bite my lip to hold in laughter.

"You're not scared, are you?" Peter calls, one arm pulled across his chest in a stretch.

Jasper's eyes cut over, watching as Peter, Cassidy, Milo, and I stand on the opposite side of the drop-off, closer to the edge. The four of us have made this jump before, multiple times. It's a summer staple in Never Harbor. Well, for everyone who isn't Jasper Davies, apparently.

"Come on, Jas. This'll be just like when we dived in the

lake as kids," Peter says.

"Isn't this the town's water supply?" Jasper asks.

"That's the other quarry. Laura just says that to scare divers away."

"What do they have to be scared away from?"

"I don't know. Rocks? Come on, Jas. Don't be an old codfish."

"Don't make me push you, Pete," Jasper threatens.

Peter grins, raising his eyebrows and biting his tongue in a taunt. "I'd like to see you try."

"He won't be the only one pushing you," I say to Peter.

He laughs, but Jasper's eyes swivel to me. I give a small, reassuring smile before we both look away.

After last night, neither of us really knows how to act. First the rain, then the nightmare ... it's been one confusing event after the other. But once I crawled back onto his couch after Jasper's cheek pressed to my stomach while I held him, I knew one thing for sure: nobody was making Jasper feel uncomfortable under my watch.

"All right, we doing this or what?" I say, shaking off the tension.

Last night keeps surfacing in my mind. The closeness. The very, *very* vivid dream I had on his couch of how I wish last night had gone. Rustling sheets. Soft moans.

I pull my cover-up over my head, tossing it into the pile of shirts the men have already deposited. But when I look up, heat runs over my shoulders.

Jasper's clear eyes are eyeing me like a hawk, chest rising and falling as he absorbs the look of the little cutouts in my one-piece. The high cut of my bottoms. The low dip between my breasts. I bite my lip, holding back the thrill shooting through me.

We're friends. That's all. But, God, that doesn't mean I

can't love his eyes on me.

Though, just as quickly as Jasper's eyes caught on to my figure, they also shoot over to someone else. I wish I hadn't been curious to know who. I wish my eyes hadn't followed. Because that's when I notice Jasper isn't the only one staring.

Peter is, too, his head lowering as his gaze wanders over my curves, my knees, my shins.

Panic eases up my neck, winding down my spine.

I used to melt under that look. But for the first time, Peter's stare feels wrong. Those beautiful mint-green eyes that would bring me to my knees isn't the same as Jasper's silver-blues. Peter's hungry expression doesn't strike the same anxiety in me that Jasper's does. I've come to like the menacing glare in Jasper's stare.

To his credit, Peter quickly clears his throat once he realizes what he's doing, gives a weak smile, then rotates away again to continue stretching.

Jasper begins pacing across the pebbles, ripping his own tee off and throwing it into our shirt pile.

My mouth dries on impact, especially when his intense look meets mine once more.

Jasper without a shirt will never fail to amaze me. Sure, all the Davies men are shirtless right now. And I'm a human with eyeballs, so it's not like I don't notice how attractive they all are.

But Jasper. God, *Jasper*.

Arms of a man constantly constructing something new. Abs from lifting heavy crates at the harbor. Light speckles of black hair coating the area below his collar. And that fishing hook tattoo that gives him a slight edge—a mark of a man that's experienced things.

I suck in a breath and look away.

"Wendy, you gonna scream like you did last time?" Peter teases.

I blink back to the here and now and not back to when Jasper had me caged against my bookshelves. Not to when he kissed my neck. Not to yesterday in the rain.

When I'm finally present, I see Peter's eyebrows hike up and down in challenge.

I roll my eyes with a forced laugh. "*Please.* You're the one who screams."

He tsks. "Not if I remember correctly."

"Hey now," Cassidy interjects at the same time Milo adds, "Come on, man."

"What?" Peter says, eyes wide, hands held up high in innocence, all accompanied with an equally innocuous laugh.

Milo shakes his head, brow furrowed. "Don't be weird."

"Yeah, Wendy's like a sister now," Cassidy adds, nudging me with his elbow and giving a brotherly nod.

"Come on. That's not what I meant." Then, he mumbles, "Scoundrels."

They might see me as a sister, but Peter and I have too much history. Everything he says, intentional or not, will sound like flirting. Plus, there's another brother I'd prefer didn't see me like a sister at all. That same brother has his eyes locked on to Peter like he's the real dead man on this cliff. I honestly worry he might push him off.

"Pete, you'll get your teeth kicked in one of these days," Jasper grits out. "And I might be the one to do it."

Peter laughs in his carefree way. "I don't doubt it."

But the look Jasper tosses me after is electric. Like he meant every word. The sick, twisted part of me likes Jasper's possession. It's very *un*-brotherly. My heart thrums to the beat of it, even in its wrongness. It's impossibility.

225

"All right, let's quit kicking the can and do this!" Cassidy exclaims. He bursts forward with a hoot and holler, catapulting himself over the cliff's edge, whooping the whole way down, his brick-like body landing with a *plunk* and delayed splash.

Bonnie and Lulu are sitting on the rocky ledge at the bottom, both laughing as water sprays over them. Bonnie shields Sam with her arms while Lulu leans her head back, as if savoring the cool water on the hot day. It's the first nice day we've had in a while.

"Seven out of ten!" Lulu calls to Cassidy once he resurfaces.

"Seven? Bull."

Bonnie skims her palm over the water to splash him. "Hey, we're the judges here!"

"Yeah, we're the judges!" Sam echoes, paddling next to Cassidy, who instantly tosses him up in the air to launch him back into the water.

I smile, waiting for Sam to come back up, which, of course, he does. Blinking through the droplets, he cackles out a screeching laugh, tackling his uncle in a makeshift wrestling match.

Suddenly, there's heat at my back, and my hair stands on end. I don't need to turn to know it's Jasper next to me, the smell of his sea salt engulfing me.

"He's doing great," I say, but Jasper doesn't look entirely present. He's tense. His jaw winding back and forth. "You okay?" I ask.

Jasper's eyes meet mine right as Milo jumps off the cliff next, twisting midair, nearly acrobatic in his fall before landing in the depths below. Another large splash.

"Ten out of ten!" Lulu says through cupped hands.

"For that?!" Cassidy yells.

"What?" Lulu says, her tanned skin barely showing her flushed cheeks. "I call it like I see it."

I ignore their continued bickering, turning around and leveling a look at Jasper. "Jas?"

He looks angry, in pain, and upset. Or all of the above.

"I ..." Jasper starts, but Peter interrupts before he can finish.

"Hey, Wendy! Wanna jump together?"

Peter's smile is contagious. It always is; it's Peter.

I can feel my brow furrowing at the same time Peter's long arm reaches out for me. I pull back before he can grab it.

"No, it's all right," I say. "I'll wait and go next."

His expression falls for a moment, but Peter quickly puffs out his chest with a grin and shrugs. "Suit yourself then."

Off he goes, exploding into a jump off the cliff, crowing into the air as he soars over the edge like a bird, arms extended through the open air, descending into a final splash.

Jasper and I stand alone at the top of the rocky bluff, looking down at his family, all floating around, immersed in conversation and dive ratings.

But it's quiet up here with just us.

Jasper looks away when I try to meet his gaze, his jaw set in a defined line that I can spot, even through his beard. He steps away from the edge. His fists are clenched tight.

I gingerly walk toward him, reaching for his arm. I wind my fingers down his skin, coasting over the tense muscles, tracing his tattoo, and landing in his palm, unfurling the fist, finger by finger.

As his fingers finally link through mine, burying between the dips and valleys, Jasper takes a deep breath and murmurs on the exhale, "I don't care that he still flirts with you." His eyes flicker to me. "I don't."

"Yes, you do," I correct for him.

His jaw shifts, but he doesn't verbally agree.

That's like a bucket of water over my shoulders. Maybe I've just been imagining things this whole time. Me instigating kisses. Me climbing him like a tree, flirting in the rain, sneaking into his room in the middle of the night.

Me *wanting*.

"Oh," I mumble. "Okay."

I turn away, walking near the edge of the cliff. But Jasper quickly trails behind me, curling an arm around my waist, tugging me back against his chest, away from the view of those below.

Jasper's warm breath tickles my ear as he leans forward to whisper, "I'm sorry. You're right." The low rumble of his voice sends sparks through me. "I care too much."

The words shoot over my chest, across my stomach, and between my thighs.

Always between my thighs.

Jasper cares. Jasper wants.

Just like I do.

"I don't ... want this," he says slowly.

"Oh."

"I don't want friendship."

My breath catches in my throat. "You don't?"

"No." He sighs. "Wendy, I want *you*."

"*Oh.*"

"Yeah," he says with an exhale. "Oh."

He dips his head to that spot beside my neck, burying it against my skin, pursing his lips into a chaste kiss. But the gravelly, painful tone that follows is less soft.

"I appreciate that you respect my family enough to not

want to get involved," Jasper says. "But I can't stay away anymore." He grips my waist tighter, tugging me against him, keeping me upright.

His palm flattens between our bodies and over my tattoo, running a thumb over the outline. I feel the length of him harden against my back as he places another kiss in the dip of my neck.

I exhale, the anxiety tickling every inch of my chest. The anticipation. The satisfaction. That knowledge that maybe I—just as I am—am desirable. That I'm not just the silly girl, tagging along. The girl who's too much or too little. The daughter who has been abandoned. I'm wanted. Just me.

"I'd let you break me, Wendy Bird," Jasper whispers gruffly. "And I'd thank God every single day for the guilt that followed if it meant I could keep you for myself."

"Jas ..."

My heart thrums as I take a step forward, breaking myself from his hold. He slowly releases me with a low groan, as if mourning the loss of my body against his. But our hands stay connected until I twist around, dropping them at the fingertips.

I walk backward toward the edge of the cliff. One step, then two, watching his eyes follow the movement, seeing those periwinkle-blues coast over my lips, my neck, my hips. Step after step toward the edge as Jasper lets himself indulge, the rims reddening. Pure possession.

When my back foot touches the edge, I halt and pull my bottom lip in, chewing on it for a moment.

"You want me? Then, come and get me, Captain."

With those final words, I leap off Deadman's Drop.

And the last thing I see before plunging into the deep is Jasper diving after me.

Chapter 27

Faith, Trust, and a Little Bit Flushed

Jasper

FALLING FEELS a lot more like flying.

The battering ram against my heart stills. The air whips against my face. The wind whistles past my ears. It's a symphony of carefree silence. A blissful jump into the unknown. A leap toward something new.

And as soon as time stops, it starts once more. My stomach drops, my heart catches in my throat, and I pull in a breath moments before I plunge into the water below.

It's warmer than I expected, heated from the day's sun. Wrapped in its embrace, I almost don't want to resurface because then I'll see the world again. It won't just be me and the skies and the water and silence. Just judgments and small-town gossip and—

When I finally do resurface, I'm greeted with something better.

Wendy Darling.

And nothing else matters.

Her blue eyes blink through the droplets of water

trailing down her flushed cheeks. Her beautiful brown hair is darkened, pooling along the water's surface around her shoulders like spilled ink. Her plush pink lips pull into a wicked smile, and I see that dip in the corner.

The recess beside her lips just for me.

Wendy swims to the opposite side of the bank, where our bags and piles of shoes lie.

"Hey, where are you going?" Cassidy calls.

Or maybe it's Milo.

Or even Peter.

I'm too focused on the woman leaving the water—the outline of Wendy lifting herself from the pool behind her, illuminated in the orange afternoon glow. The small waist, the plump peach of her backside, the slender legs ... all of it glimmering as she emerges in that formfitting suit. It's the kind of bathing suit with a high rise near her outer thighs, exposing just a sliver of a dip in her hip bone that my palms long to grab.

"I left something in the car," Wendy explains, but her eyes flash to me in an instant.

"Want someone to go with you?" Bonnie asks.

"I told her I'd go," I find myself saying.

Her eyebrows rise up to her forehead, and that subtle smile kicks up again. The sneaky thing.

I wade to the far side of the rocky ledge. Drawn to her like a magnet.

It's wrong. It's terrible. It's not a game we should be playing. But Wendy is her own woman, and that woman wants me. And nothing has my body thrumming with need more than a woman who knows what she wants.

"Anyone need anything?" I ask, pulling myself up from the water.

Wendy's eyes watch every movement. I'm not sure she notices her plump bottom lip tugging in, but I do.

"Snacks!" Lulu calls.

"Fruit snacks!" Sam throws in, and I think I hear Bonnie agree.

We quickly towel off, probably more rushed than we should be.

"Can do!" Wendy answers for us both. "We'll be back!"

Droplets of water still catch in the dip of her neck. The sun shimmers off her skin like bits of sugar. She's delectable, and I've never felt so ravenous in my life.

It's that *something* pounding in my chest.

The feeling of being *alive*.

I don't spare a glance back as she puts on her sandals and I tuck into my slip-ons. We silently trod around the corner, crunching over pine needles and cracking twigs until we reach the main trail. It's completely empty, save for the tall trees towering on either side.

I place a hand on the small of Wendy's back, barely breathing as our warm skin heats together. Water from my arm drips over the arch in her lower back, mixing with the droplets still trickling down between the space where the swimsuit cutout meets the bottom of her spine.

"Hi," she breathes.

"Hey," I respond.

"We're probably still too close," she whispers.

She walks faster, and I follow.

Our desperation to leave everyone turns into a quick walk and then a small jog until we're both racing ahead between the trees. She gains some distance on me, and suddenly, it's no longer a run, but a chase.

I'm in pursuit of Wendy through the woods, both of our heavy breaths and her occasional laughter echoing through the trees. My heart cranks into overdrive in my throat, beating like a wild animal trying to escape my chest, mimicking the rhythm of *want, want, want.*

I pick up speed, easily catching up and wrapping my palms around Wendy's waist. She lets out a noise mixed between a nervous laugh and a sigh as I pull her back to my chest, scrambling us both off the trail and carrying her deeper into the woods.

We turn a corner behind a large tree trunk. I drop her against it, caging her in with one hand beside her head.

I peer around the tree to double-check we're alone and confirm we're well hidden from the main path. I refocus back on Wendy, and my stomach drops.

What a sight.

Her body is pressed against the tree—nipples puckered in her peach bathing suit.

I run a palm over her shoulder and along the column of her neck, taking her in.

This beautiful woman stares at me with narrowed eyes in an unspoken dare.

So, I accept the challenge.

I lean down and dip my palm behind Wendy's head. But when I pull her toward me, she's already reaching for my neck and tugging me down.

Our lips meet with a crash.

The kiss is a whisper of the one we had on the couch. This one is filled with greed. We're chasing each other, my mouth pushing against hers and hers bucking back in kind. She rises to her toes, wrapping her arms around my shoulders. My palms tangle themselves in her hair. I cup her face, opening my mouth to taste her right as she does the same.

I let out a small groan. My cock strains against my

swimsuit. Her lips curve into a smile against mine. Happy. Always happy with me, for some ungodly reason.

Her palm reaches out, trailing down the bumps of abs along my stomach, over the hair leading under my bathing suit, and then over the outline of my erection. Another grunt escapes my mouth.

"No," I snap, barely able to form words through our dreamy fog. "Just you."

"Hey—" she tries to argue, but I clutch both her wrists in my palms and pin them by her sides.

Leaning back, I catch her gaze. "I caught you fair and square."

She pulls her bottom lip into her mouth and nods. "You sure did, Captain."

I snort out a laugh, and she joins in. The hissing energy between us is relieved, like steam releasing from a pot. Sex has never felt this exciting and wild and intimate, all at once.

"God ..." I muse, the word trailing off.

Because as much as I'd love to sink myself into her, to get lost in a haze of her soft skin, she deserves to have sex somewhere better. Somewhere delicate, like her. Not in the depths of the woods or against a tree, the bark grinding against her back.

I lean down to kiss the apple of her cheek.

"Maybe not here," I murmur against her skin.

"Yes, here."

"Wendy ..."

I kiss down to her chin, hearing her breathy sighs in my ear as I trail kiss after kiss along her collar, into the dip in her neck, lapping up the droplets of water against my tongue. She shivers underneath me.

Our chests heave in breath after breath. I palm her

cheek, stroking my thumb over it. She twists her head to the side and kisses the inside of my hand. But then she pulls my thumb between her lips and gives a small suck. My body is tense, the electricity between us sizzling like fire through my veins. And I want her. I need her.

"Please, Jasper," she pleads with a whine, nipping another finger.

I shake my head. "Dammit."

"Dammit?" She bats her eyes with a smile.

"Yeah," I say, placing my palms on that beautiful waist and hoisting her up, "Dammit."

I hike her higher up the tree. Her legs wrap around my waist. I trace my free hand down her stomach to her pelvis. The bottom of her bathing suit is stuck to her skin, pulled taut, showing an outline of her beautiful slit. I trace a finger along the outside.

"Dammit," I repeat again because my brain is cursing all of this.

How perfect she is.

How bad I want her.

How easily I break for her.

Her breasts are right at my face level. I lean in and roll a tongue over the outside fabric. Over her perfect, puckered nipple. She lets out the faintest of moans.

Shifting the fabric below to the side, I dip my fingers through the bottom of her bathing suit. She sighs.

God, that could end me right there. It's not her outfit that soaked; it's *her*. I groan.

"Dammit?" Wendy offers for me, and I let out a strained laugh, pressing my forehead against her chest, biting at her, gripping her thigh harder in my opposite palm.

But instead of giving an answer, I thumb her apart and bury a single finger inside.

The moan that follows is perfect—just like everything about her. Wendy's head falls back against the bark, and I hold her closer as her heels hook tighter around my back.

I curl the lone finger, letting myself explore, finding the place I need until a certain spot has her breaths leaving in stuttered sighs.

"Jasper, baby," she moans.

Baby.

Such a common pet name. So normal. And exhaled so naturally.

I want common. Normal. Natural.

Baby.

My body, though tight and hard and aching for release, feels like it's floating in a dream. In the feel of her chest rising and falling beside my ear; in the fresh, clean scent of her perfume; in the wet sounds of her gripping my knuckle as my finger pulses in and out.

I remove my finger and replace it with a second.

It grants me a whine from her beautiful lips and another, "Jas ..."

I roll my tongue over the fabric covering her nipple, pushing my finger in and out of her, letting the angelic echo of, *"Baby,"* wash over me in waves until Wendy can't form words at all.

"That's right, baby," I echo back, increasing my rhythm, feeling her start to tense around me. I growl again, "That's right."

I haven't felt this relaxed—this clearheaded—in years. This filled with energy and want.

And when Wendy breathes, "Oh God," I rub my thumb around her clit, sending my girl spiraling over the edge.

Her hands clutch my hair, tugging, as she whines. But I

keep moving my fingers in the exact same way, letting her squirm under my touch.

Because I don't want this to end. Not yet.

"I need one more, Little Bird," I command, and I'm answered with another whine, her body clutching around my fingers. Doing exactly as I said. Giving me one more.

Wendy slouches against the tree trunk, and I slowly remove my fingers, guiding her shaking thighs down as her feet unhook behind my back.

Gently, I lower her back to the woodsy, twig-filled floor. I kiss every inch of her along the way—along her breasts, her collar, up her neck, and to the apples of her flushed cheeks. I bury my nose into her hair.

We stand there for a moment as her arms wrap around my waist, as I press my lips against her neck, tracing a circle on the opposite side with the pad of my thumb.

I only move when she whispers, "Hey, look at me."

I pull back. Her blue eyes stare up at me, her cheeks more flushed than I expected. Her hair a mess. I run my thumb over her red lips.

"Just wanted to see you," she says with a smile. "Make sure you're okay."

I chuckle at the fact that *she's* checking on *me*, gifting me with a wider smile from her—the one with that beautiful dip in the corner of her lips.

"Good. I'll take that as a yes."

Chapter 28

Little Bird

Wendy

I DIDN'T KNOW I could still feel butterflies in my twenties. But not just butterflies—swarms of bees and moths and doves and literally anything with wings pummeling through me at once. The feeling of wanting *more* all the time, of daydreaming about a smile or a laugh or a groan.

It's almost nice to know that type of ridiculous school-girl crush still thrives inside me. That George didn't kill it. That Peter didn't make me jaded.

Jasper kisses differently than anyone else I've been with. Each press of his lips is suffused with his whole being, like any of them could potentially be the final, fleeting one. He puts his soul into it. Every ounce of longing. Jasper lingers, and I love it.

Little Bird.

That's what sent me over the second time. A simple nickname, and I want it said again. Every day. As often as I can get it.

After we retrieved snacks from the car, his hand on the

small of my back the entire way, Jasper and I relocated to opposite sides of the water for the remainder of the afternoon. I felt like everyone could hear how hard my heart thrummed. Cassidy glanced at me from time to time, looking a little worried, but maybe he'd just eaten too many hot dogs. Because nobody saw when Jasper's fingers traced on the outside of my arm before we walked up to jump again. When his eyes flicked over, resting on me like they belonged there.

At the end of the day, Jasper and I parted ways, and that was that. I wish there were more to daydream over, but what could Jasper do? Follow me home with Sam in the back seat?

Instead, I lay in bed last night, trying to re-create the movements Jasper had made with his fingers, having orgasm after orgasm, but none remotely as pleasing as the ones from his coarse fingers.

Since when has a man *ever* been able to beat my own hand? Don't get me wrong; my exes weren't terrible. In fact, Peter was—

No.

I won't ruin this with thoughts of Peter. Not when things are so good. He doesn't belong in my new relationship. Peter is simply one of my best friends now. Why can't we just leave it at that?

Because you almost married him, and now, you've gotten finger-banged by his hot older brother in the woods.

Oh, right.

That's why.

I sip my morning coffee next to the beautifully fixed ladder from said finger-banging brother and type away on my laptop. There are new sentences and paragraphs and pages and chapters of a certain pirate captain that has now sword-fought with Jill. Twice. It's intense; it's wild. Practically a dance.

Jasper is the best muse I've ever had because he gave me *two*—two mind-blowing, rolling—orgasms in one go.

No, he didn't give me them. He *demanded* them.

I sink into my chair and continue writing.

What was supposed to be something simple has now surpassed a normal book length by a couple thousand words, but I don't care. It feels right. Exciting.

By mid-morning, my wrists ache. I shake them out and pick up my phone, only to set it back down.

I haven't gotten a single text or call or anything from Jasper since yesterday.

He's probably busy. He's got Sam and Roger and house projects.

And it's not like I'm his girlfriend. I'm his ... something. I'm just his nanny, I guess. You don't really text your nanny —or even your *something*—on a Sunday morning. But I keep checking, writing, then checking again.

Eventually, in one of my *pick up, put down* fits, I receive a text from Maggie, asking if I want to join her for a beach day. I instantly say yes—anything to distract me from this— and walk the twenty minutes to her house.

I find Mags in the front yard, watering her haphazard bed of flowers. Her slip-on walking shoes are already outfitted, and our chairs and beach bags sit, full, on the front porch.

The moment I walk up to her, the only thought circling my mind is, *Your eldest son did things, your eldest son did things, your eldest son did the hottest, nastiest, most wonderful things.*

"Ready to get going?" she asks.

Your eldest son—

"Absolutely."

We stroll down the sidewalk to the beach, one bag over each of our shoulders, taking in the quiet of a Sunday morning in Never Harbor. The sun is finally getting its comeuppance on the rain, beaming through puffy white clouds and warming the street. We pass by Steve, the paper boy, cycling uphill—somehow always drenched in buckets of sweat. Maggie and I offer a wave. He gives an exhausted exhale back.

"Poor kid," Maggie muses, not for the first time.

We descend the creaking ramp to the beach, unfolding two plastic chairs and propping open umbrellas behind us. Maggie rests her paperback on her stomach and thumbs to her bookmarked page. I do the same.

"A Western?" she asks, glancing at my cover. "I thought you were into pirates?"

Yes, and I like them too much, I want to joke, but instead, I shrug.

"Trying new things. What about you?"

"I'm in an arranged marriage with a mafioso."

"Ooh, *principessa,*" I say, shimmying my shoulders. "And what would David say about that?"

"David can be tough when he wants to be."

I wave her off and laugh. "Enough said."

She shrugs. "I'm serious. Dave can step up and boss me around when he—"

"Maggie!" I shriek, my jaw dropping and covering my ears because the last thing I need is imagining David Davies with his cute little kitchen apron transforming into some demanding presence in the bedroom.

Although maybe it's genetic.

I bury my face in my palms as Maggie gives a little laugh.

"I'm kidding, dear. Kidding. So," she says, waving me off and changing the subject, "Bonnie told me you and Peter were close at the quarry."

My head pops up.

"What? We were?" I ask. "I don't know," I add quickly. "Not any more or less than everyone else."

I'm trying to peer past the memories of Jasper's grin and remember if Peter and I were close. But all I see is Jasper. His rough fingers. His scratchy beard along the outside of my bathing suit. His teeth grazing my nipples.

I shake my head again, letting out a nervous laugh. "Why?"

Maggie laughs. "Oh, it's nothing. Probably just Bonnie hoping."

"Hoping?"

"You're the closest thing to a sister she's ever had. I think she's always wanted it to work out between you two."

"Oh." My shoulders slouch, my gaze focusing on the water washing in toward the shore, only to drift back out.

Maggie pats the back of my hand. "Well, either way, he's lucky to have you. We all are."

"Thanks," I mutter.

Maggie shifts in her seat, squeaking against the plastic of her beach chair.

"But, Wendy, dear," she says softly. "Can I ask you something?"

"Of course."

"You're not looking to date my son, are you?"

My head jerks up.

My son.

My stomach drops. And for the first time ever, I have to ask, *Which one?*

I let out an airy laugh and say, "Peter is probably just being Peter. We ended things for a reason."

With a firm nod, Maggie turns back to her book and simply says, "Good."

Good?

My stomach twists all sorts of ways, curling out, then back, and knotting.

Peter and I had a rough breakup, but I did what was best for me. For us. Peter is a good guy, but he only has eyes for his restaurant and the people surrounding it. For fun and adventure. A wife? A family? That's not for him, and it never will be. I had to protect my own peace.

Maggie still understands that, right?

Her hand reaches out to squeeze mine, prompting my brain to tell me I shouldn't worry. Her squeezes are basically a substitute for a hug, and she gives hugs when she knows I'm drowning in my own head. She wouldn't hug me if she disliked my decision to break up with her son, but the pounding in my chest demands otherwise.

I'd do a lot for Maggie Davies, but that is nothing compared to what she'd sacrifice for her own family. And at the end of the day, I'm not her child. Peter is. And so is Jasper.

My phone buzzes in the limp cupholder. A text from Jasper flashes over the screen.

Jasper: Let's go to Main tomorrow

I curl my lips in to hide my affectionate laughter. His texts are so clunky.

Wendy: Are you telling or asking?
Jasper: Asking

Wendy: I'm okay if you're telling.
Jasper: Wendy Bird

I can practically hear his warning. Maybe he didn't mean it to sound like such a threat, but, boy, does it feel that way. My spine tingles at the thought.

Wendy: Yes, Captain?
Jasper: Your house at noon
Wendy: Can I get one emoji so I know you're a real person? This feels very spammy.
Jasper: [alien emoji]

A laugh breaks through my palm. I glance over and find Maggie's eyes roaming over my phone. My heart races as I tuck it into my chair's drink holder. Maggie slowly grins ear to ear.

"Getting Jasper out of the house?" she asks.

"Mmhmm," I say, settling into my chair because I am cool as a cucumber and totally not flirting with her other son. "Going to walk around Main Street tomorrow."

"His idea?"

I smile. "Yeah, his idea."

"Hmm," she says, her bottom lip poking out. She props her book up on her belly again, giving that screen a sly smile. "How about that?"

She's right. *How about that?*

But she just thinks we're friends. Anything more, and I'm not sure how she'd handle it. Because I can't break another son's heart. Maggie would disown me forever.

Chapter 29

The Terrible Flirt

Jasper

I CAN'T REMEMBER the last time I strolled down Main Street on a Monday afternoon for anything that wasn't running errands. Starkey jokingly emailed me, saying that I'm playing hooky from work, but he's not exactly wrong. I am. But I don't regret it when I'm beside Wendy.

It's easy to see why tourists are captured by Never Harbor.

Main is technically a two-lane road, but after a certain fork in the road, the road is too narrow for drivers. Pedestrians tend to ignore the sidewalks, and it becomes a walking free-for-all. Locals and tourists alike roam between businesses, each side of the street lined with colorful doors and shutters, ranging from teal to pink to purple. Between buildings, you can catch a glimpse of the ocean beyond, a breeze that cools, even on the hottest days.

Sam and Wendy look into a window up ahead, Roger on the leash beside them. The shop display is a screen-print art gallery, displaying areas in Never Harbor—from sailboats to the main beach and even Skull Rock. Sam's mouth gapes open in awe, and Wendy's smile beams. But she's not staring at the prints; she's looking at Sam.

My gut pulls because I know I've kept him too sheltered. But the smile on my boy is enough to make me want to visit every day now, just to see his wonder.

I crouch next to him, nodding to the print. "See one you like? We could get one for your room."

"Really?"

"Absolutely. Go pick one out."

Sam scampers into the shop, shoving Roger's leash in my palm while almost barreling over the artist coming out with his coffee.

"Sorry," I say in Sam's stead.

The artist blinks without acknowledgment.

I instantly recognize him as the tattooed guy at The Hideaway a couple of weeks ago. He's younger than me, but only just—maybe mid to late twenties at best. Murals of tattoos curl over his beige skin, peering out from his rolled-up sleeves, snaking down to his knuckles. His cheekbones are intense, high on his face with a jarringly edgy jawline. His inky-black hair is shaved on the sides, loose strands up top flopping forward. His eyes look like a mix of both sleepy and stressed, all at once. Though maybe that's to do with the pack of cigarettes peeking out from his shirt's front pocket.

"This looks so good, Rafe!" Wendy says, flashing him a smile.

I look between the two. I can tell Wendy is itching to hug him, but this guy looks like physical contact might actually destroy him.

He gives a nod of his head, and something tells me that's his equivalent of a smile.

"Thanks," he replies, his drawling voice almost just as sleepy as he looks. "See anything you like, let me know."

I squint, trying to place him outside of The Hideaway. Maybe if I'd been in town the past few years, I'd know this guy.

I used to know everyone before I went off to college. Sometimes, I wonder if me being so out of touch with Never Harbor is a symptom of growing up or if it's just my own shortcomings—if maybe living a fifteen-minute drive away from everyone else is the problem.

Or maybe I'm just not personable. Not like Wendy, who has said hi to every person we've passed and is now complimenting this artist—Rafe, I suppose—on the changes to his gallery.

Sam shuffles to me, a print clutched in his tiny fists. It's a beautiful illustration of a sailboat on the ocean.

"I want this one," he says. "It reminds me of swimming with Wendy."

I give a small smile and pull out my wallet. I hand him cash and observe as Sam runs to the counter. Rafe joins him, and Sam presents the payment proudly. The artist gives a half smile when he hands Sam back change. Sam twists to flash me the biggest thumbs-up.

When did Sam get self-sufficient? When did he become a real kid with wants and interests and a person who can see a print and buy it because it reminds him of a special day? He's growing up too fast.

"I like your tattoos," I hear him saying to Rafe at the counter. "Captain has one too."

Rafe's eyes swivel to me and then back. He digs somewhere behind the counter before brandishing a pen and clicking the end.

"Want one?"

Sam gasps. I give an approving nod, and he whips his arm out onto the counter, bouncing on the toes of his sneakers.

"Yes, yes, yes!" he says.

Chuckling, Rafe starts to sketch, drawing slow, soft lines over Sam's skin, which gradually turn into a pirate flag.

"Wow," Sam breathes.

Rafe clicks his pen again and taps his arm. "All right, now, twist your arm a little, kid."

Sam does it, and another gasp leaves his mouth because the flag *moves*. Or at least, it looks like it's waving in the wind.

"Wendy, look!" he calls.

Wendy, wandering near the prints in the back, smiles. "Magic," she breathes.

I smile to myself, watching the two of them. This feels so ... domestic. So normal.

Baby repeats in my ear like a wind chime. Soft and sweet.

I stand in the doorway, Roger's leash wrapped around my wrist, as Wendy practically dances over to me, hopping on the tips of her toes and nudging me with her hip.

"Are you gonna put this in your book?" I ask. "A moving flag tattoo on some pirate?"

She laughs and singsongs, "Maybe."

"Can't wait."

"Psht. You act like you'll read it."

I lift an eyebrow. "I *would* like to read your story."

Her once-teasing expression falls. "Really?"

"Of course. How can I tell everyone to read it if I haven't read it myself?"

"Oh, *please*," she says, pushing my arm playfully.

"My future favorite author just touched me."

"Jas."

"Best day ever."

"Stop," she says, rolling her eyes, but I love the little smile still plastered on her lips.

Sam tugs on her skirt, and she glances down.

"Hey, Wendy?"

"Yeah, bud?"

"I think I want to write a story too."

"That would be great. What about?"

"I don't know." He looks at his screen print, then back up. "A boat."

Kids' brains are so funny.

"That sounds really sweet," Wendy says.

Sam nods. "I'm still thinking about it."

"Well, I think you've got some time."

We leave the shop, giving our thanks to Rafe, who gives his nodding not-smile again, and on her way out, Wendy accidentally bumps into someone else crossing over the threshold.

"Oh, I'm sorry—"

"No worries."

My body tenses at the sound until I realize who said it.

I'd recognize Izzy from a mile away. Loose, curly blonde hair with the attitude of a bulldog.

"Hey, Izzy," Wendy says.

"Hey, Wendy."

Izzy holds her tension in her shoulders, but then she passes through without another word.

What's her problem?

We empty back onto the street, and without thinking, I place a hand on Wendy's lower back as we navigate through the crowd.

"What was that?" I whisper against her ear.

"I don't know," Wendy quietly murmurs back, letting herself blend into me as she does, relaxing her back against my chest. "Izzy's been weird for a while now."

"Hmm. Any idea why?"

"I don't know. Ever since I moved back ... it's like she hates me."

"Not sure what's to hate."

This grants me one of her adorable laughs. "You're funny."

"Am I?"

I'm not sure what was so funny because I was telling the truth. But before I can say that, Sam is tugging at my other arm.

"Can we get ice cream, Cap?"

"Sure, we can. Wendy?"

Wendy nods in agreement, but her smile looks forced.

We keep strolling, and I allow Sam to pace ahead with Roger in tow. As long as they're within my sights, I'm comfortable. He's having too much fun, looking into windows, Roger is enjoying all the nearby smells, and I'm too focused on Wendy's energy level, which just plummeted.

I don't like it one bit.

I reach out for her palm, tracing a finger down her center line before pulling away. She sucks in a breath as her lips twitch into a smile.

"Everything okay?" I murmur.

"Yeah. It's just ... I hate the idea of someone not liking me. Especially Izzy. At one point, we were friends, and I don't know what happened. Maybe that sounds stupid."

"It's not stupid."

I trace a hand over hers again. It grants me another little

smile before expanding into a full-blown grin, so I link my fingers with hers.

"You can't do stuff like that," she whispers with a small laugh.

I lift an eyebrow. "What?"

That has her rolling her eyes, scoffing.

"Wait, stuff like what?"

"Flirting. In public. Someone might see."

I look around. We're surrounded by crowds, but I drop my hand anyway.

"Lucky for you, I don't flirt," I comment.

"Yes, you do," she counters, the words accompanied by giggles bubbling out of her. "That eyebrow lift? That's flirting."

"I'm just existing."

"Well, you exist very hotly. Just toss in a few choice words, and I'd be a goner."

I swallow, my palms stretching out by my sides, trying to ease the growing tension.

"Choice words?" I inquire.

Her face flushes, and she immediately shakes her head. "Never mind."

"You like choice words?" I repeat.

Her eyes roam over my face, pausing at my lips, before she twists away, pretending she's distracted by the rows of shops. But I feel her walk just a bit closer.

"Well, you're good at it, so yes," she murmurs.

I've never been a great flirt. I'm laughable actually. Jessica hated when I tried to instigate anything.

But Wendy sees a certain type of man in me, and I don't know if it's someone I used to be or someone I never knew I could be. But I like him. I like that he's the type of man that has someone as captivating as Wendy walking closer.

So, I do exactly what this beautiful woman likes.

I lean in, my lips brushing against her ear as I whisper, "What if I told you I haven't been able to stop thinking about the quarry? That I can't stop imagining you in that tight little bathing suit?"

Wendy does nothing, but shivers explode over her skin.

"Do you like when I whisper to you on a crowded street?"

Wendy gives a small nod with a, "Mmhmm," passing a smile to Moira, standing outside her candle shop, giving a hearty wave back.

Wendy's shoulder stays pressed against my arm. Her fingers wind through the fabric of my shirt, tugging me closer when the crowds attempt to drift us apart.

I inhale and lean back in, splaying my hand over her lower back. I lightly trace over the fabric of her shirt, right where I know the outline of her tattoo is.

"What have you imagined since Saturday?" I murmur. "Sneaking around? The feeling of my fingers running over your skin? My—"

"I didn't get the chance to touch you," she interrupts in a whisper, adding in a low, almost shy, "I want to."

"That right?"

"I want to ... get on my knees for you."

I freeze, and all the blood in my body goes either to my swimming mind or right down to my cock.

Christ, I don't know the last time I had *that* happen. Jessica hated giving oral. Not that I blame her—a cock is a cock—but Wendy is standing right here, telling me she's *imagined* doing that to me.

I'm swelling against my zipper, and I have to shift behind her to hide my growing erection from view.

"Do you want that?" she asks, and that's when I realize I never answered.

"Yeah, I do, baby," I growl, gripping the fabric of her shirt in a fist and releasing it.

I can feel her tense in front of me. I run a palm up her neck and into her hair. I know it's risky. I know we're in public, but my palm needs to feel her soft hair. The tickle of her ribbon traces over the back of my hand.

I gently tug her ear closer as I whisper, "I'd love to use this little ribbon later too."

I pull back, cautious, hoping I didn't go too far, but her blue eyes are alight with fire.

"I like that idea."

"You look like you'd love that too much," I agree.

She gives me a sly smile.

"What if I tie your wrists together while you sit right on my chin? How's that sound?"

Her eyes flutter shut. She's tense next to me, lost in a daydream as she trusts me to guide her through the crowd.

"Promise me we'll do that," she replies.

Then, I take a daring leap. "I promise that if you're good for me while sitting on my face, I'll hold your hair back and fuck that sweet mouth of yours however you want."

Wendy lets out a heated pant. It's only then I realize we're at the ice cream stand. The seaside shack, with its bright aqua-blue shutters, feels so incongruous with our current conversation that it almost makes me laugh. I give her side one final grip before letting go.

Wendy's cheeks are flaming red as her eyes dart from me to the stand.

A laugh breaks through the beautiful embarrassment. She twists her hand to pinch my forearm.

"You're a fantastic flirt, Jas," she says. "I don't know who told you differently, but they were very, very wrong."

She walks past me, passing close enough that her breasts very conveniently brushes against my chest, causing me to suck in a breath to the tune of her teasing laughter. She jogs down the stone path into the ice cream shop.

I stand there, watching her and Sam order. Watching her infectious laughter carry to the employees. Watching Sam cling on to her thighs in a hug. She stares at me without abandon, giving the brightest smile, like I'm invited to the happiness party too.

I'm starting to wonder what type of man I truly am. Am I the hermit in the seaside shack? The man rattled by grief and nightmares? The overbearing dad? The terrible flirt?

Or am I the man Wendy sees? Confident. Charming. A good dad. A man able to attract someone as radiant as her. And if I'm not that man, I wonder if I could be.

Chapter 30

Jasper and Wendy

Wendy

I'VE NEVER BEEN the center of a man's attention. There's always someone prettier, sexier, and more exciting. Women are amazing, so how could there not be? But Jasper couldn't keep his hands off me. Even when we passed objectively gorgeous women in shops or at the park or on the sidewalks, his hand never strayed from my waist.

Honestly, I don't know if I should be offended that he doesn't see other women or not. Part of me thinks something must be wrong with him. He *does* know those women have longer legs or nicer smiles or softer hair, right?

George knew. Peter knew.

But when Jasper's eyes land on me, when he stares at me like I'm the first morning sunbeam over the ocean, I don't think he cares. He only sees me.

I know what we're doing is wrong—for Peter and now for his mom. But we do it anyway, and I'm soaking up every ounce of attention I can get until his vision widens to someone else. So, when Jasper invites me back to their house for dinner, I don't say no. Not with his hand on my waist. Not when that mouth made promises I have every intention of ensuring we keep.

Jasper whips up an amazing meal, using the ingredients we picked up from the farmers market. It's some type of cold summer pasta that Sam miraculously doesn't hate and that I gush over because it's Jasper and his cooking feels different, as if he uses each ingredient with care. I try to beat him to the sink to tackle dishes, but he insists on doing them instead.

Jasper tucks in Sam later in the evening after two hours of building a Lego castle.

I linger in the living room, but when Jasper's head pokes out of the door's threshold, saying, "He wants you to read him a story too," followed by Sam yelling, "Wendy! I want to hear the one about the princess!" I don't argue one bit.

Once the princess lives happily ever after, the lights are turned down. Jasper says good night and gently closes the door behind us as Sam winks off to sleep. The final snick of the shutting door echoes into the living room, and then it's just us.

I curl my lips in as I nod, and he does too.

His eyes widen, as if to say, *Here we are.*

And mine squint to reply, *Should we?*

He tilts his head toward his bedroom. *We could.*

I smile. *We should.*

In silence—me in front, him with his hand lingering on my lower back—we escort each other to the other end of the house, padding across the living room rug, over the creaking kitchen hardwood, and beyond the threshold of Jasper's bedroom, where another thump of a closed door cements our time alone.

I glance around the space. I didn't get a good look at Jasper's bedroom last time. I was too distracted by his nightmare, the scamper of my own feet to get to him, the way he curled into me, tucking his cheek against my stomach as I held him close. With the lights on, I can take in more of his space.

His bed has a maroon bedspread and an aesthetic iron headboard with a slat of polished wood centered inside. It's modern, but still non-decorative. No throw pillows. No additional blankets. The only real slice of life is along his dresser. A binder and three framed pictures.

I peek open the binder and burst into laughter.

"You've *got* to be kidding me," I say.

He chuckles. "I told you."

My bottom lip curls in as I flip through page after page of coins.

He is an *actual* collector.

"Well, now, I feel bad for joking about stamps."

"As you should."

I side-eye him as he smiles.

I snap the book shut and switch my focus, tracing my fingers over the three wooden frames propped on the dresser.

The first is of a much younger Jasper, one without a beard and slightly messier hair. He's in a group of three. Jasper is giving the biggest smile I've ever seen. The other two are a beautiful blonde and a guy with crooked teeth. My heart sinks.

Ed and Stacy.

The next photo is of him, Sam, and Roger out near the clock tower on Main. Sam still looks like a toddler, hiked up on Jasper's hip. Roger isn't the monstrosity that he is today

257

either—just a puppy with big paws he still needs to grow into.

The final in the row is a family photo of the Davies family in their backyard. The Twins are toddlers. Bonnie's hair is stringy. Milo's glasses are wired instead of horn-rimmed. Cassidy is pre–bodybuilder obsession—still fit, but not nearly as bulky as he is now. Peter is front and center, his hair brushed over and shaggy—a product of the fashion at the time. And then ...

I suck in a gasp and let it out with a laugh. "Oh my God, that's me."

On the far end, right next to David and Maggie, is a younger me. Shorter hair. Thinner eyebrows. I'm leaning in, my hand on Maggie's arm with an engagement ring on my finger, grinning ear to ear with the family I thought was soon to be mine.

I search the picture for someone else, but my face falls.

"Where are you?" I ask.

The floor creaks as Jasper walks over. I feel the heat of his chest behind me.

"I think I was taking the picture," he says.

I shake my head. "Tripods exist, you know."

He shrugs. "Figured it'd be easier."

My heart sinks.

Jasper. Always sacrificing himself for others. Always being what he needs to be for everyone else. His family can't possibly understand how much he truly cares—to keep a picture of them he's not even in.

I turn around, meeting him face-to-face. I trace an arm up his bulky one, reaching up to flatten a palm over his beard.

And then I lower down to my knees.

Jasper blinks down at me, shifting from foot to foot. "What are you ..."

But his words fade off as my hands rise to his belt. I start to unfurl the strap from its hold. The snap and groan of leather echoes through the room.

"Wendy, you don't have to."

I pause and give a sly smile. "I know I don't *have* to do anything." The metal belt clinks as I release the strap. "I want to."

He watches through hooded eyes as I undo the top button of his jeans. Somebody must have told Jasper that he didn't need attention, too, and I hate that for him.

"I want to take care of you. Is that okay?"

Jasper's palm reaches out, cradling my cheek. "Yes," he croaks out. "Yes, whatever you want."

My smile grows. "Good." I slide his zipper down, joking, "Now, all you have to do is tell me how amazing I am."

"So amazing," he says, but he doesn't appear to be joking at all.

Zips of pleasure strike through my body as I trace my fingertips along the hem of his boxer briefs. I slowly tug them down, pulling until his cock finally releases.

Men want women to say cocks are pretty, but no woman actually thinks these could win beauty contests. But a good, classic cock—one like Jasper's, which is thick, roped with veins, and hanging heavy due to the sheer weight of its need—those type of cocks sure are intoxicating.

There's something about the reddened head, bobbing with want. Something manly about the tuft of dark hair at the base. And there's something even more heady about the type of control drumming through me when this bearded man looks down at me with his head tilted to the side, taking

259

me in like I'm a goddess, blessing him with a gift, as opposed to the arrogant way other men have expected this act before.

Being on my knees for Jasper Davies comes with a particular type of power, and I don't take that responsibility lightly.

I take him into my palm, running a hand up the shaft and back down, watching his eyes grow hazy with each stroke. Leaning in, I place a kiss at the tip—one, then another—before eventually opening wide for him. Peering up, I take him inside my mouth, rolling my tongue along the outside, twisting my hand up in tandem.

Jasper hisses, followed by a breathy grunt. "Damn."

He loves that word when we mess around.

I love when he uses that word, so I repeat the motion, bobbing my head down, stroking my palm up, rolling my tongue along the side of his veins.

Jasper's hand curls behind my head, softly guiding me each time I take more of him. But I didn't ask for soft. I grip him harder, bobbing faster. His palm splays out as his gentle assist turns into more of a push.

"You like that?" he asks.

I let out an agreeable moan, staring him in the eye as a low grunt leaves him.

"That's right, baby," he rasps. "That's right."

I take him deeper, his cock hitting the back of my throat.

He chokes out a moan. "God, just like that."

I take all of him again, breathing in through my nose, pulling him closer.

"Fuck," he choruses, and I like this profanity more.

The fact that this man can't hold it together when I'm doing this to him is wild.

"So good." His words are strangled. "Baby, that's so amazing."

Amazing.

Jasper's hand behind my head curls tighter as he captures my ponytail, winding it around his fist as he pushes into my mouth. My body sparks with energy.

I like Jasper's bark, but I love his bite more.

So, when he thrusts, I let him. When he jerks into my mouth, when he tugs at my hair, I reward him in kind, pushing and licking until he's panting and groaning.

Until he's moaning out a barely audible, "Baby."

My thighs burn, and I'm slick with need and power and excitement. He tells me he's getting close, and I open my mouth wide. I allow his orgasm to empty onto my tongue, and I swallow every ounce he gives.

Through heaving breaths, Jasper blinks down at me. Hooded blue eyes grow heavier as he murmurs, "That was perfect. You're perfect."

Perfect.

Kicking his pants to the side, Jasper rips off his shirt to stand naked before me. I'm still on my knees, so he bends at the waist, dipping an arm under my legs to scoop me into his arms, giving an extra toss to adjust my position. Like I'm light as air.

"Come on," he says. "Your turn to be taken care of."

Jasper walks me to the bathroom, nudging on the light with his elbow and placing me on the countertop.

"Strip," he demands.

Grinning with my body practically humming, I reach behind me to untie my dress as he pads over to the claw-foot bathtub and runs water, dipping his hand under the faucet to test the temperature.

I watch him walk to a cabinet, admiring the round spheres of his ass, the muscular thighs, and the smattering of hair coating his calves and shins. He grabs a purple bottle, emptying part of it into the tub. Suds start to form.

"You have bubble bath?" I joke.

He turns to me with a deviously raised eyebrow, but doesn't address it.

"I don't see you stripping."

"Yes, Captain," I respond sarcastically, tugging my dress over my head and unhooking my bra, tossing it to the side.

Jasper's eyes roam over my naked torso as he slowly stalks between my legs. His palms span over my waist. He hooks his thumbs into the top of my thong, nudging it down my legs, crouching when it passes my shins to place a kiss on my freckled knee, up my thigh, then between my legs. He parts me with a roll of his tongue. I pull in a sharp inhale.

"You taste exactly how I imagined," he says.

"You've fantasized about me?"

Jasper grins up at me. "If only you knew."

He rises to his feet, and I pout.

"Tease."

"Oh, I'm far from done with you."

He places an arm under my legs again, leaning one behind my back, and carries me to the bath. Bending at the waist, he lowers me down. The water sloshes around me with the change from the cool bathroom to the hot water, hardening my nipples and sending shivers down my spine.

Jasper steps in after me, suds sizzling and popping as he rests on the opposite side. His hand reaches for my leg, pulling me to him. He runs a palm down to my knee and back again. His other hand kneads my calf. We say nothing as he massages my limbs for a minute or so, moving from one to the next with gentle motions until he's absentmindedly stroking the length of my shin, peering over at me through shadowed eyes.

"Thank you," he finally murmurs.

"For?" I ask.

"You know what."

"Oh, the thing back there?" I tease. "I mean, if I'd known you'd be so appreciative ..." My words fade as his mouth crooks up into a smile.

"It's just ..." He glances down, tracing over my leg with his palm. "It was nice."

"Can I ask you something personal?"

"You can ask me anything." His response comes so easily now, like telling me secrets no longer requires thought.

"Did your ex ever do that?"

He sardonically chuckles. "A couple of times. Jessica didn't care for it."

I inhale and sigh. "Jessica and Jasper," I muse. "It would have sounded silly if it'd worked out anyway."

Jasper's eyes flick to me. "Not like Jasper and Wendy?"

"Not at all," I respond.

"Yeah. I think I kinda like your name with mine," he says with a sly smile before it fades. "Y'know, I've always thought relationships should be more of a partnership. Not one person always doing one task, like dishes or laundry or—"

"Always getting oral?"

"That too," he says with a chuckle.

"Me too. I like the thought, but reality ..."

He runs a palm up and down my shin again. "You deserve that type of relationship."

I bark out a laugh, staring down at the suds, gathering a handful in my palm before blowing them out to fly between us. But the water shifts, lapping against the porcelain as Jasper reaches a finger out and tips my chin up so that I greet his serious expression.

"You deserve that," he repeats.

"I don't know what I deserve anymore," I confess quietly. "For some people, I'm too much." I swallow. "Others, not enough. I'm the Goldilocks of girlfriends, Jas."

"So, what do you want to be?" he asks.

"I want to be someone's world," I admit. "Maybe that's selfish. Maybe it's impossible. But I'm tired of being second best."

Jasper tilts his head to the side, lifting that single eyebrow. "You deserve to be someone's everything."

I let out a disbelieving laugh. "Yeah, well ..." My words fade out, and I shrug. I don't have the energy to argue. Not when I glance back up and he's staring at me, stroking my shin, damp hair flopped to the side. I lean forward as the water sloshes around me. I push the strand of hair back. "You're a good man, Jasper Davies. Do you know that?"

He blinks and quietly murmurs, "No," which drops my heart to my stomach.

"You are," I insist, scooting closer to wrap my arms around his neck. "You're a giver."

"I am?"

"Oh, yes. Your love language is definitely gifts and touch."

He chuckles. "And how do you know that?"

"Well, I don't know. Maybe because you now have a jar of pickles in this house. For me."

Jasper gives a devilish smirk.

"All right then," he concedes, gripping my hips in his large palms. "Stand up. Let me show you how much I truly love giving. And how much I fucking *love* touching you."

264

Grinning, I rise from the tub, water sluicing down my body, bubbles fizzing over my skin, and Jasper grips my ass, sits up, and settles his beard between my thighs.

Not even five minutes later, his palm darts up to cover my moans as I release onto his tongue, and I'm still whining into his palm when he gives me one more.

Jasper is a giver after all.

Chapter 31

Summer of Soup

Jasper

"Soups are not served in the summer," Peter says matter-of-factly.

"Is that a thing?" Cassidy asks.

"That's not a thing," Milo mutters.

I look between my brothers and my father's perfectly prepared soup, simmering on the stove. David Davies looks seconds away from tossing it over Peter's head.

"You just don't like soup," I comment.

"Well, not in the summer," Peter agrees. "No. Who does?"

Dad sighs. "It's a rainy day, son."

"All days have been rainy this summer," Peter argues back. "Doesn't mean it's the *summer of soup.*"

All five of us lean closer to the windows, watching the rain cascade down in the back of the house. Admittedly, it's a depressing sight, seeing the tree house and backyard coated in mud. Plus, both The Twins and Sam are forced to stay indoors, which, in the one hour we've been here, has led to numerous Lego builds clattering to the floor and arguments over video games. After we all lost to Liam for the third time—he's a Mario Kart genius, I swear—we sequestered ourselves to the kitchen.

Cassidy shrugs. "I don't know. I could go for a summer of soup. Sounds exciting."

"You just can't have hot foods on a hot day," Peter insists again with a shrug. "It's a fact."

Milo sighs. "Then, why do people grill out in the summer, Pete?"

My dad crosses his arms over his chest. "Yes, would you like me to stop making hamburgers? Is that only a winter delicacy?"

Peter looks around at our family before tonguing his cheek and grinning. "Fair point."

Dad claps him on the shoulder while the three of us laugh. "Summer of soup it is."

Then, a voice from the doorway chimes, "Maybe that's our next promo event."

Izzy walks through the kitchen threshold, frizzy, curly hair tied in a messy bun on her head. Her arms are full of tiny boxes, each one a different type of cracker.

"As requested, Mr. Davies," she announces, dumping them on the counter unceremoniously. "Didn't know which would go best with the soup."

"Thanks, Iz." He pulls her in for a side hug, and they give the appropriate three hug pats.

"Summer of Soup though," Peter muses. "Now, there's an idea."

"You're welcome," Izzy says. "I'm full of ideas. I expect a pay raise on Monday."

Peter snorts. "I pay you just fine. You have profit sharing." Then, he grins to the rest of us. "Remind me not to invite my *employees* to dinner again."

"Employee?" Izzy gasps with a laugh. "Hilarious. At this point, you work for *me*."

Peter rolls his eyes, but the grin on his face doesn't disappear. He likes being ribbed, and Izzy's always been the best at it.

I nod to her. "How's life, Iz?"

"Why, *thank you* for asking, Jasper," she says, playfully batting her eyelashes at me. "Life is wonderful."

"Good to hear."

"I don't see *you* asking," she snarks, elbowing Peter. "No wonder Wendy thinks Jasper's the better brother."

Blood rushes up to my head as my muscles tense and my head swims.

What the hell is she talking about?

Peter laughs out. "The better brother?"

"Wait, wait, wait," Cassidy says with a wave of his hand. "Since when is the competition strictly between those two? I want to be the best one."

"Seems unfair," Milo throws in, eyes darting to me.

But my shocked gaze is still locked on Izzy, her teasing lips tilting up at the edges.

What does she know?

Wendy and I have been careful. Our weekdays are spent apart—her watching Sam and me working—while our weeknights are spent in the bath and in bed, my face between her thighs, sometimes at the same time hers is between mine. But being in public together? We try not to be.

Although we ran into Izzy on Main a week ago. Now, I wonder just how much she saw. If she noticed my hand on

Wendy's lower back, my lips whispering into her ear, my palm traveling along her spine.

Shit.

"Just seems like she's been spending more time with you, is all," Izzy observes with a nonchalant shrug, as if she didn't just rip open the seams of our secrets.

"Really?" Peter asks.

"She's my nanny," I say.

It's too defensive, but nobody seems to notice. The perks of consistently being testy, I guess. When I actually am irritated, it's overlooked.

"They were shopping together," Izzy says. "I saw them when I went to visit Rafe."

So, she did see something.

Shit, shit, shit.

"Rafe?" Bonnie's head dips into the kitchen. "What's he up to now?"

I wait for another accusation, but the addition of Bonnie quickly shifts the conversation toward the artist and his screen prints. My body is still buzzing as I avoid Izzy's gaze, standing from my chair and leaving the kitchen.

I walk past The Twins and Sam clambering through the hallway, bumping against walls as they ascend the stairwell, and I enter my mom's office. Settled on the floral couch is my mom, and next to her is Wendy. They're clutching a photo album between them, giggling at the pages. More are littered on the floor.

"Oh, Jas!" My mom waves me over. "Come here! We're looking at baby pictures."

My face falls. "Oh no."

"They're cute!" Wendy says, and suddenly, my face grows hot.

I've never had a woman come over to look at baby pictures with my mom.

"Here's you with your fishing pole!"

"Fantastic," I groan.

"Oh, wow," Mom breathes. "And that's before the scar."

Wendy perks up. "The scar?"

"We don't have to talk about it," I quickly interject at the same time my mom croons, "He hasn't told you how he got his scar?"

Wendy shoots me a teasing look. "Are you a Batman villain?"

I roll my eyes, but I can't help the smile that forms as I take a seat in the opposite armchair.

"Can I?" my mom asks, clutching the photo album to her chest as some Polaroids inside flutter to the ground.

I wave my hand in permission. It feels so domestic for this embarrassment to happen, like a rite of passage in a relationship.

Are Wendy and I in a relationship?

It sure feels like it.

Even if we weren't, I kind of miss this. I miss my mom's messiness, my dad's fondness for the kitchen, my brothers' ridiculous conversations, and my little sister's ability to interrupt them. Jessica avoided too many of my family dinners, and I understand the urge. My family can be overbearing sometimes. But I believe it's their nosiness that makes them endearing.

My mom angles herself toward Wendy, lowering the album to her lap. "Back when it was just Jas and Pete, we would go fishing all the time."

"Oh, are we telling *the* story?" Cassidy asks, coming around the corner, shoving half a cracker in his mouth. "Have you never heard this, Wendy?"

"And she never will if you keep babbling," Mom says through laughter.

Cassidy's head jerks back. Wendy shushes him, too, adding insult to injury. I bring a fist between my teeth to stifle my laughter at Cassidy's grunt of disapproval as he shoves the rest of the cracker in his mouth.

"Fine," he says with a mouthful. "Go on."

"Anyway," Mom continues, "when Jas was just old enough to take Pete fishing by himself, Dave and I gave them a boys' day. We figured it was time to let them spread their wings. Be independent. Of course, we followed them anyway because they were just kids."

"Perceived independence," Cassidy tosses in. "I'm sure they loved that."

"Well, thank goodness we did," Mom responds with wide eyes. "Pete cast his line out with Jas standing right behind him. The hook caught in the back of his hand, and when Pete jerked it forward, Jas's skin went right with it. That boy made noises I hadn't known were possible for an eight-year-old. We almost thought he'd bleed out with how much he screamed."

"Psht. Baby," Cassidy teases me.

I flick him my middle finger. Wendy gasps and tosses a photo at me.

"Poor boy's hand was ripped to shreds," Mom continues without acknowledgment.

"Only partly," I grunt out.

But that scar remains on the back of my hand, raised and whitened and a reminder of a childhood with just me and Peter. It wasn't bad. It was full of fights and opposing personalities. But it definitely wasn't bad.

"It was then we knew we needed more bodies around

here," Mom says. "Or else Pete was gonna drive Jas insane and Jas was gonna kill Pete."

"Then, there was me!" Cassidy calls, hands extended into the air.

"And you're still here," Mom teases with a pointed look, reaching out to pinch his cheek.

He gives a small, "Ugh." Then, he says, "Hey now, I'm leaving soon."

"Right. How's house-hunting going?" I ask.

He groans. "Horribly. There's nothing out there." He points a finger at Wendy. "You got lucky with your house. Starkey cut you a deal."

Wendy's face heats, and she shrugs. "I don't know about a deal ..."

I furrow my brow. "Starkey's your landlord?"

Cassidy laughs and answers for her, "Of course he is. Why do you think there're so many flower boxes outside?"

I nod. "Ah. Marina."

Starkey's daughter, Marina, is a plant lover with a green thumb. I haven't seen her in months. Last I heard, she went off to college and joined the Peace Corps. Though who knows what's fact or fiction in Never Harbor? I once heard a rumor that I'd killed a man, but I don't think Steve's drunken state knew he was gossiping about Jasper Davies *to* me, Jasper Davies.

"Maybe you should look outside of town," I suggest.

"And leave Never Harbor?" Cassidy asks. "No way."

My knee-jerk reaction is to tell him to grow up, but that now seems too hypocritical. For the first time, I wish I lived closer to town. I want to spend more time here with my siblings and parents. I want to be near Wendy. More in tune with local events for Sam to explore, more art for him to admire.

For the first time, I can't blame Cassidy for wanting to stay close to home.

"There's only enough room in this family for one deserter," Cassidy jokes, shooting me a look.

I groan.

"Oh, come on. I'm kidding. I love that you're coming around again. I've missed bugging you."

"Yeah, we like it," Wendy adds.

My eyes flick over to her. Whenever our gazes catch, it's like the world stills around us. Like a curtain has been lowered and we're finally backstage, no longer performing our act of boss and nanny or friend.

I lift an eyebrow. She bites her bottom lip in that cute way of hers.

God, I can't wait to tease her more later.

But just behind her, I spot Izzy leaning in the doorway, arms crossed and eyeballing the both of us in a way I wish she wouldn't.

Isabel is not intimidating on the surface. She's petite and blonde. Pink cheeks and plush lips. But, boy, can she glare. She might not stand a chance in a fistfight, but I'd put money on her bringing a weapon to ensure victory. I bet she'd be a killer with only a butter knife.

"Think you'll stick around?" she asks.

I grunt in response, but Wendy's cute cheeks flush red, and something tells me I'm not going anywhere anytime soon. I don't want to ostracize myself anymore. I want to be around my family. And especially Wendy.

I wait until the conversation moves on to Bonnie's art classes and Milo's job hunt before leaning over to Cassidy and whispering, "Hey, think you could watch Sam this weekend?"

Cassidy grins. "Sure, man. But why?"

I didn't think that far. "I'm just, uh—"

"Oh my God, is Jas getting a life?" Bonnie hiss-whispers. I didn't realize my little sister was right behind me until she's leaning in between me and Cassidy, grinning ear to ear. She gasps. "Are you getting back out there?"

"What do you know about getting out there?"

"Oh my God, you *so* are—"

I purse my lips into a *shh*. She hides her smile as her feet bounce on the floor.

"You know, we should tell Pete," Cassidy says. "He knows everyone in town. I bet he could set you up with someone."

My hand twitches by my side, my eyes accidentally darting over to Wendy and back before I clear my throat. "No, I think I've got this."

"You?" Bonnie asks with sarcasm. "Flirting with random women?" She barks out a laugh. "They're gonna think you're luring them into your cellar."

"I don't even have a cellar," I deadpan.

Cassidy snorts. "Okay, but she does have a point. Sure you don't want us to set you up? There's no way you have game."

But from the couch, Wendy chimes in, "I bet Jas has game."

Bonnie and Cassidy swivel their heads over to her, and both erupt into cackles.

But my gaze settles on Wendy, who gives me her signature smile with that precious dip in the corner. I try not to grin, but I lose the battle.

Yes, I definitely like being in Never Harbor. But I think I like joking with Wendy Darling even more.

Chapter 32

Learning to Fly

Wendy

THE END.

I've never seen those words before, but now, my eyes dance over the screen to stare at my very first finished novel. I don't know what I'll title it. I don't even know what to do with it now.

But it's finished.

It's done.

I completed a book.

I shimmy in my chair, picking up my phone, my fingers hovering over the keys in anticipation. I bypass the recent texts from Cassidy, Bonnie, and Peter with GIFs and memes and scroll to Jasper instead, sending over a, *I did it.*

If anyone understands simple victories, it's him with his construction.

At that moment, my doorbell rings.

I cross the living room and crack open my front door. Jasper stands on my front step, hand hanging by his side, clutched around a bouquet of daisies. His beard looks freshly trimmed, his hair slightly damp but delectably so, like he just got out of a shower.

My jaw gapes open. His clear eyes widen as he glances down to the bouquet in his fist.

"Are the flowers too much?" he asks.

"Depends. What are they for?"

"Nothing in particular," he says, and the exhale that follows is so sweet. "Just felt right."

I tilt my head to the side, leaning against the doorframe. I love how his eyes trail over my figure. Even though I'm in a loose Never Harbor Elementary tee and bike shorts, he still can't take his eyes off me.

"I just texted you," I say.

"You did?"

I laugh. "I did."

Jasper looks behind him and then back to me.

"Can I come in?" he asks.

I roll my eyes, grabbing him by the collar of his plain white T-shirt and jerking him inside.

"You know you don't have to ring the doorbell," I say. "Nobody else does."

"How rude of them," he teases, kicking the door closed behind him with his boot.

His free hand dives in my hair at the same time I pull him to me. Our lips meet, and my stomach plummets, like I'm falling on the opposite side of a roller coaster, soaring over the tracks with Jasper by my side.

He lets out a strained groan, walking me backward until my back hits the kitchen island. I hear the crinkle of the flower wrapping as he places the bouquet down before gripping my thighs and hoisting me up and onto the countertop.

I wrap my arms around his neck. His hands capture my waist as he steps between my knees, kicking them apart to make more room for his body. Our mouths open and close in desperation, as if we didn't just see each other the day before. We did, but Sam was there, and we haven't exactly kissed in front of him yet or explained the situation. I'm not sure what our long-term plan is, but as long as Jasper is kissing me like this when we are alone, I don't think I care.

Problems for a future Jasper and Wendy.

Our kisses slow, and we pull apart, him kissing the tip of my nose, still out of breath.

"So, what did you text me?" he exhales.

"Oh! I finished my book!"

Jasper's face transforms into something new right in front of me. Raised eyebrows. A wide grin with straight white teeth—a smile that reaches his eyes, forming handsome little crinkles.

His palms grip my thighs in excitement.

"Congratulations!" he says. "Baby, that's so amazing."

Amazing.

I thought it felt good to be told that in the bedroom, but nothing—and I mean, *nothing*—compares to being told that in broad daylight.

My heart is on fire, and I'm alight from head to toe in nerves and happiness and pride.

"Really?"

"Send it to me," he says.

I blink rapidly in disbelief. "You'd read it?"

"Of course I would. I love your stories."

I've only truly gotten to know Jasper over the last couple of months, but one thing I know for sure is that Jasper doesn't say things he doesn't mean. He tells the truth.

Which is why the word *love* echoes in my chest like a drum.

He doesn't mean it.

277

He can't.

Sure, I've known Jasper for nearly fifteen years. But really knowing him, being able to figure out his expressions and know what the little grin means versus the crooked smile ... I think I might. It's only been a couple of months. At best, if you count the times I avoided him. But I understand this expression. It's pride.

I melt into his arms, burying my nose against his chest, breathing in his cologne and even the hints of a fishy harbor. But it's *him*. It's so *him*.

He loops his arms under my knees and carries me to the reading room, sitting in the armchair near the window, letting me straddle his legs.

I always wondered what he would look like in this chair, as opposed to the rest of the Davies men. However, I didn't expect to be on top of him when he finally took a seat. But I like him here, thick thighs spread, large palms kneading my ass, and a satisfied smile tilting his lips.

Happy. I never thought I'd see Jasper Davies *happy* in my home.

"Wait, where is Sam?"

"With Cass and Bonnie. I actually came over to see if I could take you sailing. If you want to get away for a night."

My stomach flips as my palms flex on his biceps.

"Are you being romantic?" I ask.

He knocks his chin back toward the kitchen. "Thought the flowers gave it away."

I grin, feeling him ghost the palm of his hand over my spine, splaying out over my bird tattoo that he loves so much.

"Then, sure," I concede. "Take me, Jasper."

He coughs out a laugh. "Pardon?"

I love catching this grumpy man off-balance.

"To your boat!" I say, swatting at his chest. "Obviously."

With a roll of his eyes, he kisses me.

Soft.

Sweet.

Then, he lowers his head, placing kiss after kiss along my neck until he settles in the dip beside my shoulder—his favorite spot. We pause there for a moment. Him sitting between my open legs and my palms holding his head against me, fingers coursing through his hair.

Jasper Davies likes being held more than anyone I've ever met.

And I really love holding him.

WE SET sail at six o'clock. Jasper has a cooler full of water, whiskey for him, and a mason jar with pink liquid for me.

"Pink drink?" I ask, holding it up to the light, like I'm waiting for the concoction to turn black, like poison. "Someone's playing with fire."

He chuckles. "I only made one, so you're safe from a hangover."

"How thoughtful."

Jasper shrugs it off. I wish he wouldn't. He's always so attentive and thoughtful.

I unscrew the cap, sipping from the rim and watching Jasper adjust the sails, wrapping rope over his arm coil by coil—motions that stretch his henley and flex his forearms. His fishing hook, just barely poking out under the rolled-up sleeve, moves in the same pirate flag motion Sam's temporary tattoo did. I wonder if Sam'll want real tattoos when he gets older. I wonder how much he'll want to be like his father figure and if Jasper will even allow it.

279

Jasper snaps open a to-go container filled with cheeses and breads and then a side container of jam.

"Fancy," I comment with a grin.

"I can't fully take credit."

"No?"

"Bonnie said if I took someone on a date, I needed a cheese plate."

"Is this a date?" I tease.

Without hesitation, he answers, "I don't take anyone out to sea, except you."

My heart runs like a wild horse, galloping up to my throat.

The sea breeze billows through my hair until I tie it back with my ribbon. The movement catches Jasper's eye, and he gives me a sly grin. I bite my bottom lip, but a thrill runs down between my legs at the unspoken exchange. It's funny how Jasper doesn't need to say anything when he can simply lift an eyebrow and portray every dirty thought in his mind. His lack of words is just as seductive.

As the sun starts to set, sending paintbrush strokes of orange across the sky, we dock at Skull Rock.

I sit with Jasper's head in my lap, massaging my fingers through his hair as he lies on the bench cushion. We watch the sun go down in streaks of pink. It's mostly quiet, but I like hearing the gentle rolling of water against the rocking boat, creaking as it bobs side to side. I like just existing with Jasper in peace.

"What's the most special item you own?" I ask.

He sucks in a deep inhale, as if in thought, then lets it out.

I laugh. "Don't tell me you've never considered it."

"I'm deciding which one."

I smile. "There's multiple?"

"Two probably."

"Well, what's one?"

"My watch," he says, lifting his wrist up, admiring the cracked face. "It's a little beaten up, but Ed gave it to me years ago, back when Sam was still a baby. He was a horrible sleeper, but with this one, you can't hear the ticking. He said it would serve me well when I babysat."

It's quiet again, the almost ringing silence of that role echoing between us—the transition from godfather to sole guardian.

"Yours is the thimble my mom gave you," he says matter-of-factly.

I grin because he's right. "It is. Your mom's hug. You notice things, don't you?"

"About you, yes. My mom means a lot to you, doesn't she?"

I nod. "She's my favorite person. Nothing like my own mom. Maggie helped me pick a dress for prom, gave me a Christmas stocking when I'd never had one, helped me wax my eyebrows for the first time."

"Is that some bonding thing I'm not aware of?"

I laugh. "Definitely. If I lost her, I don't know what I'd do, y'know?"

I expect him to say, *Wouldn't we all?* Or even the very true, *She's my mother; of course I understand.*

But he doesn't. Jasper lets me live in this moment. Lets me experience *my* relationship with his mother rather than make it about him. And that's the stark difference between him and Peter. Jasper understands individuality. He understands making space for others. Or maybe it has nothing to do with Peter. Maybe Jasper just understands *me*.

"Wendy, would you like a thimble?" he asks.

"I'd love one."

I bend down at the same time he reaches up, and we wrap our arms around each other in a makeshift hug—the best one we can manage with his head lying in my lap. We pull apart with laughter.

"So, do you ever talk to your parents?" he asks.

"No," I answer. "But I'm not sad about it. People leave your life and don't come back. Sometimes, it's friends. Sometimes, it's parents. At the end of the day, people are people."

"Life isn't a story, huh?"

"That's right. There are no redemption arcs. Just life. I probably talk to my cousin, Michael, more than I do them. But he's down in Georgia, so not a lot of hanging out really happens," I reflect with a sigh. "Life isn't a fairy tale." But then I correct myself to say, "Not always," because this right here—having dinner on a boat under the cloudy pink sky—sort of feels like one. And I wish I knew how I was lucky enough to get here.

Jasper sits up, resting his forearm on his raised knee. He blinks at me, as if expecting something.

I laugh. "Yes, Captain?"

He squints. "Wasn't I promised a book?"

My mouth dries. "What?" Then, I laugh again. "You were serious?"

The idea of sharing my own story feels too intimate. Terrifying. But when Jasper looks at me like he is now, eyes darting between mine, somehow, it doesn't feel as scary.

His mouth tilts into a half smile. "I'd love to read your work."

Your work. Like it's a piece of art.

And I find myself asking, "Really?"

Holding my chin between his fingers, he lightly traces a

thumb over the corner of my lips. "Don't think I won't find another way to get it from you."

With nerves bouncing like a racquetball through my body, I reach for my phone and tap through my apps. When I ask him his email, Jasper answers, and I invite him to my book's online document. Then, I toss my phone back onto the cushion beside us.

"Done. Happy?"

His playful grin is contagious. "I'm honored."

"Prepare for disappointment."

"I will not."

The immediacy with which he responds is astounding. I don't know what to do with his confidence in me.

"There's more," he finally announces.

"More? I only wrote one book."

"No," he says with a chuckle, reaching for my hand. "More to show you."

"Another cheese plate? Ooh, pickles?"

He snorts. "You wish."

"Well, don't ask me which kind I wish for."

"Dirty girl," he croons, his tone a low rumble.

My heart ratchets up my throat, and I choke out a laugh. "So, what is it?"

"You'll like it."

"I *guess* I'll trust you."

We step off the boat, his hand leading me down to the shore. We walk down the beach, hand in hand, the sand filtering around our shoes, his arm occasionally tugging me close so he can place a kiss on my cheek or my nose or the edge of my lips. After a couple of minutes, he turns into an alcove. In the middle is a knitted rug, lights strung between two lit tiki torches, and a propped-up beige tent.

I gasp. "Are we camping?"

"We're camping."

"Jasper! I've always wanted to go camping!"

He doesn't need to say *I know* for me to feel it through his broad smile. He unzips the front flap, and I crawl in, the wicking material swishing under my knees.

It's a simple setup. Just enough room for the two of us once Jasper crawls in after me. Some combination of mattress toppers and sleeping bags transforms the ground into a cushioned bed.

It's perfect.

"And we're staying here?" I ask, flipping onto my back.

"I also rented the cabin on the island too," he says, hovering over me with a palm steadied beside my head, "just in case you didn't want to spend the night on the ground."

"No." I grab a fistful of his T-shirt and tug him down on top of me. "I love this."

His lips meet mine on a hiss of a breath. He always does this, as if I'm taking him by surprise every time I make the first move. Every time I *want* to kiss him.

Our lips move so naturally, like they were meant to be kissing for so long and we just discovered the magic of making out. Like two feverish teenagers desperate for more touch. His hand lands on my waist, bunching up the fabric along my hip, tracing a thumb along the hem of my thong.

I pull apart from him, tracing fingers through his hair as he stares down at me through hooded eyes.

"You sure do like seclusion, huh?" I ask.

He shrugs. "I don't care for small-town gossip. Gives me hives."

I giggle. "The cottage makes so much sense now. Do you ever miss being in town?"

He trails his fingers over my skin and sighs. "I have been lately."

I swallow and change the subject. Because if I don't, my heart might beat too fast for comfort.

"You guessed my thimble," I say. "Can I guess your other item?"

"You can try."

I laugh. "Look who's being feisty tonight."

He rolls onto his side, propping his head up on his palm and looking down at me. His other hand doesn't leave my hip, ghosting fingers along my waist, up to my ribs, and back down again.

"Is it ... a gift?" I guess.

"Something like that."

And then I glance down at the bunched-up pocket, where his keys rest within.

"Is it that hotel key chain you have? The diamond one?"

He clears his throat, his face falling, surprised I guessed it maybe. Or disappointed he has to discuss it. "It is."

"Do you want to tell me about it?"

His eyes catch on an invisible area beside me, as if he's trying to find the words before nodding. "It was from spring break."

"You wild child," I whisper.

He huffs out a laugh. "We were much older than you think. It was Stacy's spring break. She was a professor of marine biology already. She, Ed, and I went on vacation, and they stayed in some bed-and-breakfast. Ed forgot to return the key. I found it on his dresser when we cleaned out their house."

I go silent before murmuring, "He kept it that long?"

"Stacy found out she was pregnant with Sam on that trip. That's also when they both asked me to be his godfather. Didn't even wait until he was born. Didn't even hesitate."

I settle my head onto my pillow, staring up at the tent. A chill blows over it, crinkling the fabric.

"Sorry," he whispers. "I didn't mean to make things weird."

"Don't be. And you didn't," I say quickly. "It's just a lot to process sometimes. I can't imagine that level of loss. But that's not weird. Never feel like you're doing something wrong by still grieving."

His grip on my side tenses. He opens his mouth to talk, goes to close it, but then speaks anyway. "You're the first person who makes me feel like I'm going to be okay."

My eyes dart to his, watching as he regards my body. Greedy, but also as if he's taking me in as a person. Savoring my presence.

I reach up, placing a hand on his cheek, and all I can think to say is, "I'm sorry."

He kisses my shoulder, right where my dress strap has fallen, lying limp on the sleeping bag below. I shift onto my side, mirroring his position by propping my head up on my palm as well. I run my opposite hand over the forearm reaching out to my hip, tracing fingers over his hook tattoo.

I glance at the scar on the back of his hand and peer back up, a light bulb flashing in my mind.

"Your tattoo is a reminder, isn't it?" I ask. "Of the accident with Pete."

"Yes."

"Your family is really important to you."

"Yes," he murmurs again, but he isn't focused on his tattoo or the intricacies of its significance.

Jasper is never focused on himself; he's concentrated on me with an unwavering stare.

He pulls my body closer, and I nervously laugh at the motion, but he doesn't. Jasper's hand continues around my body, landing over where my tattoo is, splaying his fingers out, as if delicately balancing the captured bird in his palm.

"You like my tattoo," I observe.

"I like its meaning." And then he leans in, resting his lips against my ear as he whispers, "I think I needed a little bird to remind me to fly too."

And with that, I press my lips to his, letting my heart fly out, allowing him to capture it as well.

Chapter 33

Yes, Captain

Jasper

WENDY KISSES ME, and her lips carry purpose. Soft yet searching. Needing. Chasing.

I press my palm into her back, pulling her body down to me. We're chest to chest, barely able to get any closer, but, God, if we could, I would. I'd let her melt into me.

She shifts her weight so that I'm pinned on my back, her thighs straddling me, freckled knees on either side of my hips. My palm grips her waist, steadying her on top of me as she rolls her hips forward.

Christ.

I meet her in the middle, thrusting back. She exhales against my mouth.

I run my palms roughly over her back, catching on the fabric when I grip it, jerking the dress over her head. She pulls it the rest of the way, tossing it to the corner of the tent.

Kissing down her neck, along her shoulder, and to her chest, I hook my finger into her bra strap and pull it down. I run my thumb over her exposed nipple, watching it perk up under my touch. Capturing it in my mouth, I roll my tongue over the peak, feeling her chest expand as she pulls in an inhale.

My other hand slips between our bodies, fingers trailing along the soft skin of her bare stomach, tracing the beautiful line down her center before dipping below the hem of her panties. She's already wet against my finger, allowing me to easily roll it over her, dragging the slickness with me as I tease the spot I already know so well.

Her fingers tear through my hair, gripping me closer, and she arches her back as I kiss along her chest, burying my nose into the opposite cup of her bra to bite her other breast. Her chest is already red from my beard.

She sucks in a breath, letting it out in a laugh. I love the happiness that radiates off her. Even when she's experiencing sex, she's filled with it, her joy brimming over. Barely containable. Just Wendy.

I dip my finger lower, sliding it into her. She rises to her knees, giving me room to explore, to slip a second one in, to curl them together as the heel of my palm finds its home back at her clit.

"You're so good," she breathes.

Her praise sends a shot through me as I bury my fingers deeper inside her, upping my speed, flicking my tongue over her nipple, granting me another precious whine from her. I roll my fingers slowly, as if coaxing her forward.

"Come here. Sit on my face how I like it, baby."

I remove my hand, and with a beautiful grin, she crawls forward, lowering herself over my chin. I part her panties to the side and eat my woman like I need her to survive, the taste of her like heaven.

She bucks against my chin, and I hold her steady, gripping her hips with a palm and capturing her breast between my fingers, pinching, teasing, just like I did in the bath that night, feeling her thighs tighten around my head.

What might have been a soft and intimate night transforms into something different, something heady. Like we've both been greedy for this time together, and now, nothing is stopping the rush.

She moans, clutching the strands of my hair.

"Come on," I groan. "Show me you want it."

She grinds on my face, and with a sharp breath, Wendy releases on my tongue.

Sweet, just like her.

"Attagirl," I growl.

Before I try for another orgasm, she's already crawling down my body, hands fumbling with my belt. The rattle and clink of my buckle. The hiss of my zipper. The shift of my jeans as she shucks them down. Her mouth is on my cock in an instant. My hand buries into her hair, pushing at the same time she takes more of me.

I let out an unrestrained groan. She smiles against me, and I want to *see* that smile. I cup the back of her head, tilting her face up, and, Christ, the sight.

Her plump pink lips crudely wrapped around my cock. Her cheeks flushed. Her heavily lidded blue eyes overflowing with lust.

Eyes still locked on me, she lowers her mouth down again.

"God," I breathe, running my palm through her hair, tangling in her ribbon. I give it a light tug, allowing it to release her strands.

Her hair cascades down, a curtain framing her cheeks.

"Sit up for me," I demand, and she complies, letting my cock leave her mouth with a small *pop*.

She rises to her knees, and I jerk my chin up. She follows my unspoken instruction, shimmying herself closer to me, higher on my waist until my hands wrap around her body.

I flick the ribbon against her bare back. "Hands."

I wish I could capture the look on her face. The wide smile as she puts her hands behind her back, pinning her wrists together for me. Blindly, I use the ribbon to bound them together, tying it off with a knot.

"I should have known your knot-tying skills would come in handy."

I jerk the knot tighter. "I appreciate that dirty mind of yours."

"What other plans do you have for me, Captain?"

I laugh. "You like that title, don't you?"

"I can use it more."

"Is that right?"

"If you'd like."

Her smile drives the playfulness home.

I pull her hips up so she grinds the length of me. Only the fabric of her panties separates the heavy weight of my need from finding its home. But the wetness from her still soaks through.

"I *need* you. Do you know that? I need your little teases. Your pretty smiles. Your stories. I need you."

"Then, take me, Captain."

"If I do, then I'm keeping you. I'm never giving you back."

"Never is a long time."

I sigh. "Not long enough."

She leans down to kiss me, grinding her hips forward again.

Julie Olivia

I peer around her gorgeous body, glancing at my pants on the tent floor.

I pat her hip, gesturing for her to rise up. "I have a condom in my pocket."

"Or ..." she says slowly, tightening her thighs, holding us both in place. "I'm on birth control. That's always an option."

I tense, and my palms tighten on her hip.

"My Wendy," I rasp out, dragging her down and back up my length, watching as she lets out a soft exhale.

Her knotted hands reach back, tracing along my inner thighs. I shake my head with a gruff, choked laugh.

"You always know how to break me, Little Bird."

I pull her hips up so she rises to her knees. Shifting her panties aside with my thumb and removing one of my hands from her hip to grip my cock, I trace my head over her slick center.

"Is this what you want?"

She feverishly nods. "So bad."

Without another word, I notch myself at her entrance and push in.

I hiss in at the same time she does. Rubbing my thumb over her clit, I pull out and push back, edging more of myself inside with each thrust. She's so wet, but also so tight, and when I push into her the next time, she lowers down onto me, taking all of me inside her.

I choke back a groan. The nerves zip up my chest. I'm lightheaded by the feel of her. How well we fit together. How her movements match mine.

I take her hips in my hands, guiding her back up and thrusting up at the same time she falls back onto me.

It's that desperation. That *need* to feel more of each other, to be closer.

292

"There we go," I moan. "That's my girl."

It becomes rough. Dizzying. I move faster, jerking into her. She bounces down on my hips. Her breath leaves in sharp gasps. I let out heavy groans, unable to contain myself. I wind around her back to grip her ass in my palms, reaching back to slap it in a sound that has both of us moaning. I entwine my hands with her tied ones, steadying her as our bodies move in tandem.

I thrust into her over and over, the sounds of our bodies filling the tent. I can feel her tightening around me, triggering the build of my own release, drowning any thoughts in my mind.

"Like that," I grunt. "Just like that." I shove a hand between our bodies, running a thumb over her. "Come for me, Little Bird. Make my day."

Her eyebrows scrunch in, her lips part, she tightens around me, and on an exhale, she releases.

So perfect.

I thrust harder, splaying my hand on her stomach as I savor her.

And when she moans out a soft, "Jasper, *baby*," I know I'm a goner too.

I spill into her, an exhale catching in my throat. Our hands clutch together through my orgasm, our fingers tangling in a tight grip.

I grunt out a choked breath, kissing my way up her body, up her arm, resting my forehead on her shoulder as we both exhale against each other. And when I place a kiss in that dip of her neck, she turns to kiss the side of my head.

I don't know what our endgame is here, but there's no option that doesn't include me falling harder than I already have.

Chapter 34

Five Minutes Ahead

Wendy

THE FOLLOWING week goes by too fast—a flash of memories that include staying at Jasper's house long after I'm supposed to, playing by the beach with Sam and Roger, and extended bubble-bath discussions with Jasper in his tub.

I make sure to keep an eye on Sam, and so does Jasper. We're both walking on eggshells, hoping not to disrupt his idea of normal. But Sam is ecstatic I'm staying later. It means more stories, more of his dad's laughter, and more of *us*. And I like the three of us a lot.

After only a few days, Sam doesn't look at the clock around four o'clock anymore. He just assumes I'm staying. He's following the lead of Jasper, who simply walks straight to the kitchen after work, pulls out ingredients for a meal he's considered beforehand, and starts cooking. Sometimes, it's fish he bought from town. Sometimes, it's simply home-made pizza. But every time, I make sure to join him, walking around the kitchen to hand him spices or scissors, like some meal surgeon. And when we pass by each other, our pinkies secretly link between our bodies. And if Sam isn't in the room, I might get a spicy ass grab.

It's perfect. All of it.

We eat on the back porch, watching the sun fall below the horizon, tossing a stick for Roger to chase after—down the stairs and up again. We put Sam to bed, and I continue the story from the night before until it gradually turns into collaborative storytelling. Sam interjecting situations. Me riffing off those. And Jasper looking between the two of us with a serene smile, more content than I've ever seen him.

Not surly, but content.

Maybe even happy.

On Friday night, he asks me to stay over. Well, more like demands it. After bathing each other in the tub again, like he loves to do, Jasper clicks on the light in his walk-in closet and pulls out a large, folded T-shirt, tugging it over my head.

I tilt my head to the side after sliding my arms through. "And I'm supposed to drive home in no pants?"

My dress is in the corner of the room, abandoned around the time Jasper bent me over the end of his bed with my wrists clutched in his palm, the other hand splayed over my back tattoo.

"No, you're not driving home at all," he answers, cupping my face and pulling me in for a kiss.

I smile against his mouth, causing him to grin as well.

"And what if I had plans tomorrow?" I ask teasingly.

"You do. Coming in my bed before coffee."

"You're insatiable," I say, shaking my head.

He tucks his arm behind my knees and carries me to his bed.

We lie side by side, checking our phones one final time. It happens so naturally, like falling into a rhythm that's been in place for years. I set my phone on the side table and find a charger plugged in and folded over. Maybe this is Jasper's usual side. But when I look over, I find Jasper with his phone close to his nose, a charger already plugged into his device too.

He planned for me to stay ahead of time.

I curl closer to him, tucking my hand into the crook of his elbow as his eyes trace over his screen. But that's when I recognize the words on his phone. Because they're mine.

He's reading my book.

My body tenses as he slides his thumb up to read more of the document.

"Thoughts?" I hesitantly ask. "Actually, never mind. If you hate it, I don't want to know."

His mouth tips into a grin.

"You're really talented," he says.

I melt into the cushions, tugging the sheets up to cover my eyes. He chuckles, and the mattress moves beside me. He slides the covers off my face.

"You should be proud."

"Thank you," I whisper. "For reading."

"My pleasure," he whispers back in a mocking tone.

I roll my eyes and groan, but he jerks the sheets away from me.

"Hey! I'm hiding here!"

"Did you know I have a thing for storytellers?" he asks, leaning down to nip my ear.

"Since when?" I ask with a laugh.

He moves down to my stomach. "Since you."

"So, you've got a thing for me, you mean? What kind of thing? Is it massive?"

He rests his chin on my pelvis, lifting a single eyebrow. I pull my bottom lip in to stifle the laughter at my own joke.

"You have no idea," he growls, biting at my hip. "I think you underestimate just how much I'm obsessed with you."

"Then, show me."

And I think, for just a moment, I see that bit of red his brothers always joke about. Right before he disappears between my thighs.

$$\textsf{↶}$$

"Be free!" I release the latch on Roger's collar, and he barrels through the gated dog park.

Sam races after him, and I sit on the bench, watching that crazy boy join the other dogs, like he belongs in the pack as well.

The metal entrance gate squeaks open behind me, and a brown bag plops into my lap.

I lean my head back to see Jasper standing over me, two other brown bags held in his fist.

I gasp. "Are you joining us for your lunch break?"

"Sam told me you were gonna be here today. I took a guess when, and I was right."

I narrow my eyes. "Can you read my mind?"

"Maybe we're connected like that, Wendy Bird."

His palm traces over the back of my head, threading through my hair. I close my eyes, falling into the massage. Jasper walks around the bench, taking a seat next to me and letting his arm fall around my shoulders.

We exchange grins, and I allow my eyes to trail over his collared work shirt. His pants with the nice leather buckle. His work boots that scream hard labor and manly sweat that I want to lick off him later.

But then Jasper looks side to side and removes his arm.

I follow his gaze.

He's staring out at the other dog park patrons. There's Polly, a parent of a former student and a member of Maggie's book club. Wesley, a gym buddy of Cassidy's. And Steve, our paper boy. Jasper lifts his hand to him in a wave. Steve returns the gesture, his eyes catching on me before he has the good grace to look away.

"Oh," I whisper.

Jasper grunts in agreement.

I've become so accustomed to our alone time that I forgot that being open with everything would travel like a hurricane through our small town. It would wreck the family we both love so dearly if it got back to them. At the end of the day, I'm having sex with my ex-fiancé's older brother, and he's screwing his brother's ex.

I open my bag and see two pickles, wrapped in crinkle paper, just for me. Like usual, the sinking feeling of unfairness washes over me. The knowledge that we're in a bind with the noose getting tighter and tighter every day.

"Cap!" Sam yells, running over and barreling into Jasper's chest.

With an *oof*, Jasper catches him, knocking his glasses off-kilter and making Sam laugh. Roger lopes over along with other dogs, sniffing at the brown bags. Jasper has to hold them high in the air, ordering the lot of us to go to a picnic table before the dogs ravage our lunches.

All I want is to enjoy a day in the park with this thoughtful man, his son, and their dog.

I want to be part of this little family.

But Jasper and I don't touch again for the rest of lunch.

The clock tower in the park reads five minutes ahead, and I suddenly feel like we no longer have the time we so crave.

Chapter 35

The Other Shoe

Jasper

It's the last week before Sam goes back to school and Wendy's final week with us. Wendy starts her teacher prep next Monday before school starts on Thursday, disappearing back to her life before us. Before everything between us happened.

I steal touches with her as often as I can, grabbing her waist as she walks by me in the kitchen. Lightly tugging at her ribbon when I pass her sitting on the couch. There's so much still left to say. I want to savor her presence, her ideas, her stories.

I've been reading her book before bed every night. I don't tell her that I've already finished it, nor that I went right back to chapter one after I was done. I've always enjoyed reading, but I'll be the first to say I'm no critic. I have no idea if Wendy's book is technically sound. All I know is, I love it. Her prose is composed of the same gentle nature as her spoken word. The story is an extension of Wendy, who might leave me in only a few days.

How will we find time to be together then? Will we juggle the relationship and jobs? Will we date in front of Sam, but nobody else? Is Sam even capable of keeping a secret that important? Should I even ask him to shoulder that burden for us?

Then, there are the lingering questions. Will our relationship cause the rift we're expecting? Will it split our intertwined lives irreparably? When will the other shoe drop?

It's a dangerous thought to have because it opens the door I don't want to cross through—the option of no longer dating Wendy. The first time that crossed my mind, I felt a familiar weight in my boots that stuck me to the pier's wooden planks. I couldn't handle it.

That was when the word *love* entered my mind, and I haven't shaken it since.

Our future is a mystery. But here, on our private rocky shore, we're safe. Here, I can wrap my hand around hers, stroke my thumb along the outside, lean in when Sam is down the beach and kiss along her neck. Nibble at her ear, which grants me the laughter I always crave.

I won't tell her I love her because, after only a summer, it seems too quick. But it's there, simmering in my bones.

I love her.

But when her phone buzzes with a text from one of my brothers or when my family group chat sparks to life, we both tense up. The energy gets sucked from our secret bubble, like a leak seeping through. I attempt to seal it up as tight as I can because this—this feeling when she looks at me with a small smile—is the only thing keeping me grounded. I don't want to go back to how I felt before.

"Are you going to the family dinner tonight?" I ask her when I get home from work on Friday.

It's the last weekday we have before she goes back to work, and the thought of sharing her with anyone else twists that knot in my chest tighter.

"Maybe," she says skeptically, narrowing her eyes with a smile. "Why?"

"You could stay over instead," I offer.

"Wouldn't it be obvious if we both missed dinner?"

I grunt, "I don't fucking care."

Because I think I love you.

After a moment of contemplation, Wendy walks closer and says, "Okay," right against my lips, pursing them into a whisper of a kiss before walking off to find Sam.

I love you.

After we put Sam down to bed, stories and all, Wendy and I journey to the shed behind the garden, to my workshop, where a lone light bulb bobs from the ceiling. She sits on the wooden workbench, feet dangling over the edge as I saw off another piece of wood for the porch, measuring and cutting again. The sound of Cat Stevens sings through the small space, both of us humming along, exchanging smiles through the lyrics.

I love you.

"So, what's your end goal here?" she asks.

"What do you mean?"

"The house."

I shrug. "No end goal. Just building. One thing after another."

"Sounds nice."

I love that she understands the simple things. The fact that, sometimes, there isn't a goal, but just a pleasure in living life.

I throw her a smile. "It is. It's relaxing," I say. "I actually started construction because it was something to distract me. To fill the blank space in me with distraction."

"I hate that a blank space was there to begin with, Jas."

Her smile slowly falls, and she sighs.

"Are we gonna talk about next week?" she asks.

I pause, but my heart doesn't stop its thrumming for a moment.

"Sure," I agree reluctantly.

I set my handsaw aside and lean against the opposite bench, my pulse pounding. I kick one boot over the other, linking at the ankles. Crossing my arms over my chest, I pull in a breath.

Wendy laughs, reaching across the small space to tug my arms apart. "You're already getting defensive."

I lift an eyebrow, lowering my palms to grip the edge of the table. She's right. I am on edge. I don't want to talk about this. I don't want to face the reality that I might lose her.

"Tell me what you're thinking," she says. "You're opening and closing your mouth like a fish. You do that when you have something to say, but don't want to. Come on. I can take it."

I chuff out a laugh. "I'm not good at conversation."

"I know. But you like talking with me."

"You make it easy." I walk the short distance to her, cupping her face in my palms and tilting it up. "Honestly? I'm worried. I don't know what we'll do next week," I answer. "I'm just nervous about what life will be like when you're not here."

She nods slowly in understanding, biting her bottom lip. I stroke a thumb over her cheek. Her bruise, once yellow and green, is now gone. Another memory of the summer passing us by.

"I don't know either," she admits.

"I'll miss you."

She pulls in a breath, as if my words surprise her. But how could they?

I love you, Wendy Darling.

Without another word, I lower my lips to hers. She hums against my mouth, hopping off the workbench, pushing against my chest until we're clambering backward in the workshop, stumbling over the rickety floor.

We kiss until we can't breathe. Until I'm desperate for her and her, for me.

She leaps into my arms, wrapping her legs around my waist. I walk us to the nearest wall, pushing her against it, gathering her hair in my fist as our mouths collide in force, chasing and biting.

Her hands fumble for my belt. I rip down the collar of her shirt, capturing her nipple in my mouth, abrading her chest with my beard and teeth.

With my button undone and zipper ripped down, I thumb her panties to the side and thrust into her.

A moan leaves her lips, and I capture it with my greedy mouth, tightening her hair in my grasp, jerking into her. Our bodies echo through the workshop, her unrestrained moans bouncing off the walls along with my grunts that chase after.

The feeling in my chest—the proclamation of *love*—wants to bubble to the surface, but I fight my way through, biting her shoulder, letting her nails claw down my back, and instead saying things like, "I *love* how well you take me, baby," and, "I *love* fucking you."

One crude word away from the truth.

I've never had someone who makes me feel wanted. Who loves as deeply as Wendy does. Who I can be myself with—terrible conversationalist and all. Because when talk is truly needed, I provide.

"Don't be shy," I grunt. "Moan for me, Little Bird."

"Baby," she whines.

"There we go."

But somewhere between my face burying into her neck and her beautiful, exhausted mewl tickling against my ear, I distantly hear the creaking of the workshop's wooden door.

"What the *fuck*?!"

Chapter 36

Peter's Wendy

Wendy

WAVES OF AN ORGASM spark through my body, stars erupting into constellations behind my closed eyes when the gruff words reach my ears.

"*What the* fuck?!"

My eyes snap open. Jasper's broad chest continues pressing into me with each thrust, but just beyond his muscular shoulder is Peter.

"Oh my God." The words spill out of me like a dam as my hands fumble across our bodies for something—anything—to cover us. But there's no concealing the situation. Not this time.

Jasper's cheeks and neck, already red from sex, choke into a deeper shade of maroon when he sees his brother standing in the doorway.

Jasper stops, quickly affixing my top to cover my breast. He tucks himself back into his jeans. Sweat trails down my back.

Cassidy walks in behind Peter. His jaw drops, eyes widening as he takes in the scene.

Our dirty secret.

Jasper's two brothers—my stunned best friends—block the only exit through the creaking open door. It snaps in the breeze, knocking against the wooden wall. Cassidy stares at us like we're ghosts. But Peter's clenched jaw is what makes me think we're truly dead.

I've never seen Peter so angry. Never. His face is growing redder by the moment, nearly purple. His fists clench by his thighs. His eyes flick to me, pupils like pinpricks among the sea of green.

Jasper runs a hand through his hair, taking a large step forward. "Pete—"

"We went by your house, Wendy," Peter interrupts. "You hadn't shown up to dinner. And your car wasn't there."

Peter's voice catches, so Cassidy continues for him, "We figured maybe something was wrong when Jasper and Sam didn't show up either."

"We're fine," I interject quickly, an exhale on my lips.

But when Cassidy's head rolls back in exasperation, I realize that, yes, *clearly*, Jasper and I are fine. Our tangled limbs were probably as close to fine as two people can get, but probably best to not state that now.

"I'm sorry, Pete," Jasper says. "This isn't how you should have found out."

"Found out?" Peter asks. "Found out what exactly?"

"Pete, come on," he continues.

"Found out *what*?"

"This," I say.

"This," Peter echoes flatly.

He stalks forward, and Jasper pulls in a deep inhale, taking a protective step in front of me.

Peter catches the movement, freezing in place and narrowing his eyes with a scoff. "What the hell do you think I'm gonna do to her, Jas?"

"Pete—" Cassidy reaches for Peter's arm. He jerks it away.

"How could you?" Peter says. "You're my brother. I ..."

I look up to you are the unspoken words. Though, whether Jasper can sense that or not, I'm not sure. But the knowledge is a cut to my soul.

"It's complicated," Jasper answers sternly.

"You know that Wendy's ..." Peter starts, eyes darting to mine before flicking away. "You know that she's—"

"That Wendy's what?" Jasper asks.

Peter's jaw clenches tighter. He doesn't finish his thought. Jasper's narrowing eyes tell me he wouldn't know how to finish it either.

Cassidy sighs. "Hey, Pete, come on ..."

I can see the conflicting emotions coursing through him. He stares at the workshop floor, looking anywhere but at me or Jasper.

I wonder if I've lost Cassidy. If this is the beginning of the end. My heart sinks deeper, drowning in the thought. Jasper must sense it because his arm wraps around my waist, as if catching me before I can think to fall.

Peter runs a hand through his hair, messing up the locks, pacing to the side. "So, you're sleeping with her now. Is that it?"

Jasper's eyes flick to Peter. "Careful." His tone is low, rasping in his throat.

That's when I notice just how tense he is.

Jasper's opposite hand is clutched in a fist, his knuckles stretching the skin white. The forearm around my waist is flexing in anticipation. And his jaw is popping, just like Peter's. But Jasper has a type of menace that Peter could never achieve.

I've always heard about the potentially vicious red around Jasper's eyes—a silly rumor that Cassidy spread in middle school as a prank—but I see it now. The thin lines surrounding his clear blue irises are like the shimmer of wrath.

Peter blinks repeatedly, like maybe if he does it enough, this whole situation will disappear.

"Why?" Peter asks, his voice slightly shaky.

And part of me feels bad for him. Peter's happy-go-lucky attitude, the usual radiating sun, is eclipsed by something entirely different. The shadow of pain.

"What do you mean?" Jasper asks stiffly.

I can feel the temper simmering beneath the surface, right along with the shifting fingers that stir on my hips.

Peter shakes his head. "Why would you ... we dated for years—"

"I know," Jasper interrupts.

"She was everything—"

"I know."

"I was engaged to—"

"I *know*," Jasper snaps. "You think I don't?"

Cassidy's hands rise in the air. "All right, guys, let's calm down."

"Don't tell me to calm down," Peter snarls. His eyes dart between us, his jaw tightened. "I just walked in on my brother having sex with my *fiancée*."

"Ex," Cassidy says.

But the moment Cass interjects the truth, the energy in

the small space shifts. Because Peter didn't say *ex*. The word slipped out exactly as is.

Fiancée.

As if I still rightly belonged to him.

Jasper's fist clenches tighter. "She's not with you, Pete."

Peter shakes his head, giving a small second of quiet before his lips tip up into a smile. He lets out a sardonic laugh, and I genuinely can't tell if it's cruel or not.

He shrugs. "At least we'll always know who she belonged to first."

My heart sinks into my stomach. My knees are weak, my body tilting on its axis.

But before I can process anything else, boots pound on the wood floor, and Cassidy yells, "Wait, Jas!"

And in a sudden *crack*, Jasper punches Peter in the face.

Peter stumbles backward. His hand clutches his eye. And the shock of betrayal over his features is quickly overshadowed by anger.

"Say that again," Jasper sneers.

Cassidy barrels forward at the same time I do. Cassidy grabs Peter's arms as he rears back, his large hand gripped in a tight fist, ready to strike. I hurry between them, placing a palm against Jasper's chest, his hulking body trying to press forward, but halting when it pushes into me. Peter shuffles against Cassidy's hold.

"You're mad? How can *you* be mad?" Peter asks, the words strained.

"I'm not mad," Jasper says. He takes a step forward. "I'm *furious.*"

"Why? Because I interrupted your *Little Bird's—*"

"Don't you fucking dare," Jasper barks, the words a rumble in the depths of his throat.

309

Julie Olivia

And the menace suddenly feels all too real. I think that's the moment Peter notices too.

Peter stops struggling against Cassidy. He shakes his brother off him.

Jasper clears his throat, straightening his posture. "Get the fuck out," he demands. "Before I clock you again."

Peter sniffs, taking a step back. He presses the heel of his hand to his eye and shoves past Cassidy and out the workshop door.

It's just the three of us then, looking between each other. Jasper's chest heaves up and down. Cassidy meets my gaze and shakes his head.

"Cass ..." I breathe.

"Not the time," he murmurs, exiting the workshop right behind Peter.

Jasper exhales beside me, the vein in his neck pulsing in anger.

"Hey ..." I say as calmly as I can, tracing my fingers over his broad chest and down to his forearm.

He twists away from me, and the stab of rejection is immediate.

"I need a second," he says.

"Jas, are you—"

"One second," he repeats sharply.

I freeze, my body erupting into goose bumps. To his credit, Jasper's palm ghosts over my arm, as if trying to steady me, but his hand is too uneasy. He's shaking. And his eyes are still the maroon color of fury.

"You look—"

"I just punched my brother. I'm trying to navigate," he says wildly. "To ... to navigate this situation. How to ..." He shakes his head. "How to tell Sam. Any of this."

"You can barely talk," I say, the words a near whisper.

"I can barely *think*. I'm so ... overwhelmed. God, this is *my* family, Wendy. I don't know what to do now."

"You're right," I murmur. "They're your family. And you should talk about this."

"What do I even say? *Sorry for fucking Wendy?*"

"Jas," I say, the word a warning, even for me.

"I won't apologize for that. For wanting you."

My shoulders slouch. "I know."

"But I can't ... God. Sam ..."

"I can help—"

"I can do it myself," he snaps.

My head jerks back.

"He's *my* kid. I can handle it."

"I don't mind."

"No. I'm capable of ... of parenting without you."

It's like getting stabbed in the heart. A swift kick to my soul. The area behind my nose stings with the threat of tears. And I see his face fall the moment the words leave his mouth.

"I should head out," I whisper.

His eyebrows cinch together, and he takes a step closer. "Wait, Wendy ..."

"I need to. This is a mess."

His nostrils flare, and he huffs out air. "Stay. Please. I'm sorry."

"No," I reason. "I should really go."

Jasper's teeth grit, and he gives a curt nod. "Whatever you feel is best."

I swallow, and without another word, I turn on my heel, creaking over the wooden floor and out the door. The rush of a cool breeze hits me, the smell of the workshop's freshly cut wood blown away in an instant. Memories of a summer now tainted.

311

Pacing in the garden beside the rose bushes are Cassidy and Peter. Cassidy's got his phone in his palms, fingers whipping over the keys. He's likely telling the rest of the crew.

And I'm on the outside, as always.

I wonder how long until my number is blocked from all their phones.

Peter's covering his eye with one hand. The other is shoved into his pocket. I want to sneak past, but my sniffles give me away. Their heads pivot to me.

"Leaving?" Cassidy asks tentatively.

I nod. Peter returns the gesture, as if understanding. The area around his eye is already circling in red and black splotches.

"I'm not sure what to say," he admits.

I can tell he's had time to simmer down. His voice is brighter again. Boyish. Still with an edge, but nothing like the flash of cruel anger that overtook him five minutes before.

"Me neither," I answer.

He clears his throat. "I'm sorry."

"You were heated."

"But I'm not mad at you, I promise."

"Why not?" I ask. "You have every right to be."

He sighs. "I don't know. I guess because ... you're you. I can't stay mad at you."

I don't know how to take that or how to respond, so I don't. But the sentence still bothers me. Probably more than it should.

Why is he angry with Jasper and not me? It's like we're in some twisted reality Peter floats in—a world where I, his best friend, can do no wrong. Or worse yet, his *fiancée* can do no wrong.

Because maybe that's the fantastical world he still likes to believe in.

My eyes dart back to the workshop, where the warm light from inside stretches across the yard, yawning into the moonlit grass.

"I should go."

I don't belong here. Not when there are three brothers who need to have a conversation.

They're family.

And I could only hope to be.

But the moment I get in my car, Peter and Cassidy don't go back to the workshop to speak to Jasper. Instead, they climb into Peter's car. The three of us leave Jasper's property in some awkward caravan, me trying to drive farther ahead, as if I could put distance between me and the situation that is slowly breaking my heart in two.

I came into this idyllic slice of magic and tried to integrate myself within. But if I've learned anything about fairy tales, it's that, once the pixie dust settles, it's just another world with problems you can't control. Only lessons to be learned.

The issue is, I don't think I'm a very good student after all.

Chapter 37

Black Eyes & Bad Guys

Jasper

"You punched Uncle Peter?"

"Yes."

I didn't plan to tell Sam about anything, but when I woke up with my fist red and bruised, I had no choice. I waited all day to figure out what to say, and the best I could come up with was, *I punched your uncle.*

"Why?" Sam asks.

He deserved it, I want to say.

But I don't need Sam viewing his uncle in a bad light. Even if my brother did step over the line too many times last night—enough to have my knuckles hurt the next day.

"It doesn't matter why," I answer. "We don't hit people, okay? I got angry, and that was wrong. Violence is never the answer, and I should have known better, bud. But people make mistakes, and we learn from them."

"Even you?"

"Even me."

I remove the ice pack from my hand as Sam blinks over at me from his untouched plate. It's been a long day, consisting of silence, contemplation, and the satisfaction of routine. But a day in the workshop, as Sam played with action figures on the floor, went by too fast, and our dinner of frozen pizza isn't normally what I'd make for Sam. Just another drop in the bucket of bad decisions for my kid, I suppose. I've, unfortunately, been full of those lately.

"Why'd you get angry?" Sam asks.

I sigh, then swallow. "I ... I just did. I'm sorry," I finally say through a strained exhale. "I don't really wanna talk about it yet, bud," I mutter. "But we will."

But how do I approach this with him?

How do I talk about this with anyone?

How do I make myself *not* the bad guy in the scenario when I very clearly am?

I tried to call Wendy earlier today, but she didn't answer. I also sent a text to Peter. Another swing and a miss.

I already miss Wendy. I don't know where yesterday left us or where we go from here. Are we still ... whatever we were—dating? Can I invite her over again? But if I do, how do I explain that to Sam? She's not our nanny anymore. After last night, I don't know what she is to us now.

I don't want to disrupt Sam's notion of normal. We have a schedule, and we function well. Adding Wendy to the mix, outside of nannying, would complicate things. But didn't we already complicate Sam's life with this summer alone? Aren't our lives in general more complicated now?

I remember when I broke up with Jessica and how confused Sam was when she moved out. He was like a puppy, sniffing around and sitting on the same part of the couch she'd once occupied. My solution then was to buy a whole new couch because, to me, the lingering flower scent was cloying anyway. But I can't do that—not when I'm the one taking Wendy's place on the couch this time with Sam in my lap, simply because the cushions still smell like her soft linen scent.

Ultimately, it boils down to communication. That's always been my problem. I can't even talk to Sam about Ed and Stacy. Trying to explain to him that I'm in love with his beloved uncle's ex? That loving Wendy is why my knuckles are red and Peter likely has a black eye?

How do I do that?

I punched my brother.

Christ, I'm thirty-three, and I *punched my brother*.

We fought all the time as children, but this is different. This isn't over sharing action figures or stealing baseball cards. This is because I love his ex-fiancée.

Or, in his eyes, *his* Wendy.

Always his Wendy.

I need to talk to her, but phone calls have never been my forte. Texting? Forget about it. I typed an emoji at one point this morning, but it seemed too happy. Too smiley. Was I taunting her or being more approachable? I quickly deleted it.

"Is Wendy coming over?" Sam finally asks, and, God, that twists like a knife.

"Not tonight. She's busy."

"When will she come over next?"

"I don't know. Soon," I promise, but I wish I had a real answer.

"Are we going to Grandma's next week?"

I lower my ice pack and shrug. "Bud, I don't know."

Sam's face twists in an ugly expression as he kicks his heel against the rung of the chair.

"Hey," I snap. "Don't disrespect this house."

He hops down from his chair with a start. It looks so much like a teenager move; it's almost startling.

When did he grow up?

"You never tell me anything," he murmurs.

I sigh. "Sam—"

"I wanna go to bed."

"Okay. Do you want a story?"

"No."

The word is decisive, and without saying anything else, Sam makes a beeline to his room and shuts the door behind him. Normally, I'd request he take his plate to the sink with a little less attitude, but it feels fruitless.

He's right. I don't talk to him about the important things. I can't imagine how confusing it must be.

I bury my head in my hands, leaning back and running both palms down my cheeks. I miss Wendy's hands stroking over my beard instead of my own.

God, what the hell do I say to her?

I know I was sharp last night. I was so angry, my blood pumping so hard that I couldn't think straight. All I felt was the guilt of being caught and the consequences I'd been worried about forever.

Splitting the family.

Failing Sam.

But then there's my love for Wendy and the need to guard her heart from the man who didn't put her first. Peter's my brother, and I love him. But Wendy deserves better from the people in her life. Especially him. And now, me.

I grab my phone, staring at the screen with no new texts or calls, and before I know it, my fingers glide over the buttons. I place the phone to my ear.

317

Wendy answers on the first ring, and the silence over the line feels like walking into an empty cave. Vast and unknown.

"Hey," I finally croak out. I clear my throat.

I distantly hear the creaking of wood. I bet she's walking through her house, past those tall bookshelves with no TV and her wide, open windows.

"Hi," she finally responds.

I get up, dump our plates in the sink, and cross to my bedroom. I close the door behind me.

"I want to apologize for last night," I say.

"You don't have to."

"No, I do. I was flustered, and I didn't mean what I said."

It's quiet on her end. She must be contemplating those words and whether she believes them.

I made her lose faith in me, and that guts me to the core.

"It's fine," she finally breathes out.

But it's not. I know her.

"I wish I were better at this," I admit.

I love you, I want to confess instead, but my body aches at the thought. It's not the right time—not by a long shot.

She exhales into the phone. "My first day back is Monday," she says. "I should go to bed. Get some rest."

My heart sinks in my chest, barreling down to my stomach. I feel sick. She doesn't want to deal with me, and I can't blame her. I lost my cool.

Who *would* want to deal with that?

"Okay," I finally answer because words fail me, just like they always have.

"Okay," she replies. "G'night, Jasper."

Not Jas. Not Captain. Jasper.

"G'night, Wendy."

Not Wendy Bird. Not Little Bird. Wendy.

She hangs up first, and the silence in my bedroom is deafening.

I click off the light and fall into bed with my clothes from the day still on. The comforter fluffs up around me with the scent of linens and cotton. It smells just like Wendy.

After a moment, my phone rings again.

Wendy?

I feverishly pick it up, but it's only Cassidy. I let it ring until it stops. Then, my phone buzzes again. It's Bonnie. And ten minutes after that, Milo.

All three leave voice mails.

"Hey." An inhale. "So, last night was weird, huh?" A heavy exhale. "Give me a call." *Cassidy.*

"Pick up your phone, old man! I'm literally freaking out. I just overheard Cassidy telling Mom that, apparently, you're *dating Wendy*?! And you *punched Peter*?! She straight-up looked like she was gonna pass out. I don't know. Maybe she did. I might, too, because, holy crap, we *have* to talk about this. Answer your phone, loser!" *Bonnie.*

"Bonnie just called me. I'm not really sure what's going on, but you should probably talk to Peter first. Call me when you can." *Milo.*

The word has gotten out. I sigh, putting my phone to the side.

I'll wait for them to talk among themselves. They always do.

And it's only a matter of time until the whole of Never Harbor knows as well. Normally, this would irritate me. But instead, I feel numb to it all.

I wish I could go back to twenty-four hours ago, when I was making love to the woman I'd never expected to fall for.

I close my eyes and drift off, hoping that my dreams are filled with soft linens and cotton instead of rocking boats and storms.

Chapter 38

A Pirate at Heart

Wendy

It feels like a lifetime ago when I spent every night in bed with Jasper. Since our call on Saturday, we haven't talked. I received one call from him on Monday night, but I didn't answer. It didn't feel fair to him when I still have no idea what to say.

I'm sorry I got us into this mess.

I'm sorry I split up your family.

I'm sorry I stuck around longer than I should have.

He was right. Sam is his child. This is his family. And somewhere along the way, I had wrongly assumed they were mine. I'd taken them for myself, just like Peter had taken possession of me.

I don't know where I belong now. Normally, I call Maggie whenever I'm having issues. Or Cassidy or Milo or Bonnie. But the only texts I've gotten are short.

Bonnie sent a shocked GIF of a cat.

Milo followed with, *Are you okay?*

Finally, Cassidy asked, *Are you coming to dinner on Friday?*

But I've gotten nothing from Maggie, and that hurts the most. She must know by now, and there's no way she'll forgive me.

I didn't respond to Cassidy's question. It's not my place to go to a family dinner. That is Jasper's support network. Not mine.

I've spent so many years trying to claim them as my own. And what's funny is that, now, as much as I'd love to vent to any of them, more than anything, I'd love a text from Jasper—even more than Maggie. Grumpy, silent Jasper who can't hold a conversation. I'd sit in silence with him if it felt like the right thing to do.

But I've done too much irreparable damage to the Davies family, and these are my consequences.

I distract myself through the week by going to lunch with teacher pals I haven't seen most of the summer. Our principal, Donna, already has an events calendar in place, ranging from a fall festival to pajama day and a kickball tournament. But those don't excite me nearly as much as the beach with Sam or sailing with Jasper. It's funny how life's simple, insignificant moments leave a more defined stamp on your soul than the curated events designed to make lasting memories. I think I prefer the so-called mundane.

I spend Wednesday morning finalizing my classroom decorations—twisting brown craft paper and hanging green tissue at the end to create a tree house facade. Over on my cluttered desk—overflowing with card stock, string bunting, and markers—my phone pulses on the wood.

I scramble to it, searching for the name *Jasper*, but when I pick it up, my heart sinks.

Mags: You'd better be at dinner on Friday.

It's my first text from her, and I feel like it's the beginning of the end—an extrication from my place in the Davies family. I scroll through my texts—past teacher friends, Milo's analysis of the book we're reading together, and Bonnie's *first day of school outfit* panic from last week—and find the one text conversation I've been staring at all morning.

Jasper: See you real soon, Little Bird

The last text he sent before coming home from work on Friday. The last text before the incident. Before my perfect world shattered. The reality burrows deep in my stomach. And the thoughts—the horrific what-ifs—come rushing back.

What if he regrets it all?

What if this summer was only supposed to be a fun fling?

Was the risk of losing his family worth it?

Was *I* worth it?

WITHIN THE FIRST hour of school on Thursday, I find Sam. Or maybe Sam finds me.

I come out of my classroom, hands tucked in the pockets of my long skirt, as he whips around the corner.

Like kismet.

"Wendy!" His voice echoes through the elementary school hallway, stopping a few other kids with their fists clutched over their backpack straps.

Then, that boy blazes toward me like we've been separated for years. His backpack careens from side to side. His sneakers smack down, laces snapping on the linoleum floor.

My heart, whittled down from a week without this goofy kid, balloons in my chest.

"Hi, bud!" I call, squatting down so he barrels headlong into my arms.

I steady myself on my heels, wrapping my arms around him as he hugs me tight as a python.

He doesn't hesitate before asking, "When are you coming over?"

The question is a knife wound to my already-cracked heart.

I want nothing more than to come over. To sit on the porch and eat one of Jasper's fish dinners and to share fantastical adventures.

But that's not my decision; it's Jasper's. It's his home, not mine.

Glancing down the end of the hall, I observe anyone nearby, hoping they didn't hear. I run a hand through Sam's blond locks, the hair flopping over my fingers like soft feathers.

"I don't know," I answer.

His nose scrunches up, squishing his summer freckles. "Why are you whispering?"

"I don't talk about outside relationships in school."

"Oh," he breathes, smashing his index finger to his lips in a secret-keeping gesture.

I mimic the motion with a laugh.

"I miss you," he says.

"Really?" I ask. "Well, I miss you too."

"So, when are you coming over?" he repeats.

"I ... don't know."

I think I see something pass over Sam. A childlike irritation, some emotion he can't understand.

"But we miss you," he insists again, as if it were that easy.

We miss you, so you must come over. Duh.

We.

I don't miss the *we.*

Does Jasper miss me?

In Sam's defense, none of this adds up. The magic of being a child is that complications like this don't exist. If only adulthood could capture the same frank simplicity. The worst part about growing up is the sudden appearance of nuance.

From down the hall, Linda skids into view, her lanyard jangling with keys that clatter against her teacher ID. She presses her manicured hand to her heart. Her shoulders deflate.

"Sam!" she calls before muttering to herself, "Christ."

Sam turns on the spot, eyes wide, as if he were a captive caught escaping.

"Did you run away from class?" I ask with a conspiratorial laugh.

"Maybe," he whispers back.

"You're a pirate at heart, kiddo."

Linda clomps down the hall in her loafers with one hand pressed firmly on her hip.

"First day of school, am I right?" she exhales to me, placing a hand on Sam's shoulder, which puts him in an *en garde* stance, complete with an invisible sword. I swear I see her eye twitch. "Come on, Sam. We're about to get started."

Sam dutifully follows her, his mouth twisted to the side in distaste though.

"He's a handful," I call out. "Just don't give him chocolate pudding."

"Thanks, Wendy," she sarcastically drawls.

She'll learn the hard way.

Sam spins back around, calling to me, "You'll talk to Cap, right?"

Nervous anxiety simmers in my chest like a pot rising to a boil. I acknowledge his question with a simple wave. I don't have it in my heart to promise him anything because I don't know the answer myself.

The look on his face is devastatingly sad as he turns the corner, and I've never felt more empathetic in my life.

The bell rings. I proceed back into my classroom, dropping into my seat and resting my chin in my palm, surveying the children as they chat. I catch words here and there about summer adventures.

The pirate festival. The *Survivor* competition at Skull Rock. The annual summer music festival with trombones and saxophones and the whine of an oboe. Taste of Never Harbor. Art in the Park—though it got rained out two out of three days.

I'm usually so involved in organizing one or most of these. I didn't realize how many summer events I must have missed while being wrapped up in Jasper and Sam in their cottage by the sea.

I wouldn't change my summer experience for the world though.

My boys were enough.

"Ms. Darling, are you okay?"

I shake the thoughts away, blinking back to see a kid staring at me, along with an entire row of children.

I nod. "Peachy." *Just feeling my heart break. No big deal.*

"We'll get started in five. Be thinking about your best summer memories!"

Jasper and Sam.

Jasper.

Falling in love.

Falling head over heels for Jasper freaking Davies.

My body clenches at the word.

Love.

I'm in love with him.

I've fallen in love with Jasper.

And I wish I hadn't.

Chapter 39

Not Just Happy, But Alive

Jasper

MY TRUCK RUMBLES through the car-rider line, and I'm already searching for Wendy.

Sam stands in the corner of the pickup area, kicking a rock. His eyes are leveled on me. I give a thumbs-up, which he doesn't return.

Well, all right then. Not a good sign.

I roll down my window to call his name, but another face pops up instead. I jump in my seat as Donna's bright, sunny grin stares back at me.

"Jasper Davies!"

"Donna. Still the principal, I see."

"No reason why I wouldn't be! How was your summer?"

"Fine," I answer, leaning my head back against the seat and tossing a pleading look at Sam.

I silently mouth, *Get over here and save me.*

With a twisted smile, partway laughing and still partway sad, he shuffles over to the car.

"So," Donna says, dragging out the word, "listen, I want to talk about Sam?" It comes out as a question, which has me switching my attention back.

"Okay. What's going on?"

"He spent all day trying to sneak off to Ms. Wendy's classroom."

My stomach drops as I slowly nod in acknowledgment. "That right?"

"Yeah," she says, doing that head-tilt thing with a half smile and turned-in eyebrows, like she feels guilty about delivering this news—or maybe just scared I'm the type of parent to duke it out.

Donna should know by now that I'd rather slam on the gas than stay and fight with a teacher.

"Well, I'll be sure to talk to him about it," I answer.

She gives a little tsk with a shrug. "Yeah ..."

"Thanks, Donna."

"Sure thing." Her face and voice shift to a cheerier one when Sam steps off the sidewalk. "Oh, hi, Sam!"

She doesn't have nearly as much charisma with kids as Wendy does. Sam must sense it, too, because he gives a forced smile and hops into the back seat, buckling himself in.

She closes the door and waves with just her index finger. "See you tomorrow, kiddo!"

I drive off, accidentally letting out a groan and clearing my throat of the noise quickly so I'm not too terrible of an influence on Sam. He doesn't seem to notice though. In my rearview mirror, I can see Sam staring out the window, watching the school disappear behind us with a low huff of breath.

"Hey, bud, how was your first day?"

"I tried to talk to Wendy for you."

I swallow and slowly nod. "And how'd that go?"

"She was busy," he says matter-of-factly, meeting my gaze in the mirror. "But I'll try again tomorrow."

"That's very sweet. But why'd you do that?"

"Because."

I chuckle, but I'm hoping my rising suspicion doesn't bleed through.

"Because?" I wheedle.

He's pulled an action figure from out of nowhere—probably one he left stuffed under a seat—and toys with its arm, sliding it up, then back down.

"Because you smile more when she's around," he murmurs.

I run my palms over the steering wheel.

I do.

But that's not fair to Sam.

"Bud, I miss Wendy, too, but we're working some things out right now."

"I like when she's around."

"Just because she makes me happy?"

"No. I like her stories. She's funny."

"She is funny, isn't she?"

I miss her laugh. Airy. Bright. As genuine as laughs get.

"When is she coming over?" Sam asks.

"I don't know yet."

"Will she spend the night?"

"I ... don't know." But my words don't flow as easily for that answer.

That feels like too much information for Sam. He's obviously aware of our previous sleepovers, but this is getting soberingly real. It's silent in the car as we drive down the road, and I'm not sure how to approach the truth. I don't want to lie to Sam, but where do we go from here?

If only everyone knew how she truly makes me feel.

Not just happy, but *alive.*

My family loves Wendy. Anyone who has met her for five minutes falls in love with her; it was only a matter of time before I was a goner.

Ed and Stacy would have loved her too.

God, what would they do in my situation?

I will never truly know, but I do know that Ed and Stacy were anything but cowards. Like drawn to like. When I suggested starting a band, Stacy looked into purchasing drums the following week. When we mused about studying abroad together, it was a joke for one minute before we were packing our bags the next. And when they wanted to have a child, neither of them second-guessed it. Risks weren't risks for them. They were adventures.

Mom might normally say this is an awfully big adventure. But I'm not sure this is the type of adventure she had in mind—not one where her children are split at the seams. Not when I haven't heard from her or my dad this week. I wonder if they're giving me space. Unlike my siblings, they have always been respectful of me in that regard.

My phone lights up in the cupholder. It's Cassidy again, asking how I'm doing and whether I'm going to dinner. I don't respond. But when Bonnie follows up with, *Please answer us, or we'll drop by your house,* I sigh.

Jasper: Stop

Bonnie: This isn't a newsletter you can opt out of. Are you coming to dinner?

Jasper: No

Milo asks the same thing, and I respond with the same answer.

I notably do not receive a text from Peter.

Chapter 40

Walk the Plank

Wendy

I WALK UP the path to The Davies House with less enthusiasm than usual. I feel like Jill at the end of my book, walking down the wooden plank, primed to dive into deeper waters than Deadman's Drop.

A true dead drop.

I walk through the door, and even though it's the same house with loud music from the kitchen and The Twins running past in a blur of motion, I'm uneasy. The walls feel crooked around me, like I'm walking sideways. Like my entire precious world of safety has suddenly been tilted.

I take small steps down the hall, the pictures that were once comforting now taunting in their happiness. A faded middle school picture of Jasper stares back at me, half smiling yet grumpy, even at eleven. Another one of Peter is nestled in the next frame—him standing beside the newly constructed tree house, giving a thumbs-up with one missing tooth among his nubs of baby teeth.

This is a *family*.

At one point, *they* were my world, all of them—from Maggie to Cassidy and even The Twins. But that was before I fell in love with the eldest son.

I love him, and the worst part is, I don't see him anywhere.

Outside, Milo walks with a book in his hands. He doesn't see me.

Maggie passes by the doorway, and she doesn't see me either.

My nerves flame from my chest down to my fingers.

I can't do this.

I can't bear to see her disappointment.

I spot Peter in the place where Maggie stood. His eye is surrounded by black and purple. It looks terrible.

I swallow, turning on my heel, only to run into Cassidy's hulking chest. His hands catch my shoulders before I can fall backward.

"Oh," I breathe. "Hi."

"Where are you going?"

"I'm just not feeling so well."

Quickly, as if anticipating me running, he says, "Don't leave."

Cassidy glances over my shoulder. I follow his gaze. Peter is looking back at us. His eyebrows are cinched in. He stands up and walks toward the back door.

I twist back to Cassidy. "Please, I can't be here." My voice sounds too desperate, but I can't. I can't face this yet. I'm embarrassed and guilty, and I don't *belong*.

Cassidy scans my face, his eyes darting from me to Peter, who must have just walked through the door. The outside chatter gets louder for a moment before quieting once more. Finally, Cassidy nods.

"I'll walk you home," Cassidy says. "Come on, Wen."

He puts an arm over my shoulders, and I walk out the front door with him. I think I catch him throwing a nod. It might be for Peter, but I'm not sure. But we don't get stopped.

We journey down a block, saying nothing, having the sounds of The Davies House drown out behind us. We take a pedestrian footpath off the main road, walking to the symphony of crashing waves. Tall beach grass grows on one side, creating a makeshift barrier to the cliff overlooking the rocky beach below.

"So ..." he starts.

I nod. "So ..."

"Little Bird?"

It breaks the tension, cutting a laugh into my throat that feels almost painful but relieving.

I shake my head. "Cassidy Davies, you jerk."

"Ah, full name. That's how I know I crossed a line."

He grins down at me with those kind dimples dented into his cheeks.

I sigh. "I'm sorry."

"For what?"

"For ... making things complicated. For ... I don't know ... being a—"

"Don't you dare call yourself a foul name, Wen."

I clamp my mouth shut, but he did read my mind. What else would someone think about a woman who slept with two brothers in the same family?

"You can't control who you like," he says. "Even if they happen to be brothers. So, stop beating yourself up about it. Or I'll make Bonnie beat you up instead."

"Threat noted."

"She's feisty, and she doesn't hold back."

"Has your little sister beaten you up before?"

335

"A time or two."

We exchange a smile, and I remember just how easy it is to be friends with Cassidy. This is exactly how we connected in middle school—with simple banter between two English project partners.

The dirt footpath we're following empties back onto a sidewalk. We walk until we reach my house. Climbing up the stairs, I key in. But when the lock clicks, I instead turn around and lean against the closed door, watching Cassidy awkwardly shift from foot to foot. Cassidy isn't normally a thinker. He blurts out thoughts without abandon or shame. But now, he's quiet.

"How did it happen?" he finally asks.

"With Jasper?"

"Yeah."

"I don't know. He's not what I expected."

He smiles to himself. "Jas never is."

"Are you mad?"

His brown eyes flick to mine. "I'm surprised. But not angry."

My heart flutters in my chest, and I nod. "Really?"

"Really. Heck, I didn't even know Jas showed emotion to anyone outside of Sam. I think Pete was surprised too. Well, I mean, Pete also saw—"

"How is Pete?" I interrupt.

Cassidy gives me a crooked grin, likely happy I stopped him.

"Weirdly, not too bad," Cassidy says. "I don't know. After the initial anger, it's like something hit him."

"Jasper's fist?"

Cassidy's head falls back into a laugh. "Yes, that. But when you walked away, he seemed ... I don't know. Different."

"Different?"

He levels a look at me. "Yeah. Can't explain it. And he's been weird ever since. Less like his usual self."

"I can't blame him."

"Me neither."

A silence falls over us, and it feels almost like we're mourning Peter. But I'm not sure why.

Cassidy nods his chin toward the door. "I like this house. This type of bungalow is what I have in mind. Need a roommate?" he teases.

I shake my head with a smile, happy the subject is changed.

"Not nearly enough room," I say.

He snaps his fingers. "Darn."

"But I really like this new, responsible Cass. House-hunting and stuff."

"He's got a savings account too."

"Look at you." I lightly punch his shoulder. "You're killing twenty-six."

"So are you."

I shake my head. "Not so much."

"You finished a book."

"You heard about that?"

"Sam won't stop talking about it."

"I love that kid."

"He's crazy about you too. Just like his dad."

My breath hitches in my throat, and Cassidy smiles.

"Hey. It's all gonna work out, okay?"

"I'm not sure it will."

"I've never seen Jasper as angry as he was on Saturday. If that doesn't say he's crazy about you, I don't know what does. It's the red."

"Oh, cut it out," I say with a laugh. "You're the one who started that rumor."

He points a finger at me. "Because it's true."

I roll my eyes and push his arm. "Get out of here."

"I'll tell Ma you felt sick."

"Thanks."

"Anytime."

Cassidy takes the porch steps one by one, keys jangling in his pocket until he's back on the sidewalk. I watch him walk until he disappears around the corner.

But when I enter my house, toeing off my shoes and lying face-first into my couch, I hear a knock on my window.

My head jerks up, and it isn't the man I wish it were.

It's not Jasper.

Because that man would have used the door instead.

"Wendy."

"Hey, Peter."

Chapter 41

Peter Breaks Through

Wendy

My window creaks open, and Peter steps through.

His hands are instantly in his pockets as he rises to the balls of his feet and back down. He's never been one to sit still.

It's breezy outside, closing in on the evening. Never Harbor has a stillness around this time, after most people have closed their shops and receded to their houses and families. I'm thankful enough to be one block from the ocean, but even the calm waves sound nonexistent tonight.

"Need water or something?" Peter asks, welcoming himself to my fridge.

He knows exactly where I keep the cups, so he grabs one, fills it, then sets it on the side table next to me.

"Oh," I murmur. "Thanks."

His bar-owner instinct is kicking in. Peter's love language is acts of service, especially when he's anxious. But he shouldn't be the nervous one. It should be me. I'm the friend who betrayed him. Yet Peter's the one with a bouncing leg as he takes a seat in the familiar armchair across from me.

I take the glass, and he laughs when I empty it faster than even I thought I would.

"Thanks," I repeat.

"Refill?"

"I think I'm all set, Pete."

He nods, crossing one ankle over the opposite knee.

We sit there in awkward silence. Peter looks around the room before finally resting his gaze on me. His green eyes rove over my cheeks and chin and down to my bare shoulders. He shakes his head.

"So," he starts, "Jasper."

The awkward *so* seems to be the Davies lead-in for tonight, so I nod.

"Jasper," I confirm.

He swallows, as if the memories of Friday come flooding back. He tenses in his seat, fingers gripping the ends of the armrests.

"Listen, I've been thinking."

"Uh-oh."

He huffs out a laugh, running a hand through his golden-blond hair, ruffling the ends. Even messy, it's attractive. It suits him better. "I've been thinking ... I just ... I don't know." His eyes swivel to my bookshelf, then back. "Oh yeah, you're working on a book, aren't you?"

I narrow my eyes, and my heartbeat stutters as he stands. I know this version of Peter Davies. The avoidant one. The erratic one who, like his brother, wants to say something, but can't find the words. But unlike Jasper, who stays quiet, Peter keeps talking to fill the silence.

"I am," I respond slowly. "I actually finished it."

"That's great, Wendy." He holds out his hand, like he's

340

offering the congratulations in his palm. "Wendy Darling," he muses. "Gonna be in bookstores. Wow."

Bookstores.

I sit up, the shifting cushions echoing through the now-silent room. My muscles feel tense. And maybe Peter notices because his face falls. He twists his lips to the side, pacing away, his long legs spanning the length of the room before coming back, and when he turns to me, he runs a palm over his blond stubble. It's attractive—there's no question—but it looks too much like Jasper's nervous tic.

I wish Jasper were here.

I miss Jasper.

"Wendy, I've been thinking."

I don't prompt him further, but my stomach flips.

"Okay, so ..." Peter strides forward, crouching in front of me. The playful gleam in his eyes is long gone.

I know this look. Why do I know this? I don't want to know this. I wish I didn't know Peter so well. Very few times was Peter serious in our relationship, but I remember this look clearly. It always peeked its head out at the worst times.

"I've been thinking about us," he says.

"Us?"

"I always ... well, I kinda always thought it would be us in the end. And ... I'm not sure what to do now."

My heart stops.

There it is.

There. It. Is.

And for some wild reason, instead of answering, I laugh.

I let out a small, breathy giggle at first, but then I laugh again. And suddenly, I can't stop. It's overwhelming, bubbling out of me in nervous stutters, frothing over the edge of my sanity. And once I finally come to and his

341

expression has adjusted from nervous to curious, it's only then that what he said hits me.

And it hits me hard. Like a zip of lightning. Confusion. *Irritation.*

I blink rapidly. "What?"

"Us," he repeats. "Me and you. Peter and Wendy. We were fun."

My blood is starting to pound. My heart rate is wild.

Fun?

"You can't be serious," I breathe.

"Why not?" he asks. The boyish grin slowly pulls onto his gorgeous face with his perfectly cut jaw and beautiful teeth. But his eyebrows stay tilted in, the unease still there. "I'm not saying anything happens right now, but I think we should table the conversation for later. Maybe."

But I don't want it. I don't want him.

Peter was once my world. The cool, charming boy, four years older than me. The popular, charismatic senior when I was a freshman. Cassidy's older brother.

He was—until he broke me and didn't bother to pick up the pieces.

"No. We're just friends," I say matter-of-factly. "That's it."

I shake my head, hoping maybe I'll wake up. *This is a dream, right? A nightmare?*

But I'm not waking up. And Peter is still looking at me expectantly.

My stomach drops. My face heats. And then my hands start to shake.

"Are you ... kidding me right now, Pete?"

He swallows. "No."

I can't stand the energy running over my skin. I rise to my feet, pacing over to the bookshelf wall, leaning on the ladder. But nothing is comfortable, so I stop. I cross my arms. Unbearable. I shake out my hands. My heart is pounding.

"I'm sorry," he says, and to his credit, he does look apologetic. "Are you okay?"

"No, I'm not ..." Pounding. Blaring. Angry. "No, I'm not *fucking* okay."

His head juts back, eyes wide. I hear glimmers of Jasper's influence coursing through me—forcing out the curse words I wouldn't normally say.

I shake my head again. "What you're doing is not okay. What you've always done was not okay."

He swallows, and yet still, he has the audacity to say, "What I've done?"

"Peter Davies. Please. Don't you dare. Don't you dare play this game with me right now. There's a reason our wedding was called off. You ... you didn't want me. Not then. Not now. You wanted everyone *but* me."

His face falls. "Wendy, nothing ever happened with anyone else."

"I know that," I say. And I do. "But if I hadn't seen you, would you have gone further?"

He shakes his head. "Never."

"But that's the problem, isn't it? I don't *know* that. I didn't."

I never knew what Peter's limits would be. When would I no longer be enough? If not two weeks before our wedding, would it be ten? Twenty? Thirty years, when we were tired and starting to gray? When being *old* was just too much for him?

I hold my hands in the air. "I don't care. I don't care anymore. We've moved past it, Pete. But, God, how *dare* you. I'm ... I'm with Jasper now."

His jaw clenches, and maybe, for once, a different reality than his own is cracking through his beautiful facade of a world he's made for himself. He doesn't respond.

"Breaking off our engagement was the hardest decision I've ever made in my life," I continue. "Ever. I loved you. So much. But I did what was ultimately best for us. For me."

My voice cracks more than I'd like. Peter hears it, and his eyebrows pull in. He rises to his full height, taking a step closer.

"Wendy ..."

"We're too different," I barrel on, puffing out my chest. "You know that, right? Please tell me you know that."

"You've just been around more this summer," he says. "And I really liked it. I miss it. I really like *you*."

"I was around because of Jasper. Are you hearing me, Pete? I ..." And it bubbles up again. The words I'm parsing through. The four-letter word pounding against my brain. But it feels wrong to say it to anyone but Jasper first, if I ever get the chance. "I *like* him. He sees me for who I am. You like me as a friend, Pete. Because if you wanted me, you would have made more of an effort when I wore your ring. But I'm not there anymore. I'm not *with you* anymore. And I definitely don't want to date you now."

His jaw hardens, and maybe I was too harsh, but I'm feeling bold right now. I'm standing up for myself. I'm saying *no* for the first time in what feels like forever.

Peter nods to himself. He looks away, staring at an invisible spot on the window. And although I hate this for him, I hate it more for me.

"And, by the way, my book?" I add. "I finished it. And that's it. That's all I'm doing."

His eyes dart to me. He gives a weak smile, and he looks

344

genuinely proud. But it isn't the same excitement I got from Jasper. Not even a slice of it could compare.

"That's great, Wendy," he says. "Really."

I exhale. "It is. It really is. Because, sometimes, just achieving things for the sake of saying you did it is the goal. I don't need to get a publishing deal or open a restaurant or, hell, solve world hunger. I just want to be proud of myself. Sometimes, that's it. That's enough. *I'm* enough. But it was never enough for you. And that hurts."

Peter quickly takes another step forward. "Wendy, you *are* enough. And, God, I can't believe I haven't said this yet, but I'm sorry. I'm really sorry. I didn't know you felt this way."

"Because you don't listen." Then, I feel my eyes start to sting. I turn my head away. "I'm not meant to be second best to my own partner."

Peter closes the gap between us, sliding a hand over my back and pulling me in. But it doesn't seem needy or sensual. It's something better—genuine. A hug from an apologetic friend.

"Hey. I'm so sorry, Wendy. I just thought—" He interrupts himself. "It doesn't matter what I thought. I'm sorry."

"I'm not your backup plan," I mutter.

"No, you were my first option. Always. You're my Wendy."

"No, I'm not."

I pull away right as he lets me go.

I don't know what to say now, and he likely doesn't either, based on his silence. He's not even talking to fill the space. He's letting me sit in my thoughts—for the first time in forever. This was never his strength, but I appreciate him trying.

"So, Jasper," I say quietly, echoing the sentiment of Cassidy and Peter.

"Jasper," he repeats, strained. "You really like him?"

I love him.

"I really do." The words are a cracked whimper, as if my thoughts bled through.

"Damn," Peter breathes.

"Yeah," I agree. But to what, I don't know.

He pulls back, his eyes scanning me. "I should go then."

I nod. "Probably for the best."

He backs away from me, slowly crossing the room, away from the window and instead to the front door.

"Hey," I call. "I'm really sorry, Pete." I can't help the apology from floating out of me. I'm only human. "I am."

He turns and gives a weak smile.

"Don't apologize for my shortcomings, Wendy. It's time for me to grow up."

And then he's gone, closing the door behind him, and I'm left alone once more.

Chapter 42

Father & Son

Jasper

"Pete?"

"You weren't at dinner," he says.

"Why are you here?"

He shrugs. "I'm making my rounds."

My brother stands on the top step of my porch. He even rang the doorbell. No windows were unlocked for him here, I suppose.

He leans against the railing, eyeing my scruffy beard, untouched after a few days, to my work shirt I haven't bothered to change out of yet. "You look awful."

I nod my chin toward his black eye. "Not looking so great yourself."

His hands bury into his pockets, but he doesn't respond with even a laugh.

I sigh. "Did you come here to talk?"

"Yes," he answers. "Sam awake?"

"No."

"Can we go down to the beach?"

"Sure."

I close the door behind me, and the two of us walk over to the deck, descending the stairwell down to the shore. We empty from the wooden ramp onto the sandy beach with pebbles scattered throughout.

I follow his path, stepping from one seaweed-covered boulder to the next until he sits on the edge of one with his legs bent, forearms resting over his knees, vacantly staring out at the open ocean. Lowering down on the big rock beside him, I mirror his position—squinting out at the fluctuating waves, but saying nothing. I expect him to yell at me, but he doesn't. I expect maybe even an insult, but I don't get that either. Just silence.

Finally, he lets out a hushed sentence. "How long have you been with Wendy?"

"Just the summer."

"Is it serious?"

"Yes."

His jaw tics.

The current soundtrack is quiet, an ensemble of small crashes against rocks and the shallow splashes as seagulls land on the steady surface farther out.

"Out of everyone," he utters in a quavering tone, "*everyone*—you chose Wendy?"

I feel my nerves heighten, but I let them flow out with an exhale.

"Wasn't a choice."

"I don't know what to say."

"You had your shot years ago, Pete."

His eyes snap to me in a mix of disappointment and anger, as if he can't decide which is more fitting. "That's unfair."

"No, it's not. She would have married you in an instant.

348

You know that. I know that. But you chose not to prioritize her."

"I was young and dumb. It's complicated."

"What's so complicated about it? You liked being single, and that's fine. But you dragged Wendy into your mess, and she didn't deserve a single ounce of that pain. God"—I shake my head—"Wendy deserves everything. And listen, I hate that this happened. But it *did* happen. I'm sorry. I had no intention of falling in love with her. But I do have every intention of keeping her."

The air between us thins. The flames behind his demeanor cool and deflate as he echoes stoically, "You love her?"

I didn't realize I'd said it. My chest tightens. My fingers twitch. But then all the stress and pressure releases as I allow the confirmation to fall out, as easy as water flowing through the ocean.

"Yes, I do."

He sighs, running a hand through his wild hair.

The sky overhead starts to darken. Wisps of pink clouds reflect in the water, so bright near the shore, changing to purple as it fades closer to the horizon until reaching a darker blue. The breathtaking color of Wendy's eyes.

"She is the first person who's made me feel like existing is possible," I admit. "That the world isn't going to collapse around me. That maybe I'm not failing at this whole life thing after all."

"*Like existing is possible*," he echoes in a murmur to himself. "Damn, Jasper. That's ..." Peter shifts on his rock, kicking some pebbles around and exhaling. "I really wish you'd talked to us more back then. When it all happened."

"I moved back."

He picks up a small rock and tosses it into the water.

"Yeah, but you never talked, man. You shut down. We never really discussed it, y'know? And, sure, maybe we didn't need to know every detail. That's your business, and I respect that. But I would have helped you."

"You did."

"Yeah, with Sam, sure. But we were gonna be there regardless because he's your son."

My son.

No, not mine. Ed's son. Stacy's son.

Peter's eyes swivel to me. He lets out a sardonic laugh. "Quit overthinking. I can read you like a book, Jas. You and I know better than anyone that family isn't blood. Not by a long shot. He's your kid. My nephew. And that's just how it is."

My whole body is fighting against me, wanting to argue.

But maybe I've known for a while. The defensive instinct I have for Sam courses through me like fire. He's the first person I consider. It's no longer, *What will happen to me?* It's, *How can I protect Sam?*

Sam is my kid. My child. My *son.*

Peter's right.

I let out a choked laugh. Whatever I normally keep bottled up and hidden is battling its way out. But I don't want to be closed up anymore. I want to rip the doors open.

"I miss them," I say, my words more suffocated than I'd like. "Ed and Stacy."

Peter swallows, clapping me on the back. "I know you do."

"I still get nightmares."

He sucks on the inside of his cheek and exhales. "Jasper ..."

"I think, for a while, I was ashamed," I say, my eyes stinging. "That I couldn't let them go."

"There's no timeline for grief."

"I know. I know ..."

"Jessica didn't help," Peter scoffs. "I'll tell you that."

I huff out a wet laugh, and Peter laughs with me.

"She was there for me," I defend.

"Sort of," Peter says, wincing. "But not really."

I pull in a breath and let it out.

"Sort of," I finally agree.

Acknowledging it out loud feels good. I know what support truly looks like now. It's talking about the feelings, observing the emotions, and letting them exist. Burying heartbreak only allows the vampire-like emotion to never see the sun—to never get the opportunity to fade to dust.

"You weren't given a fair draw," Peter says. "And I hate it for you. To see you struggle ..." He lets out an irritated grunt. "God, it's still that bad, huh?"

"Yes. And no." My mouth twitches into a smile. "Better."

"Because of Wendy?"

I silently nod.

Exactly because of Wendy.

Because having her around helps me breathe. Hearing her laughter is like a jump-start to my heart. Watching her with Sam—with my *son*—makes me feel again. She provides sunshine in the darkness of a world I once thought had abandoned me.

Peter shakes his head. "If Wendy ... if she's ..." He roughs up his hair again, absentmindedly straightening it afterward. "God, she's a good person. She really is. And if she makes things better for you, what am I supposed to do, huh?"

The longer he's quiet, the more my chest tightens. The more I grip my hands together over my knees. The more I wish I could help him the same way he appears to want to help me. I want to take away the pain of knowing I love someone he once loved as well.

But that isn't real life. Sometimes, things get messy. And Wendy, whether she knows it or not, is now my priority. She wants to be my whole world, but what she doesn't know is that she already is, fitting like the final, perfect piece in our little family by the seaside.

I watch Peter's mind race. Even at thirty, Peter has always kept a young look about him. But right now, he looks older than he ever has.

Finally, he lets out a heavy sigh. "I'm not happy about it. It'll take a while for me to get used to. But, Jasper?"

"Hmm?"

Peter's hand reaches to find mine. His palm rests over the back of my discolored scar—the brotherly mark he didn't intend to leave. The hurt he never truly aims to give. Because what brother would?

"Being in love," Peter says, "is an awfully big adventure."

Any bit of tightness I had left completely deflates as Peter bursts into laughter.

The tense air around us is squeaked out like a balloon. Slowly. Softly. A little annoyingly. But gone all the same. Lost to our combined laughter, echoing over the rocks and disappearing into the ocean, leaving only us to sit together as equals. As brothers.

"Jeez, Pete," I say, rolling my eyes, still smiling through the dregs of laughter bubbling out of me.

"Hey now. I think I have the right to be mean for a while, you old codfish."

I sigh. "You can take a proper shot at me, if you'd like," I say, tapping my cheek. "It's only fair since I punched you."

Peter's eyes dart between mine before he pulls back and swings forward with the force of a ... snail. His balled-up fist taps my shoulder instead.

"Nah, we're cool," he says. "You're my brother. I'll stick with jokes."

"All right then. Make your jokes."

"I'm gonna be such a menace."

I scoff out another laugh. "That's nothing new though."

Peter grins. "Nah. Nothing new at all."

$$\textrm{J}$$

I WAKE up in the middle of the night again. I'm breathing heavy, exerted from action I didn't take.

It was the boat again. Sloshing around as I gripped the rails. But for the first time, I dived in. I was swimming, making large strokes through treacherous waves, stretching my aching arms and shoulders to catch Ed and Stacy before they went under.

I can't remember if I succeeded.

But I don't feel the binding tightness around my heart, like I normally do.

I wonder if I saved them this time.

The bedroom door creaks, and moonlight spills in. Sam is illuminated in the doorway, red beanie clutched in his fist like a security blanket, Red Sox pajamas rolled up at the sleeves, and one sock missing.

"Cap?"

"Hey," I answer, wiping the perspiration from my brow, leaning up to rest my forearms on my knees. "What's up, bud?"

It's too dark to see much, especially when he disappears from the sliver of light. His footsteps are silent as he crosses the room. The mattress sinks, and he crawls into bed. My body, worn from the dream, doesn't want to move, but I still gather the strength to reach out and pull him closer. Shivers from the imagined frigid ocean or maybe just the cool, lingering sweat perpetuated by the fan overhead has me shaking as Sam curls into my chest.

"You're sweaty," he says.

I nod against his head. "I am. Sorry."

"Did you have a bad dream?" he asks.

I tense, my arms holding him tighter, as if I could shield him from the reality of my nightmares. But I feel that same water rising, and the inevitability of its outcome is ever present. Just like I can't always save his parents, I also can't safeguard Sam forever.

"Yes," I confess.

"Was it scary?"

"Not as much this time."

"What was it about?"

I swallow, the dream rising in my brain like a tide, only to wash back out.

It's time. I've waited too long.

"Your parents," I croak, and it doesn't hurt as much as I thought it would. "I feel very sad tonight," I admit. "The ocean helps me when I feel sad. Would you like to go to the ocean with me?"

Sam nods, curling closer to my sticky shirt. I take the cue to pick him up, carrying him out of my bedroom and through the kitchen. Roger yawns from his bed, following us like the dutiful dog he is. The three of us exit out through the sliding glass door, and after we step through, I don't close it behind me.

I breathe in the breeze with Sam at my chest, the overnight waves a silent rhythm as they crash against the shore. It's comforting to know they're never as loud as they are in my dreams. Calmer, a reflection of the peaceful life we've built for ourselves.

Because this is our life now. Not the rocking boat or the wild ocean. Just me and Sam.

I take a seat in the wicker chair. This moment feels so similar to the first few days with Sam, looking out from the living room at the open sea. The deck wasn't built yet. The windows didn't span from the floor to the ceiling like they do now. It was just us and a rocking chair in our seaside shack, barely keeping it together.

I loosen my hold on him now, just in case Sam wants to get a chair himself, but he doesn't budge. I tightly wrap my arms around him again, hugging him close.

"Why are you sad?" Sam murmurs into my chest.

"Because, sometimes, I miss your parents."

"Oh."

"Sometimes ..." I echo my own word in a breathy exhale, shaking my head. "Not sometimes. I miss them every single day. But sometimes, at night, I dream about them, and it makes me miss them more."

I feel Sam nod. "I think I miss them too."

I hold my breath. "Yeah?"

"I don't know."

My stomach twists. How could he miss them? He was only two years old.

"What were they like?" he asks.

I exhale. "Well, your dad, Ed, was a great man. Funny. Liked to fish. Probably would have loved playing pirates. Wouldn't be surprised if he had scurvy."

Sam giggles, and I stroke the blond of his hair, letting my fingers run through his strands.

"And Stacy, your mom? You've got her hair. You're smart like her too. Brave. And kind. Very kind."

"Would she have made a good pirate?"

I chuckle. "Yeah, I think so. I really do."

It's quiet between us, and after a few breaths, Sam whispers, "You're my dad now, right, Cap?"

A pain I didn't know could exist now courses through me. It's a grinding kind of pain, like a dull bone saw taken to my chest and scratching over the missing place where Ed and Stacy once lived, yawning open the emptiness once more.

But regardless of the pain, it's Sam who breaks through. Brave Sam, who takes the weapon from me and tucks it away, replacing the rip with a Band-Aid. Likely a Spider-Man one, if I had to guess. He shuts that wound back as best as a little kid can. And he always will.

"Yes," I answer. "Yes, I'm your dad."

Saying it out loud for the first time would hurt a lot more if I didn't have Sam tugging me closer. If I didn't have my son.

"What do you do when you feel sad, Sam?" I ask.

"I don't."

A laugh chokes out of me. "You don't feel sad?"

"Not with you," he says. "Or Wendy."

I lean my head on his, nodding.

"Yeah. Me neither, buddy."

Wendy. With her stories and laughter—a sunshine beaming through this house. With her needle and thread and cute little thimble that kept us connected. She introduced me to a life I had forgotten was possible when I wasn't busy hiding from the world, ashamed and scared.

"Does Wendy make you happy?" Sam asks.

"She does," I say without hesitation. "Very happy, bud."

I love her.

He nods against my chest. "Good."

I laugh at his confident response, pressing my lips against his head.

The past can sometimes feel like a wound that never heals, but it's the small moments in the present that pull us back together, stitch by stitch. And then, when we're mostly whole again, maybe we'll be blessed with someone who can make falling in love feel a little more like flying.

And my Wendy makes falling in love too easy.

Chapter 43

Live, Laugh, Taffy

Wendy

THE WHISPERS FOLLOW me down Main.

"Did you hear about Wendy and Jasper?"

"I thought she was engaged to Peter?"

"I wonder if Sam is her kid."

"Shut up. That doesn't make any sense, Noodler."

I love Never Harbor, but small-town life occasionally has thorns of gossip on its beautiful rose.

I open the door to Peg Leg Press, but Bobbi's eyebrows cinch in when the bell above the door dings. And, sure, she might not blame me for anything—or maybe she does—but I can't take the pity, so I give a small, cowardly wave and moonwalk the heck out of there.

Not my finest moment, but I'm drowning in too many terrible moments.

My mind is still reeling from last night—both the awkward dinner I didn't attend and the subsequent confrontation with Peter.

I'd never thought I'd have the guts to hash out our

history. When we'd broken up, the discussion had been minimal. I'm not sure how we'll act around each other, moving forward, but at least the ideas are out there. The boundaries are set, and that's a big step for me.

But the person I really want to talk to is still silent. In Jasper's defense, I've been MIA as well. I'm still unsure how to approach the idea of *us*, and I don't know if he'll even want me anymore. A lot has happened, and I wouldn't fault him for disentangling from the mess.

I bypass the park as the clock tower strikes three o'clock at the late hour of four, giving bashful waves to any eyes that follow me. I know they want to ask questions, but maybe I look just pathetic enough that they decide it's best not to. I haven't brushed my hair today, and I'm wearing a baggy Never Harbor Pirate Festival 2008 T-shirt. It might have a stain and a hole. I don't know.

Rafe stands outside of his art gallery, a cigarette balanced between his full lips. He lazily tips his chin to me without an ounce of judgment in his eyes. At least there's that bit of kindness.

But behind him, exiting through the doorway, is Izzy. Her eyes widen.

Absolutely not.

The last thing I need is Izzy's sarcastic remarks making me feel worse.

I hurry on down the sidewalk.

The only shop on Main without patrons is Live, Laugh, Taffy—a candy shop down near the pier. I push the door open, already at the counter before the bell above the door finishes its chime.

I get a bottle of water and buy some fudge I probably won't eat before sitting at the small circular table.

Alone. That's all I want.

I bury my head in my palms, and the bell above the door sings once more. Then, the chair opposite me screeches across the floor.

I peer through my fingers. Izzy sits at my table. Her arms are crossed over her chest as she bites the corner of her bottom lip.

"Yes?" I ask with zero inflection.

She snickers. "Rude."

I don't think the cutesy Live, Laugh, Taffy—with its singular fan rotating on the ceiling, two small tables, and romantically pink walls—is made for the zipping lightning between us.

"I heard about you and Jasper," she says.

"Great. Who told you?"

"Rafe."

"Rafe knows too?"

"*Everyone* knows."

"Fantastic," I deadpan, hiding my face in my palms again with a groan. "Have you come to mock me or something?"

"I could."

She might have meant it as a joke. But I'm too tired. Too stressed. First Peter. Now her. And for once, I'm set off.

"God, what is your problem?" I jerk my hands down, huffing out air through my nostrils. "Like, what did I ever do to you? I come back in town, and you're just"—I straighten my spine—"not nice."

Izzy lets out a mix between a laugh and a scoff. "*Not nice?* Come on. You can do better than that."

"I was trying to take the high road." I scan her face. "You were always better with insults anyway."

"I really am."

360

I sigh, resting my chin on my palm. "Well, let me have it then."

"Not today."

"Why?"

"You're too sad. I don't like seeing happy people sad."

"You're kidding," I say dully.

"Only I'm allowed to be mean and bitter," she says with a grin. "So, you're in love with Jasper?"

It's like being shot in the heart with an arrow.

I swallow. "I don't feel comfortable—"

"It's a yes or no question. I saw you and Jasper on Main a couple of weeks ago. And at the family dinner. The whispers. The touches. Did he squeeze your ass, or did I imagine that?"

I uncap my bottle of water and gulp it down. But somewhere in that time of me drowning my answer, something must dawn on her. Her eyebrows pull together. Her lips part.

I can't tell what flashes over her face. Worry? Concern?

Then, the words stumble out, one over the other, as she asks, "Wait, do you still love Peter too?"

"No," I say quickly, almost sputtering through my drink, letting the bottle crunch down on the table, water overflowing from the top. "No. Absolutely not." The answer comes so naturally. Peter is so unbelievably wrong for me. "No," I repeat, shaking my head. "No. He's just a friend, I promise."

Izzy's shoulders relax, and she runs a tongue over her teeth, nodding while letting out a small tsk. "Wow. Four noes."

Her sarcasm cracks a smile on my face. "I'd do five if it'd get the point across more."

"Nope. Point taken. So ... I'm assuming that's a yes?"

"To what?"

"My question. You love Jasper."

I don't know how she says such a life-changing sentence without batting an eye. But maybe things like that are supposed to be said in that way. Because it's just that natural.

I nod. "Yes." *I love Jasper.* "Please don't tell anyone."

She almost sneers, as if offended I'd even suggest it. "I would never."

She pulls in a breath and nods slowly, more to herself than me. I take another sip of water.

"What happened to us?" I ask. "We were friends."

"I ... I'm having my own issues," she says. "Nothing to do with you."

"Nothing?"

"Nothing."

And in the nothingness between us, I slide my fudge over.

"Want to share?" I ask.

She snorts. "Like we're in pre-K?"

I laugh. "I don't know."

Izzy eyes the fudge, then me and sighs. "I'm sorry, Wendy."

"It's okay if you don't want to share fudge—"

"No, not that. Trust me, I'm gonna devour this brick of chocolate with you."

"Oh. Then, why are you sorry?"

She sighs. "I don't know. Just know I'm sorry," she continues. "My irritation *did* have to do with you. But that's a me problem. I shouldn't have put that on you. You didn't deserve that."

When she isn't so serious—or scowling—Izzy looks

almost ethereal. Dewy skin. Doe-like blue eyes. In fact, in apology mode, Izzy's beauty is nearly overwhelming.

"I appreciate that, Izzy. You can be a friend when you want to be."

"Ha," she deadpans.

"I can see why Peter is still close to you."

In a single second, her eyes are on me. Hawklike. All elements of fantasy gone—unless you include Medusa with her stony glare.

"Yeah, well, I'm his bar manager," she scoffs. "Why wouldn't he be?"

But in those few words, I catch wind of something else— the softness still trying its best to hide behind her fangs. The flush rising on her cheeks. The panic in her twitching eyebrows and bitten lip. I don't know how I didn't see it before.

"You like Peter," I breathe out.

Her jaw tenses. But she doesn't say a word.

I wish I could tell her it's a lost cause. But something tells me she knows. Or that she won't even entertain her own feelings to *think* she knows. Like Izzy said, she's just his bar manager.

"You're right," I say. I raise my eyebrows with a pointed look, hoping some womanly, sisterhood connection screams, *It's okay*, between us. "You're a great bar manager."

For a moment, I see the edge of her mouth twitch into a very small smile.

She slaps the table. "You need a drink."

"I do?"

"Pink drink's your go-to, right?"

I blow out air. "Oh, I don't know—"

"We can go to The Hideaway's third floor. It's normally empty around now."

"I don't really—"

"Come on," she says, her tone sagging at the end in irritation. "Drinks are on me. It's my day off, and I'm bored. Plus, it's my bar anyway."

I almost argue, *No, it's Peter's bar.* But I'd be wrong. Everyone knows she runs the ship. Isabel is a force to be reckoned with.

I wince. "I should honestly go home."

"Nope. You can't hide from Never Harbor forever. Eventually, Donna will get ahold of you, and if you don't have a friend by your side, you're gonna flounder. And do you really want to field her questions without me?"

I grin at the insinuation. Izzy and I might be *friends* again.

Peter totally doesn't deserve her.

"You *are* a piranha," I concede.

"Exactly. So, come on. We'll hide and drink our sorrows away. It'll work like magic."

"Or poison."

"Or medicine."

"Good idea."

"I know."

Izzy presses the button on her key fob, and a green Volkswagen Bug honks from a curbside space. One minute later, with our fudge laid out on wax paper over her center console, we're flying down the road toward magic.

Chapter 44

Off the Hook

Jasper

AFTER OUR MIDNIGHT talk the night before, Sam and I slept in most of Saturday. Even once we both stumbled into the living room, taking a moment to laugh at each other's bedhead, I took us out to a lobster roll restaurant right on the edge of town. Not too close for Never Harbor gossip, but enough to feel like we weren't wasting away at the house.

But as we're rumbling back down our gravel road, bump after bump, I see another car. My heart flips into my throat until I realize it isn't Wendy's car, but Milo's, and standing on our porch are Cassidy, Milo, and Bonnie, all with their arms crossed.

I park, step out of my truck, and lift an eyebrow.

Bonnie pushes off from the porch, walking with teenage sass over to the steps. "Hey, old man."

Milo and Cassidy follow, equal looks of intimidation on their features, along with folded arms and tongues in cheeks.

"We've got a bone to pick," Cassidy says, punching his fist into his palm.

They gather closer in some weird game of sibling Mafia.

Sam hops out of the back with an excited wave. "Hi, guys!"

Cautiously—more than my son before me—I ascend the steps, stopping when Bonnie won't move from her spot. I sidestep her, then Cassidy, too, to key in the front door. It's already unlocked.

Bonnie flashes a key. "Got it from the crocodile key hider in your garden."

"We also stole some pudding while we waited," Cassidy admits.

The door creaks open, and sure enough, there are two empty pudding cups on the counter. My bet is that there were three, but Milo was the only responsible one to throw his out.

"Ooh, can I have one?" Sam asks me, tugging on my sleeve.

"Only if Bonnie gets to babysit you afterward."

Her teeth pull back in a cringe, and I shrug.

"You dug your grave, lie in it."

Cassidy barks out a laugh, and Bonnie shoots him a glare as they enter the house behind me.

"Hey, you ate one too!"

"But it was your idea," he argues.

She directs a finger toward him, then quickly shakes her head. "Wait, that's beside the point." Bouncing on her heels, Bonnie crouches down beside Sam. "Hey. We're about to have an adult conversation. Would you mind playing with Roger for a few minutes?"

"Try fifteen," Cassidy adds.

"It really will not take that long," Milo says through a sigh.

I look between them, my heart starting to pound because, while I'd like to believe I don't know what this is about, guilt stomps on my chest and insists otherwise. Blood is rushing up to my head. I think I need to sit down.

"Adult conversation?" I ask.

Cassidy gives a cursory glance. "You know."

I do.

I grind my jaw, darting my eyes to Milo, who solemnly nods his head.

"Yeah, better to not have kid ears. Just in case."

With a heavy exhale, I pat Sam's back. "Go play outside, all right, bud?"

Sam's face falls, and his bottom lip pokes out. "Ahh, I wanna listen!"

"We'll give you the CliffsNotes, if it goes well!" Bonnie says optimistically.

"What are cliff notes?"

"Sheesh, this generation," she murmurs, scooting Sam forward until he reluctantly shuffles toward the sliding glass door, pouting the whole way.

Roger, stretching his long limbs from his dog bed, follows Sam dutifully, as if he knows this discussion isn't for pup ears either.

The back door slides shut, and Cassidy swivels on his boot straightaway. He's no longer smiling. Instead, his face is downturned into a clown-like frown. And then I notice Milo's demeanor changing, too, a twitching at the edge of his mouth, as if in anger. Bonnie's lips are pursed in a solid line.

I don't let my expression show because, Christ, these are my younger siblings, and I'm definitely not intimidated by them—especially not with Bonnie's canary-yellow theme park hat twisted backward and Cassidy's red-nosed summer burn. But I'd be lying if I said my heart was beating normally.

"All right," I say, leaning on the kitchen island. "Go on."

"Stop being an idiot," Cassidy shoots out like a shotgun.

"What?"

"You're ignoring everyone," Milo says.

"And the only texts you do send have gotten more threatening," Bonnie says. "It's annoying."

"Ma's worried," Cassidy continues.

"And a little irritated," Bonnie adds.

"Also, why isn't Wendy here?" Milo asks.

I walk around the island so that I'm on one side and they're opposite me. If I'm gonna be under the spotlight by a panel of judges, I might as well be able to field questions with everyone in sight.

"We haven't talked all week," I admit.

"All week?" Cassidy echoes with wide eyes.

"Is that the longest you've gone without talking all summer?" Milo asks.

"Yes."

Bonnie shakes her head. "How long have you guys been dating?"

I sigh. "A while."

"Like, more than this summer?"

"No," I say quickly. "It only started a few months ago."

But that sentence feels wrong. The timeline is too short. I feel like I've loved Wendy for a lifetime.

Milo narrows his eyes at me. "Why do I feel like there's a *but*?"

"But ..." I start. "It's not just a summer thing. I ..." I let out a heavy exhale. I close my eyes, bringing my forefinger and thumb up to my nose. "It wasn't planned. Or premeditated. I didn't hire her for any reason other than for Sam. And I know she's Pete's ex, but—"

"Another but," Bonnie interrupts.

"Seems like a lot of *butts* happened here." Cassidy snickers.

I cut my hand in the air. "Stop."

"Okay, okay," Bonnie says, holding her palms up. "So ... are you guys not dating anymore?"

"It's complicated. Sorry."

Cassidy barks out a laugh. "Why are you sorry?"

Bonnie groans an over-the-top type of guttural sound from her throat. "Because he thinks he's ruining our family. Which is *dumb*, by the way."

I hiss in a breath, then let it out with a very heavy, "Forget I said it."

"Seriously though," Bonnie says, hopping onto the counter. "You and Wendy? That's wild."

Cassidy crosses his arms. "You should have said something."

Bonnie pushes his arm. "Yeah, but she dated Peter. Of course he didn't."

Cassidy snorts. "Yeah, like, two years ago. Old news."

"They were almost married," Milo adds.

"Married schmarried," Cassidy says. "Big whoop."

"For some people, that's a very *big* whoop," Bonnie says, giving another shove, which Cassidy laughs off. "Maybe not for you or Pete." Then, her eyes swivel to me. "So, what? It's just ... over now? Because Peter's all butt hurt about it?"

All three of them wait for my response. I run a palm over my beard, then shrug. It's the best I can manage.

"You know we're fine with it, right?" Bonnie interjects. "Like, don't feel bad."

"Yeah, you're off the hook with this one," Cassidy says.

"We love Wendy," Bonnie adds. "And we love you."

"*And* we love Pete too," Milo quickly says. "But come on. We all knew they weren't good for each other."

"Dude, he's a disaster for monogamy in general," Bonnie says. "He flirts with everyone, even two weeks before his own wedding. I mean, c'mon."

"You were only fifteen at the time," I say. "How do you even know that?"

"I remember Mom yelling at him downstairs one night," she says. "She was livid. Told him he needed to make it right with Wendy because she was a part of our family whether he liked it or not."

My knuckles tighten around the counter. "She said that?"

"I mean, Ma's not wrong," Cassidy says. "I've always viewed Wendy as a sister."

I can't help the little smile that grows on my face. Wendy would love to hear this. I wish she could.

My family is a unit. And if I'd seen through all the lies my ex told me about burdening them, I might have realized that they would show up for me—and Wendy—at any time.

It's an uncomfortable situation. It's not ideal.

But it happened.

Bonnie squints. "I mean, you're not just ... doing the dirty with her, right?"

All three of us yell, "Bon!"

"What? I'm not naive. Come on, Jas. Is this real?"

Real?

What an understatement.

Life feels possible when she's around. If that's real, then sure. But real doesn't feel accurate enough.

I look between my siblings, watching them as they stare at me in equal silence.

Milo shrugs and nonchalantly inserts, "Yeah, I think Jas loves her."

Cassidy and Bonnie erupt like fireworks on the spot, hands in the air, voices chiming in a mix of, "Holy crap," and, "Is that true?"

Love.

My muscles relax. My shoulders slouch. I exhale. And for the first time today, I feel myself smile. Just the tiniest bit. It must be answer enough.

"Oh, *hell* yeah!" Cassidy punches the air.

"Wendy's gonna be my sister!" Bonnie squeals.

I hold out my palms. "Okay, we're getting a little ahead of ourselves ..."

All our phones buzz at the same time. Milo's watch goes with it. It's the sibling group text.

Peter: Wendy's down at The Hideaway with Izzy, causing trouble.
Peter: Jas?

Peter says it like she's *my* responsibility now. And something about that eases my soul.

She's *my* Wendy.

The sliding glass door whirs on its wheels as Sam pokes his head in.

"Are you guys done?"

"Hey, Sam!" Bonnie calls. "If Jas said he liked Wendy, what would you think?"

The heightened nerves in my veins return with a vengeance.

"Whoa. Bonnie, I don't know if he's ready—"

371

Sam shrugs. "I like Wendy."

Bonnie bends down, resting her palms on her knees. "Okay, but what if he *likes*, likes her?"

"Bonnie." My tone is harsher as I take a step forward, but Cassidy pulls my elbow, trying to wrestle me back.

His arm wraps around my neck. I ram my palms up, untangling myself.

"Are you five?!"

"It was just a headlock," Cassidy says. "Don't worry about it."

But when I look down at Sam, his eyes are bright. "You *like*, like Wendy? Like, *a lot*, a lot?"

I take tentative steps over to him, pinching my jeans before crouching down in front of him. My back shields us from the group. It's only us.

"Yes," I murmur. "Is that ... okay?"

Sam starts to bounce on his heels. "Can she come over tonight?"

I run a palm over my beard as I let out a strained chuckle.

"Yes," Bonnie excitedly interrupts. "She totally can and will."

I close my eyes. "I swear to—"

"Yay!" Sam exclaims.

"Eventually, she might be over more," I admit.

Bonnie squeals again from behind me.

Sam's smile grows. "Will she move in?"

"Maybe."

If she'll have me.

Bonnie's shoes squeak behind me. "YES!"

Milo chuckles. "Bon, chill."

Sam must be absorbing her energy because he's fever-ishly nodding now. "That'll be awesome."

I feel my own smile growing to match his. "Yeah? That'd be all right?"

"Can we watch movies every night?"

"Sure," I say, the word barely coming through my choked laughter. "Maybe not every night, but yeah."

"And will there be bedtime stories?"

"Possibly."

"And can I get more screen time too?"

He cheeses at me, knowing he's pushing the limits.

"Okay now," I say, holding up my palms. "This isn't a negotiation."

"Nice try though, kid," Cassidy says, his bottom lip poked out as he gives a thumbs-up and winks.

I rub a palm over Sam's shoulder, bringing him back to our conversation, as opposed to the insanity behind me.

"Would it be weird though?" I ask. "With your uncle?"

Sam scrunches up his face. "Who?"

"Uncle Pete."

"Why?"

The fog from my brain suddenly clears, and it hits me that he has no clue what I'm talking about. Of course he doesn't. Sam was almost four when Wendy and Peter stopped dating. To him, she's simply been Wendy. Just Wendy. Friend of the family. His nanny this summer.

That's all she is.

A six-year-old doesn't understand the repercussions of falling in love with your brother's ex-fiancée, but he doesn't have to. Wendy doesn't belong to my brother.

She's ours.

My and Sam's Wendy.

I rise to my feet and make a beeline to the kitchen counter, swiping up my keys and grasping them in my palm.

"Let's go," I announce.

"Wait, why would Uncle Pete matter?" Sam asks again.

"Come on, Sam. Questions later."

Bonnie's jaw drops. "Oh my God, are we going to The Hideaway?"

"Yes."

"Oh, hell yeah!" Cassidy says as he and Bonnie high-five. "This gets better and better. Start the car, Milo!"

I narrow my eyes. "Wait. This isn't a group activity."

"Come on, Jas. You know everything is a group activity with us," Milo jokes with a smile, swinging his keys over his finger.

Cassidy claps me on the shoulder. "Yeah, you've just been living out here for too long in your little hermit shack. I think you forgot how things work around here."

A smile breaks onto my face before I can stop it.

Sam rises to his toes to snatch the leash hanging on the door and runs off with a loud, "Woohoo!"

Within less than a minute, we're leaving the cottage in a two-car caravan, Roger's tongue lolling out the corner of his mouth, whiskers to the wind.

My family is weird, but a good kind of weird. The kind that tailgates you down the cliffside with "Celebration" by Kool & The Gang blaring from the open windows. The type of siblings who honk in the street when passing businesses on Main, as if they were in on the occasion too.

Sam truly has some of the most supportive family.

I think Ed and Stacy would approve.

Chapter 45

More Than Enough

Wendy

I'm sitting at The Hideaway's third-story bar with a tiny umbrella sticking out of my glass, sipping on my third pink drink in fifteen minutes. My head is a little swimmy, but it's only from thoughts of Jasper, darting through my brain like little guppies in water.

This week has been one giant mess.

I miss Jas.

I miss everything about him—from his furrowed brow to his hardened jaw and even his red eyes that were, admittedly, kind of hot when he lost his cool. I'd pay to rewatch him punch Peter, but that's beside the point.

"I miss him so much."

"I know," Izzy grumbles from beside me.

"Know what?"

"That you miss him."

I narrow my eyes. "Can you read my mind?"

"No, you kinda, like, mumbled it or something."

Izzy's own words are a little slurred as she throws back

who knows what number of her clear-colored drink—pretty sure it's straight vodka—without even a little bit of a cringe. I swear she's made of steel. Or magic.

"Do you think magic exists?" I ask, pursing out my bottom lip in thought. "Like fairies?"

"Yes," Izzy answers without skipping a beat.

I gasp. "Really?"

"Why not?" She shrugs.

"Huh." I narrow my eyes. "Wow. I've never considered *why not*."

"That's always the real question."

"True."

I clink my glass to hers.

Why not?

I take another slurping sip from my straw before lowering my head to the counter with an exasperated groan. I don't care who sees me. I'm slowly dying, and if all of Never Harbor wants to see my Saturday evening melt to nothing, then so be it.

"Done?"

I jump out of my skin at Peter's voice.

He stands behind us. The tension between me and him is still raw from the other night, but he's nothing if not professional.

Weirdly enough, even with his black eye, Peter's still handsome. He's in a green henley, rolled up at the sleeves. Black denim. The nice leather oxford boots that blend both classiness and ruggedness effortlessly. He smells like clean tea tree cologne. Citrus almost.

It's a familiar type of comfort, stemming from years ago, yet not nearly as familiar as sea salt and cinnamon.

Or at that rate, fish bait.

"I think I like the smell of fish bait," I say out loud.

Izzy scrunches her nose. "Ew."

Peter sighs, taking my glass, coated in condensation, notably lacking pinkness. I must have drunk it all.

He points a finger between us. "No more for you two tonight."

"Ah, c'mon!" Izzy says, throwing her hands up.

"One more pink drink," I beg. "I'm fine. Really."

Though, until that sentence, I honestly wasn't sure of my state of sobriety. But the sentence came out clear enough, and when I stand up, I don't topple and fall. Except after I take one step, the floor rocks like Jasper's sailboat, which is way more than a normal patio should.

Crap.

"You're a terrible influence," Peter says to Izzy with a crooked smirk.

She gasps. "Me?"

"Yes, you." He pats her shoulder, and I swear she jumps a little under his large palm.

I snicker, and she gives me the nastiest glare in return.

Whoops.

Peter narrows his eyes at me. "Two drink maximum from now on."

"Forever?"

He leans and whispers conspiratorially, "Forever."

"You're no fun anymore." I pout.

"I'm always fun," he counters. "Now, sit."

I land on the barstool with a *thump* and a wince, saying, "Ow," as I lean forward with my head in my hands once more.

Peter nods at the employee behind the bar who sweeps by, fetching my empty glass from his hand. It's seamless, like he's some Mafia don, running this shindig.

Izzy runs her tongue over her teeth after Peter walks away, giving a little *hmph*.

"*Bad influence*," she mutters sarcastically.

"*He's* the bad influence," I say, throwing a thumb over my shoulder.

"Hell yeah."

We don't have drinks anymore to clink together, so we high-five instead.

She blinks quickly, as if coming to. "So."

"So," I echo.

"What are we gonna do about Jasper?"

"I'm gonna ..." But the words fade.

"You're gonna ..." She waves her palm, as if prompting me. "Tell him that you love him," Izzy finishes for me. "Yes?"

"Yes," I agree. "That."

But, God, it feels so daunting. So risky. So ... rife with rejection. But it's Jasper, isn't it? Jasper, who spent all summer getting to know me when he didn't need to. Jasper, who notices the little things. Jasper, who took my side, even in front of his family. Jasper, who is simply just *Jasper*.

There's so much below that surface that nobody cares to explore. He's funny. Charming. And he puts others first.

I love his eyes, clear blue like light shimmering over lake water. I love his pitch-black hair with those few strands that pop down by the end of the day. I love his beard, messy and unkempt, especially when he's between my thighs—*definitely* when he's between my thighs. I love his tongue. His words.

"*Baby, that's so amazing.*"

That he read my book without me having to ask.

"I love him," I whisper.

"Yes, I know," Izzy says again with a laugh.

"That does it," I announce, slapping my palm on the bar, only to shake it out. "I'm gonna tell him." Because *why not?* "I'm gonna march down to his house—"

"That's kind of far away."

"Okay, I'll drive—"

"You're tipsy."

"Izzy!"

"Sorry."

"I'm gonna drive down there—when I'm able to!—and I'm gonna tell him that ... that I love him."

Saying it again is so cathartic.

I don't care if Maggie hates me. I don't care if dinners are forever awkward. I don't care if I never get invited back to their home. I might love the Davies family, but I love Jasper Davies more.

If it's just me, him, and Sam for the rest of my life, then that's more than enough for me.

"Say it again," Izzy prompts.

I nod. "I'm gonna tell him I love him."

"Again, but surer."

"I love him."

"Again, but louder."

"I love him!"

That's the moment when multiple footsteps pour over the staircase on the far end. Our heads turn, and I don't have time to consider which Davies sibling might be causing a ruckus—because it's always one of them causing a ruckus —before I realize it's all of them.

And leading the charge is Jasper.

My breath hitches. It's the first time I've seen him in a week. My memories could never capture how handsome he truly is. Bearded jaw, always set in determination. Chest and large arms, stretching his wonderful flannel with rolled-up sleeves. The fishing hook tattoo. Even the scar on his hand is terribly thrilling as his fist clenches, whitening it against his skin.

Instantly, the tether between us—the connection that feels like I could reach out and tug on it—is pulled taut.

Behind him, Bonnie, Milo, and Cassidy pause in place. Sam, trailing with Roger on a leash, almost knocks into Cassidy's legs.

"You brought a *dog*?" Izzy gapes. "And your *kid*? This is a freaking *bar*."

"Family establishment actually," Bonnie chimes in.

"I'll fire you on the spot," Izzy says, but her slurred words and Bonnie's broad smile say it's an empty threat.

Sam shoves past the adults to me. "Hi, Wendy! You look sad. Are you sad? I wanted to come see you."

"Pink drink?" Milo asks.

I slowly nod, but I don't respond. I'm still stuck on Jasper, who hasn't moved an inch. His eyes are still on me as well.

Peter appears at the top of the staircase, and his arms fall.

"Jas, come on. Roger can't be here."

"This is a special exception," Cassidy says for him.

"Roger is a good boy," Sam agrees, patting the dog standing at almost his exact height.

"And we serve food, little man," Peter clarifies, ruffling Sam's red beanie.

Jasper doesn't acknowledge the mess of conversation. His eyes are still on me. Like we're in our own little world.

"I'm sorry, but"—Peter pinches his nose, the area just below his black eye—"why are you guys here?"

Cassidy and Bonnie glance at each other.

"Wings," Cassidy says. "We're ... getting wings."

"We are?" Sam asks.

Milo nudges past Jasper's frozen form. "Yep."

Jasper's gaze continues to burn me from the inside out.

I've missed you, I want to say. But with so many people present, it feels inappropriate. Or maybe I'm just used to our secrets. Does it matter now?

"Jas, you want wings too?" Izzy asks, pumping her eyebrows.

Jasper clears his throat. "I came here to give Wendy ..." His words fade. "A thimble."

"A thimble?" Bonnie asks, her nose scrunching up.

"A thimble?" Milo adds.

"A thimble," I breathe.

A hug.

My heart pulses hard, the gravitational pull toward him so magnetized that it hurts. But I've spent months getting to know Jasper, and right now, he's nervous. He's nervous that I'll reject him. That he's not enough for me, just like he constantly fights how he's not good enough for Sam.

I tilt my head to the side.

I love you though. Don't you see that? I love you, Jasper Davies.

"So, where is it?" Peter asks.

Jasper blinks. "What?"

"The thimble, Jas. Where is it?"

He doesn't even bother to dig in his pockets and pretend. Jasper has never been very good at pretend anyway.

Jasper swallows. "Oh, um ..."

The patio is as quiet as it can get. It's only then that I realize the Pirate Trio is in the corner, staring—Bobbi, Starkey, and Jukes. Officer John, off duty. Jake, after closing the hardware store for the night. Laura, taking time off from the community center. And Donna, eyes wide as saucers.

Seriously, did the entire town come out tonight?

Jasper has stepped into the pit of small-town gossip. The very reason he moved out of town. But he's here anyway.

"Jas?" Bonnie asks.

He doesn't respond. Just thinks.

Even when he's considering, he's handsome. Jasper has that little line between his eyebrows that is so beautifully tragic. I want to run my thumb over it just to soothe the hurt, but then that wouldn't be Jasper anymore, would it? And I like grumpy Jasper.

It's Jasper I want. Jasper that I need.

And in my mind, I'm yelling. Screaming. Pounding against the walls of our unspoken connection.

I love you, you big ol' grump!

Jasper's eyes dart between mine, and for a split second, I think he might hear me. The desperate pleas. The need. The fear.

Then, he moves. Work boots thump across the floor. The ends of his laces snap over the hardwood. Jasper crosses the length of the bar until he reaches me, stopping just short of where I sit.

His palm lands on my hip, and the moment it does, I sink into his touch.

"Hi," I breathe.

"Hey, baby."

Baby. I've missed the way he says it. A slightly rough edge to such a gentle nickname.

"What are you doing?" I ask.

"Stealing you away."

I can't help the grin that spreads. "I was wondering when you would, Captain."

"Sorry for making you wait, Little Bird."

And then Jasper Davies cups my face in his palms and kisses me.

Chapter 46

The Very Adult Conversation

Wendy

HOME.

That's what it feels like when Jasper Davies kisses me in front of Never Harbor's snoopy eyes.

My hands wind up behind his neck, hooking at his hairline, pulling him down to get closer. I want to melt into him. Bury myself into the crook of his neck and breathe him in. Exist only with him.

A throat clears. We both look up, hands still planted on each other, gripping clothes and clutching hair. Cassidy crosses his arms with a smirk. Milo, more respectful of privacy, stares at a random spot on the railing behind him. Bonnie's lips curl in, capturing her hidden smile.

But then I shift my gaze to Peter, standing behind them all.

My stomach coils, the unspoken words between us radiating out. But I'm not sure what else we could say that would excuse this kiss. And excusing it is the last thing I'd want to do anyway.

Slowly, Jasper nods. Peter nods back.

I squint at the secret acknowledgment between them.

Peter excuses himself down the steps to a different level, demanding something from an employee I only vaguely hear.

Jasper pulls my hand up to kiss the knuckles.

"Can we talk?" he murmurs to me.

"Of course," I answer. I'd do anything he asked.

Jasper kisses my hand again, like he's savoring that it's his, before pointing a finger to Sam. "Stay here for a second."

He salutes. "Aye, aye, Cap!"

I give a salute back, just for fun.

"Watch him," Jasper demands to the open air. One of his siblings will do it.

"Yessir," Bonnie says, swooping down to throw Sam over her shoulder. "Now, where are those wings? And bar peanuts?"

Sam kicks his little legs. "Ooh, peanuts!"

Jasper's fingers loop in mine, and without thinking, I follow where he leads. We trail down flights of stairs, journeying to the back of the bar, passing familiar face after familiar face but ignoring them all.

It's just us now.

Jasper cuts us through the kitchens—bangs of pots, calls of orders, and cutting knives—until we're out the emergency exit.

The click of the closed door silences it all.

Behind The Hideaway is a small beach leading to Crocodile Cove—a rocky place overrun with sand and too many pebbles to be viable for a proper beach day. But it's secluded. Quiet.

And just us.

Jasper runs his thumb over the back of mine.

"You've got me alone again," I observe. "How very serial killer of you."

He chuckles. "Clean house, bad texting ..."

"You're nothing if not consistent."

With a subtle smile, he runs a palm over my cheek. I lean into the touch. He does that thing again where he opens his mouth and closes it. I crook my forefinger and press up against his chin.

"Say anything you want, Jas."

"I just ..." He tsks. "I actually hated Crocodile Cove, growing up."

A laugh bubbles out of me. "Did you?"

"Yeah." He glances away, licking his lips, shuffling a boot on the ground.

"The owners of the restaurant before Peter had actual crocodiles, didn't they?"

"They did." He laughs, running a palm over his beard.

I missed that gesture. But it means he's stressed. Nervous.

"And why are we talking about this again?" I ask through a grin.

"Because I don't know how to tell you that I love you."

The words stumble out of him, rapid-fire. It's like the world shudders around us, the walls of reality fluttering with the increasing beat of my heart. One extra beat, then two.

"You ... you what?"

He tilts his head to the side and cups my face in his large, rough palm. "I love you, Wendy Darling. You know I'm not great at talking, so that's all I've got. I love you. And I hope it's enough."

Jasper huffs out a breath, eyebrows tilted in.

Waiting.

Finally, I swallow and nod.

"It's enough," I say breathlessly, and it only takes half a second more for me to kiss him.

I fade into him, gathering his hair in my hands, feeling his palms grip my hips, our lips opening and closing in any desperate attempt to get closer, to feel more.

I sigh out, like a teenager embarrassingly swooning over a crush. And I do—I have one massive crush on Jasper Davies.

He plants a kiss along my neck. My arms fold over his broad shoulders. I link my fingers behind his neck, playing with the little strands of hair extending down. He probably needs a haircut, but I kinda like the extra length. I love everything about Jasper, even the messy parts—*especially* the messy parts.

"I'm sorry if this week has been weird," he murmurs.

"Me too. I didn't want to bother you. Just in case."

He shakes his head without missing a beat, that stern expression staring back at me. His forefinger and thumb lift up my chin. "You could *never* bother me, Wendy. I just want to be with you. Only you. Like it's been all summer."

I grin. "Me too."

"Good. Because I'm done with secrets. I'm done caring about what anyone thinks, except for you. Because loving you is the only secret I have left. And it's no secret at all."

"I love you, Jas," I confess. "Secrets and everything."

I can see the moment his heart drops. The way he chokes out a breath. The eyebrows tilting up, forming that little worried line between them.

Disbelief.

Jasper might not conceive of a world where someone

could love him unconditionally, but I'll spend forever convincing him otherwise.

Our mouths meet together again, desperately placing kiss after kiss until he's kissing over the top of my head, down to my heated cheeks, and eventually to my lips, where we drift back into the abyss together, flying high on each other's presence. His palm rests behind my neck, tracing a thumb over the echoes of kisses left behind.

"It's just not the same without you," he says. "Sam misses you. I miss you. We're a mess without you."

"Okay, you can definitely function without me," I joke through a laugh. "I saw your ridiculously clean house before I got there."

"No, I mean it. When you're gone, I don't function the same. I can't imagine the man I'd be if you hadn't agreed to watch Sam this summer."

"You'd still be a great dad. A dedicated brother and son. And one *fantastic* flirt."

He chuckles. "I like the man you think I am."

"That's because you're exactly the good man I think you are. Always have been."

He presses his forehead against mine. "Why'd you agree to nanny for me?"

"Honestly? I needed a job," I say through small laughs. "I needed one bad."

His face falls.

"Living a couple of feet from the sea?" I continue by way of explanation. "Not exactly cheap. I can't exactly blame Starkey for charging high rent though. It's beautiful here. Though maybe I should text Marina about that ..."

Jasper chuckles at my rambling. "Wendy Bird, are you drunk?"

I squint. "Tipsy now. Recovering, you could say."

He slowly nods with a grin. "Ah."

"Doesn't change the fact that Starkey's rent is too high."

"Well, want me to punch him?" Jasper asks with a rakish grin.

I love when Jasper is playful. It's so subtle, so rare, that the times he does, it captures little sparkles of stars in his eyes.

"If you wouldn't mind," I answer.

He hums against my neck. The sound rumbles low in my chest. I hold him, just as he likes.

Jasper pulls back, giving a small smile and saying, "Let's get you home."

"Home?" I ask. The disappointment seeps through my voice at being *home* in my rental with just my books, but not him. Not Sam. Not Roger. Alone—again.

Jasper chuffs out a laugh and tilts his head to the side. "Yes. Home, baby. To me."

"At the cottage?"

"Yes. Home," he clarifies again, stretching the word out, grinning as wide as I've ever seen him. "Oh, and Sam would kill me if I didn't ask ... can you stay for a sleepover?"

Home.

"Of course I can."

Chapter 47

Jill's Happily Ever After

Jasper

Soft. Comfortable. And smelling like linens and cotton and rest.

I could spend every night with my Wendy Bird.

Not that it was easy to get back home.

I quickly gathered my son and dog, trying my best to make a quiet exit from The Hideaway, but my siblings weren't having it.

Bonnie hugged Wendy. Cassidy demanded shots all around, which we politely declined. And Milo said I looked happy, which Bonnie followed by saying I "sucked less than usual" this summer. I smiled, and when I did, I must have looked a certain type of content because Bonnie then hugged me, right along with Sam. Though I wasn't sure he was fully aware of what was going on, but I accepted the affection from everyone anyway. I accepted my family's love.

I dropped Wendy off at her townhouse to collect some

items, and after only a minute of her being inside, I rushed in to help her pack even quicker.

"Wow, and you didn't even ring the doorbell," she said with a laugh, leaning in to tease, "Does this mean we're serious?"

I chased her to the opposite side of her small bedroom, pinning her wrists behind her back to kiss her until both of us came up for air to laugh.

We threw her suitcase of clothes into the back of my truck and drove back to the cottage. To our home.

I let Sam stay up past his bedtime, entertaining any movie he wanted as long as I could sit on the couch next to Wendy. Though Sam overtook my spot within thirty minutes. I let him. I knew I'd have more moments with her later. Hopefully, a lifetime's worth of them.

Wendy sobered up by the time we put Sam to bed, telling bedtime stories that knocked him out instantly.

It's been a long day, so I start the tea kettle, carrying our mugs out to the workshop.

Wendy and I talk about everything. Her conversation with Peter, then mine. The lack of conversation from my mom, which makes Wendy uneasy, so I stroke her cheek while I listen to her fears. But I know—I just know—my mom would never abandon Wendy. It's just not the type of woman Maggie Davies is.

Eventually, she focuses on her notepad, feet dangling over the edge of the workshop bench while I turn to my new project. I like our little universe—just two people savoring hobbies, side by side. She doesn't ask how long until I'm finished, and I don't press on her having a deadline because it doesn't matter. We're existing together as one.

We go to bed, and I lie awake long after she's gone to sleep, stroking her back under my large T-shirt that swallows her whole. I can't see or feel her tattoo as I run circles over her bare spine, but I still feel it in my gut all the same.

The bird that flew.

My Wendy Bird.

I'm too in awe at her being here—beside me and openly mine—that I can't fall asleep. I pull her book up on my phone once more. I skim to the end, when Jill finally falls for the pirate and his own menacing heart melts into hers. I wonder if Wendy knew her ending would be just the same because she possesses my own menacing heart in the palm of her hand.

Suddenly, the bedroom door creaks open. Illuminated in the moonlight is Sam.

"Hey, bud," I whisper. "Everything okay?"

Sam runs in, crawling onto the bed before I can stop him to say Wendy is asleep.

His limbs knock into ours, and Wendy shifts beside me, murmuring something about mermaids. I rub a circle over her back, coaxing her back to sleep, but she's already turning over, squinting at Sam curling in between us.

"I can't sleep," he whispers. "I'm too excited Wendy's here."

"Do you want a story?" Wendy's half awake, and her slurred mumbling has me smiling.

"Shh." I stroke a hand through her hair, letting the soft strands cascade over my palm. "You can go back to sleep."

"No, no, I've got one," she insists, shooing me away as she sits up in the bed.

Sam, grin plastered across his face, grips my hand. "Just one? Please?"

I ruffle his hair and adjust his crooked glasses. "Only if Wendy's up for it."

Wendy, blinking awake and yawning, nods. "Always."

And then my girl tells a new story without missing a beat. We disappear into her imagined world with her hands raised in the air, painting our darkened room with her words, crafting an epic tale with ships sailing on walls and pirates plundering under lamplight.

Sam is captivated by it all, cuddling closer at the scary parts and cheering at the exciting ones.

What should have been a five-minute story turns into an hour. The clock across the room blinks a time far too late, but caring is lost to the adventures in the night.

When Wendy finishes and rightly passes out on a mess of pillows, Sam is already asleep, cuddling between us.

I inhale at the sight before me. The woman I love. The boy—my son—curled close to her, just as enamored as I am.

Jessica was wrong.

I might not be the man Ed was, but I'm doing right by Sam. He is loved, and that's all that matters. And the subtle smile on his face as he dreams beside me is enough to make my once-damaged heart feel whole again.

I glance over at my abandoned phone on the nightstand, and I pick up Wendy's book, tracing over the words that illuminate our bed in the darkness.

I smile to myself, open a new research tab, and start typing.

Jill deserves the world, and so does Wendy. She deserves it all.

Chapter 48

Jas or Me This Time

Wendy

JASPER, Sam, and I stand, hand in hand, on the Davieses' doorstep.

I already hear the chanting of loud boys, squeaking sneakers, and Bonnie's screech of, "Liam! Give my tablet back!"

"Are we going in?" Sam asks.

"Go for it," Jasper says, turning the handle to allow Sam through the door. "Wendy and I need a second, though."

The cacophony of sound erupts like a blast, muffling again when Sam closes the door behind him.

We've been outside for almost five minutes now, and I haven't even considered crossing the threshold.

Jasper nudges me with his elbow. "Wendy?"

"She knows," I whisper. "I can feel it."

I've been dreading dinner at Maggie's. It's been one week since everything went down, and I'm surprised it took until this morning for Jasper and me to get a text, sent to both of us in a new group conversation.

Mags: You two had better be at dinner—and STAY—or I'll go check on you.

Mags: And Pete and Cass advised that simply "dropping by" isn't a good idea, so I'd prefer not to if I don't have to.

She at least has a sense of humor. I expected a call throughout the week. Something with a loud voice and maybe an exile from future functions, but I received nothing.

Maggie explicitly said she didn't want me dating her son only a couple of months prior. And now, I'm here, with her other son.

What must she possibly think of me?

I also haven't heard a word from Peter all week either. After Saturday night, I received a thumbs-up emoji from Izzy, but honestly, I've been too overwhelmed to interpret what that meant. The Hideaway was a wild evening. Pink drinks are off the menu for a while.

Jasper chuckles beside me.

"What?" I ask.

He shakes his head, squeezing my palm. "You think very loud. Come on, Little Bird."

The moment we walk through the door, the sounds explode once more. The scents of baked bread and warm butter waft through the warm house. David's music follows suit.

And sooner than I can sneak off somewhere else, Jasper is guiding me down the hall, peering into each room. We bypass The Twins, who stumble by with Nerf guns, then linger on our held hands for half a second before realizing they don't care, then run some more.

"See? That wasn't too bad," he observes.

Yeah, 'cause they're not Maggie.

"We don't have to do this," I whine. "I can just show myself out."

Jasper rolls his eyes, dipping his hand around my back, pulling me closer. "I'll only chase you and drag you back."

"Hot."

He snorts, stroking my spine and peering into the last room on the right—Maggie's office. He pauses, and I can sense that she's inside. The feral mama bear snarling.

"About time." Maggie's stern voice drifts out to the hall. Sharp. Angry.

I swallow, shifting out from Jasper's hold to press my back against the wall.

"Is Wendy out there?"

I suck in a breath. Jasper meets my eyes from the open doorway, and without looking away, he smiles and nods.

Maggie groans. "Good God, Wendy, if you don't get in here right now, so help me—"

It's like getting called into the principal's office, except I was a good kid with straight A's who never actually got in trouble. Even when I hung around the Davies boys, they never let me take the heat. Karma must be catching up with me.

Jasper reaches out his hand, and I willingly take it, sinking into his comforting touch. Both of us step through the threshold.

Maggie's sitting on the floral couch, where, just a couple of weeks ago, we were poring over photo albums together. Happy. Laughing. But the air is different this week. Stiff. Photo albums are on the shelves.

Jasper turns to shut the door behind him, but Maggie shakes her head.

"You can leave, Jasper. I just want to talk to Wendy."

Oh God.

I could run. I could steal Jasper's truck keys, bolt from their driveway, and spend the rest of my life at his seaside cottage. But when Jasper meets my gaze and gives a reassuring nod, I force one back.

No, I can do this. If Jasper believes I can, then I can.

Despite being in front of the woman who is likely seconds away from murdering me, Jasper brings his finger to my chin and pulls my lips to his. It's like every star shines behind my eyes, blinking in a show of brilliant fireworks. I don't think his kisses will ever grow old.

Jasper grants me one final smile before stepping out from the room. He closes the door, and it snicks shut behind him.

Though it feels more secluded, it's far from quiet in here. I can still hear pots clanking from the kitchen. A low hum of David's radio. The boys fighting outside. It's like any other Friday dinner. Except I'm alone in a room with Maggie. Her arms are crossed over her chest, and one menacing eyebrow is raised, just like her son's.

"Hi, dear," she says, but the motherly tone is gone. "Tell me what's going on."

I swallow, unsure where to start so I say, "I'm dating Jasper."

She nods, pursing her lips. "Clearly. And you have yet to talk to me about it?"

"What would I have said?"

"Anything, Wendy. Literally anything at all."

I take a step forward, meeting her on the opposite end of the couch.

"There is no way to say what I need to."

"Try."

I swallow. "Well, I was engaged to one son, and now, I'm dating another." My eyes sting, and I hate them for it. "I can't imagine what you think of me."

"I think you should have come to me. I would have listened."

"And then what? I can't blame you for getting upset."

She shakes her head, sucking in her cheeks.

"You know what upsets me the most?" she asks. "The fact that you thought my love was conditional."

My heart sinks, barreling right down to my stomach. Too many thoughts have been rushing through my head, and not a single one considered a reality where she forgave me.

"You once told me not to date your son," I say.

"I did?" Her nose scrunches up. "Jasper?"

"Any," I correct. "I don't know. I promise I didn't mean to ruin everything."

"Ruin? Sweet girl, no."

"But I did. I ended my engagement with Peter."

Her lips straighten into a solid line. "As you should have. *He's* who I didn't want you dating again. You do know ending it wasn't your fault, right? That you did what you had to do?"

I nod because, yes, I do. But it's also not my family. It's not my child's heart that was broken.

"I just don't want to make things weird for your family again," I say.

"For my—Wendy, you *are* my family. Whether or not you date any of my sons is neither here nor there. All last week, I had a hard time trying to figure out why you couldn't talk to me about this. Yes, the situation is uncomfortable. But you're one of my children too. You have just as much right to tell me anything without fear of repercussions. And it hurts that you seem to not know that after all these years."

The words seep into me like lava, warming my muscles. A sense of *belonging* prickles its way over my skin in goose bumps.

"Family isn't blood," she says. "You'll always be my daughter. Understand?"

I nod, and I can feel the tears forming, but I keep nodding until the feeling goes away. I still give myself away with a sniff though, and that's when Maggie scoots across the couch and pulls me in for a hug.

It's full of vanilla and cookies and the fabric of her thrifted dress, pilled and restitched together. A lost item she took in for her own, just like she does with everyone in her life.

"I'm sorry," I murmur.

"Never be," she answers. "Okay?"

"Okay."

"Good. Now"—her tone is decisive—"tell me about how you fell in love with my son. The grumpy one."

I laugh through my sniffs, putting my hands on my thighs and looking away before talking again.

"Easily," I answer. "So easily that it's scary."

Maggie smiles, patting my cheek. "He's an easy man to love."

Both of us look out the window to the backyard. Jasper has Sam sitting on his shoulders, running through the grass with Cassidy roaring after them, The Twins trailing in their wake.

She's right. Jasper's a *very* easy man to love. As easy as breathing.

The back gate creaks open, and long legs extend through. Peter latches it closed behind him, running a hand through his hair as he eyes the maelstrom before him with a weak smile. But my own smile fades at the sight of him.

"Don't worry about Pete," Maggie says, watching my expression. "He's happy for you."

"He is?"

"He called me last Saturday. He said tonight's dinner would probably be awkward, but that we should all get over it because you're good for Jasper. Too good. That you just don't know it yet, but it's not our job to tell you."

I laugh. "He said that?"

"Mmhmm. Don't tell him I said it anyway."

I smile, nodding to myself, watching Peter clap Jasper on the back in brotherly solidarity. Both exchange a knowing smile.

"Wouldn't dream of it."

$\int$

EVERYONE IS WALKING on eggshells around Peter at dinner, likely watching to see if he's slouching or sighing or depressed. Eventually, Peter's fork clatters onto his plate, and he groans.

"Can we please gossip about something more interesting? Like how Bonnie drank at solstice?"

Bonnie sucks in a gasp that could deplete the entire yard of air. "What the HELL?!" She twists to Maggie. "Ma, I did not. I didn't!"

Peter cackles out a laugh. Bonnie tosses a fork at his face.

"Siobhan Margaret Davies!"

But Maggie's hollers are lost as Bonnie scrambles away

from the picnic table, yelling after Peter, "You jerk!"

David, mid-bite, narrows his eyes. "Didn't we tell her she could go?" He turns to Maggie. "Honey, we told her she could go, didn't we?"

Peter fights off Bonnie's fisted advances as they wind up the tree house steps.

"Ten bucks on Bon!" Cassidy calls.

The Twins leave the table after them. Sam joins with his fist raised around his butter knife, and that's about the time the high energy settles as Jasper apprehends the little pirate, prying the knife from his fingers. The whole yard erupts into laughter.

The rest of the evening falls into our usual rhythm. The breezy late summer weather cools the backyard, leaves already yellowing the trees as David preps brownies in the oven. It's like any other dinner, except Jasper is never more than a few feet away from me, reaching for my hand, tracing a line down my spine, pressing subtle kisses on the back of my head.

I savor every touch, every secret grab, every unspoken gesture because, though Jasper is a man of few words, his touch speaks louder than anything he could say.

Eventually, Maggie leads me upstairs to show me some new clothes. I understand where Jasper's gift-giving tendencies come from because Maggie's thrifting knows no bounds. And even if they aren't exactly my style, I still take some because it means something to her. Hugs through gifts. Just like her thimble.

I throw a few dresses over my arm, and we make our way back downstairs. But as we pass the spiral staircase leading to the crow's nest, I notice the hatch at the top propped open. Out the circular window pointing to the backyard, I count all the Davies siblings sitting at the picnic table or running up the tree house.

All, except Peter.

"Hey, mind if I meet you downstairs, Mags?"

Maggie's eyes float up to the hatch, and she solemnly nods, taking my dresses and throwing them over her shoulder. "I'll give these to Jas."

I smile. "Thanks."

I ascend the spiral staircase slowly, taking step after step until I'm crouching in the small attic space. It's decorated in an array of loose blocks, blankets, and pillows. A retired Barbie lies with pen scribbles across her cheeks. An old square television sits on a rug in the corner. A pirate flag is slung on the slanted wall. But I don't see a soul in sight. Maybe I was wrong, and nobody is up here.

A small breeze floats through the open window. I reach to close it at the same time another hand grasps it from the outside, and that familiar face from my childhood appears through the window.

I jump, clutching my chest. "Peter!"

He gives a half smile as he steps over the barrier.

"Not shutting the window on me, are you?" he asks.

Peter lands on the attic floor, clicking the window closed, leaving the cool breeze behind him. He gives a little shiver and another weak smile in my direction, pulling the sleeves of his sweater down his arms. I watch, following his awkward movements, so unlike his usual demeanor. Less boisterous. More subdued.

"Pete, I—"

"I think I owe you an apology," he interrupts.

I deflate. "I was about to say the same."

"I know," he says with a sly smile. "And I'm glad I said it first. You don't owe me one at all."

Peter takes a seat on the wood floor. I do the same, sitting opposite him with my back leaning on the wall. We don't talk for a moment, so I fill the silence.

"I used to love it up here," I say, nudging a block with the toe of my shoe. "Good memories."

"I just remember sneaking around a lot," he says.

My eyes shoot to him, and he pumps his eyebrows.

I shake my head with a smile. "Always mischievous."

"Always *clever*," he corrects with a grin. "Mom checked our rooms, but never this window."

"Trouble from day one," I say, laughing.

But instead of joining me, his face falls.

"I'm sorry," he says. "For suggesting something between us the other night. You were right. I haven't exactly been fair to you for a while now."

"It's okay. It's just who you are sometimes. You like adventure and excitement and all of that."

"Sounds exhausting."

"It's fun. You're always fun."

"I'm sorry we didn't work out."

"Don't be. You're fun, and I'm just me. I'm Wendy."

"Don't dog on Wendy. I like Wendy. She's cool." His eyes steady on mine before looking away. "And, sure, maybe I like adventure. But also, maybe I should work on being a little more grounded, y'know? Maybe it's time I grew up."

"Oh, I didn't—"

"No, I'm thirty. I'm responsible enough to own a restaurant. I should be able to hold down a normal relationship too. And I should definitely not suggest a future with the woman in love with my brother."

I give a weak smile. "Yeah. Maybe."

"Maybe," he muses. I don't say anything, but he nods in understanding. "I'm okay with you and Jas," he continues.

"It'll take time, but really, I'm fine with it. Disturbed, but fine."

We both laugh, but it fades away. Just the dull footfalls and conversational hum from the rest of the family running around downstairs remain.

"Y'know, for a moment," Peter says, "for the smallest of moments—I wondered if I had a chance to get you back. If it would be Jas or me this time."

I shake my head. "It's just Jas."

"I know," he answers with a feeble smile. "And you both deserve that. You deserve to be with someone who puts you first."

"Thank you."

"No, thank you," he answers. "I needed this. A nice little dose of reality. It's not *The Peter Davies Show* all the time."

"Oh, don't go changing on me, Peter. I like your show."

He flashes a grin. "Change comes for all of us eventually. I don't think growth is necessarily a bad thing, do you?"

I think about Sam learning to swim. About Jasper, how he's the same man he was at the beginning of the summer and yet slightly different. More open. More relaxed. I think about me. Writing a book. The pride that came with completing something. I gained confidence in myself for the first time in so long.

"True," I agree. "A little growth isn't bad at all."

"Wanna head back down?" he asks.

"Sure. You first."

Whisking out a hand, he gestures me forward anyway. "Away we go."

After Peter and I part ways, I find Jasper in the kitchen with his dad, sitting in a chair pulled out from the breakfast nook. He tosses me a crooked smile, and I give a tiny wave back.

It's never been Peter or Jasper.

It's always just been Jasper.

Because I'd choose him every time. In any reality. In any fantasy. In every fairy tale.

Chapter 49

Wendy Darling

Wendy

Three Months Later

"Did she live happily ever after?"

I pat the little boy's head. "Of course she did."

I'm surrounded by children who very much need to get to a bus or a car or something—anything but hanging out in my classroom. Instead, kids from this year, from last year, and some who just wandered their way over are crowded around my small chair in the reading area with chins in their palms.

"I want to know about Cinderella!" a kid I don't know rings out.

A second grader nudges him. "She already told that one."

Then, a much lower voice chimes in, "Did you tell them the one about the pirate captain?"

Leaning in my doorway, one boot crossed over the other,

is Jasper. Hands are tucked into his flannel coat pockets, only the glimmer of his cracked watch reflecting the lamp in the corner. An errant yellow autumn leaf somehow made its way onto his shoulder. He's got that half smile he seems to always carry nowadays, satisfied but still an undercurrent of inscrutable intrigue. He'll always be my mysterious captain after all.

There's a collective gasp.

"No! Is he cool?"

"She," Jasper corrects. "Her name's Jill."

Another eruption of hushed whispers.

"We want to hear!"

"Please!"

"All right, friends," I interject, louder than their rising pleas. I clap my hands together. "Tomorrow. For now, please go catch your buses before Principal Donna sends *me* to her office."

"She would never," someone breathes.

"I appreciate your vote of confidence. Now, go. All of you. Out. Except you," I say, pointing a finger at Jasper. "You, stay."

His grin widens as he steps into the room, crossing in strides, only to pull me to his chest, cup his hand behind my neck, and pull me in for a kiss. I melt into him, savoring the soft pecks, the scratchy beard against my chin, and even the little bites of fish bait underneath his sea salt cologne.

It's *him*, and I wouldn't change Jasper for the world.

Children filter out through my classroom door, muttering little *ew*s along the way. At the opposite end, the herd parts like waves when another child cuts through. Sam bursts through the other side, running at top speed, barreling into Jasper and me. His puffy coat deflates in our hug as he wraps one arm around either of our legs.

"Hey, bud," Jasper says, ruffling his beanie. "How was school?"

"I wrote another story!"

"Another one?" I gasp. "We're gonna have a whole novel by Thanksgiving!"

"I hope so. Then, our shelves can be full of our books!"

I smile. "Well, yours. But I want fifty of them by next Christmas, all right?"

My perfect little finished story is still on my computer. Some might think it's collecting dust, but it's not. It was something I needed to do. And since then, I've moved on to a new one. Just another story to explore. It's the beauty of a finished adventure that means the most. I don't need anything past that.

Jasper, raising a single eyebrow, opens his palm toward Sam.

"Want to do the honors?" he asks.

Giddy, Sam digs into his backpack and pulls out a brown bag.

"You packed me lunch?" I ask with a laugh.

"It's a gift from us," Sam says, bouncing on the balls of his feet.

I side-eye Jasper. "You and your gifts, Cap. What's the occasion?"

He shrugs. "For existing with us."

I lean over Sam to reach Jasper and kiss him once more.

"Ew," Sam murmurs from below. "That's so gross."

Jasper looks down at him with a chuckle. "All right then, would you like to look away or see the present?"

Sam grins. "The present."

I narrow my eyes in suspicion, but Sam extends the bag up. I part the paper handles, shuffling past the flat, wrinkled tissue paper, and what I pull out has my heart stumbling over itself, practically gushing out onto the floor.

It's a book. Hardback. Bound in fabric. There's an illustration on the front, and it's reminiscent of old adventure novels that went for a few cents, worn through time. The character is a woman, standing on the bow of a ship, loose linen shirt flowing in the wind, hand clutched around a rope, and a mischievous, determined smile over her lips.

The name *Wendy Darling* is printed at the bottom.

My heart ratchets into my throat.

I rip open the cover.

There it is again.

Wendy Darling.

My hand darts to my mouth. "How did ... what ... what is this?"

Sam rises to his toes, pointing at the name again. "It's your book."

"It's my ... how ..."

"I bound it," Jasper says.

"*You* hand-bound my book?"

He nods. And that's when I see the details. The deckled edges. The linen under the dust jacket, bound in old fabric from one of Maggie's antique dresses. And the yellow ribbon protruding from the centerfold, a swinging bookmark made from one I thought I'd lost months ago.

I run my hand over the intricate details, including the typeset with a tiny pirate ship illustration over the first chapter header.

"Where'd you find the time?" I breathe.

"While you've been busy writing the next one," Jasper answers with a smile. "I would have gotten it sooner, but I had to find the right cover designer and ..."

"You commissioned this? This is an original cover?"

"Yeah. From Rafe. Who, by the way, talks less than me. So, it took some time."

I delicately place the book down in my chair before grabbing Jasper's beautiful, bearded face between my palms and kissing the ever-loving daylights out of him—this wonderful, thoughtful man. And when I'm done making his lips red and scratching my own face with his beard, I bend down and pick up Sam, pecking his cheeks with little kisses too. He giggles, even as he's pushing my face away—because he's definitely entering the age where showing parents affection is considered uncool. Oh well. I love this boy. And I love his father.

"Thank you, you two," I say, setting him back down. "Boy, my men sure know how to give gifts."

"I know you want to keep this a hobby," Jasper explains. "But we love your stories, and I want them on our shelves forever."

I kiss him again because I can. Because he's Jasper Davies. And there will never be enough love for this man.

"I love you," I whisper against his lips.

"I love you too, baby," he murmurs back.

And then I pull back and laugh. "How am I supposed to top this gift ever?"

He chuckles against my mouth as I kiss him over and over, not even giving him time to speak, savoring his smiles against my lips.

"You could," he says between a kiss. "I don't know." Another kiss. "Move in with us."

I pull apart from him, his cheeks still held in my palms. "Really?"

"You pretty much live with us anyway," Sam adds.

Jasper takes one of my hands and kisses the palm.

"Move in with us, Wendy. Your lease is up next month. And I'm tired of waiting."

"Is that okay, Sam?" I ask.

He rolls his eyes. "Duh. It was *my* idea."

I squint at Jasper, and he shrugs, as if to say, *Give him the win.*

"Well then, I'd love to," I announce.

Sam jumps with glee, tugging at the sleeve of my dress, saying something that has to do with stories and new books and sitting on the finished porch.

But I'm looking into Jasper's eyes, wondering how in the world I can thank him for everything he's done for me.

He's given me a love I didn't know existed.

A home.

A family.

Our little life by the seaside might not look like much, but it's enough.

It's perfect.

Epilogue

Jasper

Six Months Later

"If you just move the—no, the other left."

"Cass, I swear, I only have one left."

"Okay, push and ..."

On one end, I'm grabbing the bottom of a couch. On the other, Cassidy is shoving whatever he can through the rest of Wendy's old threshold.

A few months ago, Wendy finally finished moving her stuff over to our cottage. And one month after that, Cassidy had a stern talking-to with Starkey down at the docks, where he discussed buying the place from him. They went back and forth until Starkey agreed to let Cassidy rent-to-own as a compromise. All payments would go toward purchasing. For a townhome one block from the shore, Cassidy didn't think twice.

"Okay, over there. Nope, other left."

"Only one left side, Cass," I grunt.

We shimmy the couch over to the far corner and place it down, right before Roger noses around my legs to find Sam.

Bonnie bounds through the open front door, furrowing her brow at the empty bookshelves with the rolling ladder. "Ah, darn. You'll have to tear those out."

Cassidy shakes his head. "No, I won't."

"Psht," Bonnie says. "You haven't read since high school. They'll only go to waste."

Cassidy puts his hands on his hips. "You don't know if I read."

Wendy leans on the kitchen counter, surrounded by halfway unpacked plastic plates and bowls. She thumbs through a stack of letters and magazines. "Huh. I didn't know I was still getting mail here."

"Hey, that's my mail now," Cassidy says.

She holds it closer to her. "Some of it *is* mine, thank you very much."

I walk up behind her, planting my hands on her hips and peering over her shoulder. She blows air in my face. I kiss her lips before she can do it again.

"We should check ours when we get home," I murmur in her ear, sending goose bumps trailing over her neck.

She tosses me a grin and echoes, "Ours."

That will never get old.

Projects never end with us, and we started a big one just four months ago.

After only two months of driving back and forth to my parents' house a couple of times a week and Wendy—involved in most of the town's activities—circling back to our cottage after forgetting something for the fall festival one too many times, we decided to make a change.

Wendy and I found another little house that was a

413

fifteen-minute walk from Main rather than a fifteen-minute drive, located right on the blustery coast. It was a mess and barely holding together, but it seemed fitting for a time when I wasn't either. It isn't as secluded as our last cottage, but our neighbors have a seven-year-old, like Sam, and the overlooking view of the sea can't be beat. Plus, difficult projects are the spice of life. And aside from rebuilding bits and pieces, the first decorative structure we added were bookshelves and a sliding ladder, fitted for bound stories from both Wendy and Sam.

We spend dinners on the deck, recounting real adventures from the day and fictional ones before bed. Every night, Wendy and I share a bath, talking about everything, even the stuff that hurts—because that's what partners do. I discuss what I learned in therapy and which coping mechanisms we can implement while I finally work toward healing from Ed's and Stacy's deaths. We make sure we're there for each other, through all of it, wrapped in each other's world, with her poised at my center, right where she belongs.

The front door—still open, like my family tends to leave it—is kicked wider as Peter walks through with two hulking boxes stacked in his arms.

"Where to?" he asks.

Cassidy points. "Bedroom."

"Good thing there's only one," Peter says with a nod. "Less for you to destroy."

"Who said I destroy anything? I'm not messy!"

Peter flashes me a grin, but Cassidy doesn't catch the teasing.

It's been nine months since Wendy and I announced ourselves to the family—intended or not—and it's funny how easily we slipped into normalcy. Peter doesn't make jokes when Wendy and I hold hands anymore, and the occasional loving jabs from Cassidy or Bonnie about Wendy being in our family somehow, someway have dissipated with time.

When Wendy and I moved closer in town, our transition was seamless. More early mornings spent fishing with my brothers, more evening celebrations for random events at The Hideaway, and more nights ensuring a guest room is prepared for Bonnie, who is firmly in her rebellious phase.

Bopping from the couch to the kitchen, Bonnie whips open the fridge, only to have her posture deflate. "Oh, gross. I'm used to your house, Jas. There's only bacon and eggs in here." She sighs, slapping it shut unceremoniously and waltzing over to trace a finger across an unopened brown package next to Cassidy's stack of mail. She freezes. "Wait, this isn't addressed to you, Cass."

Cassidy chuckles. "I know. Starkey's daughter keeps getting stuff delivered here."

"Marina?" Milo asks, halfway through unpacking a box.

Peter walks back in from the bedroom, dusting his hands on his denim and peering down at the address label with me, Wendy, and Bonnie.

"Yeah, Marina," he reads. "Haven't talked to her in a while. Maybe they're older subscriptions or something?"

"No, I never got those," Wendy says. "They're new. Probably some mailing mistake."

"I don't know," Cassidy says with a shrug. "I'll have to tell Starkey about it next time I see him. I'm not worrying about it. Pizza anyone?"

There's a collective agreement, boxes hastily dropped to the counter and tools for unbuilt furniture abandoned in an instant.

Wendy, looking up from her barely unpacked dishes, blinks. "Wait, but I'm almost done!"

"Finish it later," Cassidy says.

But I know my girl likes to finish what she starts, so I call for her, "We'll meet you guys at Jukes's."

"I'm not ordering stupid pickles on your pizza!" Cassidy yells back through cupped hands, already halfway down the driveway.

"Sam?" I ask.

"I'll order it," he says with a grin, clicking Roger's leash back on his collar.

"Thank you," Wendy chimes, followed by our simultaneous, "Close the door!"

Sam grips the handle with a laugh and closes it.

Always a work in progress.

I join Wendy at the kitchen island, holding out my palm so she can hand me dishes, which I stack in the cabinet behind us. It doesn't take long, but it's noiseless tranquility, only the light clatter of plates as our playlist. Moments like this are the memories I savor. I spent so much time believing the world was a mess of storms and waves, wrestling to drag me under, that something like this—simply putting away dishes together—is an inhale after a long, tiresome day.

I'm ready for more quiet breaths and easy exhales.

Once she's finished unpacking, I mosey over to the bookshelves, peering at Cassidy's empty top shelves. Though, a handful of notebooks is scattered along a bottom shelf, thick with tabs. Curious, I almost grab one, but not before Wendy hops onto the sliding ladder and glides across the wall toward me.

I catch the ladder with my palm, halting the momentum. She jerks forward with a giggle. I steady her hips with my hands.

"Don't break it again," I say with a chuckle.

"I'm not worried. I've got my old codfish to fix it for me."

I roll my eyes with a smile. "What am I gonna do with you?"

"I guess we'll see, won't we, Captain?"

With a wide grin, I cup her cheek with my hand and pull her lips down to meet mine.

And everything feels just right. Not difficult or untenable or complicated.

With Wendy, life simply feels like an awfully big adventure.

THE END

Also by Julie Olivia

HONEYWOOD FUN PARK SERIES

All Downhill With You (Emory & Lorelei)

The Fiction Between Us (Landon & Quinn)

Our Ride to Forever (Orson & Theo)

Their Freefall At Last (Bennett & Ruby)

—

INTO YOU SERIES

In Too Deep (Cameron & Grace)

In His Eyes (Ian & Nia)

In The Wild (Harry & Saria)

—

FOXE HILL SERIES

Match Cut (Keaton & Violet)

Present Perfect (Asher & Delaney)

—

STANDALONES

Fake Santa Apology Tour (Nicholas & Birdie Mae)

Across the Night (Aiden & Sadie)

Thick As Thieves (Owen & Fran)

Thanks, Etc.

I cry a lot. Anyone who has known me for a decent amount of time can attest to this. (And sometimes even people I've only met for two seconds.) I cry at songs, movies, and commercials. I cry when I get overwhelmed. I cry when I'm surprised. But I especially cry when I'm filled to the brim with happiness.

When I was struggling with writing a few months ago, I decided to pull out an old story idea I had—a little coastal town inspired by Peter Pan. I'm a big Peter Pan nerd. I've read the book far too many times, and I've committed to memory every action Jason Isaac made as Captain Hook in 2003. And, wanting that familiar comfort, I decided to give the story another go.

So, I parked myself in this coastal town. I started living in Never Harbor. And, as I sat in front of my computer with words finally forming and the Peter Pan Motion Picture Soundtrack pumping through my headphones, I couldn't fight the big ol' smile on my face.

And then I cried, as I do. Because life is so cyclical and there's gotta be some kind of beauty in writing the book that eleven-year-old me dreamed about, right? Who knows. Maybe I'm just a hopeless romantic.

I have a lot of people I want to thank, so buckle in. I've been so lucky to be surrounded by such amazing, supportive people.

First, I want to thank YOU, dear reader! If this is your

first time, hi! I'm so happy you found me! And if you're returning, hello again. I'll develop a secret handshake one of these days.

Thank you to Jenny Bailey, my best friend and soul sister. You keep my world turning. Thanks for dealing with my teary-eyes all these years.

My editor, Jovana. You make these words sparkle every single time.

My cover artist, Alison Cote. The TikTok algorithm gods were shining on me when I found your video on my front page that one fateful Sunday. I feel so lucky to have connected with you. It is an honor to have your art on my silly little romance book.

Dad. Thanks for teaching me how to fly and encouraging me to keep soaring toward the stars.

My older brother, Rusty. For always being my hero.

Allie G. My rock. Thank you for listening to me talk about book vibes and confirming that it all makes sense. I'm not sure whether it actually does, or if we've just formed our own language at this point. You get me either way.

Becca. You're the reason this book exists instead of another, and I love you for it every single day. Thank you for adoring Jasper as much as I do.

Jere Anthony. Our weekly calls keep me sane. You're the reason I have 99% of the healthy habits that I do.

Thanks to Madison Wright for letting me chat on the phone about nanny life. Sam's quiet time is totally your doing.

A special thank you to beautiful souls like Jillian Liota, Caroline Laine, and Hannah Bonam-Young for being so supportive and wholesome in this big author community of ours.

To Shaye and Lindsey at Good Girls PR for making this a killer release. Y'all are a dream team.

To my amazing beta team! Thank you to Jenny, my Allie Boo, Angie (forever a medical knowledge queen), Carrie, Emily, Elizabeth, Erin, Rebeca, and Kolin. Y'all made this book truly magical.

Thank you to my reader group! Your support, kindness, and community is unmatched. Also to every fellow romance book lover I've met through Instagram, TikTok, and other socials. Thank you for showing such amazing support for us indies. We cannot thank you enough.

And finally, to my husband. Thanks for always supporting my weird ideas, especially when it involves flying somewhere new for book research and walking around a small town without a car for two days. Thanks for encouraging me to achieve my dreams. And, most importantly, thank you for never letting me grow up. Life with you is one big adventure. I love you.

About the Author

Julie Olivia writes cozy love stories filled with humor, saucy bedroom scenes, and close friend groups that feel like a warm hug in book form.

She lives in Atlanta, Georgia with her husband who has a swoon-worthy low voice and their cat, Tina, whose meows are not swoony one bit.

Sign-up for the newsletter for book updates, special offers, and VIP exclusives!: julieoliviaauthor.com/newsletter

facebook.com/julieoliviaauthor

instagram.com/julieoliviaauthor

amazon.com/author/julieoliviaauthor

bookbub.com/authors/julie-olivia